MOUNT WONDER

MOUNT WONDER

A novel
by

Scott J. Bloch

RESOURCE *Publications* • Eugene, Oregon

MOUNT WONDER

Resource Publications
An Imprint of Wipf and Stock Publishers
199 W. 8th Ave., Suite 3
Eugene, OR 97401

www.wipfandstock.com

PAPERBACK ISBN: 978-1-6667-0562-1
HARDCOVER ISBN: 978-1-6667-0563-8
EBOOK ISBN: 978-1-6667-0564-5

JUNE 7, 2022 10:03 AM

To my wife and children. Your love spreads fire throughout the earth.
And to the three men who started it. And to everyone who was there.

Stand thou for ever among human Houses,
   House of the Resurrection, House of Birth;
House of the rooted hearts and long carouses,
   Stand, and be famous over all the Earth.

— Hilaire Belloc, "A Remaining Christmas"

CONTENTS

INTERLUDE

Book II
A STROLL DOWN MEDIEVAL LANE

INTERLUDE

Book III
THE ROYAL ROAD

EPILOGUE

PROLOGUE

BOOK OF NUMBERS

*O*F *the vanities, I know much. Of the verities, little.*
    Maybe I stopped looking. Maybe I should have listened more care-
fully when Paul Courtney told us to read a thousand good books rather
than focus on the hundred Great Books whose truths he opened up to us. All
he had to do was name the wonder: a young man riding the train of misty
knowledge—a hint there might be a means of fulfilling the inner itch toward
the unseen, the key to understanding the oral treasure handed down from
generation to generation until ours. Nobody dared to ask the questions they
asked, but we believed we could catch a train car and ascend to Beauty and
the stars.

Instead, I'm beholden to the numbers. The old clock tower on the
Drake Hotel grinds, the second hand swings two clicks beyond the Roman
numeral six, the short hand midway between the eleven and twelve. To-
night, Chicago is a Chagall dream seen through amber liquid. Nobody will
notice an overweight, middle-aged lawyer, struck with awe, sitting on his
condo deck looking over the black lake through a glass of eighteen-year-old
Glen Laphroaig any more than he would see the old clock tower on the
Drake several stories beneath or the charred journal and the Monte Cristo
with macaroon wrap sitting beside him like a loaded Beretta.

Unless he had lived as a prisoner to numbers for thirty-two years,
subtle as Fibonacci's number, wrapping you up like a deuce in a code that
only nature knows—and possibly a few inanimate objects like billboards,
scoreboards, store receipts, checks, digital clocks, movies, even court tran-
scripts—all conspiring to torture and delight like some lost dream of naked
desire.

Last time, when I still thought I could find her, the numbers appeared
on the flight board, a digital oracle telling me that I should go to Paris.
I got to the front door of a French monastery somewhere in the belly of

3

château country and stared, wondering what could make a man travel halfway around the world in search of a decades-old memory, leaving his fiancé to figure out there was not going to be a wedding, but only a barrel tasting in the Loire Valley. The French oak reminded me of perfume from a moonlit night in a quarry. Still a slave to wine, women, and numbers: ungodly trinity.

My first wife knew that when I got distant, I was going in my mind back to college—a safe place to hide. I could not talk about the mark in the middle of my palm. She liked to feel the scar. I told her it was the stigmata. She asked if that wasn't an Italian dish. She was a Polish Catholic. I knew more about the faith than she did. I was supposed to come into the Church. The second time I rang God's doorbell and ran.

I write about present things, not past things. You cannot change numbers or exorcise their hold on you. Why then do I have an old, partially burned composition book sitting next to me? Because it is not like the rest of my life with its hollowing out from too many deft business friendships, and the easy avatars that a moment will "reply to all," sipping substitute drinks to summon the flowing stream that once fed us at its font of friendship and expectation.

Because it is once again April 1. And I, a fool for numbers and April, went into a Polish church thinking I could reconnect with something. There were statues of the Virgin in there, with eyes that follow you, even one with eyes like my ex-wife's—fixed, not hateful. Midwestern. Like the eyes I saw in a waking dream one day in front of Strong Hall amid the hissing sumacs, and a face . . . a face. I opened the journal and read from it in a ritual of ecstatic hope:

> *Make us know the shortness of life*
> *That we may gain wisdom of heart.*

It is all there, every jot and tittle, my own office of hours counting my life away. Even the Latin from the Little Office:

> *Ave Maris stella*
> *Dei Mater alma . . .*

Alma mater. *How those words bring in regnant hints along with the entry in the book of saints by Hogg, that strange college spirit guide: "Together, these eight men influenced the future of Christendom for ages to come." Beneath the apse, I read aloud what came next in calligraphic script: Bishop, St. Hugh, died on April 1, 1132.*

Here on this anniversary, I feel every bit the jester as I clutch the journal containing the precious tender of my youth. It still smells of smoke. I open it to a picture pasted on the inner cover, the photo's edges wilted and charred: a younger me, standing on a porch with the inscrutable Hogg, the observant, squinting Winston, the impetuous McDarby, the golden-haired, apocalyptic Hess, and the tall, self-torturing Swensen. I am holding a cigarette and looking out at the camera with a youthful swagger, a bushy head of black hair, taller than everyone except Swensen, handsomer than I recall with only the extra freshman fifteen. No one in that picture is who he claimed to be.

The glue is flaked, the edges curling. I cannot believe it is me, or who I was. One of the masks of youth, for hiding from ourselves, the face that looks back as we look ahead of our time. Unlike the mask of middle age, a face to hide the sorrow at the passing of youth and its spell that makes all seem sensible and unified.

And the numbers behind me. 1132. Ohio Street. Just a number, just a street. What new civilization did we hope to influence? What good—or what evil—did we bring? The sea of faith retreated. I thought I could come and hear reports of her—where she had gone, a convent in Europe. A rumor of long ago, old numbers, old longings. Unrequited dreams of youth. Now again, chasing it.

If I visit the Drake tomorrow for high tea, will she really show up? Will she see that person of promise, or the faded graying lawyer in a double-breasted Burberry windowpane serge still trying to hide his gut? I pick up the Monte Cristo torpedo and light it. A few puffs and an incense cloud looms. I hold the large cherry over my palm and ponder pain as a salve for memory. Maybe this April will free me from the numbers, from what has been written, to write freshly with my scarred hand. From memory.

BOOK I

CIVILIZATION AND ITS MALCONTENTS

What is the justification of the modern American Multiversity? History is one answer. Consistency with the surrounding society is another. Beyond that, it has few peers in the preservation and dissemination and examination of the eternal truths; no living peer in the search for new knowledge; and no peers in all history among institutions of higher learning in serving so many segments of an advancing civilization.

— *Clark Kerr: The Uses of the University*

Alcuin was the pupil both of the English and of the Irish schools; and when Charlemagne would revive science and letters in his own France, it was Alcuin, the representative both of the Saxon and Celt, who was the chief of those who went forth to supply the need of the great emperor. Such was the foundation of the School of Paris, from which, in the course of centuries, sprang the famous university, the glory of the middle ages.

— *Cardinal John Henry Newman:*
The Idea of a University

I

PRAIRIE FIRE

M Y friends came to the university, some to study medicine, some law, others business or philosophy, and some, like me, to get away from servitude to our fathers. But we found immortality in the eyes of a girl, and in the ashes of our desire, we forged a bond of enduring friendship that would haunt our days.

It was the first week of class, another unbearably sultry August in Lawrence, Kansas. It was a little over a hundred years ago on this day that Quantrill and his infamous band of Bushwackers rode into Lawrence and massacred over 150 men and boys in the cross-border wars following Bleeding Kansas and John Brown's massacres. They were the Jayhawkers, freeing those in slavery, at war with Missouri—a war that continues on sporting fields.

I stood now on the steps of Strong Hall, a sprawling limestone monolith dominating student bodies for over a hundred years on Mount Oread. The quasi-Athenian edifice crowned a majestic outcropping named for the Greek nymphs. Like a Parthenon above the Kansas Prairie, it stood as a monument to an invincible administrative presence. I felt its power, we all did. Strong could not be denied.

"We are strong . . . yes we are. It's not wrong. We belong to Strong!" we used to chant, beating our chests as we ran across Jayhawk Boulevard, streaking in the winter of my fraternity discontent. As a pledge, I was a bit of a handful, hazing the elders of Sigma Chi better than they could dish out. They said go naked across the snow-packed lawn. So I led the pledges naked across campus, complete with military chants and followed by a front-page article in the *Jayhawker Daily*. But they let me in. They put me in charge of practical jokes. But the joke was on me, and I got out after my sophomore year. Seriously, I was a Jew from LA—even the girls knew the score. I was circumscribed by my past. No Greek society for me.

Across the street on the hissing, asphalt beaches of Wescoe Hall, curvaceous freshwomen loitered humidly in their white painter's pants that were all the rage, while the cicadas burned in the tall sycamores that lined Jayhawk Boulevard, waiting for dark to pour out their pulsing liturgies. In the end, what were they with all their mating rituals but bird food? And what was I but a statistic in a gross domestic product of hormones and young hopes?

So, playing my part, I perched for safety under the protective wings of the bronze Jayhawk in front of the yellow granite U-shape of Strong. I observed. I could see and not be seen. Here nothing could touch me under the symbol of the proud spirit of the student body, a one-eyed marble griffin with minatory beak, a savage bird of myth. I kissed my hand and touched it to the bird's claw. The university seal, set in the base of the bronze statue, leered back: *Videbo visionem hanc magnam quare non comburatur rubus.*

I pulled out the journal that was tucked into the waist of my faded Levi's, lit up a Camel Light in the windbreak of the Jayhawk. The smoke tasted cool and tangy. I wrote, "videbo visionem." Something about seeing a vision of a burning bush. The burning came from the "comburatur," which I knew because I had taken French and German. My father did not understand my word games. He had his numbers to hide his secrets, but my mother and I had our secret language, a cabal that protected us from his adamant materialism. His best-kept secret was my aunt Tessie in Kansas City, hidden from me until I called her when I came to school here. She was like a character from the Brontes, and something in their past had kept her from me. She called me the lout from Los Angeles, right before she let me into her heart.

As dampened freshwomen sashayed to and fro, I pretended not to notice the heavenly shapes inhabiting their jeans. Nymphs on Mount Oread indeed. My father was right, I was good with figures. But the last thing I needed right now was a girl. I had broken up with my share of bouncy brunette freshwomen; a tall, blonde, sophomore honors student; and one neuralgic, green-eyed junior who had since transferred to UT Austin. Each seemed the perfect match for me. Until I got to know them. Now I was a junior, beyond that sort of turbid relationship, sick of the futile cycles of co-ed intrigue. My overriding preoccupation was figuring out how to sidestep my father's plans for me to take over as the Carpet King of Costa Mesa and wriggle loose of the accounting program I came to enroll in at KU. I wasn't even supposed to come here. He was dead set against it, against all that "Jayhawk falderol." The more he had been against it, the more I knew I had to come here. In the end, I had to agree to the accounting degree—or I had to go to Berkeley.

I took out a book of matches to light another Camel Light. I used an old bar trick, with one hand taking the matchbook, pulling out one stick with my finger, bending it backward, then with my thumb swiping it against the black flint pad. The flame bloomed in the humid air, and I watched it form a corona. Then an image slid into the crowning flame. It hit like a shimmering shock wave. I looked up: the vision appeared as if projected on a screen across the street like a mirage of wind and heat and Jayhawk pride. It was a liquefaction of young womanhood: the eyes almonds, the lips full, the carriage supple and curving. Low-cut bangs and auburn hair framed her face like a wimple.

Then those eyes met mine. It was a moment. It was an eternity. I was hurtling through space and time, utterly exposed, out from under the protective folds of the Jayhawk. As I stood frozen—agape—the moment passed, those eyes looking down demurely. She turned away, and I helplessly followed the femme up the steps of Strong. I stuffed my class schedule into the leather-fringed pocket of my Ben Gurion jacket and put the journal into the back of my pants. The appointment I had in Strong could wait.

I plotted out every coordinate of her curves, of her graphic self, y and x splintering into an infinity of lines and points, breaking the mass of matter itself. The view from behind was another dimension entirely: wavy auburn hair billowing over her shoulders and back, a cascade of shiny allure, the milk-white skin, the shapeliness of her legs extending from muslin shorts. Her hands swinging in a synchronous ballet, waiting for my pilgrim touch. I could smell her in the stillness of Strong's windbreak. A rapture of fragrance, making all other smells impossible. As if smell itself were her subject, invented for this very purpose. I rushed forward to wrap myself in that essence. Even as I studied the spectacle of her, I felt a searing pain.

"Damn!" I flung the hot ember to the ground and sucked on my burned finger. I knew she inhabited some spaceless reach I could not—not the theoretical world of female laughter, of sweetly cloying perfume, of freshman dances and Kansas City buying sprees, of flat-belly darkly handsome boys fumbling through the Greek alphabet for a sense of fraternity. I knew she was unattainable, that I was batting out of my league again, looking for exotic beauty.

"Who is she?" I said out loud as I followed her. We mounted another set of steps toward a lecture hall; it was like entering a palace behind a princess on the way to the ball without an invitation.

"That's it," I blurted out. Other students on their way to class looked at me as if I were one of those crazy students on campus.

It was her! The girl in the painting. The one my mother had taken me to see in Florence on the carpet buying trip my father had cooked up as a write-off when I was twelve years old. I saw a lot of nudes and Madonnas, which stirred up half-formed desires in my imagination. But nothing like Botticelli's Venus on that seashell. Since that was planted in my mind, I had looked for her. I had seen many beautiful blondes on the beach and girls of the Midwest riper than a Nebraska cornfield. But never this . . . classical goddess: the pensive tilt of her head, the striking almond eyes that seem to look at you and not at the same time—almost sad—the flowing waves of auburn hair, the proportional nose and slightly pouting lips, the long neck, the soft chin, the whiteness of her skin. She was not of this realm. I had wanted her all my life.

And then I noticed the other supplicant ascending the marble stairs next to me, only he was puffing. I was better winded from swimming in chlorine-blue California waters. I looked at the Botticelli incarnation as she wafted up the stairs, then I looked back at the puffer. He looked too young to be here: gargantuan features—flapping lips, grapefruit cheeks, gibbon eyes, incongruously small nose—not quite born of woman. I could make short work of him.

I was now at the top of the stairs, a safe distance from her, steps from office of the chancellor where my futile efforts for unreachable scholarships kept playing out. I watched her bend at a drinking fountain, now holding her silken hair in one hand, now throwing it back over her shoulder. She had transmuted once more: she was a forest nymph, with a swan-white neck, sipping at a cool rock spring. The puffing boy with circles under his eyes caught up and began sniffing.

"*Benedicta tu in mulieribus . . .*"

It had not so much been said as *shared*. In Latin. He sniffed again.

"Apryl," he said.

"Whan that Aprille." He looked at me. I turned to him.

"Her name. Apryl."

"The beginning of *The Canterbury Tales.*"

"I know," he said, grave and literal, and reached out a fleshy hand and offered me a damp handshake. "Tom Hogg." After coming in from the Turkish bath outside, it felt better, but the sweating continued.

"Bernard Kennisbaum."

"Of Clairvaux?" he asked, squinting.

"No, of LA." His large, dark eyes fell.

"Do you think St. Thomas would recognize a sixth proof for the existence of God in the nature of a woman?"

"Say what?"

"Come with me into the lecture? You will find something there. I think we were meant to meet, Bernard of LA."

I looked at him, bemused.

"What would I find in this lecture hall?" Apryl stepped into a nearby room.

"Everything you are looking for."

"Scholarships, Mr. Hogg. I'm looking for money."

He didn't bat an eye. He just looked at me with those gargantuan features. "Actually, the lecture isn't for twenty minutes. There will be songs first."

"Like *Sesame Street*?"

Hogg stared at me, an intense fire burning in his dark eyes.

"She sings like an angel." A look of bliss came over his overgrown features. I guessed I could play troubadour if it meant meeting her.

"Shit." He looked at me askance. "Sorry . . . I'm late for an appointment."

Even as I slithered back into my simpering pursuit of a scholarship, I viewed the door into which she had disappeared, and I wondered: how could everything I had been thinking about seem small and without purpose? Then the stranger with big lips disappeared into the lecture room. I stared at the lecture room door and then at the chancellor's suite.

Kansas was burning, and now, so was I.

II

STUDY ABROAD

" **T**RUTH seekers."

His words came out like steam, tremulous and airy, falling down the arch of his hint of harelip. I was staring at a patrician face: a perpetual shadow of beard, padded cheeks, a jutting jaw. I had seen that arresting face enough in newspapers and on magazine covers.

"I thought I was meeting with the vice chancellor." I liked the comfortable leather chairs of Chancellor Nation Barrows even as my flesh crawled at the sound of his voice and the curl of his lip.

"You're late, Kennisbaum."

"Sorry, I was . . . detained by—"

"What?"

"A strange sight."

"I'll tell you a strange sight, Kennisbaum." Barrows was commanding in his serge Brooks Brothers suit. He walked to the window, leaned into the tinting, and looked down on Wescoe Beach. He was protected in that air-conditioned aquarium, Diocletian surveying his subjects. "A strange sight is a student on the waitlist for a Fulbright who is late to an appointment."

I sat and looked around before responding. His bookshelf teemed with leatherbound volumes: Homer, Cicero, Shakespeare, Dickens, Dante, Yeats, and Cervantes. I spied a gold box on a lone shelf, pounded to airy thinness with a sculpture of Triton crowning the top. I looked down and saw he had a thick carpet, probably Dacron 78—healthy markup, even on sale.

"I didn't realize my appointment was with you."

"It's not . . . If anyone asks, this never happened."

"It almost didn't."

"I've read your essays. You're astute, you're sly . . . not one of them."

"One of who?"

"Do you know that one of them came to me a few years ago during the riots. In this very office?" He stretched out his arms and turned to look at me. I couldn't get that hot August wind mixed with her perfume out of my nostrils. Now he was talking about another poor Fulbright wannabe?

"He stood right in front of this desk—I had invited him here out of good will. He smelled like a wet animal with that stringy long hair. Chalmers!"

"Richard Chalmers?" I said. He was something of a legend on campus, rumored to have burned down the student union in '72.

"He stood right over my desk, pulled *it* out and . . . proceeded to urinate on all my memos." Barrows stopped to let this sink in. I let slip an involuntary snicker. The idea of this student radical peeing on his desk was compelling. "You find it funny . . ." Barrows cocked a wary eye at me. I may have had the bushy hair style of the times, but after a moment of scrutiny, he seemed satisfied that I was no radical. "Now he is a disciple of the Humanities Integration Program. HIP. Don't think Paul Courtney isn't having a big laugh at us all with that name." He pronounced "H-I-P" and "Courtney" as if he were tasting bitterroot. He returned to his desk, sat in his blue leather judge's chair, and squinted at me.

"Chancellor Barrows, I was made to understand that we were going to meet about a scholarship. I don't know what the HIP program has to do with—"

"You won an English Department award?" He opened a file on his desk. He had a dossier on me?

"Yes, 'Chaucer and the English Revolution,'" I said proudly.

"Came with a cash award, a hundred dollars?"

"Yes, I took friends to Whitey's East for a mighty feast." Barrows flinched at the rhyme and began flipping through the dossier with a scowl.

"You are still an honors student, applied for many scholarships. Petefish Memorial, The Linstrom, Rice Funds. Came in second." He looked up to see my reaction. "Father is a well to do merchant of . . . rugs?"

"Carpet diem, I always say."

"What do you know about HIP?"

"Has a reputation for innovation. A medieval classics program, embroiled in controversy. There's talk of religious conversions."

"You think it is some kind of Oxford movement?" said Barrows with an edge in his voice.

"Oxford?" Barrows stared at my Ben Gurion jacket.

"Some come here to teach philosophy, chemistry, literature, humanities— some just want to write and be left alone, some to study the anatomy of sorority girls. It's a university, for Christ's sake. But these professors think they're here to rail against the culture of America and produce countercultural warriors, even countercultural priests, goddamnit. I saw Courtney do the same thing before. You know, we were both at Columbia. Then he up and left Brown to come here—after I was named chancellor!" Barrows slammed the desk. I half jumped out of the leather chair. Then he pressed his hands together and spoke softly.

"You are one of Finley's wunderkinds, aren't you?"

"Well, he did nominate me for the Fulbright."

"I know," he scoffed, "you are some kind of troubadour for him, making up music to mock the HIP program."

"I kind of thrive at satire."

"Why did you do one of HIP?"

It was 68 degrees in here, but I felt a trickle of sweat down my armpit.

"I'd read the articles in the *Jayhawker Daily*. Professor Finley thought the Humanities Integration Program was a mockery of real scholarship."

"And you always do what you think your professors want?"

"Only where Fulbrights are concerned."

Did he think we got A's just expressing our own *tabula rasas*? I had been Finley's pet honors student, but that got me no closer to the coveted scholarship. At this level, I supposed that one had to go a whole new level of groveling.

"But how much do you really know about HIP or Professor Courtney?"

"Not much, Chancellor."

"Courtney was a big name. He had published more than the entire Classics and English Departments put together, translations of Ovid and Virgil, a monograph on Joyce, a critical study of Balzac." He exhaled gravely. "The bastard insisted we give him a dual appointment with tenure. There was not a goddamn thing I could do!" He slammed the desk again. I looked at the door. "Within months, *they* teamed up and started teaching courses together. Fred Marin and Chester Whelan gravitated toward him. Like a pack of wolves."

"Marin I've heard about, apart from the news about HIP."

"Don't believe all the myths about him."

"I never had Marin. I had Chester Whelan for Shakespeare."

Every English major had heard about him, a ladies' man who had trucked with the likes of Rexroth and Kesey in San Francisco, a drinker who was reputed to pull a knife on a hippie radical who disrupted his class. I had even read some of Marin's poetry: sarcastic, earthy, working in solid traditional forms.

"They were rock stars after forming HIP. Marin even got Robert Lowell to come to campus, and some Hollywood director who was Courtney's student at Brown. Students lapped it up."

"Robert Lowell? That's a big name."

"Yes, fresh off another Pulitzer, and do you know the only class he spoke to after his memorial lecture? HIP. Marin knew him from before K.U. Drinking buddies. All of the other professors were in a rage."

"I had no idea . . ."

"Many have gone before you and have fallen into their trap. These musketeers of Western civilization can be mighty persuasive . . . talking about sophists and Plato, all the while practicing monumental sophistry."

"Sophistry?" I asked.

"By leading students to believe there can be a Truth!" He was yelling. I got up.

"Thank you, Chancellor, for this very illuminating meeting."

"Sit down. You're still in the running for the Fulbright." I sat. "Listen to some of their papers, then decide if you want to help us." Barrows shuffled through papers:

> "Our entire crisis of civilization derives from a deplorable lack of Mother Goose. The average freshman at college today cannot understand the simplest allusion in this bedrock of English verse. A generation ago, before the death of wonder and poetry, Mother was on the lips of every school child by memory—or as we say, appropriately, by heart."

"There's damsels in distress, chivalry, knights, rolling heads, Middle English romances, and monk's tales." Barrows cleared his throat and crossed his arms in a posture of superiority.

"Sounds like the Kansas City Renaissance Festival," I said.

Barrows went to my file as if following the next step in the protocol for dealing with a difficult junior. I felt a stirring in my gut.

"They have a house on the other side of campus . . . on Ohio Street. Eleven thirty-two Ohio." He had a glimmer in his eye. "One of the regents thinks this house on Ohio Street is creating all the problems." The lip curled to a fearful asymmetry. "Here!" Barrows picked up a memo from his desk. "Courtney goes there. The Subcommittee on Academic Principles—SAP—has been formed by the College of Liberal Arts and Sciences. They have appointed Finley, that godawful Tupperware salesman of Western civilization, to head a committee on Humanities Systems Search . . . they call themselves HISS."

"What do you know about the graduate program, the School for Laymen of Excellence." He looked up at me again.

"Never heard of it."

"Courtney's mocking all of us with his village at Fredonia with the hand-grown crops, no electricity. Getting my academic goat." He stroked his rough shadow of beard.

He showed me the document. I tried to pronounce it for him. "It's . . . uh . . . S-C-H-L-A-Y-E-X."

"To think I helped get the financing for the Humanities Integration Program in the first instance! This 'SLEX' has to be shut down!"

"Well, good luck shutting HIP down."

"What if certain stipends were involved, what would you—"

"A stipend?"

"It's . . . part of a fund . . . issued at my discretion." Barrows paused. "We simply want your impressions of HIP, the teachers, students, the academics."

"You want me to . . . spy?"

"We don't spy, young man. We just want your . . . impressions."

"I suppose you think you know me."

"Kennisbaum . . . be innocent as a dove, clever as a serpent."

"What does that mean?" He didn't even look up a me.

"And don't pull any stunts like you did at Sigma Chi." I went to the door, glaring at him. "Nancy will take care of the paperwork and tell you where to go."

"I . . ." I couldn't breathe.

Nancy Ellsworth was waiting on the other side of the door, with a face fresh as a spring morning, and eyes that danced. I started to walk out.

"You still have to see the vice chancellor." She pointed to a door.

III

LEARNING CURVES

I CREPT in the side door.

"You!" I stopped short in my tracks. The lecture had already started. Maybe if I just turned around—

"Yes, you—just what did you expect today, a damned syllabus of our itsy-bitsy course?"

I froze—singled out, ridiculous. I had strutted into the amphitheater on the second floor of Strong Hall heedless of all but her. On the stage stood a short, graying professor with an iron face, laser eyes, leather skin so tight it looked waxen, and a muscular frame.

Two other professors sat on chairs on the stage in academic "lotus" position. They, too, stared. So did about one hundred and fifty salivating freshmen and sophomores pivoting in their chairs. Where was she? I looked up, unable to pick her out. Maybe it was the wrong lecture room. Not my day.

Something about this tableau pleased me. I had only recently retired as Sigma Chi's in-house wit. I took stock and walked slowly, defiantly, looking at the iron-faced one, egging him on. I turned and panned the class, and as I looked back, it happened again: the girl in the vision, as ever I saw, just looking. Time stopped again.

A throat clearing on stage jarred me back.

The short leathery-skinned one rose from his chair and walked to the edge of the stage to meet me. Though of middling height, he had the presence of a giant.

"What the hell do you think you're doing here?"

"I wanted to find out if you had anything to say."

The class laughed. He grinned malevolently. His hand disappeared into his pocket and came out with what looked like a cigarette holder. I heard a sharp click and a blade materialized. With a flick of the wrist, the object went airborne. A faint current of air tickled my left ear, there was a *thwunk*, and the next thing I knew the projectile was buried in an unoccupied desk behind me, its handle fluttering like a butterfly wing.

When the switchblade stopped oscillating, I extracted it and handed it back deferentially to the professor. He received it cordially, as from a fellow vaudeville performer who has played his part admirably. He folded it expertly and slipped it back into his pocket.

Welcome to Humanities 100.

"You're asking yourself, what can I get out of this, what will school *get* me? Will I finally *get* a Great Books education, the *ne plus ultra* of university culture?" The meditative professor broke the long, uneasy silence, and let the thought take root. I stared more closely at the three professors.

I recalled seeing their pictures in the *Jayhawker*. I recognized one, Whelan, from having had him in class. It was Fred Marin who had pulled the switchblade.

I had stumbled onto the very thing Barrows had wanted me to see, part-Classics program, part-medieval dancing, poetry-reciting, and stargazing society, and part cult. Finley had openly mocked the dumbed-down scholarship and social nature of the program. I had sung for him:

> Nature in her hath wonderly wrought,
> Christ never such another bought,
> That ever I saw.

So this was what Barrows was talking about. Now I was here in the belly of the beast, where he wanted me. But all I could think about was the real creature that was wonderfully wrought. It wasn't Barrows, it was she who had led me right into this amphitheater.

The professor seated on the left did not catch my attention at first. He was thin—meditative—with dark, horn-rimmed glasses. Only when I heard him speak did I understand why the hall was overflowing. It was Paul Courtney.

The other I knew: slight, methodical in his movements, brown-haired with the beginnings of silver streaks, Irish, rabbit eyes that took in everything at a glance. Chester Whelan, just as I remembered him:

always in charge—or wanting to be. He uncrossed one leg and crossed the other in one fluid movement.

Marin lit a cigarette ostentatiously. Blue smoke plumed from nothingness. I sat down and felt the indentation the switchblade had made in the desk. I put a hand up to my ear to make sure there was no blood. Then Marin whipped around in his chair and turned on the class with lupine voracity.

"You don't have any idea why you are here. Do you?" He scanned the students for signs of dissent. "Have you asked yourselves why you are here . . . is it because *I gotta be me*? Are you just trying to please Daddy? Or was this just a nice way to satisfy your Western civ requirement? Yes, Paul, they think they are going to buy a portion of science with Daddy's tuition, a smattering of history, and what's left over will purchase a patina of maturity. Because after all, Daddy has to get some return on his investment. Oh, you didn't think you were born just for yourselves, for your loveliness as human beings. You are just investments. Ever think of that, Virginia?"

It was as if he had read my journal. I scanned the rest of the class. No one was taking notes. To my right a plain, sweet-looking girl in a purple jumpsuit stared at Marin as if she were hypnotized. I saw tears pushing at the corners of her gray eyes. Two girls to her right in sun dresses knitted as they listened. I was in an intellectual headlock, savoring every word.

"I suppose some of you even think you are going to *get* smart."

The class erupted at the mention of the icon of silly '60s television comedies, of Agent 99 and the cone of silence. Marin broke the silence with a bellicose laugh.

"Just when are you going to cut the umbilical cord . . . or didn't you think this had anything to do with Homer? When are you going to see that the child is father of the man, that you must find your father and know him before you can become a man? Or will you mistake him for a fraud and kill him on the road to Thebes?"

He let out a cackle. I noticed the fey Hogg across the hall, rapt.

"What do you think was going through Odysseus's mind when he braved the wine-dark sea? Can't wait to get home to my car and my house? Was Telemachus brooding about the loss of his father and saying, 'If only Daddy had given me the Mercedes when I asked for it, I wouldn't be in this fix'? Just what *does* it take to grow up and face your destiny?" His gritty voice cut through the air like a shard of glass. Then Courtney's turn came, softer but somehow more penetrating:

"Telemachus could have stayed in Ithaca. He could have listened to his music, eaten his Burger King, gone to the beach. Yet the gods gave him a mission to find his father. Many of you treat your parents as pariahs, except when you're using them as vending machines for money. But have you ever thought about why you are here? Is it not so that you can *find* your real parents? Who is your father? Who is your mother? Ask yourselves that. Maybe you'll discover the answer. You may come to understand that your search for your father or mother may lead to an unexpected discovery, a discovery of yourself."

I looked around at the rest of the class: all eyes fixed on the stage, breathless for what would come next. It was the short, feisty Irishman, Whelan, who broke the silence.

"They're not ready for this, Paul—why, they haven't even bought the books yet."

A flurry of snickers rose from a group seated around Hogg. One was tall and handsome, with Nordic features. He was smoking a cigarette as if it were a prop attached to his lips.

On the other side of Hogg sat another one with deeply inset eyes and a brooding brow. Next was a muscular, sandy-haired boy who smiled so hard his eyes disappeared. All they needed were pints in their hands, and they could have been a knot of pals at a tavern, itching for a good fight.

"You see, you have come to the university"—Courtney now, quiet and intense— "and you ask what that means. What *does university* mean, and what does enrollment in it mean? Well, first, *uni* stands for *one*. *Versity* implies turning. That is to say, a university is a place for turning together of many toward one thing. But you really have come to a *multiversity* with many things turning in circles, each in their own universe, with no relationship to one another. So you may think you have come to create your own universe in which you turn in on yourself ever more tightly. You cannot see the *one* because you have been programmed to see only the many. Education is about coming to see the larger one, and being able to *integrate* ideas and apply them to your lives." He smiled hesitantly. "We are here to deprogram you, in a sense, to bring the whole into focus."

"Didn't you know, there's nothing as something as one?" said Marin. "Or are you in love with fragmentation? They're all atomists, Paul. They can't wait to read ahead to Lucretius."

Marin sat down, calm and reflective. A temple of ashes had formed by his gray snakeskin boots. Several butts piled up behind his chair, leading the eye to a throbbing red sign over his right shoulder near a back exit door: "ABSOLUTELY no smoking." He fleered with his eyes, then coughed through his smoker's phlegm.

A couple of smoking students coughed as if to lend moral support.

"I see it's contagious," murmured Courtney, letting us all expel nervous energy as Marin coughed up his innards. "My doctor made me quit a few years ago, but ever since we've been teaching this class, I get enough nicotine from Professor Marin for two people."

But Marin pounced.

"What's the matter, are you afraid of the one—of the unifying principle of Truth? Don't you think we're telling you the Truth? I forgot, they don't believe in Truth. It's all opinion now." He snickered and glanced at Courtney. "Except when it suits them. Is it absolutely true there is absolutely no smoking?" He looked at the sign. Then he pointed at me. "Don't take notes—yeah, you!"

A lecture where you take no notes? I was just jotting in my journal. This was such good material. Maybe he wouldn't notice me writing if I was very careful. Then I looked at the gash in the desk left by his switchblade.

IV

VIDEBO VISIONEM

"BOOKS are shutter than books can be, with a hop skip around we go, yes, there's nothing as something as one."

I snapped the journal shut. Marin gave a sly grin.

"Now *that's* matriculation, Paul." Then back to the class: "Do you think your parents will be overwhelmed when you report that you are the first class in decades to actually matriculate at the University of Kansas?"

"I'm not sure they know what it is they are doing, Fred—matriculating," said Courtney. "That is, what Professor Marin is saying, is that this whole curriculum is serious. And unless you follow it, and not yourself, you cannot be here at all. Homer leads to Herodotus, in turn to Sophocles who leads to Caesar, then to Augustine, to Boethius, to Charlemagne, Roland, and Don Quixote." He sat contemplating his own pronouncement, looking at no one person, but apparently trying to look into each of us.

"That word, *serious*," began Whelan, pausing to glory in the susurration of its syllables. "What that means," he said as he surfaced from his masterful fillip of silence, "essentially, is that things follow each other. There is an order. It is the same root as the word *series* . . . as in world series, an order of games."

"Here, again, we are talking about *The Odyssey* in a most elemental way," said Courtney plaintively. "You ask how we can be talking about Odysseus when we have made no mention of gray-eyed Athena, wine-dark seas, or nymphs in caves." It seemed as if he spoke intimately, over coffee, to a friend in a café.

"But this is the answer: if you want that, you can sign up for Classics 101, or buy *Cliff Notes* from the union bookstore. Those things were designed for a dying culture that deals in media information. You might say we are about useless things, things that won't get you a job. The encyclopedia is a one-eyed monster you must kill. You must decide to journey back to the land of your birth, to know the real books of real human beings, not the hundred great books, but what I call the thousand good books: Dickens, Tolstoy, Balzac, Thackeray, Hardy, Stevenson, Cather, Austen, Frost, Scott, Hawthorne, Hugo, Melville, and many others."

I wanted an education. I was not going to measure out my life in carpet squares.

"Do you know where we are?" said Whelan. "This is Strong Hall— the strong box of your education. We are sitting atop the very machine that dispenses your pieces of paper. Do you think we can talk like this without any consequences? Any moment we might be blown to smithereens." Whelan sucked in the rolling syllables of the last word, a man drunk with etymology. I saw a sweet-looking, small brunette in the middle of the amphitheater pouting. Was she on the verge of crying for lost illusions about college, of neatly divided notebooks and sealed subjects, of the banality of grades?

"I bet they didn't know about Strong, Chester," said Marin. "Do you think we ought to tell them about the suicide of the architect, or will it sully their view of Alma *Mama*?"

"What might shock them more," said Whelan, "is the motto of the university: *Videbo visionem hanc magnam quare non comburatur rubus*. Does anybody know the Latin? Some of you are enrolled in a Latin course taught by Mr. Courtney and Mr. Grigson, a former student of the program. *Videbo visionem*? I will see a vision."

I wanted to pull out my journal and start taking notes. I had written in that phrase, Videbo visionem.

"Is this the promise of your college careers, that you will see a vision, or have you come here hoping for the blindness that all of our culture lives by and thinks is normal? How many of you have seen a vision?"

"They think we're talking about drugs . . . watch out: the thought police." Marin snickered and let Whelan continue. I looked over at her, Apryl. I thought I detected a blush or a look downward, like a Botticelli donna in a glance of humility. Beauty, enticement, and indifference rolled into one.

"Yes, I suppose you think of visions as some kind of drug-induced euphoria . . . well, you can't smoke the motto of the university. You have to think about it." In the interstices of silence, my bowels snarled.

"He's right." Courtney broke in. "This motto, well . . . gee, it features Moses, of all people, before what? A burning bush!"

"But I thought this was a state institution. That violates separation of church and state," growled Marin. I needed separation to a restroom. "You know, he was searching for the Truth, the Law, and what did he hear? I AM. Not 'I will be'—present progressive, see ya in the next chapter—I'm one of them gods you read about. But I AM who AM. How's that for symbolic logic?"

"That amuses you, doesn't it," said Whelan as he uncrossed his legs and crossed them again with sleight of thigh. "That is the problem. You were weaned on amusement. Yet that very word comes from *muse*, as in the muses of history, poetry, dance, song—Calliope, Erato, Clio, Polyhymnia, Urania, Terpsichore." Whelan let these names hang in the air. "That word, *muse*, has the same root as *mystery*," he continued. "It also has to do with memory. You have lost out on the mystery and muse of learning from the senses, and so you deny that anything else can exist other than brute sense. What will be in your memory for your life when you leave?"

"It takes advanced thinking and learning to really be a materialist," said Marin, "and I don't see any Bertrand Russells out there. Or do you think you're communists? Have you read *Das Kapital*?"

"Well," continued Courtney, "here you are in this university, thinking about your future, and you come upon the Truth, and it's a burning bush, and you have a vision . . . what are you going to do? Are you going to run to the nearest bar or find a girl and celebrate over a bottle of Gallo or grow a beard and live like Karl Marx? Just what would you do if you saw the Truth? What if knowledge took you that far?"

I thought about what Chancellor Barrows was offering me.

"Can you *get* knowledge?" Marin was fishing for a smart aleck. He scanned the amphitheater, filled to capacity. He lit up another cigarette, brandishing it like a *lettre de cachet*. "It is a fundamental proposition of Aristotelian logic that the thing must be in itself and that knowledge is internal. A thing cannot both be and not be at the same time, but this is the basis of your lives, is it not—contradiction?" Marin stared in my direction again. "Paul, they think they're existentialists."

"You will read Plato," said Courtney, "and we will talk about a cave, but not one in which you are trapped by nymphs. No, I am talking about being trapped in a cave by the inertia of your own soul, unable to see anything. The anything of why there is something rather than nothing."

"It turns out, you cannot *get* knowledge at all." Whelan spoke as an alter ego, a refining echo. "That is, there is no vending machine or library that has an instant dispenser of knowledge. You have been taught for God knows how long that knowledge exists outside of yourself, that it is in books or libraries. The Truth is *antithetical* to that."

"Knowledge has everything to do with you." Courtney came in with a gentle recitative. "Just as wonder brought the first inkling of knowing to you as a child when you picked a flower and asked what it was, education must come from within . . . from *educare*, to lead or draw out, as in *educe*."

"Twinkle, twinkle, little star, how I wonder what you are." Marin paused. "You find that ever so silly, don't you? That is Mozart, or didn't you know that?"

"If you cannot grasp that Truth precedes art," followed Courtney, "you will never grasp Homer or *The Odyssey*." Courtney was the pianissimo to Marin's forte. "You will never grasp Telemachus's search for his father, or the suitors' struggle to win Penelope. The steering between Scylla and Charybdis will make no more sense to you than E equals M-C squared. You see, the beginning of all real learning is coming to the realization that you do not know what you thought you knew. That is Socrates. He teaches that knowledge of your ignorance is the beginning of the search for Truth whose end is wisdom. If you start there, you may be able to progress to Dante and the love which made the stars." He turned to Marin in a drift of silence.

"I don't know if they can handle that, Paul," said Marin. "Aren't we exploding their myths? They will ask for their money back."

I thought this was something like what I got from Chaucer. Literature itself unfolded to you something rounded about how you understood life. You might be just sitting in class or reading on the lawn by Wescoe, and suddenly the veil of ordinary thought would lift.

"We hope to teach you to look up at the stars for the first time," said Whelan, recapitulating the strange journeying. "This course is not merely for your intellectual growth. In revisiting the traditions of all previous generations of students, those who walked with Socrates and observed nature, those who looked upon the hills, the seas, and up at the constellations, we are asking you to step aside from yourselves and see what is beautiful . . . to see what *is*."

Courtney jumped in naturally as in a well-rehearsed performance. "You will sense the grace and balance of your bodies in the waltz and go to places in the country for stargazing and country fairs. We want to cultivate you, as in cultivation of the soil, as in the word *culture*."

The horn moaned on campus. My stomach was calm. I felt no compulsion to gather myself up and leave or to see the vice chancellor. The rest of the class filed out silently. I stayed in my seat and watched the three men in their chairs. Just savoring it. Maybe this was my last day in this class. Maybe I was out of the university. Or maybe my future was a Berkeley business degree and Cheetos-colored shag carpeting.

Hogg appeared suddenly in my side vision, startling me out of my reverie. "She would like to meet you at the Crossing."

"Well, I have American Political Systems."

He just stood there, waiting for me to make a decision.

V

THE CROSSING

" I AM Apryl. Apryl Jovey."

Every college student needs a pub to call his own. From Quantrill's Crossing, one could go west to the stadium and other parts of campus or into the town of Lawrence. We sat at a table gouged with drunken carvings and undergraduate glyphs. The walls were bedecked with daguerreotypes and paintings of the Jayhawks and Bushwackers, the James Gang, defiant Quantrill, the burning of the Eldridge House downtown, and the rape and pillage of the town. This glorified shack sat atop Mount Oread—in the Greek myth, it was the mount of the nymphs.

She was more than art, more than nymph: I beheld Venus herself, virtuous and sexy all at once, a goddess seen in thousands of guises across the ages, skin glistening in the sultry air, her glances even deeper up close. When light filled her eyes, they were like yellow diamonds. I felt swallowed in the vortex of her gaze, mute before the muse of my demise.

"Bernard. Bernard Kennisbaum."

We shook hands. I saw how the nape of her neck met her shoulders in a perfect smooth arch of Carrara marble.

"Tom said you would join us for class."

"He did? Before I joined you?"

She pouted, nodding her head.

"Bob!" Apryl saluted the group of young men in the back of the bar milling around a juke box. Courtney's confederates shambled toward us as one.

31

That view is etched into my mind with the heat of August. They had collected a couple of others along the way. They were closer or farther from me than I could see—coming toward me or receding.

"Who's this?" said the pugnacious one I would later know as Bob McDarby.

"This is Bernard," said Apryl.

"Bernard of LA," added Hogg as he drew out a cigarette from his pocket and lit up. I was surprised to see him smoke. He had a steel butane lighter that caught the sunlight and glinted, blinding me momentarily.

McDarby, the one with the deeply inset eyes, stared at me quizzically and crushed my hand.

"Good to meet Marin's first pigeon of the year," he said with a snicker.

"I thought he was brave," protested Apryl.

"Brave, my—" She stopped him with another leer. I lit up a Camel Light.

"Well, he cooks beants like Marin," McDarby added.

"Cooks beans?"

The blond Scandanavian reached over and introduced himself.

"Peter," he said, offering me a giant hand. "It's bean–t–s. Just another name for cigarettes."

"Maybe he'd prefer to call them fags," said McDarby in a bad cockney.

Peter was taller and slender, with high forehead and capacious, carping blue eyes.

McDarby stepped between us and said, "We call him the Swede."

Another one held out a hand. I looked at a tall, imposing man with a face grooved like an archaeological dig. He looked like an extra in *The Godfather*. A white scar over his eye signaled some past brush with danger. He had a gold bracelet on his right arm and a high school class ring with an amethyst stone.

His name was Michael DeBlasio. He and McDarby appeared to be pals. I said hello and reluctantly shook his hand.

"Ross." This one greeted me as if referring to someone else. "Got up today right before class," he added, scratching his pillow-molded, red-tinged brown hair. His eyes were brilliantly blue but offset slightly, giving him the imprint of having been sublimely startled. He had a belt buckle embossed with a man's face and the words, "Bishop Fulton Sheen." Although he was handsome, with small, unthreatening features, he was invisible somehow.

"Bernard, I am Patrick." He laughed as if my very presence amused him. Patrick Winston was a sturdier member of this collegiate cosa nostra. He had an odd appeal with his squinty eyes, flowing brown hair, broad shoulders, muscular, middling frame, and dimpled chin. His bulging biceps were too big for the navy-blue tee shirt with faded yellow letters that read, "Rock 'n Roll Liberty Memorial '76." He lifted weights and read Keats. He was seventh in a family of twelve from Shawnee in Kansas City. "One of the twelve apostles," Hogg said of Patrick.

The last of the group shifted the whole time from foot to foot, hyperkinetically darting from person to person with his eyes.

"This is Clark," said Apryl. At that, Clark Zorn blushed, showcasing his innocent, clean, bushy-haired looks. He had bird legs that fit snugly into his canvas Levi's suit. According to Swensen, the auburn hair grew longer and thicker because he grew up in the rain-dappled forests of the Northwest, fed by home-brewed beer.

"Now you've met the gents of Eleven Thirty-two."

"Eleven what?"

"The address of our house," said Hogg, who up until then had remained silent, his cigarette hanging from his large lower lip. I seemed to recall something about a "safe house" that Chancellor Barrows wanted me to infiltrate.

Apryl stared at the men-in-waiting hovering around her. She looked at McDarby, then at Zorn, then at Ross. She took the half-burned cigarette from Hogg and puffed on it. Swensen grabbed it from her.

"Here's looking at you," he said in his best Bogey, with a hint of Groucho.

"I heard you laugh," she said to me. "You must have liked the class."

My heart was pumping. I made sure my journal was holding tight in the front of my pants.

"If Western Civ were a drug, that was heroin."

Apryl exhaled a full-throated warble of mirth. She flicked my collar.

"What do you call this, Bernard?"

"Yeah, what's with the safari jacket?" said McDarby.

"He's hunting us," said the Swede.

"Oh, this? It's all the rage in LA." I told about Ben Gurion and the open-chested bravado style.

"So . . . Apryl." I let her name float in the air. "Your parents must have loved Chaucer."

"They named me for the month in which they met."

"I bet that was the cruelest meeting."

Her eyes dropped, her countenance withered.

"You know, you think you're so clever, but I could take you down and pin you in thirty seconds," said McDarby, who was suddenly close to me. My heart rate shot up.

"What was it you were writing in that notebook when Professor Marin told you to stop?" asked Apryl.

Gulp.

"I—what notebook?"

"I saw it too," said Hogg, "when he was under the bronze Jayhawk."

They all looked at me.

"There," said Swensen, pointing at my crotch. "What's that in his pants?"

At that point, everybody could see the square protrusion as my Ben Gurion was open. Before I knew it, McDarby had me upside down and was yanking my journal out of my pants, beer spilling everywhere.

VI

LADY LUCK

" I TOLD you no more fights, McDarby. You all want to be barred from this establishment?" A large man in his forties with hippie-long hair, Ace, the owner, stood over us on the floor. From this angle he looked like a bulldog, all jowls.

"We're just fooling around, Ace," said McDarby. He held up the journal. "He had someone's notebook." He handed it to Swensen as I got up and tried to get it from him, who handed it off without a look to Ross, who slipped it to Zorn.

I smiled at Ace. "Yeah, just a joke, see."

"Nature hath wrought," read Zorn before Apryl grabbed the journal and handed it back to me. I placed it back in my pants. Ace looked at the bulge in my pants. He threw a rag at McDarby.

"Clean this up."

McDarby waited until Ace was gone into the back and then threw the rag at me. "You clean it up, Fulbright."

I threw the rag back at him. Apryl stepped between us. We sat down. Ross took the rag from McDarby and started cleaning. McDarby and I locked gazes for a little while.

"Bernard, what's so special about that notebook?" said Apryl.

"It's a journal . . . I have this problem with my father . . ." When in doubt, say something real.

"Girls have journals," said McDarby.

"Lots of saints kept them," said Hogg.

"Yeah, girl saints."

"St. Anselm."

35

"All right, one."

"St. John of the Cross."

"He was hardcore," said DeBlasio.

"I can't believe you're taking his side?" said McDarby.

"What problem with your father?" asked Apryl.

"There will be hell to pay for diverting from my business major," I said.

"Tell him, 'Go to hell,'" said McDarby.

"Easier said than done . . . money is an issue. I'm out of state."

"Didn't you hear Professor Marin at all?" said Swensen. I stood up, waving my cigarette.

"What's it going to take to cut the ties to Daddy," I said. They laughed at my passable impersonation of Marin.

"What did you mean, if Western Civ were a drug, HIP was heroin?" McDarby asked. The others looked at him. I suddenly chimed in, singing:

"I shot the sheriff, but I did not shoot the deputy."

Swensen suddenly roared like a drunken sailor. The others joined in. Ross still wasn't laughing. Then, as if a light switch had flipped, he began doubling over laughing and said "heroin" over and over.

Patrick Winston was chuckling, which made his eyes close. Hogg stared off. An exasperated-looking waitress, Mandy, a junior dropout who had been in my British Writers before 1800 last year, flounced over on the beer-sticky floor. She wore a tank top dappled with stains—a natural woman of the times. I remember she really liked Lord Byron. Apryl looked away. The Eagles moaned from the jukebox. Mandy dropped off more beers without being asked.

"Witchy woman," said Zorn to the music on the jukebox.

"Which woman?" I said. DeBlasio stared at me. We drank formaldehyde 3.2 percent beer in those days and counted it ambrosia.

"This round on me," said McDarby, taking charge. Apryl smiled politely at him as if he had played his part well.

"What do you think of the Latin Mass?" said Zorn to me suddenly.

"In LA, there is a Latin mass out in their cars on Sundays. We call them Chicanos, but if you prefer Latins—"

"The Mass is being chanted in the old Latin rite by the monks of Chalfontbleau," said Hogg.

"That's right," said Zorn, "and they have permission from Rome."

"And I just assumed that is common, it's Catholics—Latin, right?"

"No, it's not common, it's been pretty much outlawed," said Apryl.

"I mean, where's this coming from?"

"What if I told you that they should just have people learn English rather than read Hebrew in Temples, what would you say?"

"That would never happen. It's what ties Jews to their heritage."

"Exactly," said Zorn, "and we're bringing it back, right here, with permission for the old Latin Mass in a monastery, maybe Le Loup—"

"Don't," said Michael in a sharp tone." Zorn stopped short and shook his bushy head.

"What loop?"

"Nothing, just a farm we go to sometimes in the country," Zorn said sheepishly. "Sometimes a priest says the Latin mass there." DeBlasio said.

They were hiding something. "Wait, go back," I said. "You were saying there's some kind of controversy about Catholics being allowed to use Latin?"

"He is talking about Lefebrve," said the squinty-eyed one, Patrick.

"Lefebvre?"

"Former archbishop of Paris, the only one to stand up to the heretics in Vatican II and insist on the Latin Mass according to the old Tridentine rite," said Zorn as if reading from a tract.

"The Jews and the German bishops wanted to undermine the Tridentine Mass, as they had in the Bolshevik revolution."

"Tridentine? You mean the sugarless gum?" Patrick and Ross chuckled.

"One of the things about the program," said Patrick, "is that it is friendly to tradition."

"Like *Fiddler on the Roof*?"

"Yes, something like that," said Patrick.

"Lefebvre is a latter-day John Fisher," said Zorn.

"Lefebvre." I said his name again, pondering it. Out of nowhere, we heard a theatrical voice belt out: "Lefebvre, I would leave you . . ." We joined, singing to Apryl in the style of Robert Goulet in *Camelot*.

We encountered a pumpkin-faced black youth, a forehead higher than Apryl's, a pleasing, blinding-white smile and caramel-colored skin. He rose from his knees, standing taller than life. Apryl stepped forward.

"Jimmy, this is Bernard, from Los Angeles, the newest addition to HIP. Bernard, meet Jimmy Drungole."

"I just stumbled into a lecture by accident, I wouldn't call myself—"

"Bernard, I am HIP's token Negro. Or as we now say, *Black*. *Nigra sed formosa*. I am very pleased to meet someone from the land of the stars

and a constellation of beauties. I am from a humble place in Mississippi—
Natchez, a forgotten stretch of floodplain along the Mississippi River."

"I know that place," I said. "Twain talks about it."

Jimmy looked at the others with mocking, wide eyes. "I do declare,
we may have a literate man here. Indeed, well, well—yes, it's in *Life on the
Mississippi*."

"Who cares about Mark Twain," said McDarby. "We were talking
about a Jewish conspiracy to destroy the Mass."

"Well, it was both Jewish and German Catholic," said Clark.

"This I have to hear," said Jimmy with eyebrows raised to me in common cause. He pulled up a chair and motioned to Mandy, who brought
him a beer. She touched his hand and let it linger there as he held out a
dollar bill. Jimmy then looked at Apryl as Clark went on. I saw the Swede
catch this, as if he were a collector of potentially impure leers.

"The Masons and the Jews have been trying to destroy the Mass
for several centuries. Some Jews have converted to Catholicism just to
undermine this faith, what they see as the only true rival to the Torah and
authentic Orthodox Judaism."

I was catching them red-handed.

"And I thought we were worried about the KKK," said Jimmy as an
aside.

"The Illuminati run the world and have infiltrated the Church,
which is why the true Pope may not be in the chair of Peter." Clark had
us all captive. "It's all explained in *The Rhine Flows into the Tiber*, the
conspiracy of Vatican II coming out of Germany." Barrows would be salivating if he could hear this.

McDarby looked at Swensen, who shook his head. Jimmy's eyes
were wide. "I grew up Baptist, but that may be the most ignorant thing I
ever heard."

"What does the Jew from LA think?" said McDarby.

"We didn't attend temple . . . I was a matzah and bagel Jew," I said.

"Alas, it was the same for me," said Jimmy. "I'm just a cultural Negro."

"That lecture from the professors had more about Moses and the
burning bush than I ever got in the Pentateuch at temple."

"So what makes you Jewish?" DeBlasio spoke from under his sullen
penumbra as if he were passing time on a stakeout.

"The guilt. We didn't even have blintzes. I got all the persecution
without any of the fringe benefits."

Apryl giggled, then Jimmy joined in with a hearty chuckle, followed by McDarby's guffaw. Jimmy said, "This is my kind of guy, a little shtick, some bagel and lox, a little razmataz, yeah . . . yeah!"

"I'll put on some Waits," said Hogg as he pulled loose change from his pocket and plodded to the juke box.

"Waits for what?" I said.

"Oh, he's a scat man so white the moon is jealous," said Jimmy. De-Blasio smirked.

"Man, he's the most excellent poet troubadour we have, totally *fierce!*" said Ross, laying on the last as if he had coined the word. Apryl shook her hair back over her shoulder as she smiled, flashing those large almond eyes. There was a distant universe in that face.

"Tell me about Tom," I blurted out.

"What about Hogg?" said DeBlasio with a menacing scowl.

"I mean, does he always talk like that? Does he really have visions? He seems, I don't know—hypnotized."

"Listen, he's special," said McDarby, standing up. I sat back and looked at all of them. Apryl stepped into this incipient competition.

"We all care about him," said Apryl. "Now Bernard cares, right?" Hogg walked back over as "Ol' '55" came on.

It was immediately alluring; the groaning lyric of a leftover soul in a pickup truck with the sun at his back seemed to speak to all of us like a sacred ballad. As the music swelled and returned to the verse, I jumped to my feet and sang, barely knowing the lyrics, of the sun coming up and lady luck.

McDarby stood, bowed his back, and shouted out the lyrics with me. Soon all of us were singing, even Jimmy and the waitress.

"Come out with us, into the light of things" Apryl said, getting up and going outside. Hogg followed her.

"See you guys later," I said. The Swede shot me a tortured look.

"You're picking cherries from the wrong tree," said Swensen.

"She has his heart sorely beguiled," said Patrick, squinting.

"This feels like a scene from Tennessee Williams."

"Man," said McDarby, looking me up and down. "You're way out of your league."

"I guess that means I can't get to first base." McDarby got up closer to me with angry eyes.

"If you know what's good for you." Then he bolted out and down the hill.

"So he's dating her?" I said.

"Look," said Winston, "many have tried . . . and died."

"What about Tom?"

They laughed at the idea he was pursuing Apryl.

"He's going to pray, not court her. She's as unapproachable as Isis," said Swensen gloomily.

"Ice is right," said Clark.

I nodded sagely and followed Apryl out to the street.

Hogg was just talking to Apryl, and when he saw me, he left. I walked Apryl down the hill toward Mississippi Street across from Memorial Stadium where Gayle Sayers once played. Her house sat up from the street. We stopped on the steps below the house.

"Bernard of LA," she said, "you aren't like them."

"Neither are you." She laughed and brushed her hair back, tilting her head slightly. "Like that."

"Like what?" she said.

"Has anyone ever told you that you look like a painting from the Renaissance?"

"No. But there was this guy, an art student, who was following me around wanting to paint me."

"Did you let him?"

"Of course not. He wanted me to take my clothes off. So what painting are you talking about. And is she wearing clothes?

"Botticelli. Venus. And no."

"Birth of Venus?" she said. I could have put her on a seashell right there and drawn her.

"You know that painting?"

"Sure," she said, "Venus is born when Kronos castrates Uranus and casts his genitals into the sea. She becomes the goddess of love, pleasure. She is unattainable." I stood there with my mouth open. She stared at me earnestly, then she cracked a smile and we laughed.

"You really had me going. I need to write all that down. Good stuff about the gods."

"What were you writing before?" she had to ask.

"About striking out on my own. This is my father's life, and all his business plans for me. I guess my life's an open book." I stopped myself.

We both looked down at the journal in my pants and smiled together. Then she looked at me earnestly.

"You have a lot of comebacks, but . . . will you come back?"

"Wh-what are you saying?"

She leaned toward me, touched my arm lightly, and whispered, "See you at the next lecture."

Lady Luck disappeared up the stairs and into the house. A bouquet of fresh herbs and cinnamon lingered in her absence. I floated back to the dorm, mindless of the chancellor. Finding my old Penguin copy of Homer in a trunk, I practically devoured *The Odyssey*.

God knows, she made me feel like a god.

VII

WONDERSTRUCK

"We have been talking about *The Odyssey*," said Courtney. "I suppose we ought to look at the text. Since you are college students, you won't be happy until we dive in and analyze it."

I kept going to class wondering when I might actually speak up and drop this façade and HIP, but Apryl led me into several poetry classes. I blew it by not kissing her that first day; maybe if I had, we could have gone deeper—I could have told her more about my father and my declarations of independence.

"But do you think we're going to do that?" said Marin. I looked at Apryl resting her lovely chin on her hands. She caught me admiring her.

"In your rhetoric sections," added Whelan, "you have been reading passages aloud, rewriting speeches from Homer, retelling them. Your forebears did the same. They memorized and rewrote famous speeches and whole books. From Winston Churchill to Teddy Roosevelt to Abraham Lincoln."

"You were nothing like those giants. They translated whole passages from the Greek and Latin," said Marin snidely.

"Those generations had the experience of what is in *The Odyssey*. They had the prerequisites for it," said Courtney.

"They think you mean other classes, Paul. Is that what he means? Is it just that easy, take more classes, get the degree, then die? What about experience itself? What is Odysseus's experience, and what does it tell him?"

"That he should go home," said Courtney.

42

"If they knew what was good for them, they'd go home right now!" We laughed at Marin, but I was not sure his vinegar wasn't meant to sting. "Do you really want the Truth? Do you really want to face all the monsters of Self and find out who your parents and you really are? In the end, you just want comfortable jobs, you want a soft place to have that martini to ease the pain of death. They're into anesthesia, Paul." He paused before he pounced again. "They'd have stayed on Ogygia with the nymph. The grave's a fine and private place, but none I think do there embrace. What is Homer telling you? Stop living in your fantasies. Live in reality among humans. That's what Odysseus wants, but he is shipwrecked and finally washes up on shore in the land of the Phaeacians. What do you think he sees?"

There was silence. Marin was like an angry uncle on a bender. Courtney took a hardback out of his plaid blazer pocket. He opened it and began to read without preface:

> "And when the washing was over, and all was spotless, they flew in a long string to the seashore, choosing a place where the sea used to beat upon the beach and wash the pebbles clean. There they bathed, and rubbed themselves all over with olive oil. After that they took their meal on the river bank, while they waited for the clothes to dry in the sun. When they had all had enough, both maids and mistress, they threw off their veils and began playing ball, and Nausicaa led the singing, with her white arms flashing in the sunlight as she threw the ball. She looked like Artemis, when bow in hand she comes down from the mountains, over lofty Taigetos or Erymanthos, to hunt the boars and fleet-footed deer: round about her the nymphs make sport, those daughters of Zeus who frequent the countryside; and her mother is proud indeed, for she lifts head and brow above all the troop, and she is preeminent where all are beautiful. So shone the fresh young maiden among her girls."

Courtney looked up from the book, avuncular and urbane. "When they see Odysseus, naked and rough, they scatter, all but Princess Nausicaa. She is made bold by Athena herself. She speaks with the stranger and brings him to her father, King Alcinous."

"What's your reaction to that?" said Marin with caustic staccato. "Some excellent chick . . . Flick me your BIC?" He took out his steel butane and gassed up the grill for another chain of cigarettes. He blew out a plume of smoke that would have made Aeolus green. "Don't you think

Odysseus had graduated from dirty magazines? Is he a voyeur? You're all a bunch of puritans who like to watch. Condemn her to burn at the stake—but not before you get a peek."

Courtney jumped back in as if Marin were just a voice in a single consciousness, the id having to relent in the face of a powerful superego.

"Notice how Odysseus comes upon civilization, having fought captivity with a nymph, having spent eighteen years away from society, and he comes in this rough way upon the shore. He washes up on the rocks, bearded, browned from the sun. And what is happening? The women are tending to clothing. Washing. The women are holding civilization together. And they go to play on the beach. But not just any woman. Odysseus sees the beautiful princess, Nausicaa."

I spied Apryl for a sign, but she refused to even look in my direction.

"I don't think Nausicaa was in favor of the E-R-A.," said Marin. "She was not burning her bra."

"No," said Whelan. "You could say she was seeking support of the community." I stole another glance at Apryl. She was not laughing but deeply considering all of this.

I had to admit, so was I. Had I washed up on this shore after two decades of wandering the earth? Had she had led me to civilization, and did I live in that world of gods? Snap out of it, Bernard.

"Odysseus is a stranger," said Courtney, "a handsome stranger, and Nausicaa falls for him and takes him to the city, and what happens? They welcome the stranger. Her father, Alcinous, throws a feast. The biggest feast ever. With food and drink and games and songs and dance. Odysseus finally tells his tale." Courtney looked down at the book in his hands and read:

> "What a pleasure it is, my lord, to hear a singer like this, with a divine voice! I declare it is just the perfection of gracious life: good cheer and good temper everywhere, rows of guests, enjoying themselves heartily and listening to the music, plenty to eat on the table, wine ready in the great bowl, and the butter ready to fill your cup whenever you want it. I think that this is something like perfection.

"Imagine a world that is something like perfection." Courtney looked around at the class. Marin smoked, and I wanted to smoke with him.

"What is that world like," said Whelan, "where the food and wine are brought out in beautiful containers, just so, where the entire kingdom's arts and crafts are displayed to perfection, where hospitality is a way of life?"

"Is that better than Burger King?" said Marin. "Can you have it your way in a real civilization? Was there something better for Odysseus than a civilized meal with a beautiful princess and the best wine and food in the most beautiful gold and silver, followed by the arts of wrestling and stories? Well, he does get offered the hand of Nausicaa, so I guess he really came out on top. You get the chick—is that what you're here for?"

Well . . .

"So what is Odysseus looking for if not the princess?" said Courtney. His eyes searched the class. "Home," he said. "It is a place where all of this is unspoken, where manners and love are understood. It is an uncongenial place, really. I mean, there are no gold goblets, at least not that are brought out for you. Everyone knows your faults. Is home like perfection in a different way? You have to find out why home is uncongenial, not nearly as hospitable as the kingdom of the Phaeacians. You will find Princess Nausicaa and King Alcinous out there. When you see them, you will be born in a certain awe, born in admiration and wonder."

"Wonder, being awestruck. That is what this whole study is about," said Whelan. "If you had them in your education, you wouldn't need us. A couple of years ago, a student came up with a motto for this program: 'Let them be born in wonder.'"

"Another student," added Courtney, "put it in Latin. We won't tell you what that is. You'll have to get that when you go stargazing."

"That's a cliff-hanger," said Whelan.

"The problem with your education is that you have been getting answers to questions you haven't even asked," said Marin. "We like to dangle the grapes. Maybe we'll dangle a sword, too. But we won't cut the knot, not for you. You'll have to cut your own knot."

"I'm afraid he's right," said Whalen. "You have to want these things for yourselves. Not just because some professors say so."

Courtney picked up the theme:

"To get something like perfection, you have to look at something, don't you, and that requires you to want something, and then to choose something. That is why we built stargazing into the curriculum. When The poet says, 'Look up, look up at the stars,' don't you know, you are the only creatures who can do that and wonder who you are?"

"I don't know," said Marin, "they identify more with Narcissus. The me generation. You stare in the mirror singing, twinkle twinkle little me, how wondrous is my identity."

The way Apryl looked at them was the way I wanted her to look at me.

"Admire and wonder," said Whalen, "are two important words. *Admire* comes from the Latin *admirare*, which has the root *mir*, the same as in the word *mirror* or *mirage*. So this course is about seeing, looking, and your inquiring or wanting to know—to understand what you see."

"They're the first generation that does not want to know," said Marin. "Just feed us, give us soma, give us entertainment."

"Dervishes have wondered about these questions," said Courtney, "and they dance to the stars. They built a whole religion around dancing in concert with the constellations. The stars have everything to do with dancing. You will do that in the waltz in the spring. All of liberal education is about engaging in the dance, about looking at things as they are. Naked, with your eye."

"They understand the naked part," interjected Marin.

"Perhaps some of you have taken an interest in the constellations," said Whelan. "But do you realize you were made to look at the stars?"

"They want to get to know themselves, Chester," said Marin. "It offends them to say they were made. They like to think they sprang full blown from the head of Zeus. You're not even good pagans!"

"Well, to be good pagans," said Courtney with a sly grin, "you have to know about the gods and the nature of the universe. Pagans were intensely interested in man's place in the cosmos." Courtney pulled another small hardcover book from the pocket of his frayed sports coat. "You have read some of Ovid's *Metamorphosis* for Rhetoric. You remember it begins with the beginning of things, the void." He began to read:

> "'Of bodies chang'd to various forms, I sing . . .
> Thus, while the mute creation downward bend
> Their sight, and to their earthly mother tend,
> Man looks aloft; and with erected eyes
> Beholds his own hereditary skies.
> From such rude principles our form began;
> And earth was metamorphos'd into Man."

"What about a renaissance of your own," said Whalen, "something that takes you outside of yourself? We want you to look at what is in your own backyard. We sing the obvious. What is plain as the nose on your face. That is the beginning of rebirth."

Rebirth. Rising from the sea of troubles, of fathers, sons, girls. Plain as the nose on my face? Was I sailing away from or closer to the chancellor and his cronies?

VIII

OF VICE AND MEN

M ID-SEPTEMBER. The convection oven of August had changed imperceptibly until it gave way to fall, with its balmy sense of well-being. From my notes had emerged a manifesto to forge a new life. The HIP program opened up a doorway into a world I felt always existed but that took special goggles to see. But nothing was free. In addition to the calls from Nancy in the chancellor's office, my father was calling, and I had to talk to him.

"I enrolled in this humanities course, different from anything I've ever taken."

"I'm supporting some liberal arts frolic?"

"No, really, these three professors are incredible."

"You don't say."

"One is controversial—Fred Marin. You wouldn't believe what he did the first day—"

"Stop!" His tone had changed completely.

"Stop what?"

"Stop this nonsense."

"I'm giving it a try. And taking a little time off of the business classes." I still had Apryl on my mind, her helping me to see I could be my own person.

"Drop it and stick with business and accounting."

"Or else? . . ."

He just hung up. At least I had declared to him my intentions. I was racked by indecision as I headed up the walk to Strong Hall to see the executive vice chancellor.

"Glaze Kennisbaum in the flesh!"

I turned around to see Perry Hudson standing there, looking dapper. He had called me by my secret Sigma Chi house nickname, Glaze. His was the only real friendship, and rivalry, I had formed in the Sigma Chis. We still talked and went out for an occasional dinner or movie. He stood out here: the meticulous manner, his tortoise shell glasses, the newly minted Topsider yachting shoes, the affected New England accent . . . and now the intolerable Izod shirts. His lips curled up ever so slightly when he spoke, and the resulting half smile laced every word with double meaning. Such as when he said my name "in the flesh." That almost meant I was too fleshy. But he studied four languages and was fluent in French and Spanish. He had beaten me out for best paper in Buntrock's Dante honors seminar last year. For all his furtive ambition, I couldn't help liking him.

"Perry Mason. What case have you solved lately?"

He didn't mind the old frat nickname. Somehow, he was so unlike the fraternity that he was like an intellectual mascot. He knew I had a raw deal. He thought my donut caper masterful. Of course, he was gone home that weekend to Salina to see his family—origins he hated to be reminded of.

"The case of the missing Jew. But I forgot—you never attend temple."

"This *is* a temple, isn't it?" I said, looking up at Strong Hall.

"We are actually looking at the back of Strong, or what the architect thought was the back of Strong." He pulled out a pipe and sucked on it smokelessly as he always did.

"Well, I have a meeting at the vice chancellor's office. About a scholarship."

"I heard you were taking the HIP program and had dropped a business law course."

"I'm afraid it's true. I'm a regular cult figure, reading the great works of Western civilization and selling flowers at the airport."

"My sweet Lord," said Perry.

It was then that I realized my mistake. I always thought of Perry as a guy who stayed out of controversy at all costs, above the fray, moving seamlessly from witticism to witticism. But there was another side to him, a more determined side. He would scratch and claw his way out of Kansas and away from his dirt farmer roots if it was the last thing he ever did. He wanted that last available Fulbright and would do anything to get it. All of a sudden, I felt a spur of competition.

φ

"Bernard, please, have a seat."

Nancy Ellsworth had just shown me in. The office windows were not tinted like those in Barrows's office. Impressionistic paintings crammed the walls: a park with gazebo, an idealized vision of the campus, impostor impastos. I looked around and became aware that I was not alone. Instead of a creature with tail and horns, I saw a shadow behind a Queen Anne desk, the executive vice chancellor for academic affairs. Albert Holloway was not only thin, he was exiguous, not just gaunt but wispy. He looked like a birch bent by wind as he hunched over a mountain of paper, tucked neatly into his burgundy chair with brass studs framing him in his houndstooth. His trim mustache seemed to have its own life-support system, like a dog's tail. He was slightly walleyed, and when he looked at you, he barely blinked, as if daring you to look at one or the other eye.

I sat down in front of the Queen Anne.

"Just a moment; I'm going over budgets," he whispered.

A color-coded, tabbed dossier sat on his desk, the large seal of the university emblazoned on its cover. He flipped the budgets closed and looked up. He smiled curtly and opened another folder. He read from the dossier through diaphanous eyelids.

"Mr. Kennisbaum. The chancellor has spoken highly of you."

"He has?"

"Yes, and we are delighted to give you this scholarship." He lifted an envelope out of the dossier and handed it to me. "The first check is the stipend, half this semester, half next."

I opened it. I was dumbfounded to see a check issued by the state legislature in the amount of $2,500. I had been remonstrating with myself for a few days about this.

"There will be another in a couple of weeks for tuition."

"I can't accept it." I handed the check back to him. Vice Chancellor Holloway blinked deliberately through his pellucid eyelids. The mustache moved. His eyes were large and inviting, a kind of aquamarine color.

"It seems your father telephoned and informed Weintraub in budget that he sent his last check for tuition."

I narrowed my eyes, feeling my gut tighten. It felt like he shot me. My viscera curdled, twisting my organs into a knot. I was being put in an impossible position. Holloway looked down slowly at the dossier and pursed his lips. I rose. I had not made it to the door when I heard his voice like the horseman calling to Ichabod Crane from the other side of the grave.

"It says here you were thrown out of the Sigma Chi house."

"I left," I said tartly. Vice chancellors trolling for student peccadilloes? It was surreal. A jolt of panic coursed through me.

"You *left* because you were caught in possession of a small amount of marijuana. It's all here in the report of the vice chancellor for student affairs."

"Are you a vice chancellor or a chancellor of vice? Why stop there? Shouldn't you be hunting down fornicators as well?"

"Please, have a seat," he said without blinking, impervious to my humor. I had merely taken credit for the marijuana. The real perpetrator had never even thanked me. The dean of Liberal Arts and Sciences had said that owing to my excellent academics, the record would be expunged. I had been told wrong. On the campus, it was rare to find a dormitory room where marijuana smoke was not spilling out like morning mist. I didn't care about my father learning this fact, but my mother? The truth was worse than even the university knew.

"There's a note here that the dean suspected you were covering for another student, but you wouldn't snitch. We have an honor code. Surely you were aware then that you must tell if the . . . *cannabis* . . . belonged to someone else. That violation alone would justify—"

"What? Justify what?" I raised my voice.

"Expulsion," he said, popping the *p*.

"You look to me like an illustration by Dore of the trimmers in Dante, the people who weren't evil enough to deserve hell."

"What nonsense."

But I thought I'd struck a nerve.

"I did a paper for my honors seminar last year on the trimmers. I know about trimmers. People who take no stand, fence-sitters. Worthy of neither praise nor blame."

He looked at me as if he were judging a performance. I sat down finally.

He swiveled his chair at this, looking out a window, bringing his hands together into a pyramid.

"Have you met anyone in the program?"

He turned suddenly to me, his eyes softening into something almost human.

"I would like to meet Richard Chalmers," I blurted out, recalling Barrows telling me about his pissing on his desk.

"Arson and Old Mace," he said, nodding. "Earned that nickname during the student riots. They say he set fire to the student union."

"I have heard of some of his pranks. He's quite a legend on campus."

"If you could deliver him to us, your Dante could . . . take you places."

"*Deliver* him?"

His eyes flipped back to their bird of prey look.

"But you have met some of the other HIP students?"

"A few," I said.

"Girls?" His eyes searched mine. I felt my chest pounding. Holloway's eyes widened. He leaned forward.

"What girls?" he said, his pupils dilating.

"Just some girls. And guys." Holloway brought his hands to his chin. He finally blinked, but when he did, it was in slow-motion like a lizard's.

"They're going to try to make nuns out of the women, you know. We have Title IX problems as it is. The general counsel's office says we could lose $10 million in grants because of sexual and religious discrimination."

Nuns? Apryl a nun? My tongue loosened of its own before I knew it; my first installment of intel burst forth.

"I think they are trying to get them in a monastery where they still use Latin."

"You mean in France?" he said.

"Possibly. I'm not sure. It could be here."

"Here? That's new? Follow that."

All the noble impulses that guided my thoughts—all the high intentions of turning down the administration and devoting myself to Apryl unsullied by base interests—gone like that.

Unwillingly, my hand made a move for the check. Holloway's hand was faster, pinning it to the leather desk blotter. He put his lean body weight into it.

"You want it?" he queried me, his brows arching into horns. Then in a chill whisper: "Do whatever we ask." Blink, damn you, blink! But no blink.

Suddenly the check was free. I stuffed it into my pocket. Holloway relaxed back into his chair. He hit a buzzer.

"Yes," came up the sweet voice of Mrs. Ellsworth.

"Nancy, please give Mr. Kennisbaum the information about his meeting in Kansas City."

"Yessir."

He let go of the speaker button and turned his blinkless eyes on me. "You have a problem with that?"

"No, but what am I doing in Kansas City?"

"I not only need you to report on HIP, I need a mole with a group of people opposed to HIP, led by a Unitarian minister named Rhoden. And I need you to attend the meetings of the Student Senate with the Department of Liberal Arts and Sciences when they vote. You will report to me. Chancellor Barrows knows nothing of this."

"Yeah, the women of HIP." I was his falcon, ready to pounce for his little scraps of meat on the end of a tether.

Holloway rose ceremoniously and turned around. I leaned forward to get a look at the dossier on me—only the name on the file was not mine. It read "Apryl Jovey" in bold letters. He must have been reading up on everyone I had met, maybe even following us.

"Very good, Mr. Kennisbaum." He leaned over and opened a drawer. He pulled out three files. He handed them to me.

"Get to know these. And see if you can get closer to the group in that house on Ohio Street."

He handed them to me. I shuffled through them. Dossiers on the three professors, complete with photographs, some action taken on campus, and clippings from the *Jayhawker* and *The Kansas City Star* with sexy headlines like "Religious Controversy Stirs on University Campus," "Teachers Said to Brainwash Students with Religion." The chancellor of vice looked at me with his thin, Doberman smile and vulture eyes that never blinked. He was Cerberus, with his three files, guarding the door to Barrows.

I just wanted to look inside the file on Apryl. Was she some runaway from a wealthy family?

"And the Fulbright?"

But he simply slid the file on Apryl into his desk drawer and locked it as he flashed me the most minatory smile I had ever seen.

"All in the fullness of time."

IX

AUTO DA FE

I TRAVERSED the campus as a ghost. Its sylvan charm had turned to bleakness as I thought of my future as an informer, possibly involving Apryl in my net.

As I descended the steep hill of Twelfth Street, I looked toward the downtown hunched below the great hill of the university. Beyond the town to the north, the Kaw River snaked around Lawrence toward a blue haze of bluffs that somewhere slumped into Tonganoxie and on to Leavenworth. To the west, I scanned a limitless expanse of trees across the gauzy plain that melded into the suburbs of Kansas City. My aunt Teresa lived there. She knew my father was impossible. She warned me against coming to college here. Now I saw how dangerous it was.

Massachusetts Street ran through a quaint Main Street shopping district and on to the river. It was one of the few such places that was not a series of boarded-up shops and seedy pool rooms in small-town America. I reveled in the scaled commerce, the polite society, the proportionate justice. The town loved students. It clothed our hormone-addled bodies, provided cheap intoxication, catered to our nocturnal longings with the Campus Hideaway or the Sanctuary, and served a legal machine that was more than happy to bail us out with diversions from prosecution. Our whole existence was a diversion from the maw of ever-widening commerce. That world of carelessness disappears like Brigadoon as the veil of youth is drawn, and we are prodded on to mundane careers. I had chosen to steer clear of the Bacchanalian pursuits this year. I had already had the diversion of a lifetime with the marijuana scandal at Sigma Chi, not to mention my freshman citations for being a minor in possession of barely intoxicating malt.

After depositing my check, I went to JR's, a book exchange where the musty smell of old volumes carried me to higher planes. I had found a beautiful used copy of *The Divine Comedy* with facing-page translations and Dore's illustrations.

I had read Dante's masterpiece last year, but I wanted to own it in the original language. I found a bench in South Park near a Lutheran church and sat down to read. I had no Italian, yet I had no trouble reading him with a few years of Spanish.

Nel mezzo del camin di nostra vita . . .

Somewhere in the middle of the road of our life, I awoke to find myself in a dark wood. I was young, but that did not mean I could not find myself in a wood. For me, it was one filled with promise and cool, dark places, with paths that were both unheralded and undesirable. That was where I wanted to be, the unwanted places; a dark wood of cool indolence described my whole life.

A loud engine drew me out of my September reverie. A long black vehicle pulled up to the curb, making rickety, creaky noises as its gears responded late to the orders of its driver. It was an old Cadillac hearse with tinted windows. Smoke was pouring out of its windows. Had some drug dealer lost his way driving from Chicago?

A window came down. A pair of saturnine eyes peered through the clouds of smoke. When I saw the lips, I realized it was Tom Hogg.

"*Salve*, Bernard."

"Because I could not stop for death," I said.

"What?"

"He kindly stopped for me?"

He stared through the smoke, expressionless.

"Get in."

I got in and immediately pulled out a cigarette.

"I have to keep the windows up or the fumes from the tailpipe leak in."

"Choke or smoke, I always say."

He drove in silence as I inspected the inside of the vehicle for any sign of a cadaver. The seats were strewn with spiritual books, Greek philosophy, and pictures of monasteries. There was a pad for stretching out—maybe a little necromancy? I looked at Hogg's baggy black pants that gathered in bunches over his scuffed brown loafers.

"Moonlighting for some extra money?"

"Moonlighting?"

"You know, extracting cadavers from graveyards for the medical school."

"You're funny . . . I get in the back sometimes and just smoke, think, or pray. Can you understand that?"

"Sure." A harmless lie.

Hogg pulled up to South Park near a picturesque white gazebo. The same one in the painting on Holloway's wall. He stopped the car and rolled his window down a crack. He looked at my leatherbound book.

"A breviary?"

"Dante."

"He used Bernard to unveil the celestial light in the afterlife."

"Right, Bernard of Clairvaux." Then it hit me. "That's the saint you mentioned to me when you heard my name."

He gazed into my eyes, burning with all the smoke. He pulled down the frayed black visor. A crumpled pack of Marlboros fell into his hand. He pulled the last one out, bit the filter, and fanned his lips as his other hand searched the pockets of his tattered red jacket, pulling out a Zippo lighter. He showed me an inscription: *In lux perpetua.*

"In the light eternal. If you do not go into the light, you stay in darkness, Bernard. That's Dante in a nutshell."

Maybe he knew Dante better than I did; maybe you had to be a Catholic to really understand that poem. I handed him back the lighter. He lit up the slightly gnarled Marlboro. One was still burning in the ashtray.

"So, are all these books for HIP? Or are you majoring in philosophy?"

He looked out through the windshield.

"Plato said all philosophy is a meditation on death. Do you believe that?"

"Et in Arcadia ego . . ."

"I've heard that," said Hogg.

"It means, 'Even in this arcadian setting of education, death enters.'"

"Yes, there is an end of all of this. Until you see things under the Rule."

"The Rule?"

He reached for my left haunch. I moved away from him instinctively. Suddenly his hand was under my pants, and he pulled out a volume.

"You were sitting on it."

"I thought maybe we were getting along well," I said. Hogg looked earnestly at the front-cover reproduction of a painting of a monk working over a manuscript.

"This is the Rule of St. Benedict. It has governed Benedictine monasteries for the last fifteen hundred years." He flipped to a dog-eared passage with marginal scribblings. He began to read as if reciting poetry:

> "As far as possible, the monastery should be set up with all
> necessary things, such as water, a mill, a garden, a bakery,
> so that the various crafts can be practiced inside the house,
> to avoid the need for the monks to go here and there outside,
> as this does not profit their souls at all."

He looked up. "There is still such a place."

"Have you been there?"

"Not yet. But I will. So will you. Our house is like that sometimes."

"Your parents' house?"

"Eleven thirty-two Ohio." He turned to look at me with a penetrating gaze. It was as if he were pronouncing a holy word.

"You mean your college house." He nodded. "What about the other place, where you have not been yet?"

"Chalfontbleau," he said with an orphan French accent. "It's a French monastery."

"Is that what everyone was so secretive about at the Crossing?"

"These are things the angels want to look into, but it is not appointed to the uninitiated to know."

I nodded, trying not to overplay my hand.

"At Chalfontbleau, they live strictly according to the Rule so they can meditate on a happy death."

Happy death. It fit. All the California slang of the 1960s and 1970s paled in comparison. Here in this hearse, a chariot of death, I realized I had hit the jackpot for the university. But why did I feel like I was dying inside?

"That's a foreign concept to me," I said. "I'm not particularly happy in life."

He searched my eyes. "There is deep unrest there."

"I admit, I don't sleep as much as—"

"Wait," he said and picked up another book from the floorboard. Aristotle's *Nichomachean Ethics*. I had read about it. Hogg flipped through it.

"Aristotle said that you cannot call a man happy until he is dead. Until then, you won't know whether he has really attained happiness."

"Talk about delayed gratification," I said. Hogg looked into my eyes and began to sniff.

"The flesh is evil for those who have not entered into the true faith. They have an imbalanced relationship with pleasure and pain. For the elect, all pleasure and pain are from the one who knows."

"For me, pleasure can become pain," I sighed.

"Aristotle says that pleasure is part of our pursuit of the Good. Even Beauty is pleasurable because it is Good."

"*Cogito ergo sum* . . . I drink therefore I am."

"Only God exists in himself. You have to understand things from the perspective of first causes and then effects. You have gotten things out of order."

"Descartes before the horse."

"For the elect, purity is purity."

"Purity . . ." I repeated, sending another puff of smoke in his direction.

"I am talking about those who know the unknowable one. For them, there is no impure act."

"Like Moses before the burning bush," I said, picturing the seal of the university. The quest for ultimate Truth.

"Like Apyrl."

I sat up. He grabbed my hand. He picked up the *Rule of St. Benedict*, opened it to a page, pulled out a timeworn art postcard, and handed it to me. I couldn't believe my eyes—it was a detail of Botticelli's Venus showing her on the seashell.

"Where did you get this?"

"A bookstore at an art museum."

"You were following her as I was. Is that why you have this picture?"

"No. I always thought this looked a little like her."

I narrowed my eyes and looked into his.

"Come on, you're not serious. This is an act, right?"

"I'll tell you a secret," he said as he leaned in close. "I must pinch myself on the inner thigh when I see her," he said. "Sometimes I have to do it twice. Soon the urge to see her as an angel of lust disappears, and I realize she is a virgin who must not be defiled by my thoughts. I was reading the angelic doctor last night."

"Angelic doctor?"

"St. Thomas Aquinas."

I had read his treatise on law for Professor Finley's Honors Western civilization class.

"So what did your angelic doctor tell you?"

"*Nihil in intellectu nisi prius in sensu.*"

"Ixnay on the Atinlay."

"There is nothing in the mind that is not first in the senses," he said.

"Tell that to those curvaceous girls in the painter's pants downtown."

"They tested St. Thomas by sending a prostitute to arouse his lust. Do you know what he did?"

"Avoided a bad round of the clap?"

"He took a burning coal from the fire and squeezed it in his hand."

"A medieval Gordon Liddy."

"The impure one left him. They could not get him to do what he would not will to do. His family wanted to prevent him becoming a Dominican, prevent his consecration to Our Lady. He understood Our Lord came to bring a sword, dividing children from parents."

"I think I can relate to that."

"We are both in pursuit of purity, but we must be careful with Apryl and with all virgins."

Was Apryl a virgin for real? Her milk-white skin, the flirtations, the way guys hovered around her, the way she moved through time and space as if she were beyond it. As far as I knew, I had never met a virgin since coming to college. This endangered species was the most desirable commodity in the frat house.

"Tom, I assure you, I do not think about Apryl that—"

"We can get back our innocence, Bernard. And you shall. It may take time. There is betrayal in the air."

"Betrayal?"

He looked into my eyes. "What has to be, has to be, right, Bernard?"

My heart skipped beat.

"Don't worry, one day we will both go to the monastery, and peace will follow."

"In France?"

Hogg looked forward through the smoke and started the car. He made the sign of the cross and muttered under his breath. I needed to bail out before it was too late.

"If you keep going to Iowa Street, it is faster to get to Daisy Hill," I said.

"I'm not taking you to your dorm."

"I need to get back to study *The Iliad* because the professors—"

"We're going to 1132 Ohio."

Suddenly we found ourselves driving past Joe's Bakery up Ninth Street where several freshwomen in striped shorts mingled outside the store.

"Joe's," I blurted out. "Pretty good donuts. Excellent chicks."

"Ohio Street . . . *gratia plena, Dominus tecum*," said Hogg as he turned onto another street. I felt the car go bumpy on bricks, as if the shocks had given out suddenly.

"Must be the agitation cycle."

I thought Hogg had come to rescue me, but he was more like Charon crossing the River Styx and toward my doom.

X

ALPHA OF THE OMEGA—
A FRATERNITY

W E were going down a shady street filled with ramshackle Victorians—small-brick, turn-of-the-century two-story and three-story houses—two steps removed from dilapidation. Yet the scene oozed charm with its incarnadine-colored brick streets, its canopy of elm trees overhanging the street.

Hogg pulled alongside and parked behind a brown 1975 Toyota Celica. He turned the car off. His large nostrils expanded and contracted, and his dark eyes pulsed. He glanced up at a tall white house with black shutters that was partially obscured by an old dying elm. Gray paint was peeling off a front porch that spilled out toward buckling bricks and a heaving sidewalk.

He pulled out his Zippo and searched for another cigarette. I obliged with my Camel Light. He ignited the "beant," as the guys called them. We got out and stood at the curb to study the towering Victorian house. Its gables seemed to weep. From the way Hogg looked at it, this was no mere house but a breathing being. Storm clouds had gathered quickly. I felt some raindrops.

We walked up the heaving brick path and ascended the creaking porch as if it were an altar. A screen door obscured the interior. Muffled voices from inside filtered out, accompanied by a faint tinkle of bells.

To the right was the mailbox, and above the mailbox, the address's numerals in gold on black backing. Hogg motioned to me, putting his finger to his lips to caution me to be quiet. I crept to the mailbox where he stood. As I got closer to the door, the voices were more distinct. Hogg ran his fingers reverently across the raised numbers above the mailbox, like a blind acolyte reading holy braille. 1,1,3,2. He pointed at the names. I read them.

> ~~Richard Chalmers~~
> ~~Ellis Blaine~~
> ~~Karl Hess~~
> ~~Corey Tartt~~
> ~~Kludas Schmead~~
> Bob McDarby
> Patrick WinstonMichael DeBlasio
> Peter Swensen
> Ted (Theodoric) Ross
> Clark B. Zorn
> Tom Hogg   A Ω

The two symbols at the bottom of the names I recognized as Alpha and Omega. Fraternity letters for end times, not good times.

Hogg moved toward the door and put his ear up to the screen. I did the same. From the dull drone of conversation, an angry voice cut through. I looked through the screen at faces that were as indistinct as a priest behind a mesh confessional screen. Hogg pointed to one name— Richard Chalmers—then pointed inside. He put his finger to his large lips again and widened his eyes as if to signal grave danger.

"Hurry, will you," cried Chalmers, banging the warped oak floor with a boot, lupine eyes afire, lips parted in a snarl. He wore black leather zippered half-boots, unzipped slightly in the style of the day. His checkered shirt opened wide at the collar showing a hairless white chest and a tattered brown cloth necklace. Through the mesh refraction of the oxidized screen, I saw the others on a couch, on chairs, or standing around. I recognized them from the Crossing.

So this was Chalmers, my hero who urinated on the chancellor's desk. Arson and Old Mace. He looked to be in his late twenties, the hippest of the HIPsters, according to Vice Chancellor Holloway, one of the original longhairs turned medievalist. The tales were long, including one of him stringing piano wire across Jayhawk Boulevard and nearly killing state cops.

"Where the hell is my beer?" barked Chalmers.

Someone left the living room. I could hear a scuffle in another room followed by a gangly spectacle of motion as the supplicant emerged carrying three bottles of beer: Clark Zorn, the conspiratorialist.

"Here, Rich . . . sorry." Zorn tossed his lithe, pink face forward then backward. A bush of brown hair flopped over and behind the peak of his hairline. Chalmers snatched two beers. They looked like bottles of cough medicine in his strong hands. More bells went off, each with a different pitch, like a Viking ice rite in the middle of September.

"Goddamn bells . . . what do they think this is, Lent?"

"Maybe Pat could enlighten us," chirped the go-fer in more of a question than a statement. He giggled in his throat, like a chick learning to cackle.

Chalmers scoffed: "He's more interested in his books and verse than he is in saving the program or Western civilization."

"I'm listening," said the one I recognized as Patrick Winston. "I think this would make a great scene, a bunch of guys worrying about bells and the state of civilization while their hormones are driving them wild."

"He writes a mean limerick," retorted the blond Swensen. I could see his big knuckly hand swinging in front of him. "But I don't think his hormones have seen action this year. Not with all his money changing. You know what Chaucer said: Radix malorum cupiditas est."

"What the hell do you know about that?" said Chalmers. "A damn Swede always praying and worrying he might have a dirty thought!"

Swensen held up a large hand as if Chalmers was going too far. A guy who knew Chaucer and the root of evil couldn't be all bad.

"Wait a minute." It was Bob McDarby springing to his feet. Chalmers stood up to face the squat Irishman. Hogg and I looked at each other. Did a fracas impend?

"You come in here telling us you don't like our bells," said McDarby fiercely, "don't like our friends, man, you think we're all puritans. I'm no puritan!" He ran his stubby fingers through his jet-black hair. The phlegmatic Ted Ross stirred on the couch. DeBlasio looked like he was a match for Chalmers.

Chalmers looked around. "Man . . . you could use a little puritanism," he said.

"I know how excellent the Swede's mind is," said McDarby, "I happen to know he has impure thoughts like the rest of us!"

"Hooly sheet!" yelled Swensen in a strange midwestern accent.

"I know how *excellent* Swede's mind is," mocked Chalmers. "Don't you know any other words?"

Ross said, "He's makin' fun of the way we talk. Fierce!" He laughed harder than the rest.

"Listen," said Chalmers, "we are Roman Catholics, sons of the pagan empire that made the Greco-Roman world sit up and pray, not heirs of Knox, Calvin, and Luther. Get over this puritanical hogwash!"

"You know, Knox was a mason," said Zorn with a chuckle. "The Masons are still active in bringing down the—"

Another set of bells went off. Chalmers sat down, twisting his face into a grimace of despair and anger.

"You're a bunch of fucking Presbyterians, and you don't know it!"

Zorn slugged back some beer and winced. McDarby stared defiantly. Chalmers looked at them imploringly, speaking to them in a calmer tone: "Look, this wasn't my idea for Ellis to go to Chalfontbleau. Hell, he's been in the Church less than a year. Professor Courtney is against it, but Karl . . . well, you know Karl, he—"

"He says the end of the world is coming," Zorn chortled, "and Ellis is better off learning the prayer of heaven now and avoiding the Masons."

"Screw your conspiracies, Clark! We have a genuine conspiracy going on right here in the little river town of Lawrence, Kansas. The university is holding inquisitions! They're going to have a heck of a time making a Prot Scot into a French monk. He's got a plane to catch. Ellis!" A lone bell sounded.

"Professor Courtney says he can sing the Little Office of the Blessed Virgin better than any of us," said Zorn as he got up and paced back and forth between a blazing plaque depicting Jesus pointing to his blazing heart and a blue and pink statue of the Virgin Mary.

"You guys need to get laid," said Chalmers. Zorn stopped giggling and turned red. "Like DeBlasio. You need a little more Italian blood here."

"Heh, Rich," said DeBlasio, "you know, I'm trying to stay away from serious sins, so I won't get mortalized."

"You guys are a bunch of wannabe monks when you should be real men, willing to fight for the truth, for what you believe! Dammit! Grow up."

"Those monks are excellent men," said DeBlasio, who was rising from the couch to remind Chalmers who he was talking to.

"Yeah, they are excellent. Who do you think helped discover Chalfontbleau monastery! That's the whole point of Ellis going over there." Chalmers leaned forward, urging them to come in closer.

"All right, I'm going to let you in on some things. You are sworn to secrecy." He looked around.

"I think there is a mole who is giving secrets to Barrows!" Chalmers let this sink in as he glared at them. They all looked at one another as if to ask, "Is it I?" but no one spoke. I felt my heart pounding. "The university has formed a committee that is about to be announced to study HIP, but its real purpose is to remove the program."

There were gasps. Hogg looked into my eyes.

"I don't believe it," said McDarby angrily, his smiling face screwing up into a ball of intense purpose.

"Bastards," said DeBlasio as he balled up his fists.

"Hooly sheet," said Swensen again.

"I talked to Professor Marin. We have authorization to go all out on a counteroperation. Guys, we are going to have to move up the plans for Operation Constantine. So—"

My stomach growled like a lion on the prowl. I shifted my weight, causing a loud creaking. All heads turned at the sound.

"What the hell? . . ."

With wolf speed, Chalmers kicked open the screen door and was out on the porch before I knew it. It shot back against the side of the house. There he stood. Sweat gathered at the back of my neck. Chalmers was in gunslinger stance. I looked into his snarling blue eyes. A downy blond beard moderated the heavy lines of his thin face and unforgiving lips. It was like looking into one of my father's smoldering Brady daguerreotypes of Civil War schoolmaster-poets turned overnight colonels. The others appeared at the door.

"What are you two doing?"

Hogg was speechless, his face white as a sheet. I had to step up.

"We were just coming up to the door and heard you guys talking—"

"You were spying," said Chalmers with deadly disdain.

"We don't spy," I said echoing the chancellor. "Maybe eavesdropping slightly, but—"

"Who is he, Tom?" Chalmers looked me up and down. Hogg's mouth inched open, but no sound came out. Before I knew what was happening, Chalmers had struck Hogg square on the mouth. He went down on the porch with the ugly sound of a bowling ball hitting linoleum. Hogg's lips bloomed red with blood.

In a rage, I jumped on Chalmers, slamming him to the ground. For a moment, my weight pinned him. But my triumph was brief.

As if I were a down jacket, Chalmers flipped me over, heaved onto the porch steps, and pulled out a long switchblade knife. My eyes widened.

Suddenly, a large hand appeared on his elbow. Swensen!

"Rich, this is Bernard. We met him in the program, give him a chance to talk."

"Bernard Kennisbaum," said Patrick.

"From LA," said McDarby.

"What is that, Jewish?" said Chalmers.

Zorn looked at me with narrowed eyes. DeBlasio grimaced. Ross scanned the sky.

"Yes," said Swensen. "Definitely a Jew." Swensen looked at me apologetically as he helped in the deflection of Chalmers's wrath.

"He can speak for himself," said Chalmers

"It's Bohemian German—Jewish. I came with Tom."

"You were at the screen, listening."

I nodded.

"He keeps some kind of journal," McDarby blurted out.

"Journal?" said Chalmers. He moved in closer. He swiped at the others; the blade came dangerously close to Ross and Zorn. They backed away from me. Hogg stood by, praying in Latin and sniffing. Chalmers put the knife to my throat. My gut growled again. The pressure was building. Chalmers grimaced."You all sure like knives in HIP," I said. Chalmers looked at the others.

"Marin pulled a knife on him, almost killed him," said McDarby, exaggerating.

Chalmers's eyes widened. "You're the smartass at the HIP lecture?"

"Hogg invited me to the lecture. I was late and Marin singled me out."

"We were following Apryl," said Hogg. "Bernard then went to see the chancellor about a scholarship."

Chalmers brandished his knife again. "So *you* are the mole!" Chalmers moved closer. "You aren't very good at it."

McDarby placed a hand over my mouth, bringing in the switchblade. The others leaned closer. Hogg prayed under his breath. It was like a medieval execution ceremony.

"How did they approach you?" Chalmers looked into my eyes for recognition. I hadn't done anything yet. I could just get out, tell them everything.

"Leave him alone. I'm your mole," said a voice before I could unburden my guilt. A man with a ruddy face and shaved head stood in the doorway.

XI

UNDER THIS SIGN

"ELLIS, what the damned . . ." Chalmers relaxed, unable to complete his thought.

Ellis Blaine had a marine-style buzz haircut, rheumy eyes, and a languorous expression. Skinny, he wore a checkered shirt and baggy khakis that bunched at a pair of shined brown loafers.

"You heard me."

Chalmers jumped toward Blaine, still holding the knife. Blaine flinched. Chalmers folded the blade and put it calmly in his pocket.

"You're the mole like I'm a transvestite."

"I was very conflicted about how this program was changing my life and the lives of other friends," said Blaine. "I didn't give them much. I just couldn't bear for Professor Courtney to find out. I told Barrows last month, I'm out. So you see why I have to leave town."

I realized why Barrows had not approached me until after classes started. He was losing this guy to a monastery.

"But you converted," said Ross.

"I told them I really was becoming Catholic. They said that was fine, they just wanted more reports or they'd let the *Daily Kansan* know who I was."

"You worthless piece of shit," said Chalmers. "We were friends."

"He probably gave them a few worthless papers," I interjected. "Maybe some information about this house?"

"How did you know?" said Blaine. He looked at me solemnly.

"Yeah, how *did* you know?" said Chalmers.

"Come on, HIP is an open secret."

Chalmers inched closer to me. "I did some checking on the HIP program because I was interested in joining. I didn't know if it was a cult like they were saying."

"Who told you this stuff?"

"Charles Finley. I worked under him in the honors program."

"Honors Western civ program, no friend of ours," he said, flaring his nostrils. He turned to Blaine. "Is that all you did, give them some papers?"

"Yes, Rich, worthless stuff to get them and that rodent off my back."

"What rodent?"

"The Unitarian minister, Rhoden."

Ross and McDarby laughed. Chalmers stabbed them with a sidelong glare.

"Rhoden. He has a group of Jewish parents who have been putting pressure on that piss-ass chancellor."

Piss-ass Nation Barrows. Thanks to Chalmers's piss and my ass. Rhoden was heading up community opposition to HIP, and I was supposed to meet with him.

"You said save Western civilization before," I said, hoping to distract him. Did you mean the program Finley heads?"

"No, I meant saving your ass and the West's ass at the same time."

"How do you propose to do that?"

"Don't," said Patrick, trying to dissuade me.

"Apparently you don't think the West needs saving?"

"Leave it alone, Kennisbaum," said McDarby.

"Really," I said. I stared at Chalmers.

"Really," he said. A running discussion in the dorm from my freshman year popped into my mind. It never failed me.

"So you're trying to save the West. But how do you explain the senseless slaughter of this century, all the suffering, the rapes, the unjust imprisonment, the murders, the liquidations of Jews—if there is a God who is good?" Nobody ever had an answer to that.

"You think that there is evil in the world?"

"Obviously so."

"And you believe in the Good, and in a world where suffering is alleviated, and justice is meted out for evildoers?"

"It follows."

"But if there is no God, what would good and evil be? Without a being who is ultimately all good and powerful, *evil* has no meaning, and neither does *good* for that matter. Things are as they are, no matter what labels you put on them. Earthquakes happen, everything is in motion, people die. If there is no God, why call any of it evil?"

The others looked to me for a comeback. It was like Chalmers had made this ridiculous chess move, and I didn't know which way to go. I tried a reference.

"That was what Voltaire was getting at, and he was right I think."

"Voltaire was right to crush shallow optimism in the face of suffering," said Chalmers.

"Man . . . what are you saying, Rich," said Ross, "that Bernard is right?"

"You said it," said DeBlasio. "You can't call anything good or evil."

"Might makes right," said Zorn.

"Exactly," said Chalmers. "That's the theodicy dilemma. If you are not careful, that's where it leads—there are limits to human reason."

"That sounds like a cop out." I could see he was more than just an angry radical with a knife.

"You want easy answers to the mysterium iniquitatus," he said.

"The what?"

"The mystery of evil," he said disdainfully. "That you cannot see the reason for the massive suffering in the world does not mean it does not have an explanation that would be understandable to reason."

"So you would say, evil is a mystery that has a solution?"

"Would you say that the discovery of mathematics, or electricity or the wheel even are good things, have brought immense relief to many millions throughout the earth, making life on earth more bearable and even pleasing?"

"Sure."

"But hundreds of thousands have endured new forms of suffering never known before, including maiming, crippling injuries, and death, being crushed by heavy vehicles or under wheels, children dying in fires, electrocutions, thousands of mentally ill persons subjected to barbaric therapies, and mathematics that has resulted in the manipulation of physical reality and the atom that threatens to lead mankind and all other living things to extinction."

"But those things were not invented for evil purposes. Fire is not evil in itself but it can bring great destruction."

"Precisely, and we were not created to suffer, but suffer we do. That is the story of Job: that no person who has suffered is entitled to an easy explanation—"

A loud engine burst on the scene. I turned and looked out the window to see a classic blue Harley-Davidson Sportster, its engine belching in staccato, pulling up to the curb right in front of Hogg's hearse. A tow-headed youth in his mid-twenties jumped off. He yanked his goggles off, revealing raccoon rings of white. A case of beer was strapped to the back of the bike. He detached some bungees, pinned the beer to his side, and strode toward us, popping a foamy can of Budweiser as he walked.

"Karl!" yelled Blaine. Chalmers moved toward the door.

"Wait, finish what you were saying!" said Patrick.

"We're running late for the airport," said Chalmers.

Karl Hess came up to the porch with a sunrise smile and blazing blue eyes set in a leathery face. He wore jeans, custom cowboy boots caked with mud, and a flannel shirt with the sleeves rolled up over sun-streaked arms. We went out behind Chalmers to greet him.

"Sweet Auburn, loveliest village of the lea," said Ross.

"How thy charms are fled," said Hess with a loud, booming laugh. He flashed a pearly white smile. I recognized the Goldsmith poem that we were memorizing for HIP.

"That's the one poem I can still recite from heart," said Hess. He pronounced poem *po-aim*.

"Stick around, Karl, and Trish will have you rememorizing all of them," said Swensen.

"Trish here?" said Hess. "I ought to give that sweet thing a big bear hug for those cookies she made."

"You've done enough harm, Karl," said Chalmers. "You're late as it is."

"Yeah, I had to tend a field of soybeans all mornin'."

"I thought you were bringing the pickup," said Blaine. "I have a few things—"

"Ellis, we'll blow the stink of the world off," said Hess as he set the case of beer down on the porch rail. "Or maybe you'd rather go lyin' in the back of Hogg's deathmobile?" He brushed his hand across Blaine's flat-top for effect. "You're almost lookin' like a monk, Ellis!" He laughed with a booming crackle that nearly took your ears out. A slight twang came through in his *r*'s. He reminded me of a young Andy Griffith.

"While I was stirring soil," said Hess, "*you* been stirring them up to start the Crusades all over?" Hess moseyed right up to the fierce HIP warrior general.

"Just leave the guys alone," said Chalmers. "Stop having them out for stargazing and bonfires. They aren't ready for the apocalypse just yet."

"I plan to do lots more harm, Rich," said Hess. His defiance was all the more potent, mixed as it was with a laughing countenance.

"Filling their heads with becoming monks. Why don't you become one?"

"It's a calling," said Blaine, "you know that, Rich."

"Yeah, to go into hiding."

Hess laughed and slapped at DeBlasio and McDarby in a comradely way. Winston grabbed a beer and downed it. Hess handed out beers.

"Rich, someone's got to tend the fields for the day when there's no food, no electricity in the cities. Besides, someday we'll have a monastery in good old Kansas, right, boys?"

The others voiced their approval.

"You stupid sonofabitch," said Chalmers, "not in mixed company." He pointed at me.

"Who have we here?" He looked me up and down. He held out a beer. I took it. Hogg lit up and so did I. Hess looked at me.

"Sorry. A beant." I handed him a Camel Light.

"A what?" Chalmers looked around. The others pretended they'd never heard the word. Chalmers looked at the cigarette. "Just my style, light." He laughed loudly, and then coughed as Hogg gave him a butane flame to cook his smoke.

"I'm Bernard. Bernard Kennisbaum from LA."

Hess shook my hand firmly.

"All right, Bernie, surfer boy, welcome! I hope Rich hasn't put you off your beer. Nothin' wrong with tippin' back a beer with the world ending." He laughed again. Chalmers snarled. Hess put his arm around me and pointed at the mailbox. "See, here's my name. It's been crossed through. Hopefully, not been crossed through in the more important mailbox of life. See these symbols? That's Alpha and this here one's Omega. I put them there. Some say the world will end in fire, some say in ice!"

"There's no time for poetry," said Chalmers. "He has a plane to catch." He nodded toward Blaine.

"Always time for poetry," said Hess, and took Blaine's bag. Blaine teared up, shaking everyone's hand. He came to Hogg. They embraced.

"Why don't you two make love while you're at it," said Chalmers.

"*In hoc signo vinces*," said Blaine.

Chalmers mumbled it almost obediently.

Blaine followed Hess to the Harley.

"What's the Latin mean?" I said.

"It's the sign of the Cross on the banners of Constantine, in the fourth century at the battle of the Milvian Bridge," said Chalmers. "He converted and created the Christian Empire, stretching from Byzantium to England. 'By this sign you will conquer.'" Was that what Chalmers was talking about when he mentioned Operation Constantine?

"Listen, Bernie, we'll have you out to the farm for some old-fashioned work behind some Belgians."

"Belgians?"

"Massive draft horses," said McDarby. "He doesn't believe in electricity or using the John Deere combines and tractors his father has on the farm."

"We're making people work brickle again, you'll see," said Hess.

"Work brickle?"

"Yeah, most of you college types need time getting versed in country things so you know what work is—get your backs hard, right boys?"

Patrick and the others nodded grimly.

"Yeah, I'm still itching from throwing hay for a week before school started," said Zorn. "Give me clean hops growing on trellises in the Willamette Valley."

"Don't let him make you paint stumps," said McDarby.

"And make sure he keeps you away from that bull of his, tried to hump me," said Swede.

"You're making it all sound so appetizing," I said.

"Don't listen to them, Bernie," said Hess, "we'll have you painting the gomer bulls before you know it."

We watched as Hess strapped the suitcase against the back rest. Blaine got on behind, then Hess got on. It started to rain, another small rain. Blaine pulled his jacket up over his head, the headless rider.

"You boys don't listen to Rich, he's crazy," Hess shouted. He jacked the bike violently into an explosive start and screamed over his engine:

"Question internal combustion!"

Hess pulled his goggles over his eyes and shot out onto Ohio Street. We heard the Harley's infernal combustion, like hell's farts, all the way down the street until they cut over to Kentucky Street on the way to Kansas City Airport.

"What's he talking about, gomer bulls and painting stumps?" I said.

"He made me chop off the dicks of some the bulls and then paint their stumps," said McDarby.

"What for?"

"The bulls are still horny and mount the heifers, marking the ones that are in heat," said Swede. "Then he has his favorite stud bull take over."

"That's awful," I said as we all grabbed our crotches in a protective reflex. The rain picked up.

XII

PRANKING PRIVILEGES

W<small>E</small> came in from the rain, bringing the beer. I was questioning my own internal combustion and thinking about those poor bulls. I sat on a blue Naugahyde couch. On a side table across the room by Zorn and DeBlasio was a two-foot-tall statue of the Virgin Mary in blue and pink robes, her hands outstretched.

"He's right," said Chalmers. "I've been trying to tell you fools that the time for bell ringing, poetry writing, and drunken rosary praying is over. The time has come for a crusade!"

"We can't afford your games, Rich," said Patrick.

"Who the hell are you to talk, dreamer?"

"These guys can't pay their bills as it is," he said.

"Patrick's right," said Swensen, "my father works hard to keep me in school. We can't throw it all away to engage in your pranks."

"I can't believe you stinking Jansenists, no balls, always worried about Daddy and money!" He had gone from philosophical chess master to irate general in short order.

"It is pious to consider one's parents," said Hogg.

"Who the hell are you to come in here talking like that to me?" said Chalmers who pushed Winston out of the way. "Just like the rest of you, a mewling bunch of castrated nuns." Chalmers leaned over, pulled Hogg's cigarettes out of his upper shirt pocket, pulled one out, and tossed it in the air. It landed on his lips. Hogg drew out his steel Zippo lighter. Chalmers snapped it from him, reading its inscription out loud: *in lux perpetua.*

"Not bad," said Chalmers. The others relaxed. Chalmers exhaled blue plumes of smoke that curled around the spears of light and seemed to festoon in particles of blue, yellow, and silver in the afternoon's mellow September sun. Chalmers put the lighter in the pocket of his tattered Levi's jean jacket. Hogg seemed only to notice light streaming from the window in front of the Virgin. The smoke separated into a spectrum of white, blue, and gray fragments riding on chariots of floating dust.

"So you're not going to ask for you lighter back—your *beants*?"

Hogg stood and stared at him, lost in the moment. "St. Thomas has five proofs for the existence of God. Have you ever thought that women could be a sixth proof?"

Chalmers laughed through the smoke pouring out of his nostrils. "Just sit down, Tom."

"Despite all your earlier argument, I am partial to the cosmological proof based on the world as—" began Zorn.

"Not now," said Chalmers, still amused and half laughing. He stared at the others for a moment, then he sat down and put out the cigarette in a large tan and white ceramic mug of cold coffee.

"Hogg's all right. Maybe you puritans could learn something from him."

"His parents are against his being here," said Swensen.

"They want him to go to their psychiatrist or they will take him out of school," said McDarby.

"Then we'll prevent it," said Chalmers. "There's money if you boys care to be men. We have funds."

Could this be the secret school fund, SCHLAYEX?

"All right, Tom, no more worrying about parents," said Chalmers. Hogg smiled and took his pack of cigarettes from Chalmers's jacket pocket. Chalmers was startled. Hogg also took the Zippo lighter from his other pocket. We expected the knife, but the only thing glinting was his teeth.

"He's not a pussy like you guys."

"We're no pussies," said McDarby. "Some of your pranks go too far."

"Is that right?" said Chalmers.

"Like the one on Karl," said DeBlasio. "You made him mortalize."

"Karl's a bigger bullshitter than I am. Just because he thought he was bedding down a postulant at the convent doesn't mean he did. He still has his faith, right?"

"That was uncool, man," said Swensen.

"Totally hideous," added Ross as he adjusted his Bishop Sheen belt buckle. Chalmers paced in front of us.

"We have to act now. Everything's at stake." Chalmers stopped when he came to me.

"Are *you* still here?"

"My father doesn't like me much either. He cut off my tuition when I joined HIP."

Chalmers nodded distractedly. Then he caught himself.

"Why *are* you here?"

"I am aware your club does not admit Jews, but maybe you could make an exception."

"A wisecracker," said Chalmers.

"I always quip while I'm ahead," I added.

Swensen snickered. Chalmers inspected me.

"What kind of jacket is this?"

"David Ben Gurion."

"What?"

"You know," I said flippantly, "another Jew, a general. Started the style in Beverly Hills. Ben Gurion was a real hand at covert operations against the Arabs, helped win the war for Palestine."

"Is that so?" Chalmers became hostile again. He grabbed my leatherbound volume. "Dante?"

"*Nel mezzo del camin di nostra vita . . .*"

He came close to me, staring into my eyes. "What the hell does a Jew from LA know from Dante and generals?"

Patrick stepped in. "Hey, Rich, he stood up for Tom."

Chalmers looked at Patrick Winston and his bulging arms. Winston seemed harmless enough until his blood got flowing, then he was fearsome.

"People think of Dante as this medieval love poet obsessed by a woman," I said, "but he was really just a guy with a lot of grudges and the whole *Divine* Comedy is one big prank on his enemies, and an even bigger tribute to a girl he could never get." DeBlasio let out a high-pitched snicker that sounded like it came from a much smaller man.

"So you like a good prank, do you, Bernard?" said Chalmers. "I'll bet they teach Jews in LA to prank all the time."

"You want to hear a story of when I was a Sigma Chi?" I said. Chalmers acted uninterested. "An alum delivered about ten boxes of Joe's glazed donuts on Homecoming day. We ate until we were bursting. After the game, we still had a couple of boxes of donuts. So one of the guys who had had too much beer pulls his pants down and puts a glazed donut on his pecker."

"You call that a prank?" said McDarby as he stifled his snickering.

"Somebody told him to stop doing that," I said, "but I insisted we should all do it. I reminded them how the Pi Phi's hated us and had snubbed us. I said we should give them a pledge of our fidelity. The guys didn't know what I was saying, so I suggested we all put the donuts on our wieners, then put the donuts back in the boxes and deliver them to the Pi Phi's with a conciliatory note."

"Donuts on your wieners?" said Ross, almost falling off the couch.

"Let him talk," said Chalmers. His eyes narrowed, as if he were seeing the next move.

"The next day, we checked the trash and found the empty donut boxes. We sent over a photograph of our fraternity to the Pi Phis. I had asked a brother to take a photo of us with our, you might say, glazed members and develop a blow-up. I don't think any of them will eat donuts the rest of their lives."

The group erupted as one, bodies cascading onto the oak floor. Chalmers looked at me and nodded. Swensen laughed as hard as the others, then shouted out, "It's a good thing they weren't long johns," which caused a new round of group cackling. Chalmers joined in the group laugh.

"I heard about the Pi Phi donut caper," said Chalmers. "That was you?"

"Yep. But I am nothing compared to Arson and Old Mace," I said.

"Where did you hear that?"

"Rich's old nickname," said DeBlasio.

"I read about it," I said. "You were credited with burning down the union."

"They could never make that stick," said an insouciant Chalmers. "That was before HIP, before my conversion."

"Yes, but I also heard you micturated on the chancellor's desk."

"I did what?" said Chalmers.

"Took a leak," said Patrick. Chalmers shrugged.

"Face it. You're a legend."

Chalmers thought for a moment, then said, "Let's just say I buy all of this, you've learned a lot here, listening at the screen, Ellis leaving for the monastery and other things. Why should we trust you?"

"Hey, it's the cone of silence, Chief," I said.

"A counteroperation depends on everything appearing as it always was. Do you understand? A fat Jew shows up, that's out of the ordinary."

"Well, I—"

Chalmers did not listen to my objections to his cut.

"Even as we speak, the College of Liberal Arts and Sciences assembly is meeting and is taking action. That means we have to be ready!"

"I am supposed to be a student representative to the assembly," I said.

"You what?" Chalmers studied me.

"I am a scholarship student assigned as representative to the assembly, from the honors program," I embellished.

"Scholarship?"

I nodded. Chalmers looked at the others. McDarby leered at me. Rich handed me back my Dante.

"We didn't know anything about a scholarship," said McDarby. "He said he was going to be turned down for a Fulbright."

"Sure," said Chalmers, "and he just happened to come here just at the right time. He just happens to be friends with you."

"I never said he was friends with me," said McDarby.

"He has more balls than all of you put together. He stood up for Hogg. He stood up to me. He's willing to put himself and his scholarship status on the line."

"Well . . ." I scanned the faces of the group, who met my eyes eagerly, if not a little suspiciously. "I don't know what I can give you, but sure."

Chalmers smiled and I relaxed, but then suddenly he had ahold of my Ben Gurion collar with a knife blade pointed at my neck.

"You so much as fart in the wrong direction—"

"I won't."

He let go of me and straightened his jean jacket, calm as a fraternity council president. My internal pressure rose until something crept out.

"Hideous," said Ross. Chalmers shook his head as the others laughed, assuming this was my joke on Chalmers and his comment. Chalmers stared out the front picture window.

"Here come your little princesses."

I looked out the window and saw the ravishing Apryl leading a train of maidens.

"It's Apryl," I said involuntarily. I saw Swensen shoot to his feet and straighten up his hair. I fanned the air with Dante.

"Hey, sugar dick, you're not her type," said Chalmers on his way to the door. I started out the door with Chalmers.

"Aren't you going to stay for poetry?" said Zorn. I had not planned to stay, but in for a penny . . .

"Total pussies," said Chalmers pinching his thumb, forefinger, and middle finger together, making the sign of the cross. "Remember, *In hoc signo vinces.*" He glowered at us.

"*In hoc signo vinces!*" we all yelled. Chalmers turned to me: "Don't forget it, Jew boy!"

He stormed out, kicking the screen door shut with a back kick, trouncing down the stairs of the front porch.

Chalmers blended into the dazzling light from Apryl, who approached. He leaned toward her, too familiar. I didn't like the way Chalmers was whispering to her. Apryl looked at the window as she talked to Rich. If she was onto me, I was also onto her.

XIII

BEGIN THE BEGUILE

APRYL had several girls in tow who lived at the Beguine, the nickname Patrick had for Apryl's house at 1215 Mississippi Street. "Ole Miss" was their more common nickname for the house of young women.

I smelled something terrible. The others on the couch groaned. Zorn fanned at the air furiously with a big blue cushion.

"Mike!" yelled Patrick as they all scattered in the room.

"Saved by the belle," I said as Apryl lighted up the doorway.

"Hello, Apryl," said McDarby. Apryl smiled and said, "Hello, Bob." We all just stood there as Zorn replaced the cushion, waiting for the air to clear.

"Are you going to let us in?" said Trish. We scrambled to the entrance. Bob opened the door, then joined Apryl. She offered her right arm to him—and her left arm to Hogg. They led her into the living room and left me to hold the door for the other girls. I tried to get her attention, but Apryl walked past me, showering all her attention on McDarby and Hogg. We all shifted on our feet politely as if we were at a tea.

"Hi Trish," said Ross. DeBlasio still fanned at the air. Zorn chortled.

"Bernard," said Apryl. I quickly stood before her. McDarby snapped me a look.

"At your service."

"You know Trish Ellsworth?" Trish turned to look at us. She was shy, but her green eyes glowed. *Ellsworth?*

"I think we met in class." She nodded demurely.

"Why don't you two sit there," said Apryl, assigning seats. I sat by Trish and watched as Apryl played Miss Manners with the chairs and couch. She put Zorn next to Martha Flink, a slender girl with short blond hair and cobalt eyes.

"Hi, Martha." Zorn straightened his hair for Martha.

Apryl stared at the group as if sizing us up for a photo shoot. She pointed to DeBlasio and made him move.

"Laura," said Apryl, pointing to DeBlasio. Laura Hull, whose ample breasts stretched her long yellow dress, practically skipped up to the imposing Italian.

"Hello, Sue," said Patrick to the shapely Sue Hurlbut wearing a bright pink polka-dot dress, strutting like a Jazz-era flapper.

"Diana, over here with Pete," said Apryl.

"Diana . . . how are you?"

"Please don't make me ride a horse," she said as the other girls laughed. Diana Dietz was only an inch shorter than Swensen. She had drawn her long, sandy blond hair into a tight bun and wore overalls that covered her strong, feminine figure. She looked so different—all of them did—in this setting apart from class. Apryl, queen among the retinue, took her seat by the Virgin.

"So you are Bernard," said Trish.

"Yes. I think I sat near you the first day of class." She had worn the jumper suit and had tears in her eyes. I now saw her resemblance to Nancy Ellsworth. My heart started racing.

"Why do you have bruises?" She touched my cheek.

"It helps us get ready for poetry."

"Let's recite 'O Mistress Mine,'" said Apryl, acting the curvaceous schoolmarm. She was cold and virginal, which made it more fascinating. I wanted her to thwack me with a stick. She looked around slowly, a lovely desert flower drinking in the longing gazes.

"O, Mistress mine, where art thou roaming, O stay and hear your true love's coming," she started. We chimed in by fits and starts:

That can sing both high and low.
Trip no further pretty sweeting,
Journey's end in lover's meeting,
Every wise man's son doth know.

I thought of Apryl and the brush of her cheek against mine as I studied her again and considered her likeness to the picture Hogg had shown me.

Trish looked at me. My hand brushed against hers. I was taken in by her green eyes.

> What is love, 'tis not hereafter.
> Present mirth hath present laughter.
> In delay there lies no plenty,
> Then come kiss me, sweet and twenty,
> Youth's a stuff 'twil not endure.

Apryl stopped, looked at me, and said, "Some of us aren't keeping up."

"Let's go onto another poem." Ross's eyes rolled into the back of his head.

"Now, Theordoric," said Apryl with a scold in her voice. The guys cracked up at the sound of Ross's full name. "This is an easy one. By William Wordsworth."

I expected it would be a difficult poem, "Ode on Intimations of Immortality" or something from "Tintern Abbey." Instead, it was perfectly short, almost childlike. Apryl recited it, speaking to my soul:

> My heart leaps up when I behold
> A rainbow in the sky
> So was it when my life began
> So is it now I am a man
> So be it when I shall grow old
> or let me die.
> The child is father of the man
> and I could wish my days to be
> bound each to each by natural piety.

After we finished, Apryl pointed to me. She walked toward the door. The others stared at me as if it were some miracle that I had the poem memorized already while the others were still fumbling.

I got up and looked at the others with a querulous expression as I followed Apryl outside. The air was fresh, pregnant with the post-rain smell of ozone and earth.

"Bernard." She stood close to me. I could smell her. I trembled.

"Yes, Apryl."

"Is there something you wish to say to me?"

"I guess I'm just good at memorizing poems?"

"You did not tell us about your *role*."

"My roll?" I looked down at my stomach.

"You are able to follow the proceedings of the university committee, all this time."

Chalmers!

"Word travels fast."

She put her hands on her hips and tilted her head. Venus was having none of it.

"I just happened in . . . well I didn't just happen in, but—"

"Which is it?"

"Everybody is either on the make or trying to accuse each other of something."

"Is that how you see us, now that you're working for the university?"

"That's not the way it is."

"What is it, then?"

"It's both."

"You just happened in to HIP, and you also were there for the university."

"Not exactly. I had an appointment due to my being on Professor Finley's honors committee. I am supposed to observe the proceedings of the College of Liberal Arts and Sciences." She got closer to me, drawing the outline of some letters on my chest.

"What did you write with your finger?"

"AMDG."

"More Latin?"

"Ad majorem Dei gloriam."

"What does it mean?"

"It means, all for the greater glory of God."

"I'm not sure I can live up to that—"

"I'm glad you'll be there to warn us about what they are going to do with the program." She flashed those mysterious eyes at me. I had never been anyone's Ken doll. Just like that, she had turned me, operating me as her spy. AMDG was right.

"I'll give you everything I learn."

She smiled, and then she kissed me—not a sensuous kiss, but on the cheek. My heart was pumping again.

"And something else." She pouted. "Trish."

"What about her?"

"Well, she's shy . . . maybe you could be nice to her at stargazing on Thursday night."

I had gone from feeling like a big man on campus to a footman, and now an escort, all in the short span of a couple of days. And I had thought I could work up the moxie to ask her out.

"No labor is too great for Hercules," I said, trying to cover my devastation. She patted me on the shoulder and started back inside. I saw the names again on the mailbox.

"Who is Corey Tartt?" I asked. She turned around.

"Corey is in graduate school. He went to Chalfontbleau monastery for a year, then he came back. Why?"

"Oh," I said. "I read about HIP graduates seeking out monasteries in Europe." She looked very suspicious. "Mind you," I added to diffuse her knitted brow, "lots of people are seeking out something in Buddhist and Taoist monasteries, and don't forget transcendental meditation."

"Professor Courtney says that the monastery has been in decline but has not gone away. These people are not hippies looking for transcendental meditation or belonging to some commune." She sounded like Hogg.

"Maybe just HIP students looking for an American monastery?" Apryl faced me with a look of reproval, then she shifted into bouncy 1950's bobby-socks innocence. She touched my cheek as if to acknowledge the holy place where her lips had kissed.

"Silly. There is no American monastery."

She walked back inside. I followed. Some of the guys and a couple of girls drank Zorn's beers. Trish sidled up to me as I drank one of Hess's beers.

"Are you coming to vespers?"

"Vespers?" Was that some HIP festival? I heard they liked fairs and festivals.

"It's a chant in Latin of the little office of the Church. Like what monks do, but for everyday people."

I was being thrown into the deep end. There was too much material here.

"The only Latin I know is from literature . . . *Amor vincit omnia.*"

"Et nos cedamus amori," she said.

"Mine is from Chaucer."

"Yes, but he got it from Virgil. *Omnia vincit amor: et nos cedamus amori*—Love conquers all, and let us also yield to love."

"See, I can't compete with all of your Latin."

"You have a beautiful singing voice—I've heard it in the lectures."

"Really?" I said. Trish nodded and smiled, flashing her dimples. She looked at Apryl, who signaled to her. I puffed my chest out and sang in operatic baritone: "My love is like a red, red rose that's newly sprung in June, my love is like a melody that's sweetly played in tune!"

Trish blushed.

"Isn't Apryl coming?" said McDarby.

"I wouldn't know," Trish said. "But Diana left for St. John's early." She looked at Swensen out of the corner of her eye, and he shifted toward his comrades.

"Hey, anybody seen Tom?" said Swensen.

They looked around. I pointed toward the back porch. As a group, they stared at Hogg standing outside.

"You guys are really peculiar," I said. "A peculiar people," I added. I looked at Trish. I smelled her fruity perfume. I took out a crumpled cigarette and began to smoke it. We all pushed out onto the porch. There we saw what had Hogg so transfixed—a grand rainbow on the horizon.

"Look, a double rainbow," exclaimed Trish.

"Has it been raining?" said Ross vaguely, craning his neck upward.

"It's a covenant," said Hogg.

"It's a symbol of the uniting of the spiritual with the material realm," I said. Hogg turned to look at me. The others looked at me. "According to ancient myths," I added.

"It signifies a new beginning," said Ross. We continued staring at the mysterious phenomenon of nature, oblivious to Ross's insightful gloss. But there it was. And here I was with this group, strangely a part of them and yet not. Trish had something of her mother's compelling femininity. First Apryl, now Trish—a stand-in Apryl, a stalking horse. And they wanted me to sing some Latin chant.

Was I No Man, the clever nom de guerre of Odysseus, worming his way out of being eaten alive by the one-eyed monster of the university, or Proteus rising from the sea of Wescoe Beach, shifting shapes for each occasion?

Was I insane to get close to the chancellor's secretary's daughter, or Chalmers, or the rest? Daedalus at least had wings of wax. I had a scholarship and a world of double crosses in play.

XIV

ADAMS IN THE VOID

"*N*ASCANTUR *in admiratione,*" said Meg Neis. She had a head of wavy flaming-red hair flowing in all directions. It swished when she moved, following her like a mane. We repeated the Latin as a group. A hundred yards away, Hess stoked a huge bonfire with dead hickory limbs. It was late September; we were stargazing at Hess's farm south of Lawrence near a town called Le Loup. Normally, it was held at an overlook outside Lawrence, but this was the big event that Hess put on once a year.

"'Let them be born in wonder,'" said Roy Neis. "The motto of our program and our endeavor before the stars." He fell silent in a reverent gaze upward, his spade chin scraping at the sky. He was a skinny, credulous fellow in khakis and a yellow oxford shirt. The clothes hung baggy on him and contributed to his liberal-arts fundamentalist aura, like a Paul Courtney doll. Together, Meg and Roy were the ultimate HIP couple: fervent, natural, recently married. They taught stargazing, poetry, and oral Latin.

"We are the species who can lift up our heads and admire," said Meg fervidly. A couple of girls from Ole Miss sighed. I was trailing behind the skirts of Apryl. I was becoming her Pinocchio, an eager marionette. My nose was growing longer by the day.

"We brought you out tonight because we felt that the conditions were best to see Draco and Ursa Minor. It's cold, and greasy Joan doth keel the pot . . . but it's the stars that speak their icy language." Roy Neis was authoritative when it came to stargazing. Meg was right beside him, holding his waist. Her eyes gleamed with romantic delight at the cold canopy of stars and the light of the preternatural fire at our backs.

My head was swirling from Homer, not only *The Odyssey* but also *The Illiad*. And the ancient I had never read but was now drinking like Coca-Cola—Lucretius. His *On the Nature of the Universe* was crowding my interior universe. He saw the world as made up of a void, and atoms swimming about in that void, latching on to things and creating this whole wild circus we called life. We were all experiencing life for the first time as adults, Adams in search of Eves.

Apryl looked soft in her cashmere sweater, silken in the moonlight. The stars cast a net of silver over everything else while I worked up the courage to ask her out. McDarby shoved others out of the way to be near her. We were up against each other. Normally, the guys would not permit that kind of male proximity, but when it came to a girl in a crowded bar, or under the stars, exceptions had to be made.

"Where's Swensen?" I asked.

"What do you care?" said McDarby. "He's not drooling over Apryl."

"What?"

"She'll never go for you, L. A."

He liked calling me *LA*. Swensen had to be up to something to miss stargazing. I kept an eye on Apryl, her sweater clinging to her, as if she were painted in purple light and gossamer, her high forehead and perfect form imparting to her the regal luminescence of a voluptuous china statue.

Russ Grigson, our rhetoric instructor, wore a sweater he had picked up on a semester in Ireland with HIP. Apryl was pointing out the brighter stars to him. He looked stately, with a receding hairline, strong chin, and noble nose. A former marine sergeant, everybody looked up to him. He had taught Roy Neis about calling the stars, like belting out military acronyms or standard operating procedures.

A few of us had taken several swigs from a flask. DeBlasio groped Mary Ann Pester as they congregated on the dark mound. Jimmy Drungole stood next to Mary Anne, dazzling her with Langston Hughes. Trish Ellsworth, the solitary green-eyed beauty, stood near me. She smiled at me as we learned about Cassiopeia.

"You can see Draco, the dragon, in the right quadrant, right up there," said Roy. "Yes, that's it, the head is right there."

"Where?" I whined. "All I can see is a thousand stars."

"Be patient, Bernard," said Meg. "Now the head of the dragon can be followed back to the neck, then it loops around again into the body, then under Ursa Minor, which is also known as the Little Dipper."

"I'd like to show her my dipper," said DeBlasio. Mary Anne Pester bared teeth at that remark. Patrick giggled in stealth.

"Well, there are several galaxies in Draco," said Lucas Raleigh, the group egghead, with thick glasses and a tuft of curly black hair that stood up high on his head, "but we can see only about a hundred thirty with the naked eye. This is an edge-on elliptical galaxy, and the dust lanes are visible in larger telescopes like Livermore in California." There was a pained silence, followed by groans. Someone in the group of Chalmers and McDarby and Ross blew on their hands and made explosive fart sounds.

"Thank you, Lucas, for that highly scientific information," said Meg, "but as you know, the professors want our astronomy to be story-based."

"As you recall," said Roy, "Draco guarded the golden apples of Hesperides."

"Does anyone remember what happened to Draco?" quizzed Meg.

"He got his dipper caught by a sword," said Chalmers.

Meg ignored it. The rest of Apryl's roommates were nearby. The tall Diana Dietz looked at us disdainfully, then raised her strong hand. With her other hand, she brushed back her long, silky blond hair over her winter coat.

"Hercules killed the dragon during one of his labors," she said proudly. Trish and Sue Hurlbut stifled a giggle.

"And he got the apple from the tree of knowledge and bit into it," I said. "Almost," said Meg taking my answer seriously. "But we're mixing up our stories. Hercules got the golden apples all right, but the tree of knowledge of good and evil was in another garden."

"Eden," said Laura Hull. Trish looked at me with a cute smile. I pinched her when she wasn't looking, making her squeal.

"That's right," said Meg. "Now, let's try to spend a little silent time fixing on Draco and Ursa Minor."

Meg led us in reciting the Frost we'd learned that week, apostrophizing to the fairest star in sight.

I moved from Trish. McDarby moved toward Apryl. She did not move away. After the poem ended, the group was silent for a few minutes. Apryl turned to me, framed in perfect starlight. She broke a smile. I was ready to ask her out.

"This is from a cavalier poet," said Meg, "for all of you young cavaliers, 'On Julia,' repeat after me:

Whenas in silks my Julia goes,
Then, then methinks how sweetly flows
The liquefaction of her clothes."

I stumbled over the lines purposely. Apryl corrected me.

Next when I cast mine eyes to see
That brave vibration each way free,
O, how that glittering taketh me!

As they went back over the poem, I turned to Apryl.

"I have to ask you something."

Apryl began to walk away from me. I followed as I chanted the poetry in a trance, my eyes fixed on the liquefaction of Apryl. I got close to her.

"I was wondering if—"

I couldn't get the words out. She leaned over toward me, brushing against me, about to kiss me, I thought.

Just then, I heard a faint clop of hooves in the distance. Eyes tried to fix on the sounds coming from the dark hillside that sloped down to the Hess farmhouse and barns. Apryl raised her eyes.

"I wanted to ask—" I said.

"Isn't that beautiful?"

I looked at her.

"Yes."

She looked at me.

"I mean up there." I gazed again in the sky. It was a shower of shooting stars flitting across the sky. Together, we were transfixed. I could hear noises from the group, which was also admiring the show.

"I have to confess, I never saw this before—or a real double rainbow."

"Maybe you weren't really looking," said Apryl.

"It's Penelope!" yelled a voice suddenly. We snapped out of our starry reverie and saw a horse coming up the hill. Apryl hurried to meet it. A tall rider sat in the saddle of a bay horse. I stared and realized it was Pete Swensen, his powerful hands gripping the pommel like a blond Gary Cooper.

"Pete!" said Apryl, and he replied: "Tell me not sweet, I am unkind, that to the nunnery of thy chaste breast and quiet mind to war and arms I fly . . ."

Apryl said back to him, "True, a new mistress now I chase, the first foe in the field," and with that, the group joined in: "and with a stronger faith embrace a sword, a *horse*, a shield!"

Apryl approached the horse as it backed up, neighing on cue. I looked at Meg and Roy, who were cooing as if they knew Swensen was coming and had timed it perfectly as a great finale to the romance of stargazing.

"Yet this inconstancy is such as you too shall adore," added Swensen. The crowd held its breath. "I could not love thee dear so much, loved I not honor more!"

With the final lines, Swensen scooped up Apryl with his massive hands, placing her sidesaddle in front of him. The crowd rushed toward the bonfire. I stayed back to get a good view of Swensen riding majestically on the back of Hess's horse, Penelope, into the silver mist.

McDarby and Patrick came up alongside, forlorn.

"And this is why I sojourn here, alone and palely loitering . . ."

Patrick had begun to quote the Keats line, but I finished it as I watched her: "La belle dame sans merci."

McDarby pulled out the flask. The three of us took strong belts. Hess joined us, slapping us on the backs, smelling of hickory smoke.

"Boys, when you're one-upped like that, only remedy is a cold swim in the quarry."

We followed him away from the bonfire where the others sang, "Believe Me, if All Those Endearing Young Charms." We soon found ourselves in a woods, meandering in a cathedral of branches and undergrowth. Soon, we came out onto an outcropping of rocks.

"Been skinny-dipping here for years. Old abandoned quarry, part of the old homestead," Hess said.

Hess was naked and shone like a god in the moonlight. His splash threw water up at us as we struggled to keep our balance on the rocks. McDarby was half out of his clothes before he piled into the water, screaming at high pitch at the cold shock. Then I tore off my clothes and jumped in. When I shot up out of the dark void, I was splashing and screaming and glad of life.

"No women—just us, the rocks, the water, and the stars."

We looked up as Hess was reciting Frost, taking something like a star.

For me, the stars shone bright and fiery and full of warmth, reflecting an upside-down universe. I saw the stars that night, really for the first time, warm and personal. As I beheld the spheres in that water, without any clothes, without stratagems or parental problems or girl issues, there was just Beauty; and something else I could not then, or now, define. Yet it was a thing that seemed essential, something you could not go on living without.

XV

MURDER BY COMMITTEE

I STOOD in the middle of the College of Liberal Arts and Sciences in the ballroom of the student union, a vanity fair of egos I had only read about in French plays of manners. They lacked only the powdered wigs.

"The minutes shall reflect the vote of the assembly to delegate to the advisory committee full plenary authority to appoint another committee to study the Shaefer Humanities Integration Program." With upturned nose, Herman Gunther trumpeted his triumph in reintegrating the colleges back in the Liberal Arts and Sciences, a coup de grâce of immense importance to professors, for it consolidated power and money in his hands.

Through their dossiers on Courtney, Marin, and Whelan, I learned that Chester Whelan was able to get a lot through the College Assembly in the late '60s and early '70s. A division of the colleges into semi-autonomous units of learning was seen at that time as a way to quell student unrest. Whelan, Courtney, and Marin had joined forces and created their experimental program in the college-within-the-college system.

Perhaps if Whelan had been content to rise to his own level, to join forces with Poe and Dryden, Johnson and Donne, Willie Shakes and Cervantes, they would have let him have his little kingdom where freshmen and sophomores could tilt at windmills until they got down to real majors. He and Marin had been teaching these principles for years—the trivium—and they had tried to set up their own little Oxford movement.

Herman Gunther had a different style. He presided over the College Assembly by fear, the arched eyebrow over the glare of azure eyes.

93

Traces of his Bavarian origins lingered in his stern vocal inflections, his implacable formality.

"I have decided with the help"—he pronounced it *zee help*—"of the vice chair of the assembly, Marzette Towner, to appoint the new head of the committee." Gunther raised his nose proudly. I looked at another woman, Ms. Eleanor Rottblatt, seated next to Finley. She had a sloped nose, silken dark hair, strong hands, and roving eyes.

"Charles Finley will head the new Humanities Integration Systems Search."

I looked at Chester Whelan, who seethed. How could they appoint that prig, that lecherous climber? Whelan writhed in his chair. A hundred professors grumbled, which seemed to me their sole reason for living. Courtney stared at the floor, half smiling, unmoved, the perfect master.

I looked at Finley, the goateed roué, gloating in his arm-patched tweed. Eyes of granite, slate cheeks, a chin like a tree stump—a man of forty, with gargantuan vanity. He had an enviable physique, but muscle tone could not conceal that his jacket did not quite fit, for his upper body was overlong, giving him the appearance of a Minotaur.

Ms. Rottblatt, a carnivorous low-level university administrator in the College of Liberal Arts and Sciences under Dean Toffel, whispered to Finley. Finley then spoke:

"This committee will see what improvements might be made in the coming academic year, including reintegration with the college at large, evaluation of academic requirements and prerequisites, and funding."

"This is an unprecedented incursion on academic freedom!" Whelan stomped toward the front, boisterous and untamed.

"*Scheiss*," cursed Gunther under his breath. Towner shook her head at Whelan.

"It's a goddamned inquisition is what it is!"

I looked up at the railing above the union's ballroom floor: Fred Marin. He smoked defiantly. His voice filled the hall. "You look like a she-bear, Gunther, in your bear pit, smeared with the smell of heat."

"Now, Fred . . ." All of the English Department feared him and the rumors: Marin decking the visiting professor of comparative literature from the University of Chicago who had merely discussed his exploits among the Zuni; how he had witnessed a couple of human heads shrunken and had written about it in his book, *From Here to Modernity*; Marin pulling a knife on Dean Toffel that nearly got him canned but for the lack of any others to support the dean's decision.

"Fred, let me handle this," snapped Whelan.

"Whatever you say, Chester."

Marin stood there, flicking his ashes onto the chairman's table. I slumped in my chair, hoping to avoid Marin's detection.

"Chairman Gunther," began Whelan prosaically, "this was not even published in the *College Minutes*." I had worked in the honors-program office. I had heard of this publication being used for gossip. Professors engaged in everything antithetical to collegiality; backbiting, rumor-mongering, hatred, spite, and character assassination were the stock-in-trade of academic intercourse.

But Whelan hijacked the *College Minutes* and created a stir with his *Br'er Rabbit, PhD* series satirizing the administration and the money-grubbing of the leporine "climbers" of the College of Liberal Arts and Sciences.

I saw the rope-like hair of Eldridge Buntrock, the aging critic from the Northrop Frye school who had lost his mind over movies, who went to matinees. *Rocky*, John Belushi, Truffaut, Fellini, Blake Edwards . . . I know because I had seen him. He had seized on Unamuno, wrung his hands all across campus, and won a student award because he no longer required essays, but only asked that students observe the tragic in simple things—in objects on campus, in the stars, in nature. He professed a love for the HIP students, a genuine love of Truth, and a love of Latin. I was his star in the Chaucer seminar.

But here in the assembly, Buntrock was speechless, as were the other Catholic colleagues, who saw their HIP counterparts being roasted on one side and being turned over on the other, as I discovered later—men like Buntrock, Chaney Folsom, and Dennis Killian, who masked coward-ice behind a veneer of textual references.

"You gentlemen would not be so cavalier if it came to the court-room." Whelan had been waiting to unleash this on the assembly.

"*Vell*, you see . . ." Gunther circumlocuted about breach of assembly procedure, whimpering like a beaten hound.

Rottblatt took over. Her passionless words and arch pronouncement of procedure chilled the assembly, her eyes raking her quarry.

"A point of order . . ."

But she got nowhere with Whelan.

"You haven't even the courage to confront us directly with this an-tinomian proceeding," he said, ignoring the she-wolf. "You think your-selves the high priests of some inquisitorial tribunal. You fear us because we are radical. You who claim to be social progressives are really reactionaries. You can't abide something as popular as HIP. You won't kill us in the open, so you form little committees to euthanize us academically. Gentlemen, it is murder by committee."

There was a syncopated intake of breath, a hundred professors and underlings sucking in a zeppelin of hot air. Marin smiled. I admired how Whelan turned the tables on them.

"How dare you accuse us of conducting an inquisition!" (Gunther pronounced it *in-qvi-zition*.) I scanned a menagerie of professorial expressions from feigned incredulity, patrician chin extension, indignant beard-pulling, and physiognomic distortions worthy of Hieronymus Bosch.

"What is to prevent you from launching this type of so-called Advisory Committee investigation against any one of these other professors, say for infidelity, or . . . " Whelan stopped as his gaze turned to the Minotaur, Charles Finley.

"Now, Chester, I have the floor—"

"Bullshit, Gunther!" Marin's gravelly voice descended from above like a grave prophet of doom. He blew a defiant cloud of smoke and tapped his filterless cigarette so that the ashes drifted down into Gunther's water glass. "Let him speak . . . or forever hold your *piece!*" Marin said as he grasped his crotch, fixed above the assembly like a derisive Zeus. In his gray-blue eyes loomed the glare of Achilles, the resolve of Paris, the duty of Aeneas.

As Whelan began to speak, a voice rang out, shrill and inexorable.

"This is precisely the kind of anarchy and retrograde attitude that HIP has bred from the start. It seeks to instill a sense of tradition only to undermine all legitimate authority with the university and the world."

It was Finley, the redhead, the bearded satyr, the legend of sexual conquests—second only to Fred Marin.

"That's far enough, Finley!" Marin was giving him an order. I saw a steel object in his hand.

Finley proceeded with his filibuster when he caught the glint of steel. I saw it was just a lighter. Finley froze in his tracks. Marin put the lighter in his pocket.

"Better make a decision quick, Gunther," Marin chortled. Soon, he coughed from the ocean of phlegm in his chest.

Gunther cleared his throat. "Well, it appears as though we will have to reconvene at another convenient time and will reconsider naming the committee after . . . ahem . . . proper notice."

The assembly grumbled as one. Finley stared out at them. Nobody was going to test Marin. By the time anyone could find him, he would be gone.

"You saw him!" screamed Finley. "You can't let him get away with this!"

One by one, the body of professors began to file out of the ballroom. Finley stomped off with Gunther to a paneled room. Whelan snorted. After a few of the professors had cleared out, I saw Executive Vice Chancellor Albert Holloway. He looked at me as if to say all of this would play nicely into his plans to bring down HIP.

As I made my way out of the ballroom and down a flight of stairs, I was stopped in my tracks. Damn, it was Marin!

"Hello, Professor Marin." He was blocking my way.

"You think it went well?" He sneered. I felt my knees go wobbly.

"I liked the trick with your lighter. You had me going for a moment."

"They're going to get their pound of flesh either way. We are corrupting the youth. Or do you think we're treating you all well, Bernard?"

"You know who I am?"

"Bernard Kennisbaum, son of Norm Kennisbaum." He looked me over. "You look like her."

"Her? My mother? You know my mother?" Had he been talking with the chancellor or vice chancellor? Maybe Chalmers.

He stepped closer to me, one stair above me, until his eyes were level with mine. I could smell alcohol on his breath.

"Why are you here?"

I looked into Marin's eyes. A terrifying sea of blue anger.

"I am a student representative—"

"Yes, but why are *you* here?"

"At the assembly?"

"At the university. At *this* university."

"I want to help you."

"What makes you think I need help?"

"I mean . . . help the Humanities Integration Program."

Marin let out a sardonic laugh. He pulled out a beant. I tried to light it for him one-handed, but I fumbled my matches. He grabbed them from me and lit two matches one-handed, then pocketed them.

"You know how to do that?"

He blew a plume of smoke into my face.

"Will you really bring suit against the university?"

Marin searched my eyes. "Take some advice, boy. Get out of Dodge before the shooting starts."

Marin was down the stairs before I could ask him what he meant. What shooting? Why did Marin care what I was doing there? I looked at my hands. They were trembling.

XVI

STATE OF NATURE

F INE mists and aromas of autumn wrapped me in a blanket of forgetfulness. I too was full of the cloying, sweet scent of maple leaves, the
spices of dogwood and oak, ground in by thousands of careless feet along
the sylvan walks behind Strong, toward the Campanile and Memorial
Stadium, to worry about the Machiavellian administrators. The brilliance
of burning Moses bushes, orange-red, stirred a young man to thoughts
of spring, not fall. Nothing is known in the mind except that it first be
known in the senses.

One day, I went to my dorm mailbox and found a letter from Costa
Mesa, California. MMK. For Miriam M. Kennisbaum. She had exquisite
stationery from Benneton Graveur and impeccable handwriting, a real
epistolary female character right out of Trollope, whose massive books
were always on her bedside. She had even perfumed the letter with her
Chanel No 5.

> *My Dearest Bernard:*
>
> *No doubt by the time you read this, you may have learned
> that your father has cut off your tuition. I don't know what has
> come between you, although I can only imagine it relates to his
> plans for you.*
>
> *Perhaps you can learn to appreciate how much he has cared
> for you and me all these years and find it in your heart to forgive.
> If you only knew what he has had to put up with.*
>
> *It may be too early for rapprochement. But I dare say that it is
> not too early to find your own path that does not cut us out of your
> life. After all, his business degree and hard work have provided
> only the finest things for us.*

To that end, I have enclosed this check from my own funds and will continue to do so without his knowing. I hope you will keep this between us.

I remain,
Your loving Mother

I looked at the check. Providing the finest things may have been the problem, for her and me. What did she mean, "what he has had to put up with"?

In the program, we had finished reading Lucretius and the theories of the ancients on the nature of the universe. Now we were reading Plato, but for all his peripatetic poetry and thought, I could not get my mind off Lucretius as I watched the natural shapes of young women explode in my sight. I copied into my journal from Lucretius's *On the Nature of Things.*

Book IV
SENSATION AND SEX

I am blazing a trail through pathless tracts of the
Muses' Pierian realm, where no foot has ever trod
before. What joy it is to light upon virgin springs
and drink their waters.

I read only a few sentences before I was compelled to look again at the nubility of some co-eds. The world thus embroidered with the musty cologne of classicism was baptized, no longer lurid or shameful—sacred.

That is why I have tried to administer it to you in
the dulcet strains of poesy, coated with the sweet
honey of the Muses. My object has been to engage
your mind with my verses while you gain insight
into the nature of the universe . . .

If Lucretius was right and people were nothing but atoms in a void, this was some void. No man on campus could ignore the show of atoms known as campus chicks. Lucretius had a name for the force that brought atoms together in this pleasing way: *swerve.* I was swerving to avoid the void.

Those on the verge of manhood, in whose limbs the
seed created by maturing age is beginning to gather,
are invaded from without by images emanating from
various bodies with tidings of an alluring face and a

delightful complexion. This stimulates the organs
swollen with an accumulation of seed.

But Apryl walking into a room caused swelling with her atomic swerve, a "brave vibration, each way free." It was as if the girls in sweaters made the atoms sit up and beg in a patterned swerve. Lucretius was wrong. It was no void of atoms accidentally banging into each other to form something pleasing. It was a conspiracy of atoms. Downright impish atoms. Some criminal valence that combined so, a conspiracy of atomic hoodlums, elfin electrons, molecular Mephistopheles.

That is why you will not find it so easy to locate the
source of a smell as of a sound. The effluence
grows cold by dawdling through the air and does not
rush with its tidings to the senses hotfoot from its source.

Trish Ellsworth, Apryl's familiar, was the true daughter of HIP: soft, approachable, with mild features, laughing eyes, sweet voice. She helped me memorize poetry, learn folk songs, and understand the story of the stars. I still remember her as having the smell of autumn. Memory and smell became one. I even stood by her and tried to sing Latin chant at St. John the Evangelist Catholic Church. Apryl saw us together as the priest, a silver-haired, jovial Irishman named Father Connell, intoned the Latin of the chant, *Deus adjutorum me intende.* Every so often, we would do a half bend toward the altar, *Gloria Patri et filii, et . . .* I caught Apryl looking as we inclined.

Lately, I had begun to see Trish as lovely on her own. Maybe the electrons were conspiring. Maybe I knew Apryl was as unattainable as fall itself. That day, I saw Trish emerge through the web of autumnal stickiness and slanting light, in a cashmere sweater that made of her breasts two downy tufts. As Trish joined me, her eyes lit up.

"Hurry, we'll be late for the lecture." Trish slipped her hand into mine. I had not held hands and run with a girl since Jennie McInnes in fourth grade. I clutched Lucretius in my other hand. I felt a state of blissful forgetfulness. We skipped toward the looming granite citadel of Strong where Apryl led us in singing. She seemed to be looking at me. The charms of youth are endearing, and Apryl's charms swerved over the room.

Believe me, if all those endearing young charms,
    Which I gaze on so fondly today,
Were to change by tomorrow, and fleet in my arms,
    Like fairy-gifts fading away . . .

I was in the back row with Trish and the guys from 1132 Ohio. Right in front of us was Jimmy Drungole.

> No, the heart that has truly loved never forgets,
>   But as truly loves onto the close,
> As the sun-flower turns on her god, when he sets,
>   The same look which she turn'd when he rose.

Somehow, this poetry, put to such simple music, prepared us for a conversation. At nineteen and twenty years old, what did we know about ultimate commitment in the face of wrinkles, time's grooves of disease and weakness? Love and sensuality, so close to each other, were like twins.

Trish and I were laughing. Then Apryl fixed me with those haunting eyes. I stared, maybe a little too long.

"Look, the professors are coming in," Trish said, breaking my spell. I saw Marin come in and take the stage. I had not quite gotten over our encounter on the stairs at the student union.

XVII

METAPHYSICAL STREAKING

" S o you want to be good democrats?" Marin did not wait before going on the attack.

"What Mr. Marin is saying is true," said Whelan, "you think democracy is fair, but is it fair for the mob to rule? Plato is peripatetic." Whelan waited for us to register another inscrutable word. "He's walking and talking, you might say."

"Do you want to be happy?" Silence descended with Courtney's question. I looked at Trish, who flashed me the perfect smile of a girl on the verge of womanhood. Apryl rested her chin on her sleek hands.

"Plato wants you to be happy," continued Courtney. "What he means by happiness, and what you mean by it, are perhaps not the same thing."

"You believe in the pursuit of happiness as a right, don't you?" scoffed Marin. "You all have drafted your own little Declarations of Independence."

"What does it say?" asked Courtney. "'We believe these truths to be self-evident, that all men are created equal and endowed by their creator with certain unalienable rights, among which are life, liberty, and the pursuit of happiness.'"

"See this?" Marin lit up a beant. "This is my pursuit of happiness." He blew out a huge plume of smoke. "You don't pursue happiness, it pursues you. Chasing after happiness is like chasing after girls!"

"Mr. Marin's right," said Whelan. "Yours is the first generation that thinks happiness is a right, as opposed to a byproduct of living a good life."

"What is the Good?" said Courtney, ploughing with his Socratic tool beneath the topsoil of our minds, to the roots, without turning the whole thing into mud. "We talk in these lectures about the Good, the True, the Beautiful. Do you think those are just words?"

"Don't get them started on that, Paul," said Marin. "They think rhetoric is a bad thing. Don't you know it's part of the trivium, the ancient way of teaching that founded the university—rhetoric, grammar, and logic? And the quadrivium? They think we're engaged in sophistry. All this talk about self-evident truths!"

"Do you think that's true? That all self-evident truths are just a way of saying nothing is true?" They improvised like jazz musicians. "Is it self-evident that the sun is shining? Is it self-evident you exist? Are there things you can't prove but know exist? Like the love you have for your parents or siblings that you can't express, even to yourself?"

"They think they're in a state of nature, Chester," said Marin. "Good little Lockeans who see themselves unfettered by categories, lapping up all those rights, those entitlements of happiness and property, being liberated from any rules or governance, existing just for little old you . . . owning yourself!"

Whelan crossed his legs and spoke. "There are first principles by which, you, of necessity, live, such as the axioms that things will not be sharp and dull at the same time—that if you go faster, you will arrive at your destination sooner. Are there principles even more basic than these in the realm of the mind, in the realm of ethics."

Courtney picked up the theme:

"I don't suppose you have read the *Federalist Papers*, but you will. They said that there are primary truths or first principles upon which all subsequent reasoning depends; and these first principles contain an internal evidence that is antecedent to all reflection and commands the assent of the mind. Once you remove these antecedent realities, you are nothing more than atoms in a void of your own thought."

Marin scowled: "This is going to shatter their illusions. Don't tell them they're just atoms in the void. They don't want to believe the university is a universe of mere atoms. Pleasure is what commands the assent of their minds."

"Yes," continued Whelan, "the whole university, not just the University of Kansas, seems built on the idea that illusions are reality, that the only knowledge possible is that which can be measured in a microscope, and that power and will in the end determine how we live. If you focus only on the atoms, if you see the world only through the electron micro-scope, you'll never see anything worth preserving in the West."

"Is the Good being able to do whatever you please, whenever you please?" asked Courtney. "Rousseau says that men were born free, but 'everywhere I see them in chains.' He thinks that the Good is returning to a state of being where laws are made to fit our pursuit of nature, of the savage pursuit of happiness. Certainly, that is what Lucretius saw. But what does Plato say about that?"

We were intently participating in the conversation even though we said nothing, silent acolytes to the sacrament of pure reason.

"Why is it you are unhappy, when you spend so much time pursu-ing happiness?" asked Marin. I leaned forward. "Is it because of civili-zation and its discontents? Are you simply Freudian fruits, destined to be unhappy? Or is it *your* way of looking at happiness that sows your discontent? Instead of looking inward for the good of your own navel, how about the common good? What ever became of virtue? Ordering yourself to what is good. Or have you forgotten about that? There was a time when it was a betrayal of your country to protest in favor of your country's enemy."

"O, Fred, don't attack their war protests," said Whelan. "They're primed for betrayal of the West. They have already determined that Judas was just a guy who needed therapy. Just a higher dose of Thorazine."

Marin stood, bellicose, ready to pounce: "Is there *anything* . . . or *anyone* . . . you atomists would not betray?" Courtney came back in, res-cued us, and drew us back to Plato.

"Plato has a rhetoric. It is the pursuit of Truth through the appeal to knowledge, empathy, and emotions. This is an order of Truth, you see. So Plato's answer is to ask about the common good. What is justice?"

"Well, what is it?" asked Marin. He turned to Courtney and sneered, "They didn't read the text, did they? All of you are little Thrasymachuses from the *Republic*. Socrates tells you, mind your own business. That's jus-tice. Every person doing his own business. Know thyself, all you Greeks. Are you minding your own business, or are you poking in the business of others?"

I was supposed to be pursuing business all right, but it wasn't my business. It was the Floor King's business, and the university wanted to make my business the business of everyone else.

"We're asking you to take Plato and Western civilization seriously," said Whelan. "We're asking you to do something your generation does not like to do. It does not like to look at the past and ask, What did these people think? and take what they say on their own terms."

"To think presupposes that there is a form for thought," interjected a quiet Courtney, rescuing us from Marin's diatribe, "that there is a human nature to think about. That is, you are constantly under a barrage of democratic talk, such as 'That's all a matter of opinion.' 'One man's ceiling is another man's floor.' And while these things have some application to our emotions and the way in which we choose houses and clothes, they have no real application to reality and the ethical choices we make in our lives."

Courtney stopped and stared at the ground, just warming up.

"That is," he resumed with greater excitement, "when we make these choices, we act as if there is Truth. When you leave this lecture hall, you're going to open the door—aren't you?—and walk through it."

I walked through the door on that first day.

"You're all either agnostics or Gnostics," said Marin. "Chester, I don't think they understand the words." He smiled sarcastically and looked at the class. "You think it's all in your head—reality—don't you? You're all a bunch of damn angels. But when you drive your car, all of you follow Newton's laws to a tee. You don't jump off buildings, do you?" Marin spat the words out contemptuously. "Milton said, 'The mind is its own place and can make a heaven of a hell, a hell of heaven.' Or didn't you know that?"

"You see," said Whelan, "either this is a room or it is not. It is not both true for me and untrue for you that I am speaking right now. And when you say 'There is no Truth' you have uttered Truth, a categorical imperative."

"The square of the hypotenuse is equal to the sum of the squares of the other sides," said Courtney.

"You could not get up in the morning if you questioned that," Marin said. "You think Pythagoras is math? It's Beauty. Only Euclid has looked on Beauty bare. They're blushing, Paul."

"Plato wants us to examine Beauty," said Courtney, "and he shows us Aphrodite, the goddess of love, both of spiritual and physical beauty."

Aphrodite was the Greek name for Venus.

"Consider what Plato said, that the unexamined life is not worth living." Courtney was looking out at us now, not looking down in his usual detached way. "You read in Herodotus about Croesus. He is you. You look out on your life and wonder, 'How will I live my life? will I be successful, rich, liked by people? Will I marry, will I be a good husband or wife, a good parent?' Does leading a life dedicated to the pursuit of wealth bring happiness? Herodotus asked that question. Croesus had it all. But was he happy? Remember what Herodotus said: until a man is dead, reserve the question of whether he is happy."

"Socrates says that all philosophy is a meditation on death," said Whelan. "And that meditation is about life and happiness in light of the end of man. We dare to ask these questions. We have not given up on the examined life or on the pursuit of the Good—of real happiness, contentment, and even something the Greek and Roman culture saw as transcendent. Here's the real question: Is the West worth preserving?"

Then the whistle screeched on campus, upsetting a lacuna of silence.

"At least go to the world of poetry," said Marin. "Don't you know, your love really is like a red, red rose, and her enduring young charms are fairy-gifts fading away? Wake up, damn it, youth's a stuff 'twill not endure."

Not a body moved.

"What does Plato say about Beauty?" asked Courtney. He pulled out his Plato and read to us: "'When a man has been thus far tutored in the love of love, passing from view to view of beautiful things, in the right and regular ascent, suddenly he will have revealed to him, as he draws to the close of his dealings with love, a wondrous vision, beautiful in its nature.'" Courtney looked up: "What is he talking about? Isn't it the state of wonder, awe? And when in that state, you will begin to see beyond passion or emotion—to something more beautiful and delightful—you begin to see the Truth."

"Oh, Paul . . . you shouldn't say that word—Truth—without qualifiers." Whelan had a mocking, sarcastic tone. "I mean, it's not right—no parenthesis, no quote marks, just naked Truth. My God, it's *metaphysical streaking*."

The class erupted at the mention of what so typified this generation. The emperor may have had no clothes, but now, neither did his pupils.

"It catches up with you," said Courtney. "You will want the Good even as you realize you lack the virtue to achieve the Good. And then your life will really start. After you really read Plato, you will never be the same again."

I walked out into the hallway a little stupefied. Hogg and Apryl floated through the doors.

"O how that glittering taketh me!" quoted Hogg, reading our minds. Swensen shook his head and watched us as we watched Apryl. I patted my corduroy jacket with its suede patch, another luxury gift from my father's collection. Hogg quickly offered me a beant as we walked out of Strong together as we had walked in a couple of months before, in the shadow of Apryl's vibrations. Swensen came up from behind.

"You coming over to 1132?" said Swensen as we came out onto Jay-hawk Boulevard. We watched Apryl walk under a Dutch elm, one of the few to survive the disease that nearly wiped them all out.

"I have class," I said, mesmerized.

"That's debatable," said Swensen.

I looked at him and half smiled. I had to go to Kansas City to attend the meeting of concerned citizens against the program. Apryl flung her head back toward us with a smile, her hair slashing across her eyes. I saw something in her look—a challenge? Maybe justice was possible after all.

XVIII

TRIVIUM PURSUIT

I FOUND a picture on the front of a French medieval literature book I had. It depicted a tower of knowledge: the trivium. A knight in armor sat on a horse before the tower, and inside, at the top, was a damsel—the knowledge that leads to ultimate gentlemanly chivalry. One moment, I was Jekyll, the happy-go-lucky student of HIP consorting with the anti-modernist students, tilting at the windmills of the wasteland of university administration. The next, I was Hyde, working well outside the lines set down for higher education.

In the middle of this odyssey, I had to meet the parents committee in Kansas City. CAPUT, or Citizens Against Proselytization Under Teachers, held its meetings in the Unitarian Church of the Reverend Vern Rhoden, a man of no presence in Hagar double knit slacks and navy Unitarian blazer, which gave the impression of an umpire in the outfield. But nothing prepared me for the congeries of characters gathered there.

"Der Teufel lebt im Kellar der katholische Kirsche." The Reverend Johann Fruhling was a prepossessing man. A pastor of the local Lutheran parish, his own daughter had renounced the Lutheran Church to convert after her experience in HIP. I recognized the German from my studies: "The Devil lives in the cellar of the Catholic Church." His dark suit, goatee, and roving green eyes gave passion to this otherwise lifeless Unitarian Fellowship in Roeland Park.

"What is he saying?" This came from the wispy Father Sandy Smoot, a stick figure in priest's clothing, a member of Catholics for a Free Choice.

"What he's saying is, 'Let's get the bastards.'" Dr. Saul Littman was an imposing, porcine man with prickly hairs on the back of his neck. His large lips and fleshy nose spoke of great feats of drinking, when in fact it was just the surplusage of hormones that had this rich neurosurgeon from Mission Hills looking older than his forty-eight years.

"We should remain calm," said the Reverend Rhoden. He was short, with a bushy mustache that seemed to move all the time like whiskers on a cat. He edgily circled to the front of the denuded church where a cross in the shape of a plus sign hung sulkily. The rugs were plush burgundy Kodel polyester, designed, like the rest of the church, to give one the feeling of a modern living room. Muted light seemed a prisoner in the yellow windows that hinted of dirt rather than tint.

"I don't see what calm has to do with anything!" yelled a roguish-looking man of six feet five. He had a penetrating voice. He stood, towering over the tremulous Unitarian minister. His feet were outsized; his eyes were lodged deep inside cave-like sockets. His eyebrows were dark and angular. I had seen Dewain Schmead at Jayhawk games. A standout player from ages ago, he was a perennial figure at alumni functions and Sigma Chi fraternity rites. His son had been several years ahead of me in school. He was a regent of the University of Kansas, the building mogul of Lawrence with shady dealings with Kansas City labor.

"Mr. Schmead, I think everyone here knows your interest," Dr. Littman cut in gutturally, "but perhaps you might let them know that your involvement is purely as a regent, and your presence—"

"Yes, Dr. Littman," interrupted Schmead. Father Smoot lifted his nose in the air at this display of poor manners.

"Of course, Mr. Schmead, as a regent, is only here to advise and listen." Rhoden attempted a smile that came off as more of a snarl.

"Yes . . . as a listener," echoed Schmead with disdain. He looked at me and boomed out: "And how does that explain *his* presence—a student?!"

Rhoden's mustache twitched as he came in from right field. "This is Bernard Kennisbaum, who is reporting on HIP activities to the college assembly subcommittee. Officially . . . he is not here."

I smiled pertly.

"Well, then, I'll ignore him," said Schmead. "So, get on with it, Rhoden, and let's hear something concrete." He said the word *concrete* like no other, understanding its characteristics, its tendency to harden quickly when not properly poured or mixed, its tendency to go brittle when mixed with too much water.

"I for one insist that my son be rescued from this Chaffeeblow, or whatever they call this goyish monastery." Littman had a large cigar in his coat pocket which he must dearly have wanted to light up, as he kept pulling it out.

I immediately thought of Chalmers, of Karl Hess on his intimidating Harley with his country laugh, of Ellis Blaine and his haircut, and the innocence of Hogg's eyes in his Emily Dickinson death-mobile.

"What you counsel involves breaking laws," said Father Smoot.

"I'm sure you'll give me absolution, Bruce," said Littman.

"Laws . . . when they've broken every moral and international law?" interjected Fruhling. He stood. "There is a thing in theology, I am sure all of the clergy here would recognize it—a thing also recognized in the natural and civil law. It is called *justification*."

"Enough of the Sunday school crap," chortled Littman.

"It is no crap, and you would do well to heed its power, Herr Doctor. As I was saying, it is justification, wherein the individual—anyone in this room, or their hireling—will be justified in breaking laws, kidnapping in order to restore parents to their kids, lying and subterfuge in order to gain access to the superstitious monastery, and lying and cheating in order to discredit the Papists and Babylonians. *Selbstbestimmt*."

"Catholics know only lies, fornication, and stealing." It was an old lady in the back. "That's my experience." Sharon Blaine—grandmother of Ellis Blaine—leader of the altar society of the Country Club Presbyterian Church dead in the heart of Mission Hills, off the Country Club Plaza. She was decrepit, and yet in her plain dress was the figure of a woman of forty. I saw Ellis Blaine in her rheumy eyes.

She explained how she had disowned Ellis when he had become a Catholic. She had not spoken to him, but when he announced to the family his intention to go to a monastery in France, she decided she had to act, if not for the honor of the family, then for religious principle. She had enlisted the help of a friend of Ellis's in HIP.

"You can't do what you're proposing," said Father Smoot.

"I don't care what you do, you pipsqueak priest," said Sharon. "What you . . . people . . . do not know is that there are more than just my grandson and others here to think about. I know the child of a prominent citizen in HIP who needs this more than Ellis. I have been in touch with the parents, who are prepared to deprogram."

I had heard of students in TM and the Moonies getting deprogrammed. The professors had even joked about deprogramming us.

"Now, Mrs. Blaine," interrupted Rhoden with a frantic shift of his mustache, "we will address this problem in due course. We certainly cannot discuss anything like deprogramming in my church. What we propose is an operation, with your support and planning," he continued, "a consensus in the religious community, in our parishes, to support a rescue mission. There will be no talk of kidnapping. Nothing will be done against a person's will."

"Sure, Reverend, nothing against anyone's will," said Saul Littman with bitter sarcasm. "Do you propose that we send the milquetoast priest to parachute into this Shalfontblow monastery?" Littman laughed and whipped out the long cigar and fired it up to the shock of the gaping group.

"We cannot really have anything to do with something like this on United States soil." Rhoden gave Sharon Blaine an obsequious look. "However, if Vice Chancellor Holloway heard that a student was in HIP against his will and was then freed from the grip of proselytization, it might help turn the tide of opinion."

Sharon Blaine nodded. Rhoden smiled. They were definitely going to kidnap a HIP student. Was Apryl from a prominent family? Were they talking about kidnapping her?

Here was my opportunity to chase a new mistress—honor—and by doing so, by rescuing Apryl from their kidnapping scheme, be her knight in shining armor for real!

"This is illegal!" said Smoot.

"I'll be the judge of that," said a nasal voice from somewhere in the sanctuary. We all looked around. A short, compact man in a cheap three-piece suit came toward us. When he stopped, he folded his arms across his chest. I recognized him as the Kansas attorney general. He watched, cross-armed, over all of Kansas from billboards that read: "He knows when the law is broken." He popped out of trunks to nail KU students for possession of marijuana or LSD, showing up in disguise at parties in Johnson County, and busting rich politicians for cocaine. At the fraternity, he was the boogeyman everyone feared.

"I am here to make sure all is done in accordance with the law." He stopped in the middle of the sanctuary, as if unwilling to taint himself with full participation. "I am J. Barnett Hummer, attorney general for the State of Kansas."

"Attorney General Hummer," said Schmead. "Thank you for coming."

"No need to thank me, Dewain. I want something from this young man."

"Me?" I said. "What can you want from me?"

"Chalmers," he said. "I had him dead to rights for the burning of the union and drug activity. He slipped right through my grasp."

Clearly, he had been talking to Barrows. They really had this machine revved up.

"What can he do to get Chalmers?" said Rhoden.

"He is in HIP, you should know." Littman blew a giant billow of cigar smoke that sent Rhoden coughing.

"You are reporting on HIP to the administration, and you are also in it?" said Schmead suspiciously.

"I am taking the course. I've attended a few functions . . ."

"Are you going to be a monk?" said Schmead.

"Not if I can help it," I said with a smirk. "But I am a spy, Moneypenny," I said in my worst Sean Connery impression. "And I'm spying on the College of Liberal Arts and Sciences at the university as well. A regular double-O-seven scholarship."

"So, you wish to find out dirt on them, underhanded style, and pretend to be what you are not." Reverend Fruhling's eyes scanned me up and down. "You would fit in well in the Missouri Synod."

"Just get me Chalmers, and I'll . . . overlook your indiscretions," Hummer said to me, and abruptly left the church. Had Barrows told him about the marijuana?

"Zat man is quite surreptitious," said Fruhling.

"What can you report now?" said Dr. Littman, glaring at me.

"They know about the HISS committee's intention to dismantle the program, they're aware of the intentions of discrediting them, and they're aware of moles in the program." I told them enough without betraying 1132 Ohio—and definitely not Apryl.

Schmead nodded. I saw his Ronald McDonald feet flipping around.

"Will you tell them about what we have said here?" said Fruhling.

"You mean, can you trust me?"

"That's right," said Schmead.

"*Ich bin ein teil von jener kraft die stets das Böse will, und stets das Gute schaft.*" I could not resist quoting the German.

"What the hell—"

"*Zehr gut!*" Fruhling was laughing. The others looked on in bafflement. Fruhling translated for them the immortal lines from Goethe's *Faust*: "I am a part of that force that always wants to do evil but always ends up creating good."

I was feeling something of the power of Faust after his studies, given as it was to me to play with people's lives—their meanings, intentions, and how they were projected in public and private—and to dash the wills and drives of the willful.

"So, you know our dear von Goethe," said Fruhling, his lower lip extended in approbation. "I think we can trust him. He knows he cannot go too far or he will be damned forever."

Damned was right. I stood and bowed to them.

"If you'll excuse me, I must report to the vice chancellor."

"You will tell him nothing about what we discussed," said Blaine.

"I will be discreet," I said. I walked to the back of the church and heard Schmead say, "I have reach, young man. Don't forget."

Schmead had a lot of reach as a tall, white power forward. He could harm me, the program, my friends. Here was a group of parents, well-funded and angry at HIP, who were about to finance the kidnapping of a student.

I was going to spy on them but come to the defense of a damsel. But could I be that knight on the horse before the tower of knowledge, who had unmistakably rescued Apryl?

XIX

THE TIBER FLOWS INTO THE KAW

"LET me get this straight: the romantic man tries to get his head in the clouds, but the insane man tries to get the clouds in his head," I said.

I heard the clank of bottles as Zorn appeared at the card table from the kitchen. A game of spades was in full swing under the framed opening to the dining room. Patrick lay on the couch reading a book. A neon orange Nerf hoop and net hung over the entryway, and every so often, without even lifting his eyes from the book, Patrick threw the ball into the air, where it hung a little before swishing through the net.

"Not exactly," said McDarby. "The romantic relies on reason alone. The insane man has lost everything but his reason. Read this—it's all in there."

He threw a thin paperback volume at me. I caught it and saw a picture of an exceptionally rotund man with a monocle and a mustache. I turned it over and saw the title: *Orthodoxy: the Romance of Faith* by G. K. Chesterton.

"Chesterton," I said. "I heard of him. He wrote essays. I read one for some class. On chasing your hat. Funny. I didn't realize he was so corpulent. That makes him chasing hats even funnier."

"One day you'll be G. K.," said Swensen cruelly. Ross heard the rhyme and said: "One fine day, he'll be like G. K."

I dropped in daily now at 1132 Ohio, familiar as a cat. I was writing papers for some of them. A harmless plagiarism, not even close to the skullduggery of the university. Holloway was being coy, and I could not

115

get any official word on who the kidnapping target was. By night, I did reconnaissance at Apryl's house, watching for intruders, straight out of Chaucer's "Miller's Tale." Better than anything the Sigma Chi's offered.

"Chesterton wrote a wonderful book on Chaucer," said Swensen.

"I am partial to "The Miller's Tale," I said.

"Chaucer drank too much beer when he wrote that," said Swensen after a hiccup.

"Maybe if he had Miller Lite," I said, "he would have had better taste."

"Miller's Ale," said Patrick, looking up from a book.

"You think they had 3.2 percent beer in Chaucer's time?" said Ross.

"Pure heresy," said Zorn. "The Rhine River should have flowed with our beer, then we wouldn't have had the liberal reforms. Everything is better with beer, as the monks used to say."

"They didn't say *that*," scoffed McDarby.

Zorn plied me with his family brew, "Champoeg" beer, in little brown bottles. He regaled me with the tales of mountebanks called *periti* who had lain in wait until Pope John XXIII convened the Second Vatican Council. Then they unleashed their plot to destroy the Church by instituting a series of worldly reforms designed to make the Church more Protestant. It was all laid out in a book he held up: *The Rhine Flows into the Tiber*. Zorn's hero, Archbishop Marcel Lefebvre, stood as the lone sentinel of tradition and held out against the corrupting influences of modernity.

"Don't mind Clark," said Swensen. "All that home brew and the rain and fog in the Northwest addles their brains so that they see conspiracies everywhere."

"I don't mind him," I said, "I just don't understand what you hope to achieve with all this monastic talk. Do you all intend on becoming monks?"

"Everyone must in some way become a monk," said Hogg as if he had returned to his body after an absence. DeBlasio smoked and stared at us as if he were waiting for orders to kill me. Patrick looked up from his book and smiled. He had recently showed me some short stories he had tucked away under his bed.

"I knew that Hess said he was going to get you all out to Le Loup for some kind of monk-like life," I said.

"What makes you say that?" said DeBlasio. I just shrugged. "You ask too many questions."

"What I don't get," I said, breaking the tension, "is why they don't just market this beer. They seem to have an endless supply."

"No way," said Zorn, "my grandfather forbids it. It's a family secret."

"Reading one of the best," I said to Patrick. "*Look Homeward, Angel*, one of my favorites. A stone, a leaf, a door . . ."

"If Thomas Wolfe really meant to go home again," said Patrick, "why didn't he just go and live in Asheville and thumb his nose at the town philistines?"

An overweight retriever camped out lazily under the chair. Its reddish-brown tail swished back and forth. I petted it, sympathizing with its corporeal state.

"Fido."

"*Phaedo*," said Patrick.

"I heard you all call him *Fido*?"

"No, *Phaedo*, a dialogue of Plato," said Hogg.

"Been 1132's dog for several years," added Patrick. "Nobody knows who he belongs to."

I chugged what was left of my small bottle. I was already on my second. It was easy to lose count of the diminutive bottles. "You have to look at it like Odysseus," said Patrick. "He tried to get home, and there were all these obstacles. Then when he got there, he was not recognized, and went in disguise. We all want to go home; but the question is, will anybody recognize us."

"Deep, man," said Swensen, loosely caustic, as he threw down a useless diamond. I moved closer to Patrick on the couch.

"Let me ask you something: you love your family?"

"All twelve of them."

"But they don't understand you want to be a writer. You are like Thomas Wolfe. They don't see you."

Patrick's hooded eyes became owl-like as he reveled in the thought.

"I think Wolfe was saying that you have to leave home, in the sense that you can't ever go back to being that person they knew because . . . he doesn't exist anymore."

"I always thought that coming to college," I said, "would mean becoming an entirely different person."

"You keep eating, you will be," said DeBlasio.

"What are you saying?" asked Patrick. "That you can't be you and also pursue a new set of purposes?"

"I don't know, but my parents see only one person. They don't see that I am not meant for that world of tiles and carpet and square footage. But you have real talent. 'Birds of Privilege' is the best story I've seen in a long time."

"I can't believe he shows his stuff to *you*," said Swensen with real venom, "but me, his housemate? Nooooo."

"My father cut me off," I said. "I'm not sure he knows me at all."

"Does anybody really know what the time is . . ." sang McDarby. The impersonal banter was actually a form of intimate badinage.

"Your father flipped because you're in HIP?" Ross said as he parlayed a very questionable blind-nil hand.

"You gonna go back to California, L. A.?"

"He's resolved never to commit Californication again," said Swensen. He pulled out the ace of spades and floated it high in the air.

"You could do worse than work in your father's business," said Patrick.

"You could do worse than become swingers on carpets," added Swensen.

"Is he really that bad?" asked Ross.

"My father is a decent man," I said. "But he is lost in numbers. He holds the ledgers of my life."

"Count me out; he's milking us with the ace again," said McDarby, throwing back his chair. "Whack him," McDarby said to DeBlasio. DeBlasio just smoked, staring into space, impervious to stale mafia jokes.

"I mortalized," said DeBlasio to the air. He puffed on his beant perfunctorily with no apparent pleasure.

"An old girlfriend," said Patrick to me. "*Mortalized* is his term for mortal sin."

"She's a succubus, man," DeBlasio said with a lugubrious drawl.

"Get thee to a priest," said McDarby. Hogg looked at DeBlasio earnestly.

DeBlasio grabbed the Nerf ball from Patrick, shot, and missed.

"He's back," said Patrick. "Don't worry, he struggles with betrayal and purity—and a mediocre jump shot."

"I can relate," I said.

"It's in his blood," said McDarby. "By his age, most of his Sicilian relatives have had seven mistresses."

"I'm Neapolitan," said DeBlasio.

"He comes in three delicious flavors," said Swensen.

"Didn't your relatives in Naples have something to do with a monastery near Pompei centuries ago?" said Hogg. "Related to St. Benedict's Monte Cassino?"

"It was destroyed by the Saracens," said DeBlasio. "My family tried to rebuild it but were prevented by rivals. The feuds persist to this day."

"So they burned down your family's monastery," I said.

"I never said that." DeBlasio looked irritated.

"He's milked us," said Zorn as they all looked down at the table. McDarby and Zorn abandoned hope as they yielded their highest trump cards. Swensen raked up the pile of forlorn trumps with his giant hands.

"I'm going to St. Johns," said Hogg as he disappeared out the back.

"He underbid again," said McDarby with a high tone of indignation.

"Sandbagged," said Zorn with utter dejection.

"I've always found that Spades is a game of betrayal," I said. "First you betray your partner, then yourself."

They gathered the cards and Zorn shuffled and started to deal them out. I looked at the hecklers and turned back to Winston.

"I think you can see clearly about some things," Patrick said, "because you are detached from Catholic judgments and the familiarity that breeds."

"Contempt?"

"No, it breeds commonality."

"Familiarity breeds. Period," said Swensen archly.

"Bernard helped me with that paper," said Zorn. "I got a B plus for my insights into Sir Phillip Sydney's apocalyptic imagery."

"It might help if you actually read *The Fairie Queen*," said Swensen.

"He doesn't need to read it—he *is* a fairie queen," said McDarby.

"Bernard helped you on T. S. Eliot," said Zorn.

"Yeah, I finally got the point about Teiresias and the wrinkled dugs," said McDarby as he trumped Ross's one-eyed jack of hearts.

"I'm outta this game," said Ross. McDarby looked at me.

"All right, gents," I said and sat down at the table. "I haven't played Spades since frat days. Of course, it was Strip Spades."

"That's hideous," said Swensen.

"Bishop Sheen says nudity is a sign of the demonic," said Ross as he shot the Nerf ball perfectly through the hoop and cheered under his breath.

"Demonic?" I said. "It's a sign of lowered inhibitions. Take streaking. I think people are tired of being smothered by this wasteland of clothing—polyester, television fashions that are here and gone in a minute."

"The Levi family is part of the illuminati," said Zorn.

Swensen shuffled the cards. "I'm in prime bluffing position." I was bluffing more than they knew.

"You sound like Tom," said Patrick. "He has all these bizarre ideas about St. Francis running naked to enter into the unitive stage of spirituality."

"Yes, he has very interesting ideas about the spiritual world," I said. "He'd fit in nicely in L. A." I had a great hand.

"Blind nil," said Swensen.

"You wouldn't dare," I said, thrilled at the prospect.

"Madam Sosostris and Teiresias combine for a hundred points!"

"He's just doing it to prolong the game," said Patrick. "He owes rent." The two of clubs came out.

"Losing a hundred points would set you back considerably," said Zorn, attempting to taunt the Swedish-Jewish team.

"That burning of the church at St. Mary's . . . it wasn't an accident, you know." They ignored Zorn.

"St. Mary's? I heard about that," I said, lying. I had waded through a lot of banter to get some real dope. Zorn explained how he had been attending the Traditio Latinae (TL) group's mass at St. Mary's on Sunday and getting several of the Ole Miss girls to go, like Diana Dietz, Martha Flink, and even Apryl. The Rhine fathers had conspired against Archbishop Lefebvre.

"Why would they burn it down?" I said, looking interested in my cards. Out of the corner of my eye, I saw them shifting on their chairs.

"They didn't," said Patrick. DeBlasio shot him a glance.

"One thing we know for sure, Hogg was not there," said Swensen, "he was too busy praying for the new pope."

"That's another thing," said Zorn, "if you read the prophecies of Saint Malachy, this pope is the one for the end times."

"That corpse you planted last year, has it sprouted?" said Swensen, careless of whether anyone got the reference.

"'Ich bin gar kein Russian . . . echt Deutsch,'" I quoted as I trumped McDarby's king of diamonds before it should have gone. Swensen's eyes bugged out.

"Man," I said, aware of adopting the 1132 diction, "I just don't get why you got a Polack pope when the Italians have been great at corruption all these years."

"It's the Holy Spirit," said Patrick.

Swensen waved at the air as I blew out gray-white smoke. "It's white smoke like that," said the Swede somewhat incoherently, "signaling the election. It's the apostolic line."

The descending sun peeked behind Ohio Street's hill opposite. All at once, the card table was cast into shadows of soft autumnal yellows and grays. I was lost in that light, and for a moment, time stopped. Then we heard a stirring at the door as a foot kicked it open.

XX

GAME AFOOT

"Look at you feckless pussies!" said Chalmers.

"Don't worry, boys," said a loud, friendly voice coming in behind Chalmers. Karl Hess wore a leather jacket. Motorcycle goggles dangled from his neck. "Is nobody going to offer us a beer?" Zorn darted into the kitchen.

"We have bad news and good," said Hess.

"What is it?" said McDarby. Zorn returned with several little brown bottles.

"Do you mind?" said Chalmers to Hess. Hess smiled and sat down on the couch next to Patrick, swigging his beer.

"The university has come out with a preliminary recommendation," said Chalmers. "They're going to yank the HIP credits for English and Western civ."

"They can't," said McDarby.

"It's outrageous," said Swensen.

"Mannn, I need those credits," said Ross.

"You mentioned good news," said Patrick, ever the businessman.

"That was the good news," I said. Chalmers looked at me with scorn.

"Good news is: Professor Courtney is picking up Dom Broglio at the airport. He's giving a retreat here this week."

"Father Broglio?" said Zorn.

"Dom Angelo," whispered Ross.

"That's great," said McDarby.

"Who is Dom Broglio?" I said.

Chalmers narrowed his eyes. "What are you doing here?"

"Leave him alone," said Swensen.

"Yeah, well, does he know anything that can be helpful? Do you?"

I remained silent, awaiting the right moment.

"Just as I thought," said Chalmers. He explained: Dom Angelo Broglio was a wealthy priest from Malta, son of a Greek mother and an Italian father of royal lineage, leading back to a powerful thirteenth-century Florentine family who had to flee in the ensuing feuds between the Guelfs and the Ghibellines. Broglio's forebears saw the golden domes of Jerusalem in the Crusades, who fought alongside Bohemond and walked the parapets of Constantinople at dawn. He had an impeccable education and had taught popes at the Angelicum. Now he was being marginalized following the coup d'état of Vatican II.

"He met Courtney at Chalfontbleau," said Chalmers.

"Yeah, he says it is the only real monastery left on earth," said Hess.

"That is exaggerated," said Hogg as he entered. "The Grand Chartreuse has never stopped producing saints, Solesme has preserved the Gregorian chant in a hundred monasteries throughout the world."

"We know, Tom, and we're going to do something about it," said Hess.

"Enough," said Chalmers. "As I was saying about Dom Broglio, he is both a canon and civil lawyer."

"I didn't know such people existed except in Dante's imagination," I said, and Zorn went into a tirade, telling how in 1962, Broglio had pounded away at the Rhine fathers who were attempting to rewrite the schemas, radically changing the liturgy to make the norms more Protestant, and scrap Latin as the universal language of the Church. He had harangued well beyond his twenty minutes when the secretary general gave the sign and they turned the microphone off. After that, Dom Broglio left the council and retreated into a little known Vatican Secretariat where he encouraged traditional Benedictine monasticism.

"Fascinating," I said. "So this explains Chalfontbleau and its popularity. It's like a Latin theme park."

Zorn chuckled in spite of himself.

"Do you think you can ignore two thousand years of culture and tradition?" Chalmers asked. I was not sure I wanted to challenge his logic again.

"Ignore, no, but you can't exactly return to it, can you?"

"That depends on how serious you want to become," said Hogg. Chalmers nodded.

"Broglio's going to give a retreat here," said Chalmers, "and you boys better not screw it up. And you, LA, might learn a few things about tradition."

"Broglio gave a great retreat at my place last year," said Hess. "Seven conversions, two marriages, and one dead bull." He paused as I gave him a slack-jawed glare. "We sacrificed a bull for our food. I read a passage from *The Odyssey*, and Father Broglio sacrificed the bull right there in the field. He was better at it than me, learned from his Uncle—a cattle rancher near Pisa."

This was getting a bit strange, with crusading Maltese priests, bull sacrifices, and drunken spades. I made a change in strategy on the fly.

"I think they're planning to kidnap someone," I said flatly.

Chalmers shrugged. Hess stared at me with his clear blues. I had expected more reaction than this.

"I went to the meeting of the Committee Against Proselytization Under Teachers. CAPUT."

"That's a ridiculous name," said McDarby.

"Shut up," said Chalmers.

"Blaine's grandmother is involved."

"Is that all you have?" said Chalmers. "That old Scotch woman? She sent in a fake novice once to spy on the HIP students on retreat at Chalfontbleau—after we discovered it with Ellis on a class trip to Europe. Didn't get shit on us."

"A regent of the university, Dewain Schmead, is financing an operation to kidnap and deprogram a HIP student, to use what they learn to discredit the program, and to prove brainwashing is occurring."

"Schmead," they all said. They knew him as a basketball star.

I didn't know why I was spilling this information. Maybe to get their confidence, maybe to set up my spectacular rescue.

"Hooly shiiittt," said Swensen, slipping into his nasally Norwegian lilt.

"And they're going after the professors' tenure." What could a little embellishment hurt?

"Buuuullll—shit," said Hess.

"We'll kill them," said McDarby with clenched teeth.

"Who are they going to kidnap?" said Chalmers.

"I had to be careful how I dug for information."

"Did they give you any useful information?" said Patrick.

"Just that the parents are prominent."

"Rhoden . . . that lowlife bastard," said Chalmers.

"I think the vice chancellor is also in on it."

"Holloway?" asked Chalmers.

"What's his role?" said Hess.

"I don't know. But he has an inordinate interest in women."

"Who?" asked Winston.

Chalmers came closer to me. He grabbed the round zipper pull of my faux leather black shirt, with gold rings. He started to pull the zipper down.

"Who?" said Chalmers. "He's not going to tell me." Chalmers looked around with smoldering eyes.

McDarby stomped. Ross's eyes were big. Swensen stood tall, his temples throbbing, his hands crushing the pack of cards. McDarby moved in closer to me. I could smell his beer breath. After a grim silence, Chalmers stood up and paced. He held out his hand. I quickly gave him a beant and lighted it. After a few long pulls, Chalmers snapped back toward me.

"You find out who will be kidnapped. I want it the next time I see you."

"Okay," I said. Then Chalmers turned to the others with fury.

"Cancel the Halloween party."

"Not that," said Ross. "I'm going as Seneca."

"Hogg's going as himself," said Swensen. "I'm not sure anyone will believe it."

"Michael's going to be Caligula," said McDarby. "I was going to be Diocletian."

"I'm Didymus the Blind," said Patrick without looking up.

"Forget your goddamned costumes," shouted Chalmers, "we can't allow them to kidnap someone while we engage in drunken revelry."

Desperation dropped down on them.

"Stick with the party," I said.

"The hell we will," said Chalmers.

"Listen to the boy," said Hess.

"I can let on to the university that you're having this party," I said. "Lots of drunkenness and Latin, with costumes—a perfect time for someone to slip in and kidnap the student for deprogramming."

"That's crazy," said McDarby. "We'll all be drunk."

"Exactly," said Patrick. "We'll lay a trap, get them at their own game!"

"That's the lamest-ass thing I ever heard," said Chalmers.

"Rich, get a grip," said Hess. "Anybody lays a hand on one of us, the rest of us will grab him and take him out to the farm for some carnal education with MF."

"MF?" I said, baffled.

Hess broke out in his booming laugh. "It's my prize bull. *MF* stands for mother—"

"MF it is," said Chalmers. "A few of us can hold our liquor. I'll bring along a friend, just in case." He lifted up his shirt. A shiny revolver was stuck in his waistband.

"Playing with toys, are we?" said Hess. "You might want to talk to my friend." He lifted up his pant leg, pulled a sawed-off shotgun out of his boot, and elevated it.

"Nobody gonna fuck with us," said Chalmers to shouts of approval.

"We'll talk to Broglio about it; he'll help with the planning," said Hess.

"He'll give the retreat and make it a crusade," said Chalmers in concordance.

"*In hoc signo vinces*," I said like a good student of Constantine and Latin. I even made the sign of the cross with them. Chalmers slapped me on the back really hard. McDarby whacked me too, for effect. Then Hess piled on this spontaneous scrum. Even the dog, Phaedo, jumped in for some male bonding.

We wrestled and struggled until we heard the click of a trigger. Everyone shot off the pile. There at the bottom was a nearly crushed Chalmers, in a fetal position, holding his gun. Phaedo grabbed the gun in his teeth and hid it under the couch like a bone. McDarby helped Chalmers up as Hess guffawed. Phaedo hung out his tongue as if gloating.

For the first time, I knew I could become an insider.

XXI

HYSTERICAL HISTORICAL

P RIOR to the retreat, someone had left a copy of *The New Testament* in the dorm lounge. I figured I had best get acquainted with the terminology. But what I found in *The Gospel of Matthew* was the truest depiction of how I felt walking around planet earth: trying to work within the system but constantly upending it; speaking the sublimest poetry of the human heart I had ever heard. How a man like the writer could have simply put down his accounting books and followed that son of man spoke volumes of my own longings to abandon the business and accounting track and follow a new path. It was easy to see why they killed him who had come to earth and committed the ultimate prank—showing mankind what he really is.

"So you think you are Catholics . . . some of you, maybe!"

Broglio was short, with thinning hair. His long black cassock made him look more imposing than if he had worn the normal priestly blacks. He had a face like a library: familiar and formal at once, inviting and vast. His perpetual grin trailed avuncular understanding and superior knowledge. He laughed in basso profundo.

Next to him was Father John Connell, the local parish priest, a comfortable *Going My Way* Crosby type—a silver-haired, second-generation Irish priest with laughing eyes and lips that turned up impishly at the corners. Broglio told us he was "canon and civil lawyer, come to smite the infidels." He had explained the death of the first Pope John Paul as providential, "for now you get what you deserve, a Polack."

"And now for my next trick . . ." Father Connell pulled out a cruet containing a rusty liquid and several crystal shot glasses with similar glyph lines. The bottle contained Irish Mist. He held up the crystal to the refracted light.

"Don't worry, Bernard, I'm not going to ask about your sins," said Connell. "Not yet, anyway." I looked at him in earnest. "I mean, we don't have *that* much time!"

I joined in a burst of laughter. Broglio wailed operatically and gave me the sign of the cross as if absolving me. The he uttered a sound, "Behp," which was an offhand Italian verbal shrug. Hess cawed in my ear so loud that I heard ringing for a minute. Hogg rubbed his ears, and he was on the other side of me. Hogg told me he felt Connell had mystical gifts that he submerged with laughter, drink, and camaraderie.

Apryl was on her pedestal around priests, ignoring me. I was her manservant. She batted her eyes at Broglio and ignored Chalmers, who sat openly eyeing her shapely figure. "Come to me, my Beatrice." She did. He sniffed the air around her.

"You all smell like Dante's Paolo and Francesco," said Broglio, "floating in a concupiscent carnivale of lust." Apryl looked distressed and sat.

DeBlasio had taken a shine to Broglio. Already, there had been one convert that weekend, young Chris Kozikowski. From Polish stock in Chicago, his family had left the Church over birth control, but not before they had had eight children. DeBlasio called it the ultimate Polish defection. A Swiss exchange student, Jacques, helped him through his conversion.

Jacques Gombault was from a small town in Switzerland, La Chaux-de-Fonds, near the French border. He spoke French and German and a couple of other languages, which he made sure you knew.

Paul Courtney sat uneasily through most of the weekend, enthusiastic only at the Tridentine Mass that was celebrated early in the morning, served by Jacques "with perfection" according to Broglio, who spoke impeccable French with Jacques. Courtney sat next to an intent, cross-armed Fred Marin in a cardigan. Chester Whelan was moved to tears and was seen wiping his eyes after the *Nobis Quoque Peccatoribus*. It was a moving ceremony.

"Some more wine, Doctor Courtney?" Mary Anne sweetly held the bottle of Château Nerf, as they called the passable BG French Burgundy. The gents of 1132 had been very careful not to buy any of that California wine. Courtney preached the virtues of French wine. Only then could one taste the poetry of the vine and say truly, in vino veritas.

All about Courtney were the groupies of the program, men in baggy khakis who put on dour expressions and those flowers of youth clad in long dresses and almost no makeup.

Broglio's face was flushed from his brandy Manhattans and the rich lasagna he had eaten with the strange "illiterati"—his name for 1132 when speaking to Courtney in French across the dinner table. He was supposed to talk to us about "The Church in the Modern World."

"The best lack all conviction, while the worst are full of passionate intensity. You wish for me to tell you about the Church in the modern world? What do I tell you? Mere anarchy is loosed upon the world, and you are the worst because you are full of passionate intensity. Still you are asleep. *Nel mezzo del cammin di nosta vita . . .* But can you awake? Will you?"

Most of the gathering of thirty were wide-eyed at Broglio's intensity. I appreciated the Dante rolling off his tongue like his mother language.

"As St. Francis—no pussycat—said concerning warfare with the Devil, 'I put my dung in his mouth.' That is what the Church is lacking in the modern world. Don't be nice . . . the saints were not nice people. St. Thomas More—a favorite among Anglos when I studied at the London School of Economics—he looked at the Lutherans of his day and called them 'bags of shite.'"

He winked at Marin, who shot his blue-red eyes around the room, monitoring shock levels. Several girls from Ole Miss were noticeably flushed. Diana Dietz stiffened at the impropriety and stared at Swensen as if it were his fault for hosting this wild Maltese Dominican.

"Now we represent the Holy Roman Catholic Church . . . and no man evacuates on us. I learn tonight that a monk has gone missing at Chalfontbleau in France."

I looked at Chalmers's smoldering face. Up until this, the Halloween party plan was still good. Now I didn't know what to think.

"We must stand up and fight as the Holy Roman Catholic Church . . . Say it, the Holy Roman Catholic Church!" He shouted and chanted it until a few began to join in, then, slowly, as all movements grew to a crescendo, and then after repetition, a full-blown cheer.

"We announce tonight a crusade. There will be no yielding to the infidel and the philistine. Your world is upside down, and now you are in a dark wood, with nobody to lead you. You see, in Europe, we have lived with this kind of thing for centuries. The faith is from Europe, of Europe, and through Europe. Poland is of Europe, barely, and so the new pope is of Europe. I come from the land of many rulers but only one people. We are of the race of Aeneas, of Romulus. Now that's a melting pot!"

Broglio beat his cassocked chest and waited for the laughter. Courtney looked at the floor and smiled with a deep spiritual contentment.

"You want peace, you cannot have it without heaven itself! You have to love your mother, *vergine Madre, figlia del tuo figlio, umile e alta più che creatura* . . . virgin mother, daughter of your son, most humble and highest creature ours."

I recognized the lines. From the *Paradiso* of Dante Alighieri. But it was a canto at the end of his unscalable mountain of poetry, something I could never comprehend before.

"Is this from some Bob Dylan?" said Broglio. He looked at me. "Is this not the celestial saint in Dante's masterpiece. Is it not Bernard of Clairvaux?"

I nodded, speechless.

"Bernardo m'accennava, e sorridea, perch' io guardassi suso. Yes? Purify your vision. Not just him, all of you."

I had always glossed over the fact that my name was right there. A few of the guys laughed. I never expected a Catholic retreat to be a lesson on *The Divine Comedy*.

"Now tells us what we have to look forward to: *Nel ventre tuo si raccese l'amore, per lo cui caldo nell'etterna pace cosi e germinato questo fiore.* The heat of eternal peace brings forth this heavenly rose. Reorder your passions. Make your stand now, begin your journey up the mountain of woe now!"

A thin crack of the lips formed on Marin's face, the beginnings of a smile. Hess looked like a burnished warrior returning from the holy wars, gleaming in his gold shirt and overalls. But Apryl looked sullen. As the group's balloon was elated by the helium of spiritual and temporal desire, they were brought down by an unearthly voice at the door.

"Going to a convent or monastery won't help." The slurred words came from the hallway at the front door crammed with young students. The lone figure stood in a coat, his face obscured by a hood.

"Who are you who interrupts me?"

He pulled back his hood. It was Ellis Blaine!

"Ellis, what are you doing here?" Chalmers rose.

Blaine showed a gaunt face, bloodshot eyes, and a sallow complexion. Broglio stepped forward.

"What happened to bring you to us in this condition . . . behp."

Blaine reeled into the room, stumbling drunkenly over the girls. He let his coat fall off. He was emaciated.

"I was kidnapped, then I escaped. I hid in a ruins in Pooteeay." (He meant Poitiers.) "I have been awake for three days."

"Thank God Charles Martel did not have the likes of you in his ranks," said Broglio.

"Charles Martel?"

"Every fool knows Poitiers is site of many famous battles in 732."

"Seven thirty-two?" Blaine repeated the numbers as if in a trance.

"Know your history. It was in 732 that Charles Martel turned back the advance of Islam and defeated the Arabs. As you also know, Mohammed died in the year 632 and started a worldwide attack on Christendom to subdue it. As they are doing again in Tehran and Beirut."

"Six thirty-two! Tehran?"

"Men like Charles Martel turned back the tide that had swept all of the Iberian Peninsula."

Blaine giggled wildly and then chanted:

In 732 did Charles Martel
Turn back the infidel

"You are a latter-day Tertullian . . . *credo quia absurdum est.*"

"Transhlate."

"I believe in that which is absurd," said Broglio looking Blaine up and down. "You are not even a heretic, for a heretic must have known better."

"I'm no heretic."

"You remind me of some students I had at the Angelicum—ineducable. You have a personality flaw embedded in a malformed intellect and will. It attracts you to the irrational."

"You're out of your Italian mind."

"Maltese. Please do not mistake me for that inferior race to the west."

"Right." Blaine shook his head.

"You are so impressed with your silly Protestant battles with Christendom. A minor wave in the ocean of important battles throughout history."

"Throughout history." Blaine looked like a zombie. "Give more, tell me more history. More dates! Tell me about Constantine and his dates."

That mention of Constantine caused an agitation in the ranks. I scanned the room. Everyone felt it: the danger and exhilaration of history.

"So what about all those dates with the number thirty-two in them?"
Blaine had the bloodshot eyes of a wild beast.

"Yes . . . well, let's see. Constantine was emperor in 332, turning the
empire Christian. It is quite elementary European history. Umm . . . in
432, Patrick became bishop of Ireland and thereafter spread monasticism
in England and France . . . there have been several key dates in monastic
history, beyond the founding of Monte Cassino, of course."

Blaine sat on the couch, somewhat calmed, mumbling about seven
hundred and thirty-two. Broglio looked at Chalmers, then Courtney.

"Now you are no doubt familiar with the founding of the great abbey in Poitiers, of St. Hilarius." Blaine looked up, calmed like a child hearing bedtime stories. "St. Hilaire, as he was also known, was the teacher of
St. Martin and also a very famous bishop of his time."

"St. Martin was hilarious . . ."

Broglio worked his way into the High Middle Ages, espousing the
view that the twelfth century was the highest point of civilization in
the history of recorded time, which gave us Chartres; Notre Dame; St.
Bernard of Clairvaux and the Crusades. Blaine's eyelids were drooping,
but he sat up straight and stared angrily at us. Apryl brought him coffee.
McDarby, Hess, and DeBlasio guarded the exits.

"It was not until the twelfth century that St. Hilaire-le-Grande was
built. You understand, and it came at a transitional period, approximately
the same time as the magnificent Benedictine abbey of Cluny, finished in
1132—"

"What? What did you say?"

"That would have been around 1132 that Cluny was finished, and
for a time, it was the largest basilica—"

"Cluny in 1132. St. Hilaire, Charles Martel in 732 . . ."

"Yes, uh, that is right, 732 and 1132 . . ." He searched his considerable memory. "Of course, it would come as no surprise to you," continued
Broglio, "no surprise at all—" He was stalling to retrieve dates from his
formidable brain.

"Yes, what, what?" Blaine fairly slobbered.

"In Poitiers, a center of learning was founded, the university, in the
year 1432. The same year as St. Francis took up his hermitage near Paola."

"Fourteen thirty-two, is that really true?" He grabbed Broglio by the
collar. Chalmers grabbed Blaine who looked at his erstwhile friend as if
he were seeing him for the first time.

"Do not forget yourself, apostate—you may be burning your bridges, but you are still Catholic until I report you to Rome and you are anathematized."

"Shut your Maltese trap! Now, tell me, is this true about the founding of the university in 1432. History . . . will teach us more about history."

"If history has taught us anything," Broglio pronounced, "it is that history has taught us nothing."

Ellis's eyes rolled to the back of his head like a rapacious beast. He pulled an enormous hunting knife from inside his robe. Blood trickled from an inadvertent wound to his hand.

Marin whipped out his switchblade. Click. The blade flashed for all to see.

XXII

A SWORD, A HORSE, A SHIELD

" I WANT the truth . . . or I will kill myself right now!"
Blaine stuck the bloody blade to his throat. It began to cut into his skin, but he appeared to feel nothing. Apryl was very close. Terror spread across her face. I needed to act but couldn't.

"You have no doubt heard of the Carthusian Order founded by St. Bruno and his companions." Blaine grumbled some reluctant semblance of recognition, the kind heard from a disgruntled pennant waver turned fence-sitter. "It was St. Hugh who directed Bruno and his companions, and Bernard, to go into the desert and found the monastery."

Hogg stood up.

"St. Hugh and Bernard." And he looked at me. At that moment, Blaine stood up suddenly, waving the knife around. Apryl shrieked.

"That name, Hugh!" Blaine stumbled forward and nearly fell with the knife on Martha.

"Hugh. Bishop, St. Hugh. That's right. Have you read about him in the monastery?"

"No." Blaine was dazed.

"He died in the same year as the completion of the abbey at Cluny. Eleven thirty-two." Blaine's bloodshot eyes looked into Broglio's importunately. I felt ancient stirrings of numbers from the back room of the Floor King.

Broglio caught the look in our eyes. He stared at me and flicked his head in the direction of Blaine. Apryl gave me a "do something" look.

I shot up and slapped Blaine hard across the face. The crack sent shock waves through the rows of retreatants. Blaine humped over, weeping.

"Eleven thirty-two," mumbled Blaine, his eyes afire with confusion and pain. "Fourteen thirty-two, seven thirty-two . . ." I grabbed the knife, and Blaine passed out on the couch where I had been sitting. Chalmers snapped his fingers: DeBlasio and McDarby came over and helped me carry Blaine to Swensen's bedroom off the living room on the other side of the stairs.

Broglio had the group's attention, but everyone looked up at me on our return. I fixed my eyes on Apryl. She stared at me. There were tears in her eyes. I then looked at Courtney, who appeared downcast, deflated—even sick.

"The time is coming for you to raise the banner," said Broglio, "to smite the modernistic swine. You must call them what they are—fascists! Just like when I was in Roma during the rise of the *Fascisti*. We must go on this crusade!"

He raised his arm and the room started again to chant, first haltingly—louder, then uncontrollably. Chalmers stomped his feet, drunk with enthusiasm. I joined in. The floor began to tremble as we chanted and stomped and yelled, "THE HOLY ROMAN CATHOLIC CHURCH!" over and over again.

I saw Courtney get up. The chanting died down.

"*Vale*, Paulo," said Broglio.

"Excuse me," he said to the group, "I am not feeling well." He headed out the door. I looked at the others, who were dumbfounded.

"I never thought I'd meet a man who speaks Dante's original Tuscan and seven other languages." Courtney looked up at me without my coat, running up beside him, rubbing and hugging myself for warmth. My breath clouded the air like cigarette smoke. It was the first frost of the year.

"He believes, like his ancestors, that Truth lies in the fight."

"Does Truth lie in the fight?"

"You showed real fortitude tonight."

"So you want us to fight the university?"

He essayed a half smile—not looking at me, but it was for me.

"We are trying to cultivate hearts and souls, not generate a political movement. What Dom Broglio proposes takes years of reading, praying, and training to avoid anarchy or plain egoism."

"Dom Broglio wants a crusade."

"Your name is Bernard."

"Yes."

"St. Bernard preached the Crusades not as some activist movement but as a holy response. His motives were pure. Forget what you have read. The history has been rewritten by those who are unfriendly to Christendom. The Crusades were the result of a thousand years of developed courtesy, martyrdom, saints, suffering, and high civilization. The Crusades were necessary battles to save your ancestors and mine from annihilation. They had mercenaries and thugs but also saints like Bernard."

"The committee wants to put you to death."

"Aren't we guilty?"

"Of what?"

"Corrupting the minds of the youth?" He displayed a thin smile of sarcasm.

"They're kidnapping students."

"Maybe you should pay attention to your studies."

"What about Dom Broglio? You heard him; he wants us to take action."

He paused, then looked down. "Pray, work, and sacrifice . . . it's the saint's way—it's the royal way." He opened the door to his Datsun, then turned and looked earnestly into my eyes.

"Bernard . . . conversion must come from within. You have found your senses and are celebrating them. You see the shadows outside the cave. Your soul seeks more."

"What more?"

"You will have to decide who you are or want to be."

Could he read me like Hogg?

"You see only the shadows now; you're in the cave, but soon you will have to come into the light."

"I am not even sure what I'm doing here—not just in the program . . . but at K.U."

"You're clever," he said.

"Thank you."

"Are you sure it's a compliment? Do you want to become serious about your studies? Having a thirst for knowledge. But it begins in wonder."

"You mean . . . belief?" I think I wanted that, especially reading the classics—and not for the grade—but this was getting a bit too personal.

"See where this takes you. Ride the wave in. Don't get ahead of it. Belief itself is a gift from outside of our minds. Even believing that you could comprehend belief of Truth."

"That sounds pretty advanced."

"Of course, if you feel like it, you might try saying the Ave Maria."

I looked into his penetrating eyes. A teacher was transmitting something human. He was not quite the proselytizer people had made him out to be, but he did broach the verboten subject of religion. A forbidden tree of theological knowledge. He started to look ashen.

"I'm sorry to keep you out in the cold."

"Good night."

Courtney got in his car, started it, and pulled away from the curb. I trembled. As his car disappeared, I looked up to the stars. Could I purify my vision, like Bernard said to do in *Paradiso*? How was I, a prevaricator from L.A., going to do that?

I tried to say an Ave Maria, but it came out awkward. So many in my own tradition had uttered sacred Hebrew words before the masters of torture and mass murder. I had the strange sensation of having been given an opportunity to wander into a wood and seek the mystic wolf. Courtney had thrown down a real challenge, if I was strong enough to take it. It made sense. I had to transcend all this chasing after unattainable things and seek the most unattainable of all: self-conquest, peace, understanding, and knowledge. I felt dizzy, as if I were turning higher and higher on a Ferris wheel.

I found myself suddenly speaking from the heart: "God of my fathers, God who is, who spoke to Moses from the burning bush on Mount Sinai, you know the desire of my heart. I can't do this on my own. I don't know how to become my own man, to break free, or take it all seriously."

I thought of all the others, desperate like me—unrequited lovers—who had asked for one thing: the love of a woman. In that moment, something like complete calm came over me. I discovered what had been eating at me outside Strong. I was right: I didn't need a girl—not in the way I used to think. I needed to be strong for Apryl and try not to pursue her. To help her without wanting anything in return. I would take my studies seriously. This had to be divine. It also had to go on paper.

I reached for my journal, ever my companion, in my large pocket. I would write it down, every jot and tittle. But the journal was not there!

I ran back to 1132 and searched for it in a panic as the gathering was breaking up. It was nowhere. What if the professors got ahold of it, or the administration? Would they think I was a double agent for Chalmers and Apryl? Without my journal, I was naked. With that scribe in me, ready to write down the prophecy revealed to me, I could make sense of experience. Without my powers to reflect, I would lack the power to see or resist, to hover in irony, to hold experience at bay.

INTERLUDE

BEAT THE DEVIL

*T*HERE *I was, in that picture, suavely smoking and standing—arms akimbo—on a porch, in a tuxedo, the very thing itself. Youth. Now here I am, in the inanition of middle age, wearing another rented tuxedo, not for a dance but a wedding. At least it wasn't another faux Catholic wedding, getting married in a Polish church to reach for something missing since college. She got the marriage annulled. I saw no reason not to go along and declare what we both knew: it was not a valid marriage. I have led an annulled life since.*

So what brought me to a monastery door, dark with the fretful pounding of fists, of those seeking to wake God up at the crack of civilization? And if he were there, what would it profit a man to find a woman and repose for a livelong day along a river of love? Would it matter after all of the comings and goings; would it bring fulfillment? What would the count of all the numbers be?

Time and memory cascade around me. Yet, somehow, I think there must be another self, protected through what was written. Is time like this, a circular process of thinking and returning and remembering? By writing it, do I lose the protection from the erosion of the cascades? Do the numbers lose their mystery once written down or explicated? Do things just happen once, or is it in reliving and recollecting over and over that the image of memory itself comes into focus in the mind?

Now that I have my journal, have I been safe all these years—safe from the buffets of time, safe from the heart's clutches? In those days, it was no use to talk to me. I would not have listened even if the man standing before a monastery door could have spoken to the youth who stood at the door of unrequited love. Numbers of age, numbers of girls, and the counting of cost would not do. Once given away, the heart does not count. Reason is not the need. The heart goes where it will. I am on the train from Poitiers to another town to seek out that convent, for I came not for a monk, but a nun. I am writing for the first time in many years.

I behold that youth on the porch, trying to put on a face to meet other faces in the identity bazaar. Did he do all that I recount—complicit in kidnapping, double dealing, lies? Was this not a complete diversion from higher education, this practical joking and contravention of law? It was the initiation I always wanted, not like a bar mitzvah or a fraternity hazing. Then I was flirting with an ancient religion, a little medieval philosophy. Was it a Faustian bargain or just a game to add some spice to collegiate tedium? Or the greatest flirtation of all—ultimate love?

So be it, if it meant avoiding another vapid year, avoiding a major, and avoiding thinking of a grim career and a world of Dacron and vinyl. At least my feet were set on a path. Somewhere. Toward someone. The trick was to be a part and also maintain my distance, to flirt with it but not fall for it, to beat the devil at the game of love and lust.

BOOK II

A STROLL DOWN MEDIEVAL LANE

Past ruined Ilion, Helen lives,
Alcestis rises from the shades,
Verse brought them forth, 'tis verse that gives
Immortal youth to mortal maids.

Soon shall Oblivion's deepening vale
Hide all these peopled hills you see,
The young, the proud, while lover's hail
These many summers you and me.

— *WALTER SAVAGE LANDOR*

XXIII

CULTURE AND ANARCHY

But the Gods, taking pity on mankind, born to work,
laid down the succession of recurring Feasts to restore
them from their fatigue, and gave them the Muses, and
Apollo their leader, and Dionysus, as companions in
their Feasts, so that nourishing themselves in festive
companionship with the Gods, they should again stand
upright and erect.

— *PLATO*

"I AM not a crook, but I am a lecher," I said as I grabbed Terry Marker, the twenty-three-year-old buxom blonde who looked twenty-seven. She had come as Sappho. This was no leap for her. She was advanced in her understanding of matters of love, and only Patrick knew her to be the lecherous Roman poetess. Patrick was an early Church father, Didymus the Blind. He found himself groping and latching onto things that would have gotten him slapped if he had come as anyone other than the patristic saint. I wore a mask of the fallen emperor of our generation, Richard Milhous Nixon. I had no dirty tricks but was trying to thwart a kidnapping.

A party can be one of the more spiritual experiences in the life of a youth. At some point, a party begins to resemble a dream where heaven and earth meld into the maxims of the moment. We were all like Proteus, really, and only as we aged did we lose that power to shift forms and shapes easily. The 1132 Halloween party now lacked one thing: the arrival of the queen. And our collective need to protect her.

"Dick, what are you doing?" Terry protested with ticklish laughter.

"Looking for the eighteen-minute gap," I said, glancing at her decolletage. I had been unable to locate my journal. Before the party, I had gone to Holloway, and he had bought my scheme for a kidnapping at the party.

Zorn waited nervously by the door, dressed in a gold-fringed robe. He was the prognosticator Nostradamus.

"There they are," said Zorn, anticipating Martha's entrance. He had not expected Jimmy Drungole, and certainly not Jimmy painted to look like a white man. He brought along a white girl from Corbin dorm dressed as Angela Davis in blackface and Afro wig.

"We're here to crash and smash your party smarty, 'cause we're a couple with dash and interracial panache and we're very hearty." He had shiny white teeth and spoke better nonsense than ever.

"Haime and Blackie . . . we love ya mammy." I sang my best Al Jolson in a Nixon voice, got down on one knee.

"Ask not what you can do for your university . . ." Jimmy wore a white tie and had that effervescent Boston-untouchable look.

"Jimmy the poet!" Zorn had drunk only about five Champoeg beers.

"The spade of Isis . . . a card-carrying member of the Mississippi Black Panthers. Your country club does admit us?"

Zorn regaled Jimmy with talk about the pope who comes during the third moon after the tide is red and Malachy's general prophecies. Ross had brought Rick Wakeman's album *The Six Wives of Henry VIII* from home. The synthetic sounds engulfed us with a metallic-orgiastic thrum, a crypto-medieval thesis and antithesis. DeBlasio was Caligula, fresh from confession with Father Connell. A few were dancing in various disguises, in Roman togas or antlers, as medieval damsels, and one skinny crusader in a Templar outfit replete with cape and hood.

"You said Catholic . . . sheesh!" said Jimmy as he scanned the gallery of statues. "This is idolatry central." Jimmy pointed to an odd couple, Stacey and Kim, two prominent fixtures of the Gay and Lesbian Coalition. Stacey and Kim relished the medieval aura of the program and had attended parties at 1132 for years. The isle of Lesbos, as DeBlasio called their house across the street, was a tame venue compared to this religious house. Two kids from the freshman class came as Iranian terrorists, faces caked with brown shoe polish and holding a sign: "Death to Satan Americans."

Swensen burst out into the party, large with alcohol. He was dressed as a hairy knight, a big rusty sword hanging sorry at his side. He had picked it up from Penshurst, the landlord, whose wife ran a junk/antique shop downtown, Brick-an'-Brac.

"Hooly sheet," said Swensen as he looked at Jimmy turned watermelon man next to me in the Nixon mask.

"Hieronymo . . . I'm mad again," yelled Swensen and grabbed my shoulder.

"What did the thunder say?" said Jimmy in a dramatic way as he turned around and hiked his butt in the air.

"Shantih . . ." I whispered in Swensen's ear. Swensen pulled back.

"How'd you know I'd been reading 'The Waste Land'?"

"You're so . . . wasted." Swensen suddenly staggered backward against the dining room wall. I turned to see what jolted him: it was Apryl.

Just as I had seen her in front of Strong Hall, only more radiant, with sprigs of olive in her hair and oil on her face that made her sparkle. A diaphanous sheet wrapped her sleek figure so that she looked like Aphrodite/Venus. As she wafted toward us, I smelled that rapturous smell again. My resolve crumbled in the face of this pulchritude. I was back in Florence standing before a painting.

Swensen, still in a trance, dropped to one knee. His rusty sword clanked against the dulled oak floor.

"My lady . . . I will that you would let me carry your scarf into battle." Swensen's red eyes looked up into hers.

"What white ritual is this?" asked Jimmy, marveling at the train of damsels hovering glassily behind Aphrodite.

"This is Aphrodite," I said. "But if we're being purist, we might say, Venus after the Romans."

The girls behind Apryl-Aphrodite giggled. Apryl held out her hand to us; I took it and kissed it.

"Hello, Mr. President. Where's Trish?" she said.

"She's with David Eisenhower in the Millard Fillmore memorial bathroom."

"I mean Trish, Bernard."

I was not letting go of her hand.

"Are you going to hold my hand all night?"

"That was my plan. Not to let you out of my sight."

"A little possessive, even for a disgraced president."

"Angela Davis is in the house, and we can't be too careful."

She chuckled with that low, sensual, throaty sound that vibrated through my bones. She left me with a "come back for more" goddess look. I got her a Champoeg beer.

"Ambrosia for a goddess."

I stood there with her observing the others.

"They all seem to know their place."

"Yes," she said, "and my subjects know they can seek my help any time they need it. That goes for you, Mr. President." She pushed me playfully. I got down on one knee to recite:

> Yet this inconstancy is such
> As thou too shalt adore;
> I could not love thee, Dear, so much,
> Loved I not Honour more.

"Oh?" She looked askance at me as if she caught my attempt to distance myself from the pursuit of her. She broke off the look.

"There's Diana!"

"Just in time for the hunt," I said. Her retinue from Ole Miss was taking over the party. A lusty Teutonic girl rounded the column leading from the living room into the dining room—Diana Dietz, the fine blond specimen, the puritanical German Catholic from Peculiar, Missouri. Swensen bowed to her curtsy. She just now had taken her first drink. Mere alcohol could not contend with her will.

McDarby rolled his eyes and said in a salacious tone, "Bei-sucker." Belinda Beisecker walked into the room with an older couple. I gathered that Belinda was one of Chalmers's old flames. Dressed up and with a Jacqueline Kennedy bouffant, she was tempting. Russ Grigson, the graduate student who taught rhetoric and Latin in HIP, strode alongside Belinda. He possessed a quiet military confidence.

Belinda and Russ were our "chaperones." But they were also reinforcements. After Blaine's untimely arrival, we weren't taking any chances.

Right behind Grigson was the one in the shining armor, clanking around inside it. Grigson flipped up the visor, revealing the severe-looking HIP grad, Corey Tartt. He had started the Society for Creative Anachronism, another HIP offshoot. Corey loved only one thing more than the stars: fencing. Slender, intellectual, and with wire rim glasses.

I looked across the room at Roy and Meg Neis, the celebrated HIP couple. They had come as Aragorn and Arwen, in the same glittery outfits they had worn to another costume party where they had fallen in love, now famous at Ole Miss. They both had a passion for Tolkien and spoke in elvish words in the language called Sandarin.

An amplified scratch across the nylon brought the room to silence. Ross started singing the Ben Jonson song we had been learning in HIP to Roy and Meg: "Drink to me only with thine eyes, and I will pledge with mine." We all joined in:

> The thirst that from the soul doth rise,
> Doth ask a drink divine;
> But might I of Jove's nectar's drink,
> I would not ask for thine.

McDarby raised his eyebrows at the word Jove. I nodded. We were both thinking of the goddess Jovey, not Jove.

"Martha . . . hi . . . I'll get you girls beer. And Meg, you look so . . . radiant." Zorn chortled and slid past Swensen. Martha Flink, with her short sandy hair, intelligent face, and small pointy breasts, was dressed appropriately as a shepherdess. She had protested at abortion clinics in Missouri. Zorn was arrested at an abortion clinic protest, and this had made him a hero to her, as she wanted to become a lawyer to argue abortion cases.

"Not the same old 1132 you remember, eh?" I said to Roy Neis.

"It's not so different, although your music choices are . . . interesting." Roy said this ruefully as he noticed the volume of Baudelaire sitting on the lamp table underneath the Sacred Heart. He had lived there when it was known derisively as "the cloister."

DeBlasio belched slightly, and Laura socked him in the arm.

"When in Rome," said DeBlasio.

Several girls moved in a bevy near Apryl, vestal virgins basking in her glow. Apryl ignored Swensen. Zorn went to the door. I heard a foreign accent.

"Jacques!" Zorn waved him over.

"'Allo."

"Jacques Gombault . . . Martha Ingersoll," said Zorn.

"You're the one from St. Mary's?" said Martha accusingly. "I've been wanting to meet you. You're famous in Traditio Latinae."

Jacques had clear green eyes, dark Gallic features. He wore a make-shift robe declaring himself to be Duns Scotus.

"I heard you said that TL needed the sanctuary burned. Is that true?" inquired Martha, a born cross-examiner.

"I was pointing out that the Church was built and used by those who never understood this great divide between the American Church—a heresy—and true Church. The Lord brought it down."

"I hardly think he lit the match," said Martha.

"That is still a mystery," said Jacques.

A hand went to my shoulder. I turned.

"Preppy on the Hudson!" I yelled. Sure enough, it was Perry.

"Glaze!" yelled Perry and slapped me on the back. "I see you're up to your old tricky dicks." He flashed a grin and gave the double peace sign.

"What brings you to these parts?"

"Someone has to check up on you in your intellectual devolution." He turned up an urbane smile. "I dated Martha last year," added Perry as a confessional aside for everyone to hear. Martha blushed. Zorn shook his hair like a lion. I was relieved to hear this friend from my fraternity days was not poaching on Apryl.

"He used to come over here sometimes," said Zorn.

"I had no idea you consorted with this house," I said.

"I see you're thick as thieves now," said Perry.

"I don't live here, if that's what you mean," Of course, I didn't say that Hogg had invited me to take Blaine's spot.

"No one would want to reside in this hovel," said Perry. "But it can be amusing. And I like old structures . . . They smell like the history of wood and human smells and must."

A strange cadence wafted through Ross's Bose speakers. I recognized the throaty, grainy scat voice from the Crossing's juke box. Couples were slow-dancing now, drinking in the desperation and beauty of the song. I started singing with the music of "A Little Trip to Heaven," but more to Apryl, the goddess transplendent, goddess sparkly, goddess with a raven shine—Aphrodite come to make a beauty contest and thereby start a war, come to find her doting Paris. She turned an eye in my direction.

Swensen caught the goddess's eye. He saw its flutter, the iris and the lovely diamond lake, saw it vibrate. He crept up to me. He started to put his hands around my throat. I felt the vise grip of his hands shutting off my windpipe. "There's something you're not telling us." I could not talk. "Why are they attacking us? Who is getting kidnapped?" I am sure my eyes were as big as saucers as I struggled and kicked. I started to panic for lack of air.

Perry came up to me, and Swensen let go. Perry leaned close and said, "We need to talk, old boy." In that tuxedo, he was like a secret agent. I took off my mask to get some oxygen.

"Who is that ridiculous couple with the glitter?" he asked.

"That's Meg and Roy Neis."

"They were talking some gibberish."

"I think it's elvish, from Tolkien—*The Lord of the Rings*?"

"I have heard of it. He's the one who's popular with the Dungeons and Dragons crowd."

"They really know their way around the stars."

"*Ad astra per aspera*, I always say."

"And her aspera isn't bad either," I said to complete the old joke on the motto of the State of Kansas.

He caught me looking at Apryl, then he looked at me. "La femme? ... *très joli*."

I put on the Nixon mask again to cover my blushing. "Don't look at me—Kissinger's the ladies' man."

"What did that drunk giant mean about kidnapping?"

I looked into Perry's eyes through my Nixon mask. It was curious, my running into him outside Strong after my meeting with Holloway.

"What do you know about this graduate program, SCH-LAX."

"It's SCHLAYEX: School for Laymen of Excellence."

He nodded. At that point, I looked around, and Apryl was gone. I could not find her anywhere.

Suddenly Swensen yelled, "SCHLAYEX! This party sucks!" He was going berserk. I tried to say, "What about Apryl?" but he had backed me over the sink, choking the life out of me. He had impossibly vise-strong hands. Perry backed away. Under that mask, the world was going black.

XXIV

CHRISTENING

J UST then, the basement door slammed into the refrigerator. Swensen released his grip on me. I ripped the mask off and gasped for air.

Tom Hogg burst from the basement in tonsure and robes, looking every bit the studious Dominican, wearing a pillow over his stomach. The Dumb Ox of Paris University. Young St. Thomas of Aquino. Stranger still, he had a woman on either arm, flashy as Christmas trees, dressed as hookers. One had sparkles on her halter top. The other, a fake platinum blonde, wore a strapless bra and a short dress that made her look like a young Carol Channing.

Hogg was playing the role of Aquinas in the moment of temptation from the prostitute. He was having me on all along. Swensen watched as Apryl drew near. She seemed to ignore everything around her, as if a spotlight had appeared over Hogg and its center was the tonsure. Was it real, had he cut out a circle of hair on top of his head?

"So Anselm has challenged me to objectify my proofs for the existence of God. He will never know the *in esse* that I have found tonight . . ." Hogg pronounced this with a near-Parisian accent. The one in the halter top laughed with an uncouth rasp.

"Garrigou LaGrange says that in order to leave the purgative stage, you have to abandon silly pursuits standing between you and God."

"Yes, Jack," said one of the girls with the platinum hair, touching Hogg's chin. She pronounced it *Jock*. Hogg lit up a Marlboro.

"Who are your friends, Thomas?" I asked.

"I found them in the West Bottoms of Kansas City, on the street."

Perry gathered around, smirking. McDarby shook his head at DeBlasio.

"That's not an area of town you should be in," said DeBlasio. He had been looking out for Hogg. It was already after midterms, and Hogg had barely cracked a book. All he did was read Garrigou LaGrange and St. Thomas, smoke, and pray.

"Rich challenged me to do one thing St. Thomas did. Quod erat demonstrandum," he said with a luminous glare into the distance.

Patrick/Didymus the Blind threw back his head and laughed. "Who cares what Chalmers thinks." He grabbed blindly for one of the Ole Miss girls. His hands landed on Sue Hurlbut. She shrieked with chaste glee.

"You wouldn't say that if he were here," said McDarby. He hopped up and down, a libidinous Robin Hood making eyes at Aphrodite. Apryl, unimpressed, took Hogg's arm.

"I can't believe you really shaved that spot for this party." She teetered and grabbed for a half-empty bottle of Zorn's Champoeg beer.

"Hey, get your own john, Jack," said Carol Channing.

"Party? . . . I have done it for sanctification," said Hogg.

"Bernard, Apryl, I'd like to introduce Margaret," Hogg said. "She is from Quebec." The one with the platinum wig glared at me, looking me up and down with cold blue eyes. "He's the one I told you about," Hogg said.

"Yeah, Jack, well, he'd better have the fare for the ride. And I don't recall giving you my name. Call me Martinique."

"I thought it was Jack," I said.

"Remember that there is only purity for the elect," said Hogg as he passed her off to me. Hogg followed Apryl out into the warm October night, in back, where the dogwoods swayed.

I turned to Martinique. DeBlasio, McDarby, and Swensen scampered toward Apryl, her bodyguards protecting from possible kidnappers. Perry turned to me and cocked an eyebrow:

"I'll let you handle this one." He walked off. I turned awkwardly to Martinique who was lighting a long, thin cigarette.

"You've come a long way, baby," I said. She blew a large plume of smoke into my face and studied me.

"So what's with the bitch?"

"What's with the long beant?"

She laughed in a nasally way. "Puppy love—seen it before," she said.

Hogg suddenly appeared. "Margaret, do you know about the three ways of the spiritual life?"

"Hey, Jack, don't call me that." Hogg wandered off. "So what's with the stuck-up goddess? She have a thing for Tommy?"

"You might say that. But she really does look like a goddess."

"How did he know my name?"

"How does he smell sin?"

"What?"

"I think he's an idiot savant or something."

"Kinda cute. Been bugging me with all kinds of old-world religion in Kansas City." I studied her face. Behind the Carol Channing wig and sparkles was a hard, attractive girl. Twenty-five, maybe older. Under the wig, she also had platinum blonde hair, flecked in places, edging to a dirty blond. Her slinky, green dress pulled at her breasts and made the outline of her nipples show. She reminded me of a rough-around-the-edges mermaid.

"So you met Hogg in the West Bottoms?"

She turned and poked out her posterior at me. "Which one you like—the West or the East Bottom? Depends which side of the street I'm working."

"You really are good in this role."

"I'll give you a roll, Jack."

She grabbed my arm and snuggled against me. I was intrigued but wondering about Apryl.

"You and Tom?" I said.

"Purely platonic," she said, blowing smoke and rolling her eyes around the room.

"We studied Plato's *Republic*. Were you in the program?"

"Yeah, Jack, I was in the program . . . the methadone program in Montreal. But the nuns of Saint Mary's College drilled us on Plato, Aristotle, and Aquinas. The unmoved mover, *De Anima*, the *Metaphysics*. The simile of the cave. More like a cage. Until I flew the coop for Chicago. What about you, how'd you get mixed up with this bunch?"

"Hogg sort of found me. I was standing around, and there he was."

"Yeah, well, we got that in common." She paused. "So, you in this program? Heard they're brainwashing students."

"That's what they say."

She lit up another skinny beant. I looked out the door, and a figure emerged in a white sheet. Was this ghost coming for Apryl? I put the Nixon mask on.

"Holy shit!" I said.

Chalmers banged open the door, appearing from behind the ghost. He wore a fancy ruff collar from the Elizabethan era that turned him into a Mercutio.

"I have had six crises, and now I believe in Isis," said the short, older guy under the sheet. Eyes appeared through two slits. Whoever he was, he was drunk as hell.

"Luther is a bag of shite," said Chalmers to me.

"You're Thomas More?"

Martinique let out a whiny laugh, smoke seeping out of her nose and mouth as she watched the show.

"Close. I'm Erasmus, his friend," said Chalmers, slurring his words a little. "It was Saint Tommy More who said that about Luther, but More and I were friends and didn't mind plagiarizing. You know about plagiarizing, Mr. Nixon."

"You dumb-shit ex-president," said the sheet. Chalmers leaned over into my face. "What do you know?"

"Liddy is to blame," I said.

Grigson came by and looked at Chalmers with a swashbuckling sneer then proceeded to ravish Belinda, take her into his arms, and swinging her round and round to the strains of Todd Rundgren.

"Who put on this crap?" shouted Chalmers. Belinda blushed. She had wide, dark eyes, fair skin, and ample breasts. Chalmers looked around the room. He saw Swensen grabbing for Sue, but Patrick had her in a close slow-dance embrace, even though the music was throbbing.

Hogg and Apryl were back inside. Hogg was declaiming on the inferiority of Duns Scotus. Martinique saw this and instantly narrowed her eyes.

"What's she got that I don't?"

Apryl shot us a glance as if she had a sixth sense for when people were talking about her. Martinique pointed her cold, blue eyes at me.

"You really want her?" She raised her eyebrows.

"Actually, I've sworn off that futile path for the alabaster road of Truth."

"Well . . . I'm going to get some monk. He can't resist *my* alabaster ass forever." She snickered and pinched my butt. She walked off, sashaying toward Hogg.

Chalmers looked at her; she looked back. Swensen lifted his middle finger indolently and brandished it in the general direction of Chalmers. I waved Swensen off.

"Some outfit, eh," I said to Chalmers.

"Outfit, hell."

"I mean, she's equipped for the role, if you know what I mean."

"She'd take you on rides you're not old enough for."

"Why does Apryl cling to Hogg like that?"

"You mean, why is she not threatened by him?"

"I suppose."

"No heat-seeking missiles," said Chalmers drolly.

I frowned, but then a picture of SAM missiles and go-go girls flashed before my mind. Apryl could be herself with Hogg without fearing probing hormones, without the sense of being pursued like quarry.

"I don't like that she's here," Chalmers said, pointing to Martinique, who flirted with McDarby as he performed on an invisible guitar to Rundgren's solo in "I Saw the Light."

"What are you saying?"

"It's just coincidental a lady like that shows up."

"There are no coincidences," said the sheet.

"You just better be right about Apryl being the target, G.K."

"I never said for sure she was the target, but who else?"

Chalmers shrugged. "Ever think she might just be a prick tease?"

"You don't get her."

"Yeah, well, neither will you. Besides, we have other things to talk about tonight. We've made arrangements to protect your goddess."

I saw McDarby right in front of me stealing the show, flat out on the floor like some ballet dancer, splayed and cavorting to "Boogie Oogie Oogie."

Martinique danced in her high heels like some solitary European dancing queen. I pulled on the Nixon mask, jumped onto McDarby's stage, high-kick dancing alongside her. The sweat was pouring off me; the people were clapping. McDarby was grabbing for my ankles for a take down, but I was too quick for him. We were all on a medieval Soul Train.

Martinique bounced against me on purpose, bumping her hips to mine and looking very sassy.

"Oogie," sang McDarby as he grabbed the ankles of Martinique. She went down. Then I saw the large paws of Swensen grabbing Laura, then Terry, until a mound of female bodies formed over him. The knight in shining armor crashed to the wood floor in a heap of breastplates and chain mail. I went down purposely by Martinique.

DeBlasio the Roman emperor came down on me with the other West Bottom babe and yelled out, "The die is cashed!" Somewhere in the pile, the sheet was pinching behinds.

McDarby got up, jumped through the air, and smacked down on the pile. I heard Zorn under me. The air went out of him like an old bellows. Swensen grabbed the buxom Terry Marker, embracing her. The two of them were enjoying this pagan rite. Somewhere in that melee, I heard Perry.

"I've been working on fractals at the computer center," he said, adjusting his Steve Allen glasses and staring at the ceiling. I reached out from the pile and grabbed Perry. He caved in like Tinker toys and folded into the pile.

"SCH-LAY-EX!"

The word rang out as some kind of primordial urge, a recognition of Dionysian dissonance. The word from my first interview with Barrows.

"SCHLAYEX!" I joined in.

"Isn't that from the German?" called out Jacques. He had been speaking in French to Martinique, who obliged him with some sort of curse.

"*Lache-moi, baiseur Suisse.*" But her giggling grew louder. Swensen crawled out from under the hem of a maiden's dress and took a swig of vodka. He reached into the pile, extracted the merry Terry Marker, and picked her up in his arms. She kicked and giggled.

"German? That's an acronym," said Chalmers, who was sitting in a corner now, his puffy shirt all torn.

"No . . . it is like German word for sex," said Jacques, "*geschlechts.*"

"Yes, I would have to agree," added Lucas Raleigh, a HIP egghead, as he rubbed his glasses against his shirttail. "Definitely related to *Geschlechtsverkehr.*"

The music reached a crescendo, after which the pile relaxed its grip and we all got up.

"I don't like you," Chalmers said, leaning toward the Swiss intruder, "I don't like what you stand for."

"And what would that be?" said Jacques with amusement.

"You are a Lutheran with fewer theses."

"It was tasteless, if you ask me," I said to distract him and hopefully force him into his party role, "for that German to nail his ninety-five feces to a door."

It stopped Chalmers in his tracks. "Yes . . . Luther's arguments *are* feces!" Aphrodite-Apryl frowned. At least we had her in our sights.

"That's wholly scatological," said Perry, who had crawled from the cupidinous pile and straightened his glasses and bow tie. "I was a Lutheran and resent the mere reduction—"

"Shut up," said Chalmers, "let the Jew talk."

Apryl approached. Chalmers whipped off my Nixon mask. My hair was matted and sweaty. Apryl wanted to hear what I had to say.

"The German monk says that we should 'sin boldly . . . no sin will separate us from Christ, even though we commit fornication and murder a thousand times a day'!" I had written on that for Finley's Western civilization class.

"I know who you are," said Chalmers, taking me by the arm.

"I know who you are. Erasmus."

"You fat . . . G. K . . ."

"Pardon me," I said, feeling the humiliation.

"You need a name. Not Jew or LA. G. K. That's who you are."

I heard laughter all around, and chants of "GK."

"From now on, you are G. K.," said Chalmers referring to the rotund British writer. They seemed to approve. I looked around and recited a line I knew from Chesterton, having perused his book about orthodoxy:

"'I tried to found my own heresy, and it ended up being orthodoxy.'"

They laughed. I tried one more, putting on the Nixon mask, and rattling my jowls:

"'The madman is one who has lost everything but his reason'!"

They hooted, cheered, and chanted "GK" over and over. Chalmers gave me an evil grin. The drunken sheet extricated himself from the pile and grunted, "GK." The room responded "G. K.!" and chanted it like "rock-chalk Jayhawk." Chalmers grabbed me.

"Let's go. We have to talk."

"You won't have G. K. to kick around anymore," I said and held up the peace sign. DeBlasio shouted, "Party in the basement!" People started to flood to the stairs. I saw Apryl in the throng on its way to the basement. Hess stood apart from the group, observing all the partygoers. Apryl was being hustled toward the basement. I had to get down there to protect her.

XXV

ALL SAINTS

" H EY, wait," I said with crapulous urgency. I tried to resist Chalmers as we were going out. I wanted to go back to protect Apryl, and Hogg. But Chalmers held my arm insistently.

"I think it's best to stay and protect Apryl."

"The girl is protected," grumbled the sheet.

"You sound familiar," I said.

"Yeah . . . what the hell you doing in Kansas, boy?"

"What better place than Oz to play the odds?"

"Don't give me that Dorothy shit." In the boozy haze, everything and everyone sounded familiar and distant at once.

We trundled down Twelfth Street past St. John's, its spires splitting the dark departing October sky. I heard the cooing of doves under brick eaves.

"I have to take a leak," I said.

"I thought you plugged all the leaks," said the drunken sheet.

"All in good time," said Chalmers.

"What good can come from Kansas?" said the ghost.

Chalmers grabbed the sheet by the arm and hastened down the sidewalk. I followed.

"This is . . . beautiful," I said. "It must be true if it's beautiful."

The sheet started singing "LA Woman" off key as we stumbled down brick-lined streets on Mount Oread, drifting gradually from the hill toward the flats of downtown.

We came to the outskirts of South Park. A breeze wafted eerily through the arching oaks. I stared through the branches. Things looked hazy to me, the silhouette of the sleepy town, the quaint shops in 1890s-painted white brick and tar. The Southwestern Bell microwave tower loomed in the dark like the enduring face of a medieval bell tower.

"Those are big . . ."

The sheet looked up at the trees and laughed gutturally. He put a beant through the slit. Smoke oozed from the eye and nostril holes.

"Only God can make a Watergate!" said the sheet, raising his hands to the towering branches.

"This way . . . that's right." Chalmers was directing the sheet. We passed through the park. The spire of a church poked up through the dark haze.

Was this some Catholic rite? I found myself ascending the steps. It looked so faceless, like so many dark churches I had passed in LA nights on freeways, like the body of knowledge of Western civilization my education had been driving by at ninety miles an hour.

We stood before a great old door, which seemed to be made from some majestic dark wood. I heard mellow sounds as of running water. I became aware of a pool of liquid forming at our feet. Then the man under the sheet snickered.

"G. Gordon Liddy is no democrat." He was urinating on the door of the church. Then he looked to his right, and Chalmers was doing the same, forming a steady stream.

"I thought you had to pee," said Erasmus. I started my stream.

"*Sola scriptura!*" yelled the sheet.

Soon I was spraying across Nixon's and Chalmers's streams. "I'm not sure what we're doing."

"Matriculation," said the sheet.

"The first class to micturate," I added. The sheet finished and lowered his sheet. He started to leave.

"Where are you going?" I said.

"Where you cannot follow," said the sheet. I grabbed the sheet and started to take it off. A ghostly hand grabbed me and pulled me close.

"I think . . . I know you."

"Bastard," said the gravelly-voiced sheet. "You don't know your daddy." I let go of the sheet. He was gone into the ghostly night.

"What church is this, Erasmus?" I asked.

"Lutheran," said Chalmers.

"Why piss on the Lutheran church?"

"Wittenberg is too far."

"This is Fruhling's church, isn't it?"

Chalmers nodded. We started walking back into South Park. Stars poked through the canopy of oaks like a thousand tiny lights strung through the balding branches. Chalmers's severe expression turned serious, as if honesty poured through the cracks in the armor created by the alcohol.

"History is dying on the vine, G. K, nothing is important anymore."

"Is this another chancellor's desk?" I said.

"I have found that there is something worth caring about, worth peeing over." He started walking again, stumbling slightly.

"I once thought Luther was a great individualist," I said.

"Now you've marked your territory; you've crossed a line." Chalmers's face took on the puckish, angry quality it usually had. "We crossed the Rubicon."

"I'm the rube and you're the con."

"Luther wasn't Luther," he said.

"Damned straight. It's a paradox. To be radical now, you have to appear old-fashioned."

"You're okay, G. K."

"He okays all this?" He knew I knew the sheet was Professor Marin.

"Fred wants to make sure about you."

"What did he mean about the masks?"

"He's drunk."

"Why does he drink?"

"Why do you drink?"

"What does he want from me?"

"He wants to watch out for you, but I don't trust you."

"Does he?"

"You think we're idiots?" Chalmers stared. He seemed suddenly sober. "I know you have been following Apryl, watching her window."

Chalmers grabbed me by my collar.

"You've been writing it all down, how lovely she is, your dream," he said. I was jolted into awareness.

"You . . . have my journal."

"If you don't want others to know what's in that journal, you'll do what I say."

The die really was cast.

"Right now, we're arranging to have Apryl removed."

"Removed?" I was panicked. It was all in there, how I saw Apryl's file on Holloway's desk, how I suspected Holloway of having an affair, how I loved her.

"I want you to tell me about Apryl," he said, sober as a judge.

"Listen, I'm not thinking about her like that anymore, like . . . That's just idealistic stuff."

"Tell me what you really know about the kidnapping scheme."

"Holloway directed me to the committee in Kansas City. I saw Apryl's file. I put two and two together."

"Hess should be slipping her a mickey about now."

"*You're* going to drug and kidnap her?!"

"Not us. *You* are going to kidnap her. You have written things about her in your journal. They'll connect you to the kidnapping if you say anything."

"That was fantasy, nothing but my musings about being alone with her."

"By the time it got sorted out, you'd be ruined."

"It's Perry you want."

"Who?"

"Perry Hudson. He was at the party. He was in my fraternity. He's the master spy."

"You mean that faggot in the tuxedo?"

"He's Barrows's boy. Check it out . . . he's the one in line for the Fulbright."

"I knew you were a snitch. You two are peas in a pod."

"I'm no snitch. I took the blame."

"Why'd you fall on the sword for him?"

I paused, perhaps too long under the circumstances.

"He covered for me at the frat."

"For the glaze donuts? And now you snitch on him to save yourself? Real noble."

I explained how I was nearly thrown out of school for the marijuana caper, how Perry was selling the stuff, and how I had been caught with only a small amount.

"So this Perry, is he operating you for Barrows?"

"I think so. You have to give me back my journal."

"I think we'll make quite a team. You and me—and your journal."

"You'll give it back?"

"In time. You will go back to 1132—to the basement. Don't try any-thing with her."

"I'm Lancelot, the chaste knight."

He grabbed me, leering into my eyes with his savage gaze.

"You don't touch her, you got it? We have plans for her." I nodded. "After this, you're ours."

"Are you going to tell the guys at 1132? Or Apryl?"

"You are the perfect double agent now. Hess will give you instructions."

Chalmers started to walk away.

"Rich." Chalmers turned around and stared at me. "I'm going to get Apryl to love me."

"That's rich," he said, laughing. "Stick to your spying, Mr. President." He gave me the peace sign, turned, and walked off.

"Give me back my journal!" I yelled.

He mocked me in a girl's voice: "Give me back my diary."

He walked off. As I stepped back out into the eve of all souls, a blade of wind cut across my roseate face. Spirits were abroad, the face of youth was downcast, I was in the very snare of my own making.

I gazed up at the campus looming over the town and me to Mount Oread and the shining lights of Fraser Hall where the Kansas state flag snapped proudly. I would have to face the world now without my journal to guide me. I felt sobriety touch my face like the first rosy fingers of a Homeric dawn. I had to do something to turn this situation in another direction. I couldn't let Chalmers kidnap the girl of my dreams, even to protect her. If anyone was going to do that, it was me.

XXVI

SHADOWS IN THE BASEMENT

"G. K. . . . come in!"

Swensen had a red nose and flaming eyes that looked unusually wide. He too was part of that alcoholic mystical dream quest. At 1132, it was not so much escape as it was a sacrament to the overwhelming vision.

"Thank you, Pete."

"Call me Swede, you big G. K."

Hogg had told me to come to the party after he had sniffed me and prophesied that I would be a convert within the year. The Jew who converts. What an idea—conversion! Like a perfect disguise. To have been one thing, and at the same time be something else—but not entirely.

I could hear it now. "You're a goddamned Catholic? . . . your mother will shit, she'll positively shit." I would say something wry like, "Nice image, Dad." And then I'd lose the car for graduation and still have to sell carpets. In my last call home, he had gotten on the phone, grabbing it from my understanding mother. He mentioned opening a flooring outlet in Anaheim. I said, "Why don't you call it 'Lie Like a Rug.'"

Here I was with this motley crew, being led toward the creaky stairs to a dank, musty basement. There were a few freshman girls passed out on the couch. They no longer looked like damsels, just available bodies.

"Where did you go?" Swensen glared at me from the stairs. I thought he was going to strangle me again. Instead, he hugged me.

"Solving problems of history . . ."

He yelled into the basement, swaying and laughing. "I've got G. K. Chesterton up here."

"Tell him to get his fat British ass down here!" It was McDarby's voice.

"In the basement?" I asked.

"Where base is meant." Swensen wagged his eyebrows.

"I'm not going down there . . ." I really wasn't sure about the enveloping darkness. I could smell the dank organic must.

"You can't do that . . . you can't." Swensen grabbed me by the scruff of the neck with his powerful Nordic paws. "She is down there—Apryl."

"You lead the way." I felt woozy as I surveyed the stairs melting into darkness. But Swensen steadied me.

It seemed that once I entered the dark space, I did not really awaken until an hour later. I remember hugging and kissing the shy girl named Mary Ann who sang with Trish before the lectures. She planted a tender kiss on my lips and disappeared like some fairy. I heard a faraway music . . . like some chant—but more mellifluous, a lady singing from a place beyond time.

Then I was dancing with Swensen and Hogg and drinking from a bottle of Jayhawk Everclear grain alcohol. Swensen smelled of exotic perfume. The music then took a more worldly turn. Someone was playing it over and over, and we all joined in singing to Rundgren's "Hello, It's Me."

Shadows played on the moldy walls of the basement. But the female form was nowhere to be found. All forms seemed to be revealed within and without in my own view. There was no male or female, free or slave.

Where had McDarby's voice come from? I heard the cackling of Clark Zorn, the chirping, hiccupping cackle, and then Ross's maundering laugh—as if coming from an echo chamber. Hogg had his eyes closed as if in a rapture. Patrick Winston, the poetic skinflint, was doing a jig to Rundgren. We had our arms around one another.

"I'm dancing with G. K.—I think I'll live another day," chanted Patrick over and over, laughing impishly and swigging the Everclear grain alcohol liberally. I had this vague idea of a corpulent British humorist . . . but I could not have appeared that way. Youth, in its drive to see black and white, exaggerates everything, is Procrustean.

Patrick laughed impishly and called me GK as if I were a long-lost friend. Hogg gripped me tight and said something to me in Latin; Swede wagged his tongue, and still no sign of her . . . of Apryl.

"Where's Aphrodite," I asked as I began to sweat from the dancing and the musk-choked air.

"Combing her Aphro." Swensen gaped at his own joke. Patrick spit out a mouthful of alcohol on Hogg as he was trying to light up a cigarette, and a hellish flame erupted from his butane lighter like some magic act turned horrific. Winston threw his leather jacket on Hogg's head, and the little St. Thomas survived the flames of purification.

"You must come to live here."

It was Hogg's voice, raspy from shouting about St. Thomas all evening over the eclectic music.

"You have not worked with the agent intellect," he said.

"I think that Agent 99 worked with him," I said.

"Chief, we'll comprehend the forces of evil under a cone of eternal silence."

In this euphoric state, dancing with males in some ritualistic rite known to all youth, I felt—unified? It was dark and you could say what you felt. Even the women did what they wanted in this realm of dispensation.

Hogg took me by the hand and pronounced the name, "G. K.," and it was as if he were part of a naming ceremony. Now I was no longer being called GK, I *was* GK. And Hogg led me through the dank, dark shadows around a corner, into blackness, where I heard the chanting of voices.

Then I saw the spiraling flicker of light thrown against the moist black walls. I could see in the pitch dark with eyes of night. It was a candle, judging by the way the light leaned and bent in rhythmic waves. As I entered a cave, the voices grew slightly louder. I felt a presence alongside me. It rubbed against me, soft and warm. I hoped it was not Swensen.

"Finally, I found you . . . my dear G. K.!" It was the sweet voice of Trish Ellsworth. I leaned over and smelled her youthful breath. I kissed her. I felt her quiver and sigh.

Figures bounced in the muted candlelight. I could barely make out a strain of Latin as slurred voices stepped over each other. McDarby was in the front, leading in this puckish underworld of prayer and sensuality. Bodies kneeled, prayed trampled-over Latin. There was another body— Jimmy Drungole, praying in Mississippi-Latin. And standing watch, I saw the burnished face of Hess, trimming his lamps.

I smelled the unmistakable scent from that hot August afternoon outside Strong Hall. I saw only the sheen of her hair from behind. Yes, it was Venus, goddess of the night, this votary of pursuers on their knees in the catacomb.

Aphrodite turned, as if in the motion of a dream, fluid and pure, and I saw the large eyes like Andromeda peering out brightly in the dark nebula of desire. Her pupils were dilated, which made the beauty of her eyes more intense. Chalmers's drug was working on her. She made contact with the darkness, made it visible, and those eyes penetrated and entered my space. I saw that the others were staring with equally holy fervor as Clark pounded out the rosary in Oregonian-Latin while the rest of us seized on the eyes as a burning altar lamp in this secret temple.

I felt an intense happiness in that basement because I was just *there*, blinded with some inner sight among the shadows of that cavernous world. Courtney had described the Truth from Plato's cave. Indirectness appealed in this half-light.

Hogg came alongside me. He pulled out a rosary with wooden beads that looked hand carved, and he handed them to me and whispered in my ear.

"Pray to her, Our Lady of the Happy Death."

I took the rosary, began to finger it, and prayed haltingly—only I was looking at the angelic lifeform of Apryl, as were Swensen, Winston, Ross, Zorn, and McDarby. I turned to Hogg and watched his eyes flit back inside his head as he kneeled before the statue of Our Lady of the Happy Death. *Bien mourir.* It sat in a little niche that had been carved into the wall.

Hess cleared his throat. I looked up. He nodded.

I took Apryl by the arm and raised her up. She did not resist. The others continued praying. McDarby got up in a flash, and just as quickly, Hess stood in his path and shoved him back to his knees. Apryl's eyes registered dismay. She looked into my eyes and smiled.

"G. K." She planted another kiss on my cheek. "What's happening?" I whispered in her ear.

"Don't worry, I'll take care of you."

Hess shepherded us to Hogg's car and into the half-morning of All Saints' Day. I had all the saint I needed. I was going to maintain my resolve to be honorable, but every cell of my body screamed otherwise.

XXVII

QUARRY

I DROVE Hogg's hearse through the darkness south of Lawrence, to the countryside near Baldwin and Ottawa, where the world resembled a Grant Wood painting, farms with old Victorian wraparound houses, dilapidated red and white barns imploding from heat and cold and the weight of their beams. I knew we were near Hess's farm, as we had been there for a bonfire and stargazing, followed by skinny-dipping under the stars in an old rock quarry nearby.

Apryl sat between Hess and me in the front seat, leaning on my shoulder, woozy and dreamy. Hess had me veer off the main road, past broken-down homesteads. We bounced like rocks in a tumbler. Apryl giggled as she bounced against me. We came to a ramshackle homestead, long abandoned.

"This is good, stop here."

I did, relieved to stop the agitation cycle but sad that I could not be jostled with her more.

"Where are we?" said Apryl slowly.

"We're going to play a game of hide and seek," said Hess. "This place belonged to a real pioneering family. Later, it was a stop on the underground railroad. They took the freed slaves from here to Lawrence."

We went inside to creaking boards and broken windows. An old, disconnected wood stove stood sentinel in the middle of the room. Hess jerry-rigged the pipe to the roof with his strong rancher's hands. He broke some old boards from the side of the cabin and found some old newspapers and wadded them up in the stove. He shut the door. He felt his pockets.

I pulled out a matchbook and lit a match one-handed. Apryl looked amazed.

"Courtney says someone has to smoke 'cause you'll always need matches when the Dark Ages come." Hess laughed heartily. "This will tide you over while I go back to my place and get you supplies. I'll take the keys, G. K."

I handed them over.

"Don't go anywhere. She's not in any shape, and you ain't versed in country things."

"What does he mean?" said Apryl with an imploring gaze. The makeup and glitter had faded and formed little stripes on her cheeks.

He left, started the car, and was gone.

Apryl looked at me for explanation. I stood up and paced.

"I think the university was planning to kidnap you."

"The vice chancellor?"

"You know Holloway?"

She looked down. "I don't feel right."

"Chalmers must have slipped grain alcohol in your punch. I saw him doing that." How could I tell her she was drugged, that Chalmers had my journal and would spill everything to her if I didn't do what he wanted? Tell all the truth, but tell it slant.

"I have to get out of here."

She began to cry.

"I have been standing watch outside your house for a week and a half."

"You *have*?"

"I have been afraid for you."

"Who told you I might be kidnapped?"

"I saw a file with your name on it, and I knew the university was financing a private group to have the child of a prominent citizen kidnapped and deprogrammed."

"Who had the file?"

I hesitated. She looked so beautiful, so vulnerable.

"I . . . Apryl, I did not want you to know this. I figure you'll hate me if I tell you. You can't feel anything but disgust for me after I tell you. It was Vice Chancellor Holloway."

Apryl shot up straight. Her face was twisted in nervous anger.

"What did he tell you?"

"Not anything specifically."

She seemed to calm down.

"What would the vice chancellor want with me?" She paced in a wobbly way. I sat her down again.

"That's what I asked myself. He seems obsessed with HIP women."

"Why would you be asked?"

"I was asked by the university to spy on HIP. That is partly why I joined the program. The chancellor offered me a full scholarship to get information."

"What was the other part?"

"You."

"Me?"

"I was attracted to you before I knew anything about Barrows and spying on HIP. Chalmers knows what I say is true. He has my journal."

"So he took it from . . . there?" She pointed to my crotch.

"Uhhh … no, I think it fell out in the scuffle at the retreat at 1132."

"I know about the spying and counter-spying."

"You do?"

"Rich told me."

"No wonder."

"Why are you with us, really?"

"My father." I couldn't tell her about my passionate desire, or my struggles to be platonic.

"Your father. What about your father?"

"I hate him."

"You do?" She stood, made me sit by her, and leaned against me.

"So do I. I hate my father," she said.

"He was against my coming to school here," I said.

"So was mine."

"He was?"

"I did it partly to spite him. He wanted me to go to Sarah Lawrence. Well, I went to Lawrence, all right." She laughed.

I told her about the Floor King and my secret desire to break free of him, but at the same time, to come to school at Kansas to annoy him and still to break free of the past.

"You're weeping," I said.

"My father left us when I was twelve. I have hated him ever since. But I can't stop wanting to get back at him."

"Yes, it's like an irresistible urge," I said, "a craving that is with you from the time you wake up to the time you go to sleep. And even in sleep, in dreams, it's there. He's holding everything . . . over me."

"What does he hold over you?" she asked. I held her head in my hands.

"I was just ten. A kid. I thought I'd make pancakes for my family. They were all asleep; everything was going fine until the skillet caught fire. I threw water on the fire, but it only flamed up more. Soon, there was smoke everywhere, and the fire spread. My father came down screaming. He had called the fire department."

I went over to the wood stove; the fire was dying down. I tore off a piece of floorboard and violently tossed it in the stove.

"The fire was put out, and then they questioned me. After that, he always brought that up whenever it suited him. It made me question myself for years, thinking maybe I set the fire. Sometimes I would light a match and let it burn my flesh . . . not sure why. Just to spite him, I guess.

She wept openly. I embraced her. The fire in the stove crackled. I couldn't believe I told her about the fire. I felt great relief. I felt her hand go up my back, stroking and embracing me, and I felt such warmth, such arousal, beyond the purely carnal. Two souls fueled by a common hatred and sharing painful secrets.

I don't know why, but a song that had been playing earlier came to me, and I started singing to her, quietly, as one might sing a lullaby to a child. I sang "I Saw the Light."

I just kept singing and humming when I forgot the words. She was humming quietly with me in perfect harmony.

Before I knew it, our lips were touching, and then we melted together in a kiss. We were fully part of each other in that kiss, and all of my senses, all the cells in my body, were awakened.

Apryl had turned on a switch. I knew I could have her, completely, without hesitation at that moment. I knew I could fulfill the wildest fantasy of my dreams. She was not only Botticelli's Venus, but Bond's femme fatales, Dulcinea, Becky Sharp, Tolstoy's Helene rolled into one. Most of all, she was Apryl Jovey, and now she was not a distant object of desire. She moved toward me, and soon, she was sitting on my lap, and we were twisting into a deeper embrace. Her smell filled me, was new, not just her perfume, but her smell, vanilla and cumin—inside me now.

"Will you rescue me?" she said between kisses. "From everybody, from everything."

"I already planned to take you from this place to somewhere they can't get you."

"You did," she said with slight alarm.

"When I realized they wanted to do something else with you."

"They?"

"Chalmers. I am guessing taking you to Europe."

"Where are you going to take me?"

"Better than a nunnery—the Plaza." She looked alarmed suddenly.

"What's wrong?"

"I don't think your fire skills have improved."

I glanced at the floorboard that had fallen out of the stove and had caught the floor on fire. It was spreading already.

Her eyes widened with nervous excitement as the boards began to catch fire.

"Let's get out of here," I said.

"We have to put this out."

"With what?"

As we fled from the cabin, I started to run for it. She was too weak to keep up, so I picked her up. I looked back at the ramshackle cabin. The tinderbox cabin was soon an inferno. I looked down at Apryl in my arms, light as a feather. We went off into the woods.

After a few minutes, we came upon a farm and crossed over a fence. A sorrel horse cropped at the long grass from the Indian summer that had followed the rains. The horse did not budge as we approached. It just looked at us as it ate.

I patted the horse. I put Apryl up on her, and then I led them out to a road. I used the fence to hoist myself up on the horse. Then we rode off at a slow pace.

"My chevalier," she whispered. Apryl clasped my waist and leaned her body against mine. I looked back at the smoke from the homestead cabin that formed plumes over the hackberries and cottonwoods.

Soon we were in a deserted woods. The horse walked quietly amid the cottonwoods. The harvest moon seemed to be following us like a large lantern held by some genial overseer.

"This reminds me of lines I memorized in high school from Lord Byron:

> *There is a pleasure in the pathless woods,*
> *There is a rapture on the lonely shore . . .*

Then he says something about loving Man not less, but Nature more."

"I am happy being alone," she responded. "I know that sounds weird, but loneliness can be joyful. Nobody defining you, nobody to let you down."

"Yes, it's about realizing yourself in taking a path that is uncharted."

"Stop," she said abruptly.

I pulled back on the horse's mane. It stopped. She turned and pointed. "The rock quarry is over there."

"You know about the quarry?"

"Sure, been swimming there with the gang a few times."

We led the horse up over an outcropping of boulders and came onto an idyllic scene of rocks and water enclosed by walls of granite. It was still. The water was black except for where the large harvest moon hovered over the water like a messenger. The blood orange moon got larger as we got off the horse as if it were growing inside us. The horse wandered around the rocks to crop at the place where the vegetation ended.

I was out of my shirt already. She was feeling my chest. I started to slip her out of her Aphrodite blouse. I could feel her shape.

"No . . ." She spoke softly. "It's wrong." I stopped.

"I understand . . . Professor Courtney wants me to pursue the—"

"Good life . . ." she said.

"Right. So, I understand *no.*"

"Yes," she whispered in my ear. The hot, sweet breath ignited me again. She unzipped my pants. I was tugging at her bra. She stopped me and took it off herself.

Soon she was entirely naked. Then so was I. Her skin in the moonlight was like pearl. She was a work of art, Venus Rising on granite, more beautiful naked than I could have imagined. We just looked at each other, hardly aware of what to do.

"You look like you want to paint me."

Then she jumped in the water, suddenly, as if to cover the sheer exposure. I jumped in after her. The water was cool. We ducked underwater. When we came up for air, we were very close. We frolicked but soon were intertwined in a slippery embrace.

I felt an incredible urge, a great ecstasy in being near her. I was pulsing, and she felt me. Then, suddenly—was it over? I felt ashamed. I don't know if she realized what had happened.

Was it the water temperature? Was it that I was done? I swam away and she swam after me. She grabbed onto my ankle, but I made it to shore and flopped onto some rocks near my pants. I felt the slipperiness of water all over me, the dripping of dark quarry liquid. I was suddenly overcome with a feeling—of taking advantage of her. She came up next to me, shiny and naked and heavenly in the moonlight. She was rubbing me. Then I was aroused again.

"I can't . . . not like this." Something in me would not let me take her under the circumstances. Maybe it was something I had never really felt before—love? She would hate me, not love me. I stood.

"I trust you. I don't know why. We were so intimate . . ."

I grabbed for my Camels and lit up a beant. I was still on fire in my body. I turned around.

"What is it, Bernard? Don't you want me?"

I had to master the situation. I did not know what to do. I gazed down at the cherry on my beant, a burning ember.

"You've been drugged," I said.

"It was just too much alcohol, like you said."

"No, they put a mickey in it."

"A mickey? You mean, like, Quaaludes?"

"You've heard of Quaaludes?"

"Who hasn't?"

"So you rescued me from them after they drugged me?"

"Yes."

"That makes me feel different about you."

"I understand."

"No, I mean, you really protected me from them and now from yourself. Like a real live knight."

I wanted to go back to her, but the moment was gone. I felt my left palm burning. I saw my right hand holding the cigarette to my left palm. I felt the pain of the cherry burning my flesh and smelled the burning of my skin.

"I promised Professor Courtney."

"Bernard! What are you doing?" She ran over to me and grabbed my hand, seeing the wound it had made.

"My God," she said and looked up into my eyes.

"I . . . didn't mean to . . ."

It was only then that I felt the excruciating pain. She ripped a part of her goddess skirt and bandaged my hand. I continued to smoke with the half-smashed beant, pacing the rocks. My hand throbbed She was clothed in a hurry. I slipped on my pants.

"What promise?"

"You know, stop seeking happiness in creatures, as Augustine says."

"We forgot ourselves," she said as if reporting a past event. She was more beautiful than ever.

"I took advantage, didn't I?"

"You rescued me."

"And perhaps myself," I said. I started around the rocks and brought the horse back. I placed my hand on her buttocks and helped her up. I got on a rock above the horse and got on behind her. My hand hurt like a bastard.

"Where are we going?"

"Kansas City."

"On a horse?"

"True, a new mistress now I chase."

Apryl gave me one of her throaty Lauren Bacall laughs.

"What's in Kansas City?"

"The oracle of Seville Square." There was silence. "That's what I call my aunt Teresa. You'll love her."

She leaned back against me as we rode toward the interstate. When we got there, I put the horse in a nearby field to graze. I got off and helped Apryl down. The pumpkin moon skulked overhead, watching us in this early-morning masquerade. Apryl, this force of nature with her glistening legs, transformed the shoulder of the interstate. A car stopped in no time and took us to Seville on the Missouri.

XXVIII

DON QUIXOTE AT THE MALL

I RECALL the waning sun as it splashed across the Spanish-tiled roofs of the Country Club Plaza, a brush stroke of fire. We had passed the opulent estates of Mission Hills on the Kansas-Missouri border, a land of Roman fountains, jewelry, and fur. Kansas City was the test-market city, lustrous, shiny—a three-dimensional Hallmark card. The familiar temple of Seville Square shopping center was its centerpiece designed in Moorish Revival style. Apryl looked around at the ornate buildings like a lost princess in our little Roman Catholic holiday.

Aunt Teresa lived in the Robert Browning, an ornate stone apartment building. The other buildings were named after other authors—Twain, Keats, and Hemingway.

She immediately embraced me and kissed me on the lips. I was embarrassed. She wore a sharp yellow dress that gracefully highlighted her attractive figure. I saw Apryl look at her with admiration. Here were two women who had become important to me. One was twenty, the other around forty. For all of that, I could scarcely tell their ages apart.

"Aunt Teresa, this is Apryl Jovey."

"My dear, look at you . . . come in."

"How do you do, Miss Kennisbaum?"

"Call me Tessie. You're not at all like the others he brings here."

I gave her a gimlet eye.

"I can see the family resemblance," said Apryl as she looked us over.

Aunt Tessie was a spinster who painted and wrote poetry while the lights slowly went out due to her cataracts. She had been left the bulk of the money from the estate of my grandfather, Mortimer Kennisbaum, a shoe designer and distributor. Tessie had a transparent quality, not conniving, as my father thought. She was candid and courageous. Fiercely individualistic and careless of political trends and fashion, she had no use for the vanity of men or the blandishments of shallow women. Through her, I saw the world clearly.

Despite the tastefulness of her apartment, Tessie lived as if poor and gave a great deal of money to charity and art. In the last five years, my father had talked about almost nothing else. "How could Papa leave her the money! Why doesn't she give some to me—she gives it to everyone else!" I never knew my grandfather. Yet for him to deny my father money, the thing he dearly loved, must have come from some hilarious place in the heart of this rich Jewish shoe designer.

She looked at Apryl, sized up the situation, and put on tea.

"I have a spare bedroom. You can use the shower on the other side of the hall. Come this way." She disappeared with Apryl.

I heard the screech of boiling water and ran to the kitchenette. I turned around as Tessie grabbed the tea pot from me and started making tea.

"I see you are in some kind of trouble." She sat down at the kitchen nook, a table illuminated by sunlight and brimming with flowers. She was a handsome woman—green eyes, sleek nose, and a longish face. She had had her fill of male suitors and found them lacking. She almost married a greeting card writer who was later indicted for embezzlement at Hallmark Cards. She said it was his bad verse that got him.

"What's that?" she said.

I put my hand under the table.

"I'm not entirely blind, you know."

"No, you see everything."

She wore little makeup, preferring to be seen as she was. Her look was direct, and her words were direct, often brutal.

"Nice begonias." I sat down at the kitchenette and looked with squinty eyes into the zenith of a bright sun. My head was pounding. I took a sip of tea. It was herbal lemon.

"They're azaleas . . . never cared for dark apartments. Too much to hide. I prefer things being out in the open." She gave me another direct look.

"I burned my hand."

She took it in hers.

"You're playing with fire."

"You're telling me. I'll never hold someone else's bomb while they go to the bathroom."

"Ha-ha," she said. "This is some fraternity stunt?"

"A dare. I dared myself to be like St. Thomas."

"What?"

"Nothing. Just an accident over temptation."

She left and came back with salve and bandages and ministered to me.

"You're playing with fire with the girl."

"Oh, Tessie, please," I said as if it was utter nonsense.

"If you don't like my honesty," she said with a smirk, "you know the way to the door."

"Yes, Aunt Tessie."

She grabbed my hand and forced me to look at her. I winced in pain. She let go.

"I haven't seen this look before. You're in love, aren't you?"

I looked away toward the room where Apryl was. I looked at Tessie and she gave me one of those knowing looks, half smirk, half frown. She patted my arm to show me she had taken care of my wound.

"I'm not sure what I would call it, but this is something new."

"You're not in one of those snits with that lout of a father?"

"It's not exactly that."

"So is this some disguise, or has she beguiled your heart?" It was the right question. It was always the right question.

"I'm in over my head . . . doing things for the university, and now, bringing Apryl here because a parents' group wants to kidnap and deprogram her. This is just not anywhere in the college catalog or hazing playbook either."

"You always did love the secret agent toys I sent you."

"That's not the half of it. I really like these guys, and I feel I'm going to betray them and my parents—everybody."

"You aren't thinking of converting?"

"What?"

"I've heard they brainwash you until you cry 'hail Mary!'"

"The university is trying to ruin HIP, and they want to kidnap Apryl. And the people opposed are using her, too."

"Are you one of those?"

"I'm just helping her out. She needs a place to stay for a few days until we can sort this out."

"Come on, Bernie, you don't have to temporize with me," she said.

"I had to kidnap her . . . to protect her."

"Dear God, she has you tilting at windmills." Now her eyes betrayed a girl's playfulness. "In my day, the guy drove you out to the lake to make out."

"In this case, it was a quarry."

"I see."

"It's pretty mixed up. There's a plot at the university. I'm supposed to find things out."

"Oh, dear, you are in deeper than I thought."

"It started out that way, but now I don't know. She's part of this new group of friends. I sometimes go to the church with them and sing in Latin. I hardly learned Hebrew, and I'm chanting Latin."

"At John Connell's church in Lawrence."

"You know Father Connell?"

"Known Johnnie since he was a brand new priest just over state line, and he would come to the Cafe Regal with parishioners, and they would drink coffee and laugh and tell jokes. I would be in there reading. And he noticed I was reading Yeats. He recited 'Easter, 1916' by heart. I don't know about this Catholic stuff . . . pretty dangerous. But I do feel there is a terrible beauty about Apryl, and about you now."

"What is so terrible about her beauty?"

"College is the most dangerous time of your life," she said with a sparkle in her eyes, "and therefore the most fun. There are more things than are dreamed of in your . . . destiny. But be careful of these beautiful Apryls."

"You're cheerful."

"You've always been a romantic. I see your heart being broken, Bernie."

I told her how much fun it really was—the women, the stargazing, being drunk with wonder. Beauty and Truth were no longer abstract.

"Now I love you and you love me, and books are shutter than books can be," she said.

"Cummings. Professor Marin quotes that." When I said his name, I noticed her eyes change. "Aunt Teresa! You're blushing." She smiled at my accusation.

"When I was at KU, I was one of his devotees."

"E.E. Cummings?"

"Fred Marin!" She hit me with a girlish tap of the arm. I smoked a beant. She bummed a few hits off mine. I was overcome with a sense of knowledge of something I wasn't supposed to know.

"Sounds like your father's experience at KU."

"What? He didn't want me coming here."

"Surely you knew about your father's friendship with Fred Marin?"

I shook my head. I heard the shower running and savored the memory of Apryl at the rock quarry.

"Fred was older than I. Your father introduced me to him—this naive, skinny Jewish girl. He was charismatic, worldly, and incredibly brilliant. He had all of the university administrators running for cover. I began taking all of his classes and painted and read poetry and wrote it. Your father drank with him. He helped your father a great deal in his art."

"His *what*? Norm Kennisbaum partied with Marin? This is more than I can take."

She looked out the window onto Brush Creek where the cars were teeming madly in Kansas City's morning rush.

"He was a young man, like you—a very different man. Norm was a promising young student of literature and painting at one point. A bit of a carouser too."

"We can't be talking about the Carpet King?"

"Uh huh. He even studied to become a Catholic at one point." She acted like a little girl tattling on her older brother. It was making some sense, his intense dislike of my decision to go to KU, his attempts to get me to transfer the year before.

"Why didn't he tell me? Why didn't *you* tell me?"

"Secrets haunt us all. He never succeeded with art; he resented Marin and all of his type for trying to lead him into the Truth when life was so harsh."

"He sure got his revenge on Truth through carpet."

"You, my boy, have scratched the scab."

She rose from the table and went to a closet, returning with a canvas. She dusted it off and showed it to me: a simple still life, apples and oranges in a bowl behind a transparent veil. It had a quality about it of real art, not accomplished but possessed of expression and soul.

"Your father painted this for me when I was in high school. See the inscription?"

I turned it around and read: "To the loveliest flower of them all, Teresa." "He was quite a tender man, you know."

"What happened?"

"He blamed me for his estrangement from your grandfather."

"Why?"

"You ask a lot of questions."

"I'm sorry."

She breathed in and exhaled deeply.

"Your father became bitter after our father died and the trust went to Mother. And then she died, and he got very little. The terms of the trust are fairly strict. I got most of it. He thinks I'm hoarding it."

"Hoarding? You practically give it away on the street corner." She had helped me out of a couple of scrapes in my first year when I had no money and could not go to my father and she hired that lawyer.

We sat there in silence and contemplated the still life as if we were peering into another world—of her, my father, Fred Marin, and now Apryl.

"Tell me about these friends." She stared at me and turned up the corner of her mouth into a quizzical smile.

"It's like being in Plato's Academy. I feel I can actually become . . . myself. Professor Marin talks directly to me, severely. Professor Courtney is a musician. We are his instruments, or it feels like that. And this house, 1132 Ohio Street, and the guys—it's a real fraternity."

"Slumming through the classics in a run-down house. A place of magic and unlimited possibilities. Independence without responsibility. Your grandfather called it a fool's paradise. Norm inherited his pragmatism."

"I would like for you to meet them. They really are Catholic . . . they embody the whole thing: its holiness, its imperfection, the original sin, the corruption, the inner circle. Like art." I did not think of telling her about the bacchanal of the evening before or of Chalmers's enlistment of me in his corps of pranking men.

"Do you think she will love you back?"

"I don't think of her that way . . . or, I'm trying . . ."

"Don't kid a kidder, kiddo."

"Maybe it's just poetic. But something's happening to me. She was just a part. Dad is conspiring against it, the university is conspiring against the program, and people think the whole idea of looking for the truth is absurd."

"Tell the truth, but tell it slant." She smiled slyly.

"Marin likes to quote that. How did you know?"

"Your father used to talk nonstop of Marin when he was at KU. He dragged me to a few lectures. I'm half Catholic myself."

"You considered becoming Catholic?"

"Wherever Jews live, they are pushed to become what the locals are, to assimilate. I am on speaking terms with the Almighty. I suppose I was too independent to assimilate like that."

"But what did Marin have to do with it?"

She fell silent. I could tell we had come to some threshold, and the door was shut. The gods might be laughing at Dad now, but with Teresa—there was some tragic veil there.

"I hope I'm not like Dad. I want to be happy." I was lost in a rhapsody of tangled dreams.

"I didn't say 'happy' before," she said. "For all I know, he would have been miserable as hell. Pursuit of the truth is no guarantee of happiness. There was a guy named Jesus Christ who showed that, if nothing else."

"If it all ends in heartbreak, that's the point?"

"The hurting is how you know you're human."

"And you call me a romantic."

Apryl walked in just then, her hair wrapped in a towel, wearing a terry cloth robe, stunningly au naturel.

"I was just going to sleep, if that is all right."

"Yes, you go ahead. I won't disturb you."

"I'll have some things brought for you," I said.

"Thank you, Bernard."

She kissed my cheek then disappeared into the spare bedroom. Aunt Tessie gave me the keys to her car.

"I'm too blind to drive it anyway. Bring it back in one piece."

"I will." I kissed her on the cheek.

I drove to Lawrence and thought about what she had said and about Apryl and our night of ecstasy—or near ecstasy.

Along the highway near DeSoto, I looked up at a billboard of the Kansas attorney general J. Barnett Hummer, the wizard of pop-up prosecutions, and the long, crossed arms of the law: "He Knows When You *Brake* the Law."

As the mound of earth came into view, on fire with the silver and gold of the descending sun, what I came to know as Lawrence, that demi-monde, that little universe was a miniature map of the brain. It was shaped like something I was just on the verge of understanding, perhaps a shape my life could take. I could feel the vibrations coming from the mountain as it appeared to me: Mount Oread, the center of the organism, sweetest auburn, loveliest village on the plain. Mount of birth, mount of wonder and renewal.

I had a few minutes to get to class. I wasn't going to waste this sense of enlightenment, this high, on sleep. Outside, a few vagrant flakes of snow told of coming winter, waltzing gaily on the evergreens surrounding Dyche Hall.

XXIX

THE SHAPE OF THINGS

"HEIDDEGGER and Kant are the most influential of the thinkers of the last two hundred years." Courtney was trying to coax us. "Although you may not know it, you identify most closely with them in your own life."

Marin picked it up, looking really hungover.

"I think they like Nietzsche. They want the will to power. They like nuclear energy—or is it pronounced nukulur? They like the machine, the engine, internal and external combustion, thrust. Don't you?!"

We had finished with Plato's simile of the cave and were onto Aristotle's *Ethics*. It was not the easiest book to think about in this hungover state. There were a lot of empty chairs. McDarby, Patrick, and DeBlasio were there, but Clark and the others were missing in action. Swensen was sitting by himself, his head down, hands over his eyes.

Whelan guided us to the text:

"Aristotle says that our irrational passions can be governed by choice. That is, reason can be a guiding factor in your life, and in the life of the society. Although your passions may govern you at, say, this moment, you are still tending toward a Good, or what you perceive to be a Good."

"You have been shaving with Occam's razor," said Marin. "You think you can reduce everything down to the simplest explanations. You're a bunch of nominalists. You don't believe in the forms of things, only in what is front of you. You're Enlightenment philosophes. But you didn't earn it. You can't even explain what is going on inside you. The biggest truths have no explanation, let alone a simple one."

I wondered if Marin ever thought about what drugging a girl would do, kidnapping her—or just about making us all feel like intellectual dwarfs.

"You want to be virtuous people," said Courtney, trying to moderate Marin's assault, "only your reason fails you, or you lack the proper habits and choices. Freedom is the state of being free to choose to do the right thing in the right circumstance."

"If you could choose it," noted Marin, "would you? Would you choose to do the virtuous thing? Do any of you even have the idea of temperance in your minds?"

A drunk talking temperance.

"At some point, you have to admit some reality outside of yourself exists. That's right . . . *adequatio rei et intellectus*. Aristotle didn't make it up. Truth is the mind coming to the realization of the 'real' that is. Or are we wasting your time, Narcissus? You aren't looking at yourself, Virginia. The knower must be adequate to the thing known."

Courtney jumped in for a solo.

"The problem is not Aristotle. You know he is right about the mean. You know if you could push a button, you would choose the balanced action. It does not come from reason; it comes from your understanding, which is different from pure reason. Kant thought it was pure reason, but it is not, it is perception, experience, sensation, and above all, intuition. You have to learn to trust your own instincts. First, you have to discover them."

In all my other classes, we were dancing around reality, dancing around the question of personal accountability, private virtue or public.

"It is Plato who tells us that there are forms, that the soul knows things due to an innate recognition of forms. He was a universalist, an idealist, you might say." Courtney paused. "But then, Immanuel Kant also asserted a different form of Platonism. He said that full, perceived objects and not mere sensations were given to the mind by the sense organs. But he went beyond Plato when he developed an ontological system that said it is impossible to think of anything in the world or even beyond the world that had goodness—except a good will. That is called voluntarism and you have been saddled with that philosophy ever since. And it holds that you are incapable of knowing ultimate reality, the essence of things."

"That's a mouthful," said Marin. "Paul, I think they will all just say *I. Kant.*

Maybe I got the larger point, that we were phonies, thinking we could fake it all and be clever and it would all just work out. My passions were ruling me, but I had somehow followed a higher instinct, or had I?

"Just watch out with all this knowledge," said Marin. "It's dangerous. You all want to know all about everything but especially about yourselves. How far back do you want to go with your heritage?" It was like he had heard my conversation with my aunt.

"You read Sophocles—Oedipus the King wanting to know the prophecies, wanting to know about his past. The very thing he's looking to avoid, he meets on the road to Thebes, but it only is shown to him later what he has done. Caught in a web of fate, he puts out his own eyes. Maybe you don't want to have your fortune told after all. Have you ever thought what a Freudian nightmare it is to know? Can too much reality be a bad thing?"

He was really playing with our minds. I did not care what Marin thought—or what Chalmers, or Hess, or the others at 1132 might think. Apryl was safe, not only from the kidnappers but from friends who drugged her against her will.

"Aristotle was the apostle of reality," said Whelan as he shifted in his chair. "He catalogued nature; he saw into the meaning of reality because he observed it. Do you observe? This is why we have you go out into nature, to look at stars, and engage in the arts of culture. This is a gymnastic education where you taste and feel knowledge. Why we have you memorize poems like 'The World is Too Much with Us.' You internalize it and perception is aided." He recited the first few lines, and we all uttered it in a whisper with him.

> The world is too much with us, late and soon,
> Getting and spending, little we see in nature that is ours.
> We have given our hearts away, a sordid boon.

Then Courtney broke it:

"You see, we had you read the most important parts of the *Ethics*. And the last part is the culmination of the whole, for there, Aristotle directs us to the chief Good to which all of this virtue directs us. You must know what it is: friendship. It is the Good of your education. It is the opposite of getting and spending. The Good of the other is not for your pleasure, not for the Good the other can do for you, but because the other is a friend. That is happiness and the considered life."

The whistle howled. In that time outside of time, I prayed I still had friends.

McDarby, Patrick, DeBlasio, and Swensen were waiting for me outside near the bronze Jayhawk.

"How about this weather," I said. "Indian summer one minute, snow the next."

"You know what they say about Kansas weather," said Patrick. "If you don't like it, stick around for a few minutes."

I grinned uneasily at them as Michael and McDarby circled me. Swensen would not look at me.

"Friendship is a virtue, don't you think?" I said.

"So is loyalty," said McDarby. His feral eyes bore down on me like some lonely beast who wanted to be admired but refused to be touched.

"What did you do with Apryl after you drugged her?"

"And kidnapped her," added McDarby.

"Chalmers has been feeding you a load of crap. I didn't drug her, he did. Hess knows what happened. He won't lie for Chalmers."

"Do you deny you took her from the woods?"

"I don't."

"You were supposed to protect her, not kidnap her," said Swensen.

"Sonofabitch," said McDarby, speaking like a James Cagney wannabe.

"I wasn't going to let them do anything to her. I took her to safety."

DeBlasio stood close, looking down on me through his reptilian eyes. Then I saw what was really in their eyes. McDarby and the others were jealous.

"Look . . . nothing happened, really." I lied like a cheap Dacron square.

"We're supposed to believe you're a hero?" said DeBlasio. My heart was beating fast. Nobody knew about the quarry, I hoped.

"You think she will fall for you?" asked McDarby. "Why would she?"

"Look, I was supposed to take the fall for Chalmers—and the rest of you—in case everything went south. She is safe with my aunt on the Plaza."

"Screw Chalmers," said Patrick. "Now we're holding the cards."

"She's still going with me to the waltz!" said McDarby. He looked at Swensen, whose face was a mix of fury and guilt. He stomped off.

"Pete almost killed you last night," said Patrick, rubbing his puffy, bloodshot eyes.

I said, "Other than that, Mrs. Lincoln, I'd say the play was most entertaining," and they broke up laughing.

"What's up with Swensen?" They looked at each other.

"He thinks he mortalized," said McDarby.

"Swensen?" I said. "Purer than Caesar's wife?"

"Except when Caesar puts out the honey wine," said Patrick. "I've only seen him like this one time before, when he was a freshman and he got in too deep with a girl from the dorms. He was guilty for weeks, going to Mass daily, confession twice a week, praying. Turned into Padre Pio, beard and all."

"Yes, dorms," I said. "You can cut the guilt with a knife on a Sunday on Daisy Hill, everybody holding their heads in shame, hoping the girl, whoever she was, doesn't show up at the brunch line."

"Speaking of dorms, what are you doing living there?" said Patrick.

"Just lucky, I guess."

"Why not live with us?" he said. "You practically live at 1132 already."

"I have a contract to pay through the school year."

"Yeah, that settles that," said McDarby.

"He did help me with my English lit paper," said DeBlasio. "Otherwise, I would have flunked."

"I guess I could use someone to write my papers, too," said McDarby reluctantly.

We headed out onto Jayhawk Boulevard. The sky was blanketing the campus in a downy sugar cap.

"If they won't let you out of the dorm contract, I'll have my uncle talk to them," said DeBlasio.

"All for one," I said and held up an invisible sword.

"And one for all," said McDarby. They all thrust their arms in the air, stabbing at the elusive snowflakes. As we came to the crest of Ohio Street, we were met by the angry face of Chalmers coming up the street.

We all ran in the opposite direction toward my dorm, doubling back to 11th Street through alleys and taking the long way around to 1132.

XXX

BOTTOMS UP

W E doubled over, panting at the bottom of the hill on Eleventh Street in the alleyway behind 1132 thinking the coast was clear. But Chalmers popped up, sneaky as ever.

DeBlasio tried to block him, but Chalmers tripped him. He came up to me and slugged me on the cheek, knocking me down on the slippery pavement. I slid a few feet down into the alleyway in a gangly glissade.

McDarby jumped Chalmers. They fell into a slippery pile. Chalmers shot back onto his feet but then fell on the slick pavement. We started laughing at the flopping.

"He took Apryl to safety, you asshole."

Chalmers finally got up and stood in gunslinger stance.

"Listen, pussies. G. K. got it all wrong. It's not Apryl. It's Hogg. He's gone missing."

"What do you mean?" said Patrick.

I wiped a trickle of blood from my face.

"He didn't show up for class, did he?" We looked at each other. "His car is still at the house."

"Just where Hess parked it last night."

"Maybe he's still partying with those girls," I said, thinking of Martinique.

DeBlasio laughed. "Yeah, for sure . . . the West Bottoms, man."

"You may have something there . . . that's it," said Chalmers, snapping his fingers.

"What?" we said in unison.

"Let's go to the West Bottoms and find ourselves some hookers."

191

"Fierce," said DeBlasio.

"Hookers? It's All Saints Day," said a bloodshot-eyed Swensen who had already been to confession. We followed Chalmers as he raced toward Hogg's hearse alongside the curb in front of 1132.

φ

Seedy would have been a monumental understatement of the West Bottoms along the Missouri River, set between an old-world theme park of Kansas City, Kansas, called Strawberry Hill, and the glowing cherry of the Kansas City Power and Light Building. This was not the Country Club Plaza. There were no apartments here named after famous writers. In this lacuna of the old, fringed by the squalid reminders of the stockyards, the smokestacks cast a judgment over the old redbrick warehouses and broken windows.

As we arrived at the Bottoms, I explained the night past; at least, an abridged version.

"How did that cabin burn down?" asked McDarby.

"Hess had a hell of time explaining things to the county," said Chalmers, eyeing me.

"We had a fire in this old wood stove when we left," I said. "It was a rickety contraption."

"Why would you walk all the way to the interstate?" said McDarby. I had left out the part about the horse and the quarry and skinny-dipping.

"Rich, I had to get her out of there. She was drugged, confused, angry, and she needed a place to stay away from all of this."

"I get that," said McDarby, "but what about the cabin?"

"When in doubt, burn it out."

Chalmers looked at me in the rearview, nodding his head in near approval.

"I don't buy it," said McDarby, "I still think you're—"

"There she is!" I pointed at a shiny blue sequined dress. Unmistakably Martinique. Part of me held out hope that she was somewhere in a sociology class at KU thinking about Darnell Valentine and the Jayhawks' chances in the Final Four.

"This is your show, G. K.," said Chalmers.

"Why is it my show?"

"He's right," said McDarby. "You were wrong about Apryl being the kidnap victim."

"Been wrong about everything," said Chalmers. "We'll pick up Apryl next."

I thought about my aunt Teresa. I couldn't bear the idea of bringing a prostitute to her and Apryl.

I leaned out the window as we slowed. The exhaust was sickly cloying.

"Martinique . . . it's Jock."

She snapped her head in my direction. She was not wearing the Carol Channing wig. Her dirty blond hair made her look more hardened.

"Tricky Dick . . . how's it hanging?"

I flashed her the peace sign. Chalmers slowed the hearse. He got out and opened the back. Martinique sashayed over and looked at all of us.

"This your secret service? Group rate is five hundred."

"Your bail will be five hundred," said Chalmers. She got in. We drove around the old stockyards as Martinique played footsie with us. "Where's Tom?"

"You mean St. Thomas?" she said. "How should I know? Couldn't get any action with His Holiness. Though I did learn about the five proofs for the existence of God."

"Where's your friend?"

"Tammy's working Troost today. I catch the morning johns on their way downtown."

"So you really are . . ." I couldn't even say the word. Hogg had actually sought out a hooker and brought her to the party. Two hookers. I looked in her eyes.

"What's the matter, Jack, you never seen a *fille a pied*?"

"A what?" said McDarby.

"*A pied*, you know . . . on foot, on her back—streetwalker, Jack."

"For sure," said DeBlasio. "They aren't usually as hot as you."

"Yeah . . . well, I used to be high-priced and, well, never mind."

"And what?" snapped Chalmers.

"Nobody owns me, Jack."

Chalmers pulled into an abandoned stockyard building. "Right now, I do."

"What's with the tough guy?" she said to me.

Chalmers stopped, got out, opened the back of the hearse, and grabbed Martinique. She started kicking him. He got hold of her midriff, picked her up off the ground, and carried her inside. We walked inside the burned-out rooms to the abattoir where the cattle were slaughtered.

Martinique was red-faced, kicking and scratching at DeBlasio and Chalmers.

"Let me go, Jack! You don't know who you're messing with."

"You don't know who *you're* messing with." Chalmers looked at De-Blasio, who stepped forward. He began to grab her leg and acted as if he were going to break it.

"Just tell her who you are," said Chalmers.

"I don't care who you are, Jack."

"I'm Mike DeBlasio."

Her eyes became saucers.

"My uncle is Freddie DeBlasio. He's also my godfather. Owns all the bars and rackets here in the West Bottoms."

Martinique let go of her grip.

"I didn't mean anything," she said with contrition. "I was just play-ing with you guys."

"We aren't playing around," said DeBlasio, all business. "He doesn't like to get involved, but if you're messing with my education, that would concern him."

"Is he really your uncle?" she said.

"Yeah. He has been good to me, as he has to all the people under his care. His father, my grandfather, was in charge of this whole area in the forties and fifties. People took care of each other in those days, and they didn't let neighborhoods go to shit like this."

"That's more words than I've heard from him in four months," I said.

"You were the last one seen with Tom," said Chalmers. "He's miss-ing, damn it!"

"Guys, I'd like to help . . . but—"

"Listen . . . someone's gonna get hurt real bad," said DeBlasio.

"We're just trying to find our friend," I said

"There's two forces down here," said Martinique. "One is Mr. DeBlasio."

"Who's the other?" asked Chalmers.

"The unions. DeBlasio has the rackets, bars, prostitution, gambling. Labor controls the rest."

"Who?" said Chalmers.

Martinique took out a beant. Her hands were trembling. I took out Hogg's lighter that was left in his car and gave her a light. She looked up into my eyes with fear and hesitation.

"I tell you squat, I'm rat food."

"You don't tell us, you'll be worse," said DeBlasio. Martinique took a few drags and threw the beant to the floor.

"I tell you what happened to your friend, you gotta hide me."

"Hide you?" said McDarby. "Where are we gonna hide a hooker?"

"Right on campus," I said. "She's been meaning to finish her degree, haven't you?" She looked up at me and smiled.

"Yeah, Jack, me and Plato were real tight in Montreal."

"It will take a little doing to get her enrolled," said Chalmers. "Tell us what happened."

"Hold on, tough guy. You got somewhere for me to stay in the meantime?"

Chalmers's nostrils flared. "On the Plaza, the Robert Browning building, right?"

"No, Rich, my aunt would never—"

"I like the Plaza," said Martinique as she put a hand up to her cheek and made a fashionable pose.

"Get on with it," said Chalmers.

Right there in the old boneyard, Martinique laid it out. How these men had noticed Hogg coming to see her a few weeks before the party. They paid her to go along with his routine of spiritual advice and platonic companionship. It was her idea to come to the Halloween party and blend in so that in the wee hours, they could slip him out of town to a waiting car.

"It makes sense," I said. "We were all played."

"Who are they?" said Chalmers.

"They are with the union," Martinique said.

"They don't have names?"

"They're johns, so the names they give are no good anyway. One of them, a big man, tall, I don't know who he is, but the union guys do what he says."

"Where did they take Hogg?!" Chalmers yelled.

"I don't know. Some kind of programming center. They took Interstate 70."

"You mean deprogramming?" I offered.

"Whatever."

DeBlasio grabbed her leg. Chalmers kneeled and held her.

"My uncle Freddie is just a phone call away," DeBlasio said.

"Go ahead, Mike: break my leg. I don't know where the flying frog they went. I just delivered him."

Chalmers got up. "We want to know who approached you."

"I *told* you, I don't know names. I'd recognize him if I saw him again."

DeBlasio looked at Chalmers and shrugged. Chalmers motioned to us. We started to leave.

"What about me, Jack . . . you are taking me, too, aren't you? I'm sure they probably seen me with you by now." Chalmers stopped her.

"Listen, slut, you belong down here."

Martinique grabbed my arm, scared.

"Take me with you, please. I'm serious, man."

All of the outer shell of anger, street smarts, and the lingo was gone. Just a scared girl with imploring eyes.

"We said we'd help her."

"She's your problem! She likes the Plaza, so let's take her there."

I looked at Martinique, then at Swensen, who was shying away. She clung to me like a child. We brought some things for Apryl. McDarby accompanied me and Martinique. Tessie let me in, and I introduced her to McDarby.

"One of the famous gents of 1132, I take it."

"Yes, Bernie's become a regular at our place."

Apryl walked into the room. She hugged McDarby and nodded at me coldly. I exchanged a glance with Tessie. I guess the drugs had worn off, leaving only the sordid memory.

"The goddess from the party," said Martinique, catty and smooth. Apryl looked right through her.

"I brought a few things," I said, trying to break the ice. "Laura packed them." I handed her a small case. She wore an attractive, close-fitting eggshell-blue sweater that perfectly set off her shiny hair. I saw McDarby was enjoying her attention—and Apryl's snubbing of me and of Martinique. He grabbed the bag and handed it to her.

"You can probably come back this week," said McDarby.

"I'm having a wonderful time here," said Apryl, smiling at Tessie. Tessie said to me, "Who is your friend?"

"This is . . . uh . . . Martinique."

Apryl crossed her arms and narrowed her eyes.

"Maggie," said Martinique. "My real name's Maggie." She extended her hand to Apryl. Apryl obliged as she would the paw of a dog.

I imagined instantly a plan to get it all back. To redeem myself from those Medusa eyes.

"They've kidnapped our friend," I said.

"This isn't the time or place," said McDarby, but it was too late.

"Tom?" Apryl said as her eyes widened.

"What are you going to do about it?" said Tessie.

Apryl grabbed my arm. "You have to get him back."

"I'm helping with that," said Maggie.

"Maggie needs a place to stay," I pleaded with Tessie.

"Bernard, do you think I'm running a girls' boarding house?"

"Tessie, this is real trouble. We have to get Tom back."

Apryl then did something I did not expect. She took Maggie by the arm.

"I can put her up for a little while," said Tessie.

"Just until we can get her something in Lawrence," I said.

I saw Apryl's eyes, those large pools of feminine sense, opening to me, telling me to help. A knightly challenge. The labors of Hercules. If I had kept my eye on the ball at 1132, maybe Hogg would not be at a deprogramming center.

All I had to do now was rescue Hogg, and then she would love me. I could do what Courtney said, rise above it all, and at the end of the self-conquest, maybe—the prize.

Had I ruined things between us by seeing her in her naked beauty and coming that close to being her first lover? How far was I willing to chase after this chimera, if all it came to was a mirage of my love-parched psyche?

We went out and got into the fumy hearse. Chalmers, beant dangling from his lower lip, sat behind the steering wheel and shot me a rearview leer.

"Now you got yourself a cathouse on the Plaza, G. K."

If I had a rope, I might have garroted him. McDarby stared at me, wordless. What could I tell Holloway? That I had been naked with the one he wanted? That now we wanted to bring a French-Canadian prostitute to campus and possibly the wrath of the mob?

In the midst of all this, I could not think of calling my mother and trying to explain the complicated web into which I had fallen over a gentile woman and a course of study in Western civilization. Or that I was about to find myself on the receiving end of the largesse of the Kansas City mob.

XXXI

WINTER OF MY DISCONNECT

A BITTER wind rose from the Wakarusa plain, overtaking the campus, flashing it into fine bits of memory. Looking from the living room picture window, I saw a blasted landscape, white and lifeless, in a kingdom of recurring dreams: stasis in nature, as in my soul, moveless hills and trees, stark scenery that obstructs the ventricles of madness for an instant. If I could go back to that winter dream, I would stay there a thousand years. But a thousand years is a day, and I am forced to awaken to memory and indigestion.

It was as simple as a call from Michael's Uncle in Kansas City to someone in student housing. I moved into into Hogg's room at 1132 Ohio. St. Thomas and St. Francis pictures hung haphazardly, along with one tacked up that was supposedly of the Blessed Virgin herself as drawn by an Italian mystic.

1132 was a haven of intellectual inquiry, a gentleman's club of elevated conversation alternated by sudden lapses into its former antic disposition. Everyone at 1132 was flunking except for Winston and Swensen—and me. Zorn's papers were riddled with eloquent pleas to expose the conspiracies behind science and history.

Food at 1132 wasn't exactly food: wretched combinations of Velveeta cheese on Wonder Bread, on noodles, Top Ramen, peanut butter, bologna. Only Hogg could cook, and he was gone. I lost ten pounds in a month and a half, smoking and drinking coffee. I had not spoken to my parents once I left the dormitory and told my mother I was moving in with friends from HIP. She suggested I not talk to my father.

I spent Thanksgiving with Patrick and his family in Kansas City, swimming in a spectacle of the football team that were the siblings, crashing and pulling and tackling for attention and the upper hand, ribbing, hugging, abrasive and connected.

Back on campus, we watched Jayhawk basketball at Phog Allen Fieldhouse and concocted pranks for the administration through Christmas break. I recall the day I spray-painted the concrete gray over a huge ice patch in the university executive parking area. I hid in some bushes with binoculars and watched as Vice Chancellor Holloway walked out of his car and blithely skated onto a patch of pure ice, skidding, turning in a spastic pirouette, and splaying out into a classic pratfall, all the contents of his briefcase flying up into a whorl of white papers.

Swinging freely between the sublime and the ridiculous, we stood ready to bank a Nerf shot in the middle of a Yeats stanza. For some inscrutable reason, the center held as we wondered who would gain the ascendancy with Apryl.

I dreamed of Apryl—sometimes of her and Maggie together—in bed, turning down the sheets, and beckoning to me. Some days, that was all I thought about, even when I was supposed to be thinking about G. K. Chesterton's *The Everlasting Man* or the latest off-course book. I was reading in *Everlasting Man* to see if my eponym had anything important to say to me and fell on this: "There are two ways of getting home; and one of them is to stay there." That sunk in. Maybe I had found a home and I needed to stop thrashing about. Only Aunt Teresa would understand.

The Plaza was a brick Christmas tree with an aurora of lights strung along its Spanish tiles and towers—a little city unto itself. Flocks of Christmas shoppers were gliding about, careless, footloose, indulgent. I wondered what it might be like to suddenly jump into their skin. Somehow with all of this span of years living in Kansas City, even shopping on the Plaza, then Chicago and the Gold Coast, I have never become carefree like them.

I stopped by the Robert Browning building. The girls were not there. Aunt Tessie said they were out shopping on the Plaza. I sniffed the air like Hogg, hoping for some trace of the bewitching one, and instead was treated to the clarity and grandeur of Handel's *Messiah*: "Every valley shall be exalted, and every mountain and hill made low."

"Apryl has really taken Maggie on as a project," she said as she turned down the volume.

"Damaged goods tending damaged goods?"

"Bernard, watch out, you are venturing into things you know not of."

"Know not of . . . that sounds a little scriptural for you, Tessie."

"Someone has hurt her deeply."

"Look, I admit the other night was a bit—"

"You're going to get burned, nephew."

"Burned?" I hid my hand under the table. "That's not fair."

"Did you burn down a cabin?"

"That was an accident. It was older than Abe Lincoln."

"Uh huhn . . . I see her pulling you down a hole."

"The heart out of the bosom was never given in vain.."

Her eyes burned. "Housman's right—keep your fancy free. Take it from one who knows. But don't think poetry will blunt the pain."

"Has she said anything about the university and the vice chancellor?"

"She thinks you can rescue Tom Hogg."

"That's me, her knight in shining armor."

"Leave that for Broadway musicals."

"You've given me much to think about."

She put her hand on my chest.

"She said it was you who insisted on rescuing Maggie." Tessie approved of at least one feat of mine.

My fondest memory: the hand on my chest, a woman of all women to me, saying I was something to her, something even noble. And Apryl thinking of me as responsible for rescuing a woman from the street, not to mention preserving her virginity on All Hallows' Eve. This was the grail.

Who did I think I was, Sir Gawain? How did Tessie expect me to keep my fancy free, knowing that I could rescue Hogg and take Apryl's heart?

I walked out onto the Plaza and looked up at the clock tower, a replica of one in Seville, Spain. The iron hands of the clock pointed to the time: 11:32 in the morning. Time to get back to Lawrence.

I picked up a book by Hogg's bedside. Hilaire Belloc, *The Great Heresies*. He was G. K. Chesterton's comrade in arms, Edwardian England's fearless Romish duo. Nothing in there about Jews from LA who didn't believe in anything. I read about Saladin's decisive thrust that turned back the West and nearly turned the whole world Muslim. Belloc's truculent, finely honed prose appealed to me in that frozen world. It contained certainty, stone-cold reason, knowledge of real things, real places, no Lucretian swerves; hot and appealing like Dante's chambers of punishment, penetrating through my confusion.

Zorn caught me reading. "Fierce, G. K. Belloc tells it like it is."

"Yes, he is like a British Hunter S. Thompson."

"Who? . . . I love what he says about the Church." He held up an arm and gestured like a declaiming British statesman: "'The Catholic Church is an institution I am bound to hold divine, but proof of its divinity can be found in this: that no mere human institution run with such knavish imbecility would have lasted a fortnight.'" He left.

I got up, thinking about what I was reading, thinking about my own crusade of the heart. I was pacing the creaky wood floors and driving Patrick crazy, smoking my fourth Camel Light. I went back into Hogg's room and flopped on his bed. I felt something hard as I hit the lumpy, nicotine-impregnated mattress. I felt under the mattress. My hand struck something.

I yanked. A small notebook appeared. I opened it greedily and scanned the rough cuneiform style of Hogg. Like most of the male youth in HIP, he had not internalized its calligraphy no matter how hard the maids of Ole Miss tried to get them to practice better penmanship. Only here, one detected an attempt not so much to write as to inscribe, like a novice monk trying to copy a Twelfth Century manuscript. Page after page about souls in turmoil, souls being saved, souls damned, monasteries, convents, St. Bernard and St. Thomas in dialogue—with little corner sketches of gargoyles and demons.

I skimmed, rushing ahead to the place where I entered the story.

> As Shakespeare said, there is a tide in the affairs of men which taken at the full leads onto fortune. Dame fortune is smiling on us . . . I still see the image of Apryl, the Quentyne, standing before Bernard, by water, and I am seeing her pudenda through his eyes and trying to hold onto the coals of St. Thomas to avoid impurity. And even as I hold the burned area of my hand, I place it in the water to cool the burning.

The image of me and Apryl at the quarry was vivid.

> I have not wished these faculties . . . I did not want to see into the shape of things . . . Bernard has seen my antic disposition. I have prayed that in the moment of this impurity, that Mary help Bernard, as she

helped the Saint of that name in the Middle Ages, to see the real light, to overcome temptation and to save civilization.

Was he feigning crazy like Hamlet for a purpose? Was it all some elaborate prank—or part of a larger plot I could not see?

> Their love will be deeper than a lake, more solid than the rocks surrounding that lake, more dependable than a horse. Through a woman all have been tempted, and through a woman will he be saved in the fullness of time. Is he part of the Chosen people, and if he is, is he chosen? Or part Chosen. Only he can see at the sign of Quentyne.

This planted a seed, an idea for a way to get back at them. Patrick walked in through the cloud of smoke. I immediately hid the journal.

"Someone on the phone."

"Tell them I'm preoccupied."

"It's Strong Hall . . ."

I panicked. Patrick glared at me until I got up and followed him to the living room and the black rotary phone.

"This is Nancy Ellsworth. The vice chancellor wants to see you right away."

I shriveled up all over. I felt terrible for spurning her daughter.

"Can you be here in a half hour?"

"I really need to see the chancellor . . ." There was a silence.

XXXII

THE IDEA OF A MIDWESTERN UNIVERSITY

A SHARP northerly breeze slashed my face as I slogged up Twelfth Street. The sun came from behind a mass of gray clouds, and as it struck Memorial Stadium and the snow-covered hill above it, they sparkled like jewels and dazzled me with amazing light, with silent stillness.

Strong Hall loomed. The proud bronze Jayhawk was half-covered in a powdery snow, but I could see Moses kneeling before the bush. My waffle stompers sunk into the three-foot drift and flattened the million flakes. I paused to look down the expanse of the campus, onto the snow-fed Wakarusa plain.

I encountered Barrows alone in his office, posing behind his desk in a blue turtleneck sweater. The office was just as before, with the tidy files and the pounded gold box with the figure of Triton on top. Barrows was hunched over a gold-leaf leather-bound volume. He snapped it shut and looked up:

"I think I am the only person who came to work."

"Does anyone work in the administration?"

He stiffened, threw his head back, tilted his chin.

"You seemed dead set on this meeting, so have a seat, Kennisbaum."

I stood and looked down. A gold key lay next to the leather volume. The key had a loop at the top, etched with a figure, like the Triton on the gold box. I looked at the box, then at the key, then into Barrows's dark eyes.

"Suit yourself. I am told you have moved into 1132 Ohio Street."

"Not bad for an amateur agent provocateur."

"Is that what you are?"

"Is there something missing in the reports?"

"You are missing. You can act aloof with me, son."

"I'm not your son."

"Are you anyone's son?"

I stood, silent, feeling the venom.

"The vice chancellor is concerned you're losing focus."

"Maybe I'm too good at this." I looked around his office, then at his estimable jaw with its five o'clock shadow.

"That would not be in the spirit of our . . . agreement."

"Spirit? You mean, like the spirit of illegal eavesdropping, or perhaps the spirit of slander of three professors?"

"That is the work of vicious academic jackasses."

"But you're purer than Caesar's wife. No, wait, you are Caesar, so anything you do is already pure before you do it. It's a kind of elect status such as the Catholics and the Calvinists never imagined."

"You're even talking from a medieval point of view."

"There's much to recommend the medieval life. They had no potatoes, but then they had no suicide either." I doubted he got the reference to Belloc.

"I know all about classical education, the idea of the university just as Newman conceived it, the discarded image, the scholastic ideal. Courtney is trying to make gentlemen of you, educated gentlemen, souls with longing for beauty even in an ugly world devoid of true desire."

"When did *you* give up on that image of education?"

"What use is it to you in a world gone mad, what good is it when the weight of technology and the crush of progress scream for something else, a pact with the devil, a pact with modernity?"

He looked out on the Persephonic freeze outside. A blonde girl in a white ski outfit hurried along.

"You're sounding more medieval all the time, Chancellor."

"It's an unfortunate thing when the world has absolutely no use for gentlemen . . . when females prefer barbaric fops, when employers settle for learned ignoramuses."

"Maybe students want alternatives to the campus *carnivale*," I said.

"Used to think so myself. Before anarchy was loosed in the sixties."

"You didn't have to be so . . . promiscuous with knowledge." He snapped his head around.

"All of society became soft," said Barrows. "It abandoned any of its institutions that offered resistance to change."

"Keep this up and Courtney will have you in as a guest lecturer."

"*I* wanted to start a great books program. A national honors program, to bring fine minds here. Like yours."

"What stopped you?" I asked.

"The three of them. I don't know if Courtney knew, but somehow he wanted to . . . upstage me."

"Upstage? It is not his style."

"Au contraire, my fair Junior from the City of Angels. He's every bit the calculating Iago. Behind that univocal view of Truth lies a man who sees all angles. I knew him when, like me, he saw the university as a marketplace of many ideas."

"What about Finley? He is hogging the stage now. He's not open to the idea of medieval truth, the unity of truth, of taking Aquinas's view of Beauty and Truth, say, and not Heidegger's."

"Yes, I lament the retreat of the sea of faith. I am Episcopal. I read Eliot. I know the attraction of these higher things. But today . . . education is all politics. And money. The regents want only to avoid more trouble on campus. Then there's that hick attorney general, Hummer. Did you know he calls Lawrence 'Red Square.' And the legislature eats that up. We just don't have the luxury to pursue truth purely."

"So it's all about appeasing Chalmers and legislators?"

"You've gotten to know him quite well. How is the permanent graduate student?"

"Still full of piss and vinegar, sir."

"The truth is, I don't mind so much the content of the HIP program."

"Why try to kill it?"

"What makes you think I want it dead? Kennisbaum, there are more things in education than are dreamt of in your pedagogy."

"Chancellor, do you think that education should be something that so enthralls you, that crawls into every fiber of your being, into your nerves and into your mind, and your desires—"

"Desire is a dangerous thing. Knowledge, even more so. There are things you don't want to know because at your age . . . it's best you keep your nose out of this. That is why I called you here."

"You called me here to tell me to stay innocent?"

"You were supposed to have this conversation with Vice Chancellor Holloway." He fingered the gold key, drawing my eyes to it. "I brought you here to tell you, your work is done. At the end of this semester, you will end your involvement with HIP. You have served your purpose."

"What exactly is my purpose?"

"I think we will be able to avoid the hearings altogether, to bring peace to the university and graduate you with honors. Stay with this any longer, and it will tarnish you academically."

"I think we're beyond that . . . I need to know what you did with Tom Hogg."

"I have heard his parents wanted to help him."

"Does that involve using mob influence to kidnap students?"

He clenched his jaw. "You must keep your nose out of this."

"Everybody keeps telling me to stick my nose into things, then not stick my nose into other things."

Barrows leaned toward me. "You let Chalmers know about our arrangement, didn't you?"

"They have their moles inside just as you do."

Barrows shrank back to the interior contemplation of his own universe.

"The vice chancellor has been acting without my authority. I am putting an end to this."

"Do you know Tom Hogg's whereabouts?"

He just shook his head.

"I'm supposed to believe you're shutting this down?"

"Don't you understand, Kennisbaum, you are still in the running for the Fulbright. Don't you want to study in Florence after graduation?"

"When will the Fulbright be announced?"

"All will be revealed in the fullness of time."

Right now the only fulness I was interested in was in my gut.

"You must withdraw from HIP at the end of the semester."

He opened the leather folder and placed his hairy paw on the golden key.

"If you don't mind, I have to prepare the final exam I am giving for an honors Western civilization class. I'm composing a question on Cicero's essay on friendship. Do you think that will be provocative?"

"Friendship is the most provocative thing there is," I said. I started out the door, then paused.

"Don't you think the *Kansas City Star*, even the attorney general, would want to know if the university is mixed up with the mob?"

He laughed—not the reaction I was expecting. He narrowed his eyes at the sound of reverberations from my nether parts.

"What is it you want, young man? You are being offered the world."

I grinned and started out the door.

"Where are you going?"

"To rescue a friend."

"Is that a no to the Fulbright?"

I turned, holding the door. He was holding up the golden key. He set it on his desk.

XXXIII

MY SALADIN DAYS

"The most misunderstood time in all of history," said Patrick with pompous aplomb.

"Dead right," replied Chalmers, "the Crusades brought culture, saved all these little shits from having to go around in robes and dump along the side of the road." He cocked his eye at me as I came into the Crossing, out of breath.

"Or put their asses in the air five times a day," I added to slip right into the spirit of things, blowing my frozen snot onto a handkerchief. Chalmers downed his beer and ordered another from Mandy, the cunning brunette.

"Isn't the Holy Father coming next year?" said McDarby.

"Yeah . . . that will solve everything," said Chalmers with a sneer as he lifted the cigarettes from my top pocket and snatched a smoke.

"You watch," said Patrick, "they'll accuse this pope of being medieval, just as they did Paul VI. It's the only curse word left: you're mid-evil."

"You're middle evil," said Ross.

We cracked up. Ross was proud of coining another HIP phrase. He went to the jukebox.

Mandy walked by; her symmetrical derrière casting a spell. McDarby's eyes followed her movements to a neighboring table where she cleaned up a sticky mess of popcorn and beer.

"Enough," said Chalmers. Ross had just put a quarter into the machine. We went silent as we heard the raspy lyricism of Waits singing "I Hope that I don't Fall in Love with You."

208

Even Chalmers was moved by the rhapsodic ballad that conjured desires buried in the soft places of young men.

Ross chirped in: "I don't understand why we don't have Clark here . . . he's done a lot of abortion-clinic protesting; he's not afraid to do anything. And Jacques. He's acquainted with automatic weapons."

"Clark is a do-gooder. Abortion clinics . . . what about senseless acts of destruction? Clark would not approve of things I've done."

"Like peeing on the door of the Lutheran church?" I said. The others were jealous that I got to cross streams with Marin.

"Karl said that—" McDarby began before being interrupted by the dominant Chalmers.

"Karl . . . sheesh . . . he wants to found a village and wait for the Apoca-lypse. He should just farm and leave the action to us."

"Found a village?"

Chalmers looked at me, then at the others. He took out his switch-blade and fingered it.

"It's some dream of Courtney," said Chalmers, "where we all live off the land and have a church, a square—a village idiot and a mayor and a cow and three acres. Karl's an idealist. He's the only one who can lead that life out there."

The barmaid shot us a glance, winking at the infamous Chalmers, the fiery blue-eyed outlaw with the narrow nose and angular jaw.

"When I was a student of the professors," he said languidly, "you wouldn't have believed Marin. I followed him to every bar, drove his Triumph, shot guns with him."

"We're better than the last group to live at 1132," exclaimed McDarby, holding up his glass and motioning to the brunette vixen.

"Yes . . . they were real Jansenists. They come out of the woodwork like termites to chew up a perfectly good structure. They wore khakis, talked like Courtney, pretended Marin wasn't drunk. It wasn't like that when I lived there."

We wanted to hear the legends. Chalmers began to tear up. "It wasn't like that when Todd lived there."

I had heard stories about the death of Todd Livermore when HIP had gone to Ireland's west coast for an entire semester. Todd's derring-do was legendary. He climbed medieval towers in France to impress girls. As a dare, he stayed out all night on an outcropping of rocks on the Aran Islands and was swept out to sea and drowned.

Some girls kept his picture in their lockets or held relics of his dead body—a shred of clothing torn up by the relentless rocks of the Irish coast. Karl told me Chalmers's heart was broken by Belinda Beisecker, who still carried a torch for Todd.

"You know, man," said DeBlasio, "we've asked you a million times to come back to the house."

"My time is past." He wiped his tears and looked away, embarrassed. I thought about Patrick reading Dylan Thomas on the divan and spouting about how the deep words of this twentieth-century master were cutting to the quick. We would stay up late and wait for the muse to get us drunk with understanding.

"Eleven thirty-two is no shrine. It's just an old house." Chalmers fell silent as the ballad came to an end.

"Yes . . . you guys think you can hide in that house and worship Schlayex?" Chalmers stared at me, took out a beant, and smoked. "You can't honestly expect Apryl to be your girl, Kennisbaum?"

"Definitely not his girl," said McDarby.

"You too. You're all kidding yourselves," said Chalmers. "You want the lie, but you can't keep up with her games. This ain't Camelot, and she's not Lady Guinevere."

"You mean, she's not Belinda Beisecker," I said. The others looked panicked. Chalmers flicked open his switchblade.

"What do you think you know?"

"I know that Barrows is the one playing a damned game."

"Yeah, what game is that, G. K.?" demanded Chalmers.

He picked up his knife deliberately and brought it to my arm as De-Blasio and McDarby held me. Here he was, an anarchist masquerading as a traditionalist. Chalmers came from St. Louis at seventeen, a real rebel turning into a hippie, then into HIP.

"He wants me out of the program," I confessed. "He says I've served my purpose."

Chalmers leered like a wolf. "How can we trust you?" He lifted the knife. I had to think quick.

"Barrows offered me the Fulbright."

I looked into Chalmers eyes. He stared into mine.

"It's been nice knowing you," said McDarby.

"I didn't say yes."

They all stared at me, incredulous.

"You didn't say no either," said Patrick, reading my eyes. "Who could blame you?"

"Maybe I don't like what they're hiding. I can't just leave with my friends in trouble."

"What are they hiding?" asked Chalmers.

"There's a box in Barrows's office," I said. "It's a gold box, about so big, and there's a key. There's something significant in there."

Chalmers licked his thin lips and swilled his beer.

"This is why we're here, to fight the administration," said Chalmers.

"What about Courtney . . . the ideal village, our true calling?" Ross was bleary-eyed.

"Leave that to the dung lovers in Fredonia. I came to bring a sword, not a clod of dirt!" Chalmers laughed. I didn't know anything, what was in the box. But there was something about the way Barrows was talking about Chalmers.

"I say we go look in that gold box," I said, and rose to leave. McDarby stood as well, squaring his shoulders to Chalmers. DeBlasio edged his chair back. Ross stared at Chalmers, whose eyes thinned as they darted at me.

"I burned the union."

"Fierce!" said DeBlasio. It was all reputed, never spoken.

"Barrows knows it too," I said as if I knew.

"He didn't give me the book of matches, if that's what you mean," said Chalmers with suave resignation.

"Why didn't he have you prosecuted?" said Patrick.

"It put Barrows on the map," I said.

Chalmers shrugged.

"What about all the commitment to the radical life?" said Ross.

"It was the times," said Chalmers, his face glowing. "If the man needed you, you needed him. I made him important, like the chancellors who got attention at Columbia, Berkeley, Kent State. The sit-ins, the newsreels, Clark Kerr, the Black Panthers, the riots."

"What stopped him?" I said.

"I did." We looked at him, waiting for the next revelation. "I heard about this revolutionary new program to study the classics, and a few of us went to a lecture. Courtney explained the truly radical, how to go against the whole institution, against the whole society's attempt to get us to buy things and settle down. And Marin challenged us, saying we thought we were righteous longhairs, when all we were was pawns of the university and the establishment. Courtney spoke to us, man, like nobody else. He was our Richard the Lionhearted."

"He does that," said Patrick. "Right to the core."

"More radical than rock 'n roll," said McDarby.

"Cooler than Terry Bradshaw," said DeBlasio.

"He's a star," said Ross. "Like Sheen. Most excellent."

"Barrows just let you thumb your nose?" I said.

"He didn't mind my burning down the union, I suppose, as much as he minded my joining HIP. He didn't want anything that stole his limelight."

"I think Barrows wants us to help bring down the enemies of HIP," I said, "but also to bring down Courtney."

"Bullshit," said Chalmers. "He is the enemy of HIP. We have to get whatever's in that box."

"Break in?"

"That's right. He may have evidence against you—or Courtney. Maybe there's something in there that will help us find Hogg."

"I'm in," I said. The others nodded eagerly.

"First, I must insist on your oath to keep all of what you have learned or will learn tonight secret, as Knights of Mount Oread."

"Knights of Mount what?" I said.

"It was started by Grigson. There are only ten knights in all of HIP from seventy-one on."

Chalmers grinned and pried the knife out of the table and pricked his thumb. A trickle of blood bloomed up from an invisible wound. He reached for McDarby's hand, but it was withdrawn before he could grasp it. McDarby grabbed me again.

"Let me go!" I yelled.

"If you want to become a knight, like the Knights Templars in *Ivanhoe*, you have to swear an oath of blood," said Chalmers. "Repeat after me . . . hic hoc in agitorium, videbo visionem, nunc et in hora . . . in tres partes, vini, vidi, vici."

One by one we offered our hands sacrificially. He pulled DeBlasio's strong hand to the middle of the table and cut into his index finger. Chalmers had cut himself. He grabbed my hand to draw blood. He stared at the middle of my hand.

"What the fu—"

"An accident," I said, withdrawing the hand and substituting my other hand. He grabbed it, looked deep into my eyes.

"Boys shouldn't play with fire," he said as he cut my finger without looking down from my blank expression, daring me to wince. I did not oblige. We mingled our blood together. Chalmers sucked on his finger, tasted the albumen and salt of all his comrades' blood mixed together in his seeping wound. Then the others followed suit and they all chased it down with a swig of beer. I only pretended to suck the injured finger, substituting a clean finger.

"I declare you Knights of Mount Oread, select men among a crowd of imbeciles. As Belloc said, 'Noel, Noel, Noel, here's to all who wish us well, may all my enemies go to hell!'"

"Noel!" we shouted as we left.

When we hit the street, it was dark, and we were drunk. Chalmers looked into the gray, starless sky and recited the Frost we had all memorized, and the star that was the fairest one in sight.

We joined him, twisting our necks and thinking of a world under those same stars where the Truth was honored.

Ross and McDarby started pushing each other, soon DeBlasio and Chalmers joined, and I was the first to go, slipping on a patch of ice hidden under the snow, taking off into the air and landing on my ass. The others squealed laughter, and, one by one, they fell.

"You aren't like those old pantywaists," said Chalmer. "You give 1132 character. You are knights." He got up and held out his hand, helping me up. I looked down; a trickle of blood splashed against the bright snow.

Looking back, I count that moment on that mount, under the stars, in that frozen state, as a rebirth and a benison of memory.

XXXIV

ATAVISTIC ACTIVISTS

N OT since the break-in at Democratic National Headquarters had
there been such a group of bungling burglars. Nobody could get
the door to Strong to work until Chalmers pushed us aside and simply
twisted a latch: we crashed inside, falling onto the marble floor with our
slick boots, then sat up, listening.

"I am not a crook," I said, echoing my Halloween performance.

"You keep this up, you will be," Chalmers said. "Now quiet." He
knew what he was doing. Of course, he did. We mounted the stairs on
tiptoe. I imagined what awaited us—a trap, armed guards, newspaper
photographers. I traced in my mind the interview with Barrows. If he
didn't want me to come back here, why was he so mysterious about that
box, the key?

I started to turn around. Chalmers stopped me.

"What's the matter, second thoughts?"

"It's a trap."

"Really?" said Chalmers sarcastically. He proceeded up the stairs,
snickering, as if he thought the idea of a trap made this more appealing.
We followed. We were now part of a great fraternal tradition of pranks,
false leaks, destruction of property, burglaries—in other words, part of
the grand American tradition of politics, law, and business.

Barrows's office was unlocked. I pushed the door open, looking for
our reception party. A steady rush of warm air came from the window
register. It was dark. Chalmers pushed past me, sat in Barrows's chair, and
kicked his feet up on the desk. We left the door open a crack to allow in a

wedge of light. My eyes adjusted to the shimmer of gold coming from the shelf. McDarby reached for the box, but it would not open.

We felt around the desk. DeBlasio was rifling aimlessly through a filing cabinet. Ross looked out on the dark snowy world of Jayhawk Boulevard and the desolation of Wescoe Beach.

"Shit, it's not here," I whispered. I palmed the key, opened the middle drawer, and sloshed around the contents of paperclips and pens while Chalmers gleamed in the dark. I moved the contents around again in a kind of random shell game, then started to close the drawer. Chalmers grabbed my arm.

"Wait." He reached in. "This what we're looking for?" He held up the gold key. He threw it up into the air where it caught the moonlight streaming in from the window.

"Amazing, Rich," said McDarby.

"The key to the kingdom," I said as I grabbed it and walked to the box. The others gathered around. Even Chalmers had large eyes as we gazed at the glimmering box. He pulled out a single piece of paper, old and yellowed, with cursive handwriting. He read aloud:

> *Louise, why are you grieving—*
> *Over April's beauty unrelieving,*
> *Over time and change and ends,*
> *over this time of useful friends,*
> *so youthful, strong, and unbelieving?*
> *O Miriam, what is this impeaching*
> *In the act of student teaching?*
>
> *Campus crackers, without the cheese,*
> *Create a breeze and whisper disease.*
> *Helen, chemicals are the real price;*
> *For a little more, they'll throw in rice.*
> *Then come live with me and be my lease,*
> *We'll have our fill of sin and blame*
> *(If you recall whatever became of them).*

"Who wrote that?" said Patrick as he grabbed for it. I took it.

"Let me have it," said Ross. Chalmers grabbed it from me.

"Who's this chick?" said DeBlasio.

"The writing sucks," said McDarby.

"What do you expect, man, he's a chancellor," said DeBlasio.

"Then who's Miriam?" said McDarby.

"That's my mother's name," I said, motionless at Barrows's desk.

"How does Barrows know your mother?" said McDarby.

"This looks like Holloway's writing," I said. "Barrows thinks he's off the reservation. I think Holloway's obsessed with Apryl."

We exchanged looks of chagrin.

"Miriam is biblical," said Patrick. "Probably not your mother."

"Whatever became of sin and blame sounds familiar," I said. "One of the professors said that, didn't they?"

"No," said Ross. "Bishop Sheen." We all turned to him. "Karl Menninger wrote a book, *Whatever Became of Sin?* Sheen talks about it on one of the tapes."

"You're a genius," I said.

"I am?"

"Don't you get it?"

Chalmers moved toward the door. "Let's get out of here before we all get it."

"No, wait," I said, "Barrows put this in here for a reason. He wants us to know something. Off I-70 she said. It goes through Topeka, doesn't it?"

Chalmers stopped in his tracks.

"Remember the girl, Martinique, she said they took Hogg on I-70," said McDarby, who was hopping up and down.

"If you were going to deprogram someone," I said, "where's the best place in the Midwest to take them off I-70?"

"That's it," said DeBlasio.

"Menningers," said Chalmers.

"And they said poetry is useless." I rose from the desk. Chalmers grabbed my arm and stopped me.

"We're forgetting something." I looked into his eyes as they narrowed and a thin smile split his face. I heard the sound of a zipper. I looked down. Slowly he began to take out his member. Then I heard a chorus of zippers.

"Rich, not this," I said.

"You know, zipper is an onomatopoeia," said Chalmers. DeBlasio laughed in a high-pitched squeal. Chalmers climbed on Barrows' leather chair. The others started repeating the word, emphasizing the "p" and laughing too loud for this operation.

Pretty soon we were all partaking in the ritual, part of Chalmers's wolf pack. It must have been colder in there than I thought because clouds of steam rose from Barrows's desk, just like the door of the Lutheran church.

φ

"Ever see *The Dirty Dozen?*" I said, looking up, stretched out like a corpse in the back of Hogg's hearse. We were on a back highway somewhere between Lawrence and Topeka. We had found Hess at 1132. He hadn't needed to be asked twice. Patrick napped with one eye open.

"I don't know about dirty dozen," said Hess, "but all of you could use a shower." He smiled in his white smock, looking like a young Lee Marvin with his toothy smile, his wheat shocks of hair, his leather face, his big blue eyes.

"I never could memorize the count where Lee Marvin goes over the plan," said Patrick as he devoured a map under the glare of a flashlight in the middle seat. Ross was asleep, snoring next to DeBlasio and McDarby—who were also passed out—shielded by a Jayhawk hat, proudly clutching his Bishop Sheen belt buckle.

"I think we need to come up with some lines to remember what to do," said Hess.

"Good idea," I said as I worked on some lines. I looked up at Chalmers. "Now that I'm a knight of Mount Oread, can I have my journal back?"

Chalmers snickered.

"You don't trust me yet?"

"Don't let that bother you," said Hess, "he doesn't trust nobody."

"Or anybody," said Patrick.

"That's a philosophy to live by," said Chalmers. I kept staring. Chalmers looked up into the rearview and saw me staring.

"Besides, I don't have your journal anymore," he said.

"What do you mean, don't have it? Who does?"

"Someone took it. I don't have it, dammit!"

I was not sure if I believed him. We memorized the rescue plan, and I drifted off.

We came up a drive and saw an ominous clock tower rising up from what looked like an old brick college. The headlights of the hearse exploded on the snowy mound in bluish spangles and a sign: *The Menninger Clinic.* Chalmers cut the headlights

"There," said Patrick. He jostled McDarby, DeBlasio, and Ross.

"Wake up, sunshine," said Hess, laughing thunderously. DeBlasio winced.

"Where are we?" said Ross as if he were coming out of anesthesia.

"By the Ganges or the Humber," I mumbled.

"Topeka's the pits, man," said McDarby.

"To-puke-a," said Patrick.

"Now remember everything I said," whispered Chalmers as if someone were trying to listen in.

"We remember," we said as we chanted: "Chalmers gives the word, G. K. flips the bird, Michael fires up the hearse, Hess takes Hogg without a curse."

"Good. I'll do the talking . . . the extraction team will be at work finding Hogg's room."

Chalmers held a clipboard with some official-looking papers. As we entered the building a large security guard scanned us.

"You from St. Francis Hospital?" The security guard was taking in the strange suits, the hearse. He was huge, with a kind, receptive face. Patrick chatted him up. He was an ex-football player, a third stringer at Nebraska. "I dunno, the super isn't here, uh, not 'til 7:30 . . . if you could wait."

"No waiting, we have our orders . . ."

Chalmers pointed outside. He had parked the hearse as far away as possible so the security guard could not tell if it was official. The guard nodded and stood up.

"Hogg . . . yeah, I know this one. I held him down for EC. Always seeing angels. We get a lot of weirdos here, but he's a real boogey wigger. Nothing fifty thousand volts didn't cure."

"Yeah," said Chalmers feigning humor. I could see he was tensing up, ready to spring on this ogre. DeBlasio flexed his fists as he and McDarby disappeared.

"I'm not supposed to . . . look, wait here, I'll be back."

The guard left. Chalmers pointed out the security cameras to Ross and me.

"What's EC?" said Chalmers.

"Electroconvulsive therapy. Shock treatment," I said. Chalmers's jaw clenched.

"Give the signal, G. K."

I stuck my arm out the door and flipped the bird at Hess, DeBlasio, and McDarby, who waited around the corner. They started around the back of the building. Patrick and I went down a corridor to find a door to let the others in. DeBlasio was inside in a flash. Hess, in his cowboy boots, skidded like a dog gliding over the finely polished parquet floor.

"Whoa, horsey," said McDarby, catching Hess.

"Thanks, Bob," said Hess.

"Where to?" said McDarby. Patrick motioned, not seeming sure where to go. We came down a corridor and saw Chalmers behind the hulking ex-lineman. Just as they walked past an administrator's office, DeBlasio whipped around the corner and was face to face with the guard.

"Mike, he held Tom down to give him electroshock," said Chalmers.

The security guard realized what was up and started to swing a large club of an arm at the agile DeBlasio. DeBlasio ducked and came up under the guard, landing a solid right to his breadbasket. The guard doubled over and gasped for breath, then took one to the chin that knocked him out cold. DeBlasio rubbed the knuckles of his right hand.

"He was a two-bit bench warmer for Nebraska," said Chalmers.

"Come on, here's an office," said McDarby. They went inside and rifled through some files. We split up to look for Hogg, peering into rooms with patients of various ages, some in sleep or half-sleep, some just staring restlessly from their pillows, strapped in, their eyes showing neither despair nor hope, only psychotropic torpor fit for another circle of Dante's hell. Then I heard a familiar voice.

"It is only when the pope speaks ex cathedra, that is, from the chair of Peter, that he speaks infallibly. We have to assent with our will. The will is a faculty of faith, as St. Thomas points out in the second argument of . . . or is it the third . . . do you have a copy of the *Summa*?"

I held up an arm to signal to Ross to stop and listen. It was Hogg, pulling madly on a Marlboro, sitting in a lime green beanbag chair. The coal on the end flashed a bright amber. The smoke hovered over a pale strawberry blonde in a matching beanbag the color of bubble gum. Hogg held the cherry of the Marlboro in front of his eyes.

"St. Thomas did it . . . the prostitute tried to seduce him, and he took the burning coal from the fire and squeezed it in his hand." Hogg brought the cherry closer to his hand. Ross was opening his mouth as if to tell Hogg to stop. I held my finger up to my lips to keep him quiet.

"You have been released from Reverend Moon—into Our Lady's moonbeams," said Hogg. The girl looked up at him with the admiration of a disciple. He began to bring the cigarette closer to his hand.

"Why do you have to burn yourself?"

"So you do not have to burn."

Hogg moved the glowing ember closer to his flesh. Suddenly, the Moonie put her hand between Hogg's hand and the beant. As it began to burn her flesh, Hogg withdrew it. She took Hogg's hand and put it around her neck. The girl cried. He brought his hands to his head in pain. The strawberry blonde hugged him.

"Why do you sniff all the time? Do you have a condition?"

"I smell something in your hair."

"It's Herbal Essence."

"Essence of soul."

"I don't think they make that."

It was my fault that Hogg had been kidnapped. The committee would never have had the information, would never have had a basis for obtaining a court order to commit him—to convulse his brain, to turn him into a tossed spiritual salad—without my reports. I thought they were harmless, stories of mad prophetic utterances.

Finally, DeBlasio came up behind us at that moment with McDarby. Hogg and the strawberry blonde snapped around in our direction.

"Quick, Tom" I said, "we're here to rescue you. Let's go."

"What about her?" he said.

"Forget her," said Chalmers as he walked in. She looked at us vacantly, tears running down her cheeks.

Chalmers pulled Hogg up. Hogg threw a rosary at the girl. We helped him out to the car. As I sat next to him on the trip home, he prayed under his breath. I looked at Patrick.

"This is my fault," I said. Nobody responded. Ross was asleep again. Courtney was right about Aristotle and the urge toward friendship. The ethics of friendship was no longer in an essay. It was before my own vision and experience. I pledged then and there that I would not betray Hogg or my blood oath to my comrades. We had him, habeas corpus.

However weird I found it, I would try to do what Hogg said, no longer pursuing what was base. I would pull myself out of the basement, out of the shadows of intention, into the light of action. It was something I didn't need to write in a journal.

In this dark wood, I was finally coming to myself.

XXXV

BEAUTY SO ANCIENT AND SO NEW

I HAD chased an image of scholarship, but now I was chasing a new mistress, something buried in the past: an image—a girl, a triptych of civilization in the perfection of Beauty, Truth, and Goodness. The university had played the great game of spades and had discarded all its other suits: it now held only high spades and they were milking all of us of our heritage.

Hogg babbled and smoked. His parents called; the university sent spies. We hid him in the basement or at Ole Miss. Finals were a blur, easy and perfunctory. I took Hogg's and mine. Chalmers provided cover through SCHLAYEX funds with payoffs aplenty. A couple of principled professors held out until we slipped them an all-expenses-paid weekend at the Raphael on the Plaza, and tickets to the Eagles concert at Kemper Arena.

I was taking both the freshman and sophomore HIP classes. In the freshman class, we were reading *The Aeneid* and I was floundering on the shores of the new Rome, journeying with Aeneas through his passion for Dido, her tragic end, and Aeneas forging ahead to found the destined race. The sophomore class had just passed beyond the Romans, beyond the readings of Seneca and Horace and Cicero and Virgil. Of Origen, of Tertullian, the Bible, Boethius—and now it was the dawn of Christendom, of the Bishop of Hippo himself, God's Hippo, St. Augustine, merging in his thought the spirit of the whole Greco-Roman world. I recall that crisp February day when the sun was strong and warm against my chapped face. I ran to Strong Hall where Courtney lectured on Augustine.

"There comes a point in the individual life when the straight way is lost in spite of learning, worldly achievement, popularity, even success. It is a fork in the road." Courtney's music had given way to a sinewy philosophical strain, as if he were trying to name the craziness around us.

"You want to be pure, do you?" Marin stared at us with a wolfish grin. "Augustine knew about desire. His mother, Monica—she knew about desire. Do you think Augustine brought any of those Carthaginian babes home for Thanksgiving? Was it because dear old Mom couldn't understand his loins? Or was it because Augustine started to see the error of unbridled lust?" He snickered. "They don't like that word, Paul. They think you can just love God and do what you will."

"Mr. Marin is right," said Courtney in a conciliatory tone. "There is the understanding that something is wrong, the apperception of the intellect. And then there is the will. I don't know if you can hear this, but we have come to a place in society where not only is the intellect diseased, but there is a widespread epidemic disease of the will. Knowledge of the wrong, inability to act on the right. Augustine said it perfectly, 'Lord, make me pure, but not yet.'"

"Did you hear that?" broke in Whelan. "He is asking God to bring him chastity, but he acknowledges he is still too chained to his senses. He wants the ultimate good. He is an intellectual. But he is lost in hedonism. You might say he was a dormitory man."

"Did you know," said Marin in the voice of a wise uncle, "that George Washington said the country cannot exist without moral and God-fearing men. It is hard to believe but you can't have America and individual freedom without recognition of these essential truths in Augustine. He lived while the greatest empire in history was crumbing under the weight of its decadence. Or are you too afraid to acknowledge what you know in your hearts—that the party has to end, you have to pay the piper, a civilization can't live on Coca-Cola, Disneyland, and free love. Love, like freedom, comes at a price!"

There was a hush as these barbs landed on those of us who lived in a brave new world free from moral imperatives.

The Confessions held a strange allure; the powerful need of a whole civilization to confess. It seemed in tone much like the music of Lucretius, a figure at a time in history, at a place in the cosmos, accomplished, attuned to civilized things, yet mired in carnal pursuits. Other teachers seemed to have given up on it, had treated it as the mob had treated the king, the culture, the Church, in revolutionary France.

"Augustine is a prism through which to view that refracted light of the ancients," said Whelan. "He was the best the ancient world offered. He represented its privilege and philosophy, its rhetoric and law."

"Did you know about Augustine's college days?" said Marin. "Lest you think him too inner-lectual, I mean for you to know that he too understood the frivolous streams of a man's soul, he too was part of a group of cruel and hilarious pranksters known as the Overturners, young men who went about pranking the conventional order."

Overturners. What were the Knights of Mount Oread but a bunch of young men overturning the conventional order? We wanted wisdom, but we also wanted those who thought they had it, the sophists and philistine administrators, to be overturned, just as Vice Chancellor Holloway was turned upside down in that parking lot.

"Augustine was like your modern-day graduate student," continued Courtney, "who finds himself courted by GE, AT&T, or Standard Oil. The giants of Augustine's time knew him and wanted him. But in that future, he saw the clouds of destruction. He had given in to youthful lust and it had burned him up."

"Look at his mother," said Marin. "Do you think she gave up and became liberated? Did she burn her bra, or her eighteen-hour netting or whatever the hell they used in Roman civilization? Did she say, 'Boys will be boys?' No! She prayed and wept for Augustine, that his *restless* heart would fix on the beauty not of sex but the ancient beauty. You are not up to his level of sin. You have to enjoy sex to really sin, with a full appreciation of the act. You're no damned good at being pagans!"

"Well, you see," said Courtney, rescuing us, "you face taking the road. There is a thorny road, filled with troubadours and drunkards and snake-oil salesmen, where it is acceptable to stumble into the ditch. And then there is the royal road. El camino real as Teresa of Avila called it. If Augustine is right that we have restless hearts, then we have to walk a certain path toward a certain place to find rest, to find the object of our search. Augustine heard it in a garden."

A silence descended on the class, feeling the pinch of that dichotomy: the easy way of silliness, loutishness, working in the world like high school students with money, or choosing a serious life with all that it implied.

"This was the *highest* civilization the world had ever seen," said Marin, "and the best and the brightest were going to watch blood sport! Are you even up to that decadence? You're all too sentimental. You'd report them for cruelty to animals."

"Augustine was a master rhetorician," inserted Whelan, aware of the sapping of energy in the class. "He set the tone for two thousand years of civilization."

"What did Augustine hear in the garden?" asked Courtney. "*Tole lege.* Take up the book and read. This was a practice known as bibliomancy, the opening of the Bible or a sacred text to find answers wherever your eye or finger landed. Augustine had practiced this, along with numerology, the mystical association of numbers. And when he opened the book, what did he see? Not in drunkenness or in wantonness, the passage told him. It spoke directly to him. Let me read it." Courtney picked up a worn hardcover of *The Confessions*:

> "I grasped, opened, and in silence read that paragraph on which my eyes first fell, Not in rioting and drunkenness, not in chambering and wantonness, not in strife and envying; but put ye on the Lord Jesus Christ, and make not provision for the flesh, to fulfill the lusts thereof. No further would I read, nor did I need; for instantly, as the sentence ended, by a light, as it were, of security infused into my heart, all the gloom of doubt vanished away.

"That single passage was sufficient to go to the heart of his restless life. Stop your wanton life, he heard, and he heard singing. A beautiful voice. There is always a beautiful voice that will bring you back from the brink and set your feet on the road. And he wept. This is the pinnacle of the ancient world: to have this education, to live in a civilization that has everything but the one thing you need and to come to this point of pity and to weep."

"It culminates in those most famous of lines in all classical literature," said Whelan. "'O, Beauty, ever ancient, ever new.' You can read his passage over and over for the rest of your life, and it will never lose its freshness or its power."

"Margaret, are you grieving over golden grove unleaving?" said Marin, "Things like the leaves of man . . . Will you ever grieve or weep for your own loss?"

Holloway's poem sprung into my mind: Louise, why are you grieving? I wanted to approach Courtney for further elucidation on this royal road, to explain the numbers. They were the id, superego, and ego to us. Even at 1132, we were taking sides. We needed the insults to our ego that Marin gave us. Winston went with Courtney because of his mysticism and high sense of philosophical poetry. I was torn between Marin and Courtney as dual opposites of passion and the life of the soul.

And had it ended that day, I would have gone and taken up the book. But another book entered the picture, the book of nature. Apryl was returning to school.

XXXVI

UNRAVISHED BRIDE

M ARCH sometimes feels like April when the rains fade and a strong
sun warms the soggy world. I was walking downtown in that pre-
venient April when I encountered Perry coming out of Drake's Bakery.
He was wearing a brown tweed jacket with leather elbow patches and the
ubiquitous Topsiders sans socks.

"As I live and breathe, Mr. Hudson," I said.

"Brother Glaze," he said. "No shows for Joes?"

"Chased them out of town . . . I think they left on spring break."

"Beware the ides of Munch," he said.

"We must take the currants when they serve them," I quipped in
return.

"You look more lean and hungry than when you were a freshman. I
would almost call you slim."

"I don't live among the philistines of the dormitory race with their
unclean cafeteria food."

"Yes, I hear you are quite hip these days."

He adjusted his tortoise shells and looked me up and down—the
baggy khakis, the burgundy sweater vest, the loafers. No more signs of
Ben Gurion. "Transformed," he said gravely. "A Courtney disciple?"

"Just trying to become more like you. But I draw the line at socks."

"Alas, only a few can do prep proper. Say, did it ever work out between you and that tart?"

"Apryl."

"Whan that Aprille." He laughed.

"You might say we reached a separate peace."

"You always went after the ones who didn't want you."

"I'm done with all that. Why don't you come along, see what I'm talking about, we're singing Gregorian chant."

"That I shan't."

"Always the wit, Brother Hudson."

"*Piece* be to you."

He turned down a side street. As I looked back toward the bakery, I saw Vice Chancellor Holloway exiting and walking toward his car. My stomach turned. Perry had been schmoozing the administration for that Fulbright. I walked quickly the other way toward St. Johns, pondering how I could stay true to my path.

φ

"*Deus, in adjutorium meum intende . . .*"

"*Domine, ad adjuvandum me festina . . .*"

I had learned the chant enough to lead it now in front of Courtney, Roy and Meg Meis, Corey Tartt, Belinda Beisecker, Hogg, and most of 1132. Patrick stood next to me. We sang vespers from the Little Office of the Blessed Virgin toward the front of the church, by a stained-glass window of the Annunciation. There, the young maiden was wrapped in a brilliant green robe, with pale skin and auburn hair—like Apryl. Above her hovered Gabriel with flaming wings and a luminous face asking the maiden to take on the assignment of all time.

I loved the beauty of the chant, the plainness of it, how it filled the space of the church, all the way up to where the picture windows of saints lined the vault.

Iam iams transiit

The rains, over and gone. True, it was nearly April. I noticed how the tone of the chant slowed, or stayed on one tone for certain poetic interludes, when the lover sang to his beloved. I wanted things to stay just as they were, time held captive in the arms of plainsong.

Nigra sum, sed formosa

I am black but beautiful, daughters of Jerusalem. I looked around at that, seeing Jimmy Drungole, who had joined us. I imagined him scat singing chant, "The winter is past, spring is here, O April is near." Nearby were Diana Dietz, standing with Swensen, and Miss Bernadone, with dark eyebrows and piercing blue eyes. The lovely Trish sat near me. Since Apryl's departure, she walked with me from class.

It was during these reflections that Apryl arrived. We had inclined a half bend as we sang the "Gloria Patri," so I was viewing her behind me, upside down, the image of the one who had transfixed and startled me out of my old life. She swished her hair. There was no way to avoid being shrouded in her smell as I considered the burning coals of lust Augustine felt. Swensen turned red as I caught him looking at the beauteous wraith. I righted myself. She was paler, white almost—not like alabaster, more like a china doll.

I was staring at her, but then I saw in her wake a maiden—Martinique, whose real name was Maggie. Only she was different. Apryl could have no more made herself less than spectacular than she could have passed as a man. Yet because she had this other with her, we somehow transferred her glory to Maggie, who no longer bore the etched features of time. She appeared young, with scant makeup; her skin was milky— her features French. She had nothing like glittery attraction or ordinary beauty. Something had been done to her.

As Apryl passed, I looked at her. She looked at me and the others. She blushed. Her one magic, her feat: she knew she could beguile when she walked by. But now another interrupted this arc of timeless fragrant light and shadow.

Maggie was not Apryl. Could all of that be conveyed while inclining and saying *sicut erat*? The world seen from the upside-down perspective and then righted showed Truth. Newness of sight. The mingling of incense, of Apryl, and now Maggie—whose perfume, a new scent, was filling the space. I could not say it was musky, nor sweet, nor cloying, nor mysterious. It was simply Maggie.

Apryl showed her a little office, and she followed along the best she could. Perhaps what we had was a dream, one rapturous night in the pathless woods, in the lovely moonlight reflecting off her marble body.

Nisi Dominus aedificaverit domum

Unless the Lord build the house, they labor in vain who build it. Did I labor in vain in this house of 1132?

Rubum quem viderat Moyses incombustum . . .

In the bush Moses saw burning without consuming, we acknowledge thy admirable virginity preserved. I had seen a vision, oblivious to the base politics of the university, in the ache of my youth, in the hope of my future, and there by a fountain of sweetest-smelling nard and the smoothest leopard skin and silkiest hair and most liquid eyes and being. I was leading in this song. Ending with an unquenchable longing.

> *Ave Maris stella*
> *Dei Mater alma,*
> *Atque semper Virgo,*
> *Felix caeli porta . . .*

Bright Mother of our Maker, hail, Thou Virgin, ever blest; the Ocean's Star by which we sail and gain the port of rest.

I needed a port. I had grown tired of looking in the mirror at my tired old self. An image of life could not be greater or a better cure for obsession with oneself. I saw sunlight streaming through the green robes in the window. Late had I loved her, Beauty so ancient and so new!

Afterward, a group formed around Apryl. She saw me trying to get close to her, but she pretended to be wrapped up with the girls as if she were at a shower or birthday party. Swensen and McDarby looked at the ground, trying not to let on to the other girls that they'd have preferred to look at Apryl. Patrick shook his head.

"Let the games begin," I said.

"Games?" said Swensen.

"With you bringing up the rear," said McDarby.

"She doesn't look well," said Patrick.

"Really?" I said.

"She's not feeling that good," said a voice. We turned to see Maggie.

"Sorry to hear that," said Swensen, barely acknowledging her.

"She took good care of me. Lately, though, she's had la grippe." Maggie said this with a French accent. A song had replaced the drone of her sarcasm, a certain girlishness peered out. I looked at Apryl, who was trying to make cheery with her bevy of maidens-in-waiting from Ole Miss. Patrick was right. Something about her was off.

"I have to thank you," said Maggie.

"For what?"

"For taking me to stay with your Aunt Teresa. She is a great woman."

"That I know," I said.

"I mean, she sees much."

"Tell that to her eye doctor."

"You like telling jokes," she said, showing me a big smile. "Apryl really helped me."

"Yes . . . and I would not be here if not for her."

Swensen and McDarby moved toward Apryl, and I was left standing alone with Maggie. I looked over. Apryl spied us together. Something in her eyes made me wonder if she had not planned this. I wondered if she was playing a game with me here as she had with Trish, acting as Demeter to ensure the fertility of mortals.

"You all are like a pack of dogs wagging your tails around her," Maggie said.

"We are just friends."

"Il faut qu'un porte soit ouverte ou fermée."

"Another one of your French cliches?"

"It means roughly, you can't have it both ways."

"Thanks, I'll remember that." I walked over to Apryl and the group.

"It is wonderful to have you back since we rescued Tom," I said, smiling at her. She grabbed my arm and took me to the vestibule, into the cry room. She pulled the shades.

"Is this going to make me cry?" I said, bracing for the heave-ho.

She approached me and stood very close. My stomach growled. Then, all of a sudden, she was kissing me—and not a sisterly kiss, but a deep, full kiss.

"Apryl . . ."

She kissed me again.

"I never properly thanked you for the rescue of Tom and also of Maggie. And me."

"I am now a freelance knight in the rescue business."

"I have to go."

"Wait." She turned. "Is this just a kiss handed out in thanks or something else?"

"Everybody's after me. Sometimes it's too much, you know? But with you it's different. You're special to me."

"I'm special to you?"

"Aunt Tessie said you are an ardent and idealistic young man."

"What else did she say?"

"That you'd never really had a girlfriend."

"Most of the girls I've been with lack insight. But I thought we exchanged something . . . incredible that night. We opened up to each other, for real."

She put her hand on my arm.

"All my life I've had this thing nagging at me, am I really someone to them? They all say, you're so pretty. But my father left me. I'm not a woman in a Botticelli painting."

"Okay, so you're not a goddess."

"And I don't want to be owned . . . at least not yet."

"Okay."

She squeezed my arm, smiled, and walked out. I felt embarrassed. Exhilarated but also off balance. Maybe this was how she wanted me, locked in a passionate pose on an urn. Maybe it was how I wanted it. Nobody gets hurt when glazed in poetry.

I saw her take McDarby's arm, and the two of them walked down the aisle like a newly married couple. I licked my lips just for a little of the finish of her wine.

I knew what I must do to prove myself to her.

XXXVII

MIDDLE EVIL

Now that Apryl was back, it was spring. We read *Don Quixote* in HIP's second-year courses. In the first year, we were reading Boethius and *The Consolation of Philosophy*. Both dealt a blow to looking at the world and the affairs of men pragmatically. For Boethius, there was chance, as in Lucretius, but he did not stop at the fountains of lust; he saw beyond the chance pleasures of life to the great queen of arts: philosophy. Don Quixote saw through the pretense of modernity, and while he seemed antic, he saw clearly what a man must do.

I was on my way to the most medieval place one could think of in our age of bronze—the college assembly. I took my usual path by the stadium and Potter Lake, dressed out in verdure, a fountain feeding the turtles and mallards in the cattails and sedge, amid the tulip and water lily. I thrilled to the songs of red-tailed hawks circling overhead in the oak and willow trees.

"Little we see in nature that is ours." I was startled to see Chalmers sitting on a bridge by the lake, dangling his legs, holding a green bottle and smoking.

"Wordsworth would have written an Ode on Potter Lake if he had been here." I walked over to him.

"I come here to meditate. Sit down, have a swig of wormwood." He held up the bottle, it was light green.

"Vermouth?"

"It's good by itself."

"It's too early for me, and I have to be at the College Assembly."

"It's not for twenty minutes, sit awhile and take in this beauty."

232

I sat and lit up a beant. I took the bottle from him and washed down some dry vermouth. It was bitter but warmed me up.

"What are you going to say to the Assembly?"

"Not sure if I'm going to say anything."

"Professor Marin thinks you're up to it."

"This is a perfect setting."

"Leisure is the basis of culture, don't you think?"

"If we had more of it, maybe we'd have more culture."

"Do you believe in permanence of perfection?" said Chalmers.

"Like a monastery?" I recalled what Hogg said to me.

"It stands as something permanent, something timeless, more than just a place to find peace. It preserves learning and culture, it brings order to society that otherwise would not be there."

"You think you can go back to that kind of order in the vanity fair of modern culture?" I ventured.

"We're not the only ones who see the new order coming out of the old. Jacques Maritain, Frank Duff, Dorothy Day, and you and I can take the chaos and find the old and new together. Waiting to be watered and grown afresh."

I took a swig.

"You and I?"

"If you have the courage to look for a new world."

"You mean like Constantine turning the empire Christian?"

"In hoc signo vinces," he said, evading the issue. I was starting to feel a little high from this late morning conversational cocktail. I got up.

"I'll be late."

Chalmers just smiled placidly like a hermit I had merely stumbled upon.

"We have come to the vote and have concluded we must have the hearing this semester!"

Herman Gunther let a thin smile protrude from his tight lips and terse face. There was much hubbub and whispering. The hearings were supposed to take place over the summer when there would be little press attention and minimal effect on the students. Finley looked smug and commanding from his chair at the front with Gunther. Holloway sat a safe distance away, pretending to be an objective observer. I watched him keeping the Reverend Rhoden in eye's reach, a wary predator.

Whelan stood, containing himself, and looked around at the assembly, making remarks to Broglio, who sat with them in full black cassock and hat, *una brava figura*. Courtney seemed contained also, staring at the ground. Marin was fidgety but clearly following a plan of saying nothing, though his seething eyes looked ready to shoot bolts of lightning.

I looked around and saw Barrows jutting his jaw in the shadows, standing with the tall regent, Dewain Schmead. There was another man and a woman with them at the periphery, standing by a column. Among the spectators above were Sharon Blaine and Reverend Rhoden. This inquisition had all the clerics it needed to make it resemble the Diet of Worms or Wolsey and More before the Parliament. Whelan broke in:

"We will have Dom Angelo Broglio, a lawyer, sitting here, represent us in this proceeding. We reserve our right to file in another forum, at a time and place of our choosing."

Fear enveloped the assembly like a plague. Professors and administrators went back to low whispers, raised eyebrows, and florid gestures. The tide was full, a perfect moment to speak. They turned to look at one who rose. A student representative? It was me.

"There is a tide in the affairs of men . . . which taken at the full leads onto fortune. Shakespeare wrote this of Julius Caesar."

Buntrock cowered under his bushy eyebrows. Gunther glared. Finley whispered to some feckless professors who rolled their eyes at my simplistic utterances. Marin sat back and smoked.

"I am merely a student representative. Bernard Kennisbaum. You know, my name means tree of knowledge in German." I looked at some German professors I had, and they grumbled under their breath. "I would have thought that knowledge would have flourished, firmly planted by the river of thought. Instead, it has withered in the drought of March. Why have we not together gone on to greater academic and personal fortune in such a full tide? Why are we divided, you in your cliques and opposing camps—for and against HIP, for the administration, against it, for the chancellor, against the vice chancellor. The arts and sciences are now in the service of taskmasters and pimps."

The hubbub rose to a crescendo. The mob was angry, and it wanted to kill me. I looked at Chancellor Barrows and Holloway. They knew we had rescued Hogg; they knew we held the keys to their destruction. If they weren't going to stop me, I was not going to stop myself. I would be Pericles to the Athenians, Washington to the Continental Congress.

"The tide of affairs has come full circle. Fortune is fickle. We do not often control our own destinies. We look for something to control them. But do you not know that you allow your destinies to be controlled by others? Many come to college unsure of what they are—or who they want to become. They expect changes, a taste of culture, new beliefs, books, experimentation with all manner of things. You turn a blind eye to the saturnalia and all the moral experimentation. You overlook temporal infractions, the drugs and sex in the dorms. Some of us were seventeen when we arrived. I've taken classes that taught the Bhagavad Gita, I had a psychology professor who invited us to experiment in sexual pairing. Some of you participate in it yourselves."

I looked at Finley. I saw one young, bearded assistant professor who took tickets to a Billy Joel concert. We had him on film with a co-ed, not his wife, living it up at the Raphael courtesy of SCHLAYEX.

"And you seize on the crimes of three professors of whom you are jealous. You come after them for daring to take seriously the texts of great writers and thinkers. You condemn them for corrupting the youth."

I was riding high on the muses, and some wormwood. I looked at Barrows, then at Marin and Courtney. It was why I came to this embarrassing and freeing moment. It was my chance to tilt at these windmills that kept me from Apryl. I was now going to tell them about my complicity in the inquisition of HIP, of the kidnapping, of CAPUT, and of Attorney General Hummer.

"You have let me be a representative here, an honors student. But I have to tell you professors that I lack honor just as you do, for I am guilty of not caring about principle. This scholarship I did not earn . . ."

Two faces emerged from the shadows. They stood with Barrows above. I stopped in midsentence before I could implicate the chancellor. Before I could unburden myself of my crimes.

There, standing with Barrows, was my father, Norm Kennisbaum!

I found myself stammering, talking nonsense before I could even make sense of what I was seeing.

"The Jayhawks were number four in the country. Yet they did not play in the NCAA tournament that was played here! Have I not reason to lament what has become of KU? Yet we are supposed to feel consolation in Magic Johnson from Michigan State."

Schmead paced in his giant Florsheims. The assembly was confused, expecting some great revelation.

"We sometimes hide who we are. There is a tide in the affairs of men. Do not fail to take it," I said faking a peroration of some kind before I ran out.

The guys caught up with me. We ran all the way to 1132. As we approached, we saw a large Buick sitting in front.

XXXVIII

CARPET DIEM

W E entered the living room of 1132 cautiously. There was my father, Norm Kennisbaum, standing before the statue of the Blessed
Virgin, studying it as if it were a piece of inscrutable pop art. Almost
six feet tall, he was slender of frame with an emerging pot belly concealed by his usual stylish LA shirt, a velour pinstripe under a belted,
double-breasted aviator leather jacket. He turned around. He beheld me,
slimmer, no longer wearing Ben Gurions. Patrick, Clark, McDarby, and
Swensen greeted him and then left the room. I assume they eavesdropped
at the top of the stairs.

"You live with a fine bunch of idolators," he said, admiring the Virgin and the picture of the Sacred Heart of Jesus.

"Dad—"

"I was going to New York on a buying trip, incredible price on 50
percent nylon and polyester mix from Shell, and I had a layover in Kansas
City, so I thought . . ." He still had his back turned.

"I was going—" I began.

"You're not eating, I can see." I smiled. I suppose this was his way of
complimenting me. "So you're taking nothing but poetry, rhetoric, and
humanities curriculum with who—Fred Marin!"

"Well, two other professors, also."

"I've heard about them." He collapsed on the couch. His hair was
flecked with an autumnal ash. His large brown eyes were circled by sag-
ging flesh.

"Your mother is sick with worry. You haven't written once; you
skipped the holidays . . . to stay here?" He looked around with a sneer,

just as he looked at textiles when he was trying to maneuver a wholesaler down in price.

"You're the one who cut me off."

His baggy eyes searched the Catholic paraphernalia.

"So you fell into the clutches of Fred Marin, now that he is some kind of alcoholic Catholic professor. Now you're a radical."

"What about your friendship with Fred Marin?"

"Phooey."

"Aunt Teresa told me."

"Ha, ha!" He got up and laughed as he neared the statue of the Blessed Virgin. "Teresa? Always the *truthful* one. She had the luxury to do that." He suddenly turned back to me. "*She's* the one with the crush, sonny."

"Did Teresa . . ." I let my voice fall off. He nodded as if to completely close out the subject, the way he always did.

"You had to come here and had to sniff your way to the worst possible professor and fill your head with nonsense." He paced and huffed.

"Professor Marin is only teaching things I already thought about, ideas and a world of study that I've longed to embrace. You once thought him great."

"Sure, when I was addled with alcohol and turpentine. But life takes over. You took over."

"Yes, my life."

He turned and walked toward me.

"You always did go googly eyed for that world of King Arthur, even as a little shit." He had been to see Barrows. I wanted him to hear my side.

"I think it was because you showed me that somewhere, at some time, you thought that stuff was true also. I have discovered orthodoxy."

"With the curls? The phylactery, Shabbat, the whole works? Well, it beats being Catholic."

He seemed almost pleasantly surprised.

"I don't mean that kind of orthodoxy. I mean accepting old truths in a new light, ever ancient and new, not to buy into Dacron, replacing everything every few years, like the carpet or kitchen floor or one's mind—what you sell is impermanence."

"We're number one in Costa Mesa now."

"I think there's more to life than shiny linoleum. Even the ground we walk on now is unreal. But to see into things as they are, to accept that there is a world we have dismissed, like the world of Chaucer or Cervantes or *Le Morte d'Arthur*—the stars and nature. Getting and spending we lay waste our powers—don't you recall reading that?"

"I haven't the foggiest idea what you are talking about, Bernard. This HIP program has turned your head—like the chancellor said."

"Turned is right. We took a wrong turn. It's the most progressive thing to turn around and go back to where you lost your way, don't you think?"

"Turn back how? Where? You want to go about in a carriage?"

"Question internal combustion, Dad. Question your Cadillac. Visualize industrial collapse."

"What are you, some kind of Luddite? I can't believe my son would talk to me like some hippie, after all—"

"After all what? After all the lies, all the coercion?"

"That's the way it is?"

I didn't want to leave it this way. I had opened up the floodgates of emotion, and it would not stop.

"You're worshipping a false god," I said, "after you betrayed your ideals and Fred Marin. At least they tell the truth."

"Listen, sonny," he shouted, "you don't know nothing from truth. You don't know about sacrifice, you don't know . . . what the truth will do to you!"

"I'm sure you do with your sucking up to rich bitches in Costa Mesa, Encino and Tarzana, lying like a carpet."

He glared at me, then suddenly slapped my face. My eyes teared up. I was speechless. I heard feet scuttling overhead.

I knew he would try anything to take back that savage act. But I would not say anything. We were locked in a battle of gazes, eyes like coals.

"I'm going to marry a girl, a shiksa," I said.

"I suppose you'll become Catholic," he said, and walked to the door.

"I'm studying it, if that's what you mean." It was the first time I had said that aloud. I wished I could take back the whole conversation, start over.

"You're no son of mine."

He exited the hallowed house and the screen door slammed behind him. I listened to a car engine roar and the screech of tires. The sounds gradually retreated as the world of Ohio Street fell back into silence. I sat down and looked down at my hands. They were shaking. Then I choked up and began to cry.

"Bernie," said Patrick as he came into the room. Embarrassed, I sat up and feigned a cough. Patrick went into the kitchen and put the kettle on.

"I sure hate it when my father blows through town unexpected."

"I see where you get the clothes," said Patrick. In a few minutes, he came in and handed me a mug of tea.

"Yeah, he thinks he's a disco floor king."

"I couldn't help overhearing what you said about marrying a girl. Are you talking about Apryl?"

"Oh, that." I felt suddenly exposed. "I just tried to think of what would really piss him off." I was really thinking of that kiss at St. Johns. He squinted, looking at me closely:

"What happened between you and Apryl? She isn't the same."

"We were able to connect." That was true, in more ways than one. "I think she has a lot to sort out."

"Bernard . . . I need to tell you something, but I don't want it to come between us."

"Patrick, you can tell me anything. I simply will not let it affect our friendship."

"Well . . . last year, Apryl and I, we were going out."

"What happened?"

"She . . . sort of burned me. Only she tells others I burned her. Anyway, I am really over her. Believe me."

"I do," I said.

"Maybe you need to get over her. Did you mean what you said about becoming Catholic?"

"It's a process."

"Getting over her or coming to faith?"

"Both."

"Let's keep this all between us," he said.

"Yes, and please ask the others to keep the marriage comment between us."

Now I was deep in it. I had declared for Apryl and Church. I would ride the wave and see what shore I washed up on.

XIX

NIGHTS AT THE CASTLE

Nor, in thy marble Vault, shall sound
My echoing Song: then Worms shall try
That long preserv'd Virginity:
And your quaint Honour turn to dust;
And into ashes all my Lust.

— *MARVEL, "TO HIS COY MISTRESS"*

T HE last of March was going out like a lion. We had a raging snow-
storm, but by the end of the week it melted away; flowers were peek-
ing out from green stalks; incomparably fresh girls were starting to stalk
Wescoe Beach in tight shorts. Swensen would say, "It's time to go to confession: 'Bless me father, I was on campus five times this week.'"

We had all gone to Ash Wednesday Mass at St. Johns. As the only
non-Catholic, I was at least allowed to get the blotch on my forehead.

Apryl had her hair in a braid that day at the lecture. She was in every
poem. We had memorized "To His Coy Mistress." The ultimate carpe
diem. Faces were flushed, hands became fidgety, palms sweated.

"If you haven't had your heart broken by someone who didn't love
you in return, you shouldn't be in this class!" Marin's eyes were fiery red.

"Do you think Don Quixote is insane?" said Whelan. I sat next to
Patrick, who rested his chin on his powerful fist. McDarby's eyes burned.
I knew he had been successful with Apryl, getting her to allow him to
walk her home and go with him to the spring waltz. Swensen sat apart

from us, brooding. Apryl was wan, appearing detached and sickly. We all thought she had mononucleosis. Apryl saw me with that charcoal mess on my forehead and half smiled.

"He is right, you know," said Courtney. "The world thinks chivalry is dead, in Don Quixote and Miguel de Cervantes's time, as now. Is it dead? The pragmatic world of affairs says it is not even a relevant question. The idea of going off on quests is dangerous, leading to psychological breakdown."

McDarby looked at me. Hogg sat in the back of the room with De-Blasio as bodyguard.

"Are you insane because you believe in love for another, the most illusory and useless thing of all?"

"I think they're insane, Paul," said Marin. "You're reasonable people, aren't you? Don't believe in knights and crusading and jousting. Quaint, isn't it? What about honor? Is that quaint too? Is there anything worth questing after? Cervantes thought that you must attempt the absurd to attain the impossible. Whatever is he saying?"

"'The lunatic, the lover, and the poet are of imagination all compact,'" said Whelan. "Maybe some of you have been in a midsummer night's dream."

"Do any of you have a Dulcinea?" asked Courtney. "Someone who represents the ultimate longings you have for honor, for goodness? When you meet the right person, you want to be honorable and good."

"We're not talking about Robert Goulet and dreaming the impossible dream," said Marin. "We aren't going to break into a musical comedy here."

Apryl had all our attention with her paleness, her hair up, her mystery, and disappearance. Now it was time to move. While the iron was hot, while the poetry was running. Winston was turning out a passable poem every day. He had gotten off O'Neill and was onto Tennessee Williams. And he was writing lyrical pieces to some unknown girl who I suspected was a literarily transformed Apryl.

"Are any of you willing to drive straight at the monsters of modernity, the windmills of industry, in the name of your dream?" asked Marin.

We had an adventure all right. Kozikowski now wanted to be a knight of Mount Oread. Chalmers denied the very existence of the knights and told us to do the same. Ever since my encounter with my father, Chalmers had tried to take me under his wing even more, taking me for drives in Marin's yellow Triumph TR 250. He would race around Clinton Dam at breakneck speed and shout about freedom from parents, about liberation of soul when one isn't bound by duty.

I heard that Marin had finally converted. Like Chesterton, he had written and spoken like a Catholic for thirty years, but he had never really crossed over the English Channel. Marin was a father figure, not because he advised us but because we saw in him the ability to become a man, to take the licks, to pound on and beat the odds—even intoxicated—and tell the real story.

Marin growled, "You're better off with simple lust . . . you can't handle love."

"There have been Dulcineas throughout history," said Courtney, "and there always will be. You have lost something essential in your heritage. Don Quixote wants to recover it, this romance of the West. That is why you are learning to waltz. The entire romance of the West is to be found in the dance. The waltz reflects the constellations, in harmony moving together, seemingly fixed yet independent."

"It's too much intimacy, Paul," said Marin, "moving together in harmony. It's too human. The touch of another in the dance is too real. You prefer something more intellectual because you think you're angels. Well, I have news for you. You are not angels. In the dance, you are relating to your nature and another's. Get it?"

"I have students in another course," added Whelan, "who read Huxley's *Brave New World*, and some of these students think the book is a prescription for a better world. They don't know that Huxley is satirizing that world in which romance is outlawed, babies are not born but hatched, where love is considered subversive, and where all of your physical needs are satisfied by the state. Some of the clever ones realize it is a critique of scientific materialism, but they ask, 'What is wrong with that?'"

"What's wrong with free sex, food, jobs?" said Marin. "If you have to ask, you don't get it. They have a little blue pill for you, called Soma, and that little pill takes away all your madness. You won't tilt at windmills anymore after taking it. You won't have any cares or worries. You won't have anything to quest after, no fights to fight, no reason to go on living! The end of romance is suicide."

Courtney looked up at us and finally broke the silence.

"You have to mount the horses of your life and be like Don Quixote. If you want to avoid madness, you will have to see the beauty, the romance of living. You will have to see the monsters in society, even when nobody else knows they are there, eating away at the fabric of your families and your country. We have to have Don Quixotes, or we all die. That is why it is among the greatest books ever written."

I could understand the quest for the Virgin Mary as long as I found my unattainable Apryl, the far-off and sweet-smelling diva of Mount Olympus who had no flaws other than her capriciousness. Not for sex, not for pleasure, but for romance.

I stopped Apryl after class, determined to confront her. My eye grasped an opening in the crevice of Lady Fortune's garden wall. But when I tried to ask her out, the words were not there.

"As the most valiant knight in the realm, I am honored by your presence, my lady," I said in the words of Don Quixote.

Hogg had gathered with Chalmers, Maggie, Swede, and Marin in a corner, and other HIPsters were busy trying to pat Hogg's shoulder or commiserate. I had Apryl in the hall in the press of traffic between classes.

"Bernard, it is Lent."

"You forget," I said with an impish smile, "nobody is supposed to know you are fasting, right?"

"You're right," she said and tapped her index finger on my chin. I almost fainted. She twirled her hair between her thumb and index finger, and widened her eyes.

"Pick me up tonight at eight—we can go to the Castle Tea Room."

I didn't even ask her out.

"Uh . . . tonight? Yes, I will pick you up in my Chevy Rocinante."

Color returned to her face as a smile appeared around her cheeks and spread to her eyes.

"I heard about how you rescued Tom, and then how you stood up before the college assembly and spoke out against the university. You *are* a knight, Bernard," she said.

"Well, I kind of lost it when my father showed up out of nowhere."

"See you at eight." We all watched her glide down the stairs. I strode after, past a scowling McDarby, a bewildered Swensen, a distressed Hogg, and a gawking Maggie. I felt like a big man on campus.

φ

The Castle Tea Room was an old stone mansion on Massachusetts Street, built in the nineteenth century ornate Romanesque style, with crenellated stone turrets; inside were dark oak paneling, a potpourri of china, nondescript paintings of trees and miniatures, doilies, old plates, a century of memorabilia crowding the walls. Only the classiest students dined there. Apryl wore a tasteful outfit: a skirt, a blouse with a lace collar, her velvet black shoes, and white stockings that led all the way up to her Venus's thighs.

"Aunt Teresa tells me you have not been well."

"*You* certainly look well," she deflected. I had brought a bottle of B&G red French wine. We ate by candlelight in a bay window, occupying our own universe. I loved the way the light licked her cheeks and danced about her eyes.

"Apryl—"

"Bernard."

My stomach started to sink. Something in her tone said we were not here just for pleasure.

"I don't want you thinking that that kiss meant . . ."

"What about all that happened, the cabin, the quarry, our night . . . ?"

"That's what I wanted to come to dinner to talk about."

I nodded cautiously.

"I cannot marry."

"I never asked." Did Patrick tell her what I told him in confidence?

"I didn't mean that . . . I just feel . . . I can never marry. Unless . . ."

"Are you talking about being a nun?" She laughed. "I thought something happened between us."

"Yes, exactly," she said. She stopped. "I think something happened."

"Yes . . . We shared real honesty."

"You're not listening, I think I'm different . . . physically."

I stopped talking and reached for my wine. Clumsily, I knocked over the glass and some of the ruby liquid spilled on her. I started wiping her sleeve, dipping my cloth napkin in the water glass, making more of a mess. A couple across shot us looks of irritation.

"'Spilled wine, dig this girl,'" I said to the censorious couple.

"Do you think it's possible for two people to connect and then to have something happen that cannot be explained scientifically?"

"It's like the professors are always saying, it's beyond the material and scientific."

"I know about that intimacy of soul. I mean, the other," she whispered.

"You mean, we did not actually finish . . . in a traditional way." If only we were more fluent in French, we could have dispensed with the code.

"Didn't we?"

"Well, I, uh . . . the connection was not as sure in those parts." It was embarrassing to talk about what happened under the water.

"This is not funny."

"I'm not the one who kissed you at the church."

Then she became more pale and thoughtful.

"What if it was more than that?"

"What are you saying, what is more than that."

"Could we have a child?"

"Are you saying what I think you're saying?"

"I don't know if it's true."

Could it be true that our underwater encounter could produce pregnancy? I had never heard of this. If it had ever happened, it would have been in the unwritten warning manual at the fraternity house where they doled out advice for evading such feminine traps.

"It's probably nothing," I said recalling one bromide from the brothers of Sigma Chi who said you can't hit the fire alarm until they miss a few periods.

"Well, I wouldn't call it nothing . . ." She leaned forward, whispering. "I haven't had a period for several months."

Just the mention of that word made a part of me shrivel. But then I recalled another brother bromide.

"Has this happened before? Are you sure?"

"Yes, it has happened before. I have a tendency to miss periods. Especially when I undergo great stress." There it was.

"You look so relieved, as if it's all nothing."

"You're asking me to believe something unheard of in medicine or even to college students."

She looked down. There was the Botticelli gaze. She was radiant even in this moment of despair, able to ponder things like Venus and birth.

"How about this, let's talk to somebody."

She looked up, panicked. "Let's just see what happens."

I thought that's what I was saying. She changed the subject.

"Has Tom talked to you about Maggie?"

"Maggie? Why?"

"He thinks you should help her."

Here came the needle in my balloon.

"I want you to take her under your wing, show her what happened to you."

"What did happen to me?"

"I heard about you and your father . . . I know how that is. But we have to think about conversions."

"Conversion . . . that's easy for people who are certain," I said.

"Even Augustine says conversion of the heart is a lifelong process."

"So you doubt?" I asked.

"Faith is not having no doubt. It's acting in spite of it."

"So maybe if I just have faith, things will work out between us?"

"Well . . . if you pay attention to your studies for the Church."

Just a vow, a splash of water, and I could remove the bagels and lox from my pockets once and for all and gain admittance to Apryl's club. She gave me a long, lingering look, searching out my eyes. It was as if she were saying to me, "Pass this initiation."

"Father Connell said I could come in." I had not actually gotten his consent, but Patrick had said Father Connell would give it. "Of course, I have to do more reading."

"You will."

She placed her hand on mine: you will do what I want, you will be my vassal, you will win me by winning yourself for Christ. I caved in wholeheartedly. I would be her Mercutio. She could choose her own Romeo. That night, I recalled that her hand sat so lightly on mine and blessed the very skin. We were bonded, blushing pilgrims. But was it just one more manipulation of my coy mistress? Or was she asking one more labor, and I would be more than Hercules? I could clean out the Augean stables of my own duplicity, the pall of pretense. Maybe if I did Athena's bidding once more, I would come home to Ithaca and find myself at rest.

XL

LENTEN BULL

To the Israelites the glory of the Lord was seen
as a cloud consuming fire on the mountaintop.
But Moses passed into the midst of the cloud as
he went up on the mountain; and there he stayed
for forty days and forty nights.

— *EXODUS 24:16–18*

"Boys, I'm hell when I do penance," boomed Hess, the apocalyptic agrarian who had just come in from unsuccessfully trying to get rid of his troublesome bull at an auction. The bull was still in the trailer behind his pickup outside making quite the racket.

"What penance? You smoke more than us," said the ever-vigilant Swede. He was just waiting for the stroke of midnight that would bring the sound of milk flowing in cereal bowls and the roar of the stove as bags of noodles were dumped into pots of boiling water. It was the cruelest six weeks of the year. Still crueler for me, looking not only for the glories of the rising of Easter but for a personal rising.

"It's incense, and I hate it, so I started taking up smoking for Lent," retorted the farmer-turned-Luddite. Hess shoved a cigarette into his mouth; I drooled for one puff. I had lasted a total of three days without a cigarette.

"That's crazy," said Ross.

"Bernie here gave me his carton of Carmelites to hold for him during Lent," said Hess, "Carmelites" being the name he gave to my Camel Lights. "I hate smoking. Been around it all my life, hell—what better penance?"

With that, he blew a gargantuan blast of smoke and taunted the denizens of this bleak Lenten house. Swensen had been studying his book of saints in search of another forgotten feast day.

"Sounds like you have stumbled onto another good loophole to Lent, Karl," said Swensen.

"We don't need any more loopholes," said Patrick, who was reading.

"Where's Bob and Michael?" asked Hess.

"I think Broglio's giving another retreat in Tonganoxie."

Hess nodded. "Spades anyone?"

They gathered hurriedly around the spades table and spread out the cards: Hess, Ross, and Swensen.

"GK, your spot," I looked up from the couch where I was engrossed in a book of modern poetry.

"Not now, I'm trying to read 'Ash Wednesday.'"

"That was a couple of weeks ago," said Ross. Patrick put his Thomas Hardy down and took my spot. I recited to nobody in particular:

Because I do not hope to turn again
Because I do not hope . . .

"That doesn't sound like a mediation on Ash Wednesday," said Hess.

"It's T. S. Eliot," said Patrick.

"St. Tobias," said Swede. "We can use St. Tobias for a feast."

"St. Tobaccus?" I chirped, delirious from nicotine deprivation. "I think what Eliot is trying to say, is that we place too much emphasis on the moment, on place, and on emotion."

"Hogg! Come out here. Karl's here," yelled Ross.

"He ain't coming," said Hess.

"In that poem, Eliot is in process of converting," said Patrick. "He finally sees the blessed sister, spirt of the garden."

"Nope, Karl," said Swensen. "He isn't right since you brought him back."

"He knows I'm here. He was outside, preaching to MF."

"MF?"

"You know, Bernie, that crazy mother-effing bull of mine."

"He isn't normal, preaching to bulls and the like," said Ross.

"He should pray to Augustine of Hippo," I replied.

"Hippos aren't the problem," said Swensen. "Hogg's been talking to Phaedo about *Clouds of Unknowing* and *Imitation of Christ.*"

"Are you sure the dog doesn't understand St. Thomas à Kempis better than we do?" I said, going back to the Lady of Silences. The author of "Prufrock" was a perfect guide for impostors on a path to authenticity.

At 1132, I was living at the Academy of Plato, where Dionysus was celebrated under various names: wine, women, song, cards, wrestling, Nerf, writing poetry and prose, Irish exploits. Father Connell knew us as kindred spirits, but he also knew my confreres by their sins of impurity, gluttony, lust, and sloth. How was he to know that one woman could launch a thousand confessions? Maybe the sly priest had connected the dots and just kept his counsel.

"At least he's not listening to Bishop Sheen tapes three times a day," said Swensen.

Ross's rosy features flushed instantly. "Sheen is . . . excellent."

"And I can quote him word for word. He's in my head when I'm walking on campus." I took on Bishop Sheen's theological-thespian voice. 'The problem with birth control is that those who practice it believe neither in birth nor in control.'"

We heard the clatter outside of the bull kicking the truck fencing.

"Maybe Hogg needs to preach to MF about the virtue of silence," I added.

"St. Francis himself could not do nothin' with MF," said Hess expansively as he blew a large plume of gray smoke across Ross's face. "I just came back from the auction. Nearly sold, but he went nuts and kicked the auctioneer right in the oysters."

The sounds outside stopped.

"Not great cards, eh?" Swensen had been acting cocky ever since he had announced to the house that Apryl might accompany *him* to the waltz. He had scripted an invitation to her and made it rhyme in Middle English.

"Cat got your tongue, Old Swedy?" said Hess. Swede raised his arm and batted Hess's beer off the table.

"I was wondering how we were going to handle the finding of the HISS committee," I said. "They're proposing to gut the program, take away distribution requirements."

"Chalmers says the hearings won't determine anything," said Patrick.

"I have no choice but to go nil . . . *blind nil!*" said Swensen. There was a brewing of outrage, uprising, murder in the air.

"He's going blind nil on his soul . . ." Ross was afraid of losing this one.

"That's your soul," said Swede to me, pointing to the large blue ashtray. I had been practicing a slightly British voice to use when I went in front of the veil of the confessional, channeling G. K. Chesterton who, when he was asked why he would become Catholic, replied, "To get rid of my sins."

As the talk drifted to the university administration's injustice to HIP, Chalmers rushed in. The screen door slammed behind him, and he relaxed his swagger.

"Rich, come in . . . sit down."

"I need to talk to G. K. Where's Bob and Mike?"

"I don't know," I said. I suspected McDarby went to see Apryl.

"Now." Chalmers motioned to the door.

It was a warm and blustery spring evening. We headed toward Ole Miss.

"Only a few people can know about this. Not even Courtney knows. Only Whelan and Marin, and Whelan doesn't know Marin knows."

"The cone of silence."

"I have a draft copy of the HISS findings," he continued, out of breath as we crested the hill and coursed down the incline toward Memorial Stadium.

"It's worse than we thought. They have witnesses, including a monk."

"Someone other than Ellis Blaine?"

"Yes, Frere Joseph Marie at Chalfontbleau."

"Frere Joseph Marie?"

"You haven't heard of him. Rhoden was there posing as a priest."

"Rhoden canceled the last few meetings of CAPUT. This makes sense now."

"That's not all. They have evidence on financial aspects of the program that could bury us."

"Financial?"

"We've used some of the SCHLAYEX moneys for operations."

"Sure, graduate study issues, that's easily characterized—"

"No, diverted from the university for . . . helping get people to and from the monastery."

"What? Do they know you've embezzled university funds?"

"I wouldn't call it that."

"I know a little something about financial books. If you can't rechar-acterize those expenditures . . ."

"You're an English major."

"With a business minor. Also, I balanced—or cooked—my father's books. There are ways to cover over certain things. I need access to the ledgers."

"You can fix it?"

"On one condition." He looked at me with fire coming out of his eyes. "I need my journal back."

He nodded reluctantly. "One other thing," he said. "You need to stay out of the Church."

"Stay out of the Church? Conversion is a personal—"

Chalmers grabbed me, ripping a button off my peach oxford shirt.

"Listen, LA boy, many are called, few are chosen. You have to suffer trial by fire, you get it? That Clarence Darrow stunt you pulled in the college assembly didn't help anybody."

"Apryl said faith will be given if I ask—"

"Who do you think you're fooling with this piety act?"

I stared ahead at the buckling sidewalk.

"Right now, we have to find Bob," said Chalmers.

Chalmers put his finger to his mouth as we came up the steep step. I saw the stately pillars bracing its inclined porch. Chalmers walked past the statue of St. Joseph and touched it gently. We crossed into the living room. The wood slats creaked. We started up the tall stairs leading up to the holy chambers of the women. The smells of competing perfumes were like so many invisible branches, slashing our eyes.

"Here . . . Apryl's room," said Chalmers. Finally, the sanctorum of Apryl's boudoir. Had he been there?

"Bob . . . Michael?"

"There's nobody here?" I said. Sounds of a shower came from the hall outside her room. Chalmers walked up to the door to Apryl's room and opened it. I peered inside. It was dark, the shades drawn, a faint musky smell of perfume wafted out. I felt sick at the thought of finding one of them with Apryl.

"Bob, if you're in there, come out, and get Michael, wherever he is. We have a serious situation," said Chalmers.

There was a rustling of bedclothes. The clearing of a throat.

It sounded familiar to me, like Marin under the sheet at Halloween.

"Who the hell is in Apryl's bed?" demanded Chalmers.

A crimson, angry face appeared. It was not Michael or Bob, not Marin or any face of any youth. It was . . .

"Professor Finley!"

I grabbed Chalmers as he lunged for the half-naked Finley, who was gutting HIP and overseeing the upcoming hearings. Caught in flagrante, in my Apryl's bed! Finley sat up in bed, looked in the direction of the shower, stroked his beard. Rage spread as I jumped Finley. Chalmers pulled me off.

"Let's get out of here."

I looked in the direction of the bathroom and the sound of the shower. Chalmers yanked me out of the room to Finley's laughter. All the way back to 1132, I cursed and told Chalmers I felt betrayed.

"Listen, poetry man, this ideal chick thing is a fantasy."

"I'm going to get Finley if it's the last thing I do."

"You're going to see Holloway and tell him you're still on board."

I was too angry to respond. When we got back to 1132, we found Hess looking out the back window of the house.

Hess said: "I can't imagine anyone being stupid enough to mess around with him."

Hess checked his boot for the shotgun as he stood up. McDarby and DeBlasio ambled over.

"Damn, I left the gun in the truck."

"You brought a fucking bull *here*?" said Chalmers.

"Yeah, and we think Tom let him out," said McDarby.

"Where have you been?"

"At the retreat in Tonganoxie. Where were you?"

"We don't have time for this," said Chalmers.

"Where did Hogg go?" said McDarby.

"Where would Hogg go at this hour?" We looked at each other.

"St. Johns!"

We ran out into the dark alley behind the house. We could hear Phaedo's intermittent barks. When we arrived at St. John's, we saw the gentle flicker of candlelight coming through the stained glass. We tiptoed into the sanctuary. There stood the bull, as tall as a black pickup, nearly as wide as a small sports car, positioned on the altar, leaning back on its haunches toward the statue of the Virgin. Its sinews were heaving like inexorable cogs of a giant engine, breathing a sough of steam.

Father Connell joined us. Swensen, Hess, Chalmers, DeBlasio and McDarby tried not to hyperventilate. Hogg kneeled before the pounded copper tabernacle. A rosary was strung in the beast's horns.

"Now look what you've done, Brother Bull!" said Hogg, "You've displeased Our Lady . . . you've disgraced the sanctuary by tearing the banners."

The bull snorted and shook his head. Hogg bowed his head and continued to pray. Then the bull's front legs buckled, and we all saw what we would later tell as myth. MF, despoiler of Herefords, wrecker of fences, and kicker of keepers and auctioneers, bowed down on the altar.

The fear and wonder at this sight took my mind off Apryl and the recent scene of carnality. We kneeled down and pulled out rosaries at the sight of Our Lady of the Bulls. Chalmers prayed like a Sunday school girl. Was it a miracle or another practical joke? Like the miracle of Apryl's virgin pregnancy. I needed some answers.

XLI

APRYL FOOLS

Whan that Aprille with hir shoures sote
The droughte of Marche hath perced to the rote.

— CHAUCER, THE CANTERBURY TALES

A PRIL does things inside you, stirring up desires, bringing up the
roots; it can even drive you to speak in Middle English.

I marched righteously to Vice Chancellor Holloway's office on that
misty afternoon. The wrens sang loud fusillades on Mount Oread in a
tangle of dogwood blooms and sycamores. The white and blue hydran-
gea and wisteria blazed across campus, dainty handmaids to this cyclical
conjugation of nature. When I barged in past Nancy, a tired, baggy-eyed
Ichabod Crane stared up at me.

"The HISS report is out. You helped us after all."

"I care about what you did to Apryl."

Holloway shrugged, paused, and said: "They will lose the credits
that make the students sign up. They will lose their funding."

"What about Apryl?"

He flashed his patented thin smile. "You lost your scholarship. Do
you want it back now?"

I felt a roseate rash spread across my face.

"No more!"

"Calm down, Mr. Kennisbaum."

I started to pace. I told him everything: the kidnapping of Hogg, the counteroperations, SCHLAYEX funding, the lost money.

"How much money?"

"I don't know."

"Find out."

"So J. Barnett Hummer can make a dramatic arrest?"

"I don't know what you mean."

I had had it with him. I leaned over his desk.

"I think I caught Apryl sleeping with Finley."

He looked up, imploring me to go on and stop all at once. I went on, explaining the whole sordid scene.

"So as you can see, we left before I could confirm, but the circumstantial evi—"

"Enough!" His blinkless predator's eyes were wet with tears.

"And there is this." I pulled out the poem I had stolen from Barrows. "We know about you and Apryl." Devastated, he looked at the poem.

"Why are you so upset? I'm the aggrieved one."

"Why? Did she break your heart, too?"

He turned around in his chair, facing a credenza and the usual lumber on the wall—rotary plaques, teaching awards.

"She was so . . . perfect before Courtney got ahold of her and corrupted her."

"Who hasn't she slept with?"

Holloway stood up out of his chair, trembling. He lifted a bony finger and pointed it at me like a pistol.

"Don't talk about her like that!" he shouted.

I found it difficult to believe this tortoise of academia could come out of his shell long enough to have an affair with Apryl. He probably had a file on her two inches thick. I picked up the poem from his desk.

"So this is about you and Apryl. And *the chemicals* is a reference to abortion. Did she have your baby at one point?"

"You don't know what you are talking about."

I circled around behind his desk and raised my fist.

"Stop this, stop your lies. Tell me about you and Apryl!"

He looked up at me, drooping, defeated.

"I love her. I can't go on without her love."

"So it is your poem about her, and the references—"

"I didn't write this poem."

"I thought you said you loved her."

"I do, more than you can know. But I didn't write this."

"Who did?"

"It looks like Fred's handwriting. The small letters, the swirls, not what you would expect from him."

"Fred Marin?"

"Yes. Marin wrote in this style of poetry twenty years ago."

"But it mentions her."

"April is just a poetic device. And he spells it wrong. But the names of these other women are professors' wives. Louise Courtney. Helen. Might refer to Helen, my ex-wife."

"I see . . . I'm sorry." I sat down again.

"Apryl won't speak to me."

"She's not talking much to me lately."

"Quite the heartbreaker."

I saw Holloway's plight. He was bitten bad. It must have been some honors sophomore seminar he taught. I didn't need to hear the sordid tale. I could see in his fallen face the ultimate victim of this belle dame, and she was burning him worse than any of us.

"So you blame HIP for taking her from you."

He just stared at me.

"And Marin and your wife—"

"I cannot believe she slept with Finley!"

"You must get rid of Finley," I said.

"It's easier to fire Brezhnev than to get rid of a tenured professor."

"Goddamn it, find a way."

I wanted Finley's red beard plucked, his highlander arrogance stuffed into his puckered mouth; I wanted to see the look on his face when he was revealed for the pervert he was. Holloway let me twist for a while, his hawk eyes boring into my soul.

"Maybe . . . with your help," he said.

"You want my help to bring down HIP in return?"

"It is self-preservation, Mr. Kennisbaum."

"What have *they* done?"

"It's not what they have done, but who they have offended."

"Athens's ruling elite think they are corrupting youth, so they must die."

He smirked. "I taught Plato's *Apology* last semester. Don't think I don't see parallels. But we cannot do anything to Finley until the hearings are over," he said as he snapped back to his impersonal self. "Then we turn to your professors. In the future your reports had better be more revealing."

I lowered my head and started out of the office.

"Kennisbaum." I turned to look at him. "Don't pull any more stunts like the other day at the college assembly."

I nodded.

"And say nothing to Apryl about me."

As I made my way back to 1132, I was trying to make sense of the poem I had purloined from Barrows's office as being written by Marin. Did Apryl know her mother had had an affair with Marin? If so, were her involvement in HIP, or her whole mystique, just a complex disguise? Was she on a revenge mission of her own?

There was only one way to find out: Apryl needed some schooling, the kind you could get only in the university of pranks. What I thought up was no mean April Fools' Day joke.

Everyone knew Swensen wrote little rhymes in Middle English. It was as if the cover of an archaic language allowed him to say things he never could otherwise. It was the language of practical joking on love, lust, faith, marriage, chivalry, usury, and all manner of human vanity and pretension.

In his room, I found some of the Swede's scribblings on Chaucer and love. He was in one of his strict phases, trying to convince himself that Apryl was no goddess, only a female of about twenty years, 34 cup, false lover of Chaucer. She was denying him as she had denied me and McDarby, although McDarby was in denial, wearing the ribbon of her consent to escort her to the spring waltz.

"Fronk!" I heard DeBlasio unleash some afternoon gas, pent up from Whelan's British Writers before 1800. It was in that class that Swensen had studied more Chaucer than in an entire Chaucer seminar. I tried to concentrate on Swede's scribblings, but the ruckus they were making distracted me.

"Man," said DeBlasio, "how about a game of Nerf . . . double or nothing." Already Swensen owed fifty-seven dollars to various members of the household from Nerf and unending spades games.

"Anon he leet fle a fart as greet as it had been a thonder-dent!" Swensen quoted impeccably from Chaucer's "Miller's Tale."

"Heinous anus!" I yelled. Swensen shook his head and pulled the *Collected Works of Geoffrey Chaucer*, which he had borrowed from me, from his bookcase, and began to reread the "Prologue." He saw all of my notes from Buntrock's seminar.

It came to me: "Whan that Apryl . . ." Yes, it would work! I realized Swensen, the Swede, had ridden the colorful clouds of duplicity.

I simply had to insert myself into that identity. It was strange gift, assuming the role of so many, to spy for Apryl, spy for Chalmers, spy for CAPUT, spy for Barrows and Holloway—like some Galapagos mutation, allowing me to blend.

"Where are you going?" said DeBlasio as I headed out the door.

"I need the fresh air of poetry." I had no intention of going to poetry memorization before the sophomore lecture. I already knew the Crispy-Crispian's day speech from *Henry V Part I*. Shakespeare had plumbed the depths of a young man in disguise just to be among his men as a friend.

But I had a different kind of poetry in mind.

XLII

EROS ALL AQUIVER

"O, give me a home where the beer has no foam," said Jimmy. "I could use some natural piety with whipped cream on top," I said. Hogg smiled. We had rescued him from his depression. Jimmy put on a Neil Young song. We were on our third Coors.

"Is eternity going to be like this?" said Hogg.

"It's a long road to eternity, Hogg, my man," said Jimmy. "It's best not to knit your brow but focus on the here and now."

"Pretty soon, we'll have vespers," I said.

"Bernard," said Hogg, looking deep into my eyes. "What do you feel when you sing the 'Ave Maris Stella.'"

I looked around. A few sultry senior women eyed us indifferently.

"I think heaven must be like this. Your friends together, singing in harmony—one voice, one tone. Everything understood without having to explain."

Hogg nodded. "That's why I want to be at the monastery. You don't have to leave the monastery after the 'Ave Maris Stella' is over."

Hogg walked over to the senior girls. Their hard shells seemed to crumble after he spoke to them.

"Bernie . . . you know that boy ain't well. He's living in hell."

"You'll have to tell me which one you're talking about. I'm a little hazy on who's crazy."

"He's going to be doing well just to stay out of some institution."

"He has . . . powers."

"Don't tell me you buy all that bull about . . . the bull?"

That bull thought there was something to it. I'd seen MF at Hess's farm, and that was no praying menace.

"I don't know," I said.

"It's a miracle he's still in school."

Out of the corner of my eye, I saw a beautiful blonde enter. She went over to Hogg and bent over him and the senior girls.

"My heart leaps up."

"Something's leaping up," I rejoined.

Then she stood up with Hogg and turned to us. It was Maggie. She wore tight jeans. Her hair was let down, and the natural curls seemed to hover gently over her like wisteria. She sashayed to our table. Her eyes were cerulean. Her mouth was pouty, giving her a sassy look.

"You remember the Lady Margareta of Cordova," said Hogg.

"They remember me. It's Maggie."

Maggie made no secret that she had grown tired of Hogg's antics with Apryl and had begun hanging around Bob, Michael, Patrick, and me.

"Sit, lovely lady," I said.

She sizzled. I snapped my fingers. Mandy shot me a withering look. I winked at her; she came over.

"Your Grace," she said with a laughable curtsey.

"A beer for my lady," I said.

"Make it two," said Maggie.

"We don't have time," said Hogg.

"We have to do some Latin riff in a jiff," said Jimmy.

Maggie put her hand on Jimmy's arm. "You danced well at the party," she said.

"We were all bewitched that night," said Jimmy. "I could show you other moves—"

Hogg stood up with a panicked look. He grabbed Jimmy.

"We have to go."

"What about them?" he said.

Hogg rushed out with Jimmy waving his arms in protest. "I feel like we're in a chapter of *Pudd'nhead Wilson*," said Jimmy. He left with Hogg.

"Looks like they've abandoned us for plainsong."

"Speaking of which, we could use a song," said Maggie.

I stood and put a quarter into the jukebox, hitting a new Waits song: "Martha."

"Waits," she said wistfully.

"I never heard this one. You know it?"

"Used to listen to him in Chicago."

"If I might say, Maggie, you are looking lovelier all the time."

She gave me a practiced coy look and pulled out a long Virginia Slim, and waited for me to light her. I obliged. She was like the younger sister living inside her.

Mandy came with three beers. Maggie blew out a cloud of smoke.

"I say, 'il n'y a que premier pas qui coute.' The first step is always the hardest."

"Another nostrum from the North?" She slowly cracked a smile.

"No, it's from Belloc's *Path to Rome*. Belinda gave me her copy."

She dragged on her cigarette and looked around at the other girls who could see she was not part of their world.

"Young bitches," she said. She looked into my eyes with a hard glare. "You're probably wondering why I'm here."

"You get right to the point."

"Why waste time?"

She stared at me and blew smoke as we listened to Waits and his nostalgic groans.

"Look, I know why you're being nice to me," she said.

"You do?"

"You're her lap dog."

"Lap dog?"

"I see how you wag your tail around Apryl. I spent time with her, remember—she gets people to do what she wants. Hell, she had me shopping like a sorority girl."

"At least you learned something valuable."

"I have learned something more valuable. That life is salvageable, that you are your own agent."

"My agent takes 10 percent."

"Ha, ha."

"I'll admit, I have been her agent."

"You think she's gonna love ya, eh?" I heard the Canadian coming through. "She's working the street harder than any two-bit from Quebec."

"Funny you should call her that."

"She struts her stuff like nothing."

"I used to think she was . . . innocent."

Maggie pulled her chair closer to me and placed a hand on my arm.

"Listen, Jack, I don't want to stir up trouble or nothing, looking as how she's been helpful to me and you have all helped me."

"But . . ."

"She's playing you for a fool."

"What does that mean?" I dreaded what she was going to say.

"She doesn't look so good lately." Maggie paused, as I pondered her meaning. "I think she's . . . enceinte." I stared at her. She whispered. "Pregnant."

"Pregnant?"

"Your purest Dulcinea was ill the whole time I stayed at your aunt's. Throwing up in the early hours. She hasn't been *réglés* since."

"My French isn't very good."

"No period."

"She may just be stressed."

"Did you two . . . you know?"

I didn't respond.

"You look as pale as her."

I put my head down. It made sense. How pale she was, how detached, and her affair with Finley. This was not like those tense moments at the fraternity when young brothers paced the halls and we were on "tampon watch."

"You want to have some fun?" She looked at me quizzically. "I mean, things that get under other people's skin."

"Farces . . . pranks?"

"I wonder if you would be interested in accompanying me."

"Like your escort."

She wiggled her eyebrows. She was pretty and saucy, and I thought perhaps she could be useful in a Canterbury geste.

"You know any Chaucer?"

"Whan that Aprille with his shoures soote . . ."

"Where'd you learn that?"

"Ursuline nuns, then Jesuit high school in Montreal. We also read *Chanson de Geste* in old French. That's *Song of Roland* to you. I ran away in my senior year."

"Something tells me that beneath that street paving lies a—"

"Heart of gold?"

"I was going to say, lies a high school girl who loves a prank."

Her eyes seemed to sparkle.

"What did you have in mind?"

"It's still percolating."

"Shit," she said looking at her watch. "The sophomore lecture is starting in three minutes."

φ

"You believe in the erotic, don't you?" said Marin. Maggie and I sat together. We thought we could overcome mutability. The professors imparted something like an erotic impulse, but it was toward knowledge.

"What is it going to take for you to learn depth? Don't you realize that the erotic is not about sex? Eros requires longing, and you lack that. You can't wait for the beat of rock 'n roll. But some of you think Chaucer, Cervantes, and Shakespeare are a little pornographic."

Maggie smiled, pulling her pink sweater against her breasts and curving hips, and snuggling in the chair. I looked at Apryl. She was in a jump suit.

"It's true," said Courtney. "We have tried to bring something out of you in this course, to direct you to these great writers like Shakespeare and Chaucer and Dante who occupy the firmament of the West. But the question is, are you up to it? You come from puritanical backgrounds, and despite your wholesale abandonment of rules, it still runs in your veins, thinking everything dirty and leading to naughtiness. All of the music, the advertising, the movies, the magazines—everywhere you turn, it is an attempt to act out this naughty thing, a fetish of society. But behind it is a void. Into that void we're trying to shoot some eros."

We knew we had lost the sense of the sacred and of Beauty in architecture as in letters. But for God's sake—tell us at least we had the erotic.

"You see around you people madly trying to get back to Chaucer, with hot pokers and sex toys and marital aids and complexes of every type," said Whelan. "We are being candid with you; you have to know that erogenous zones will not substitute for the complete loss of understanding of eros and Beauty."

"Chaucer understands your world," said Courtney. "The question is, do you understand his? All of these people have stories in the *Canterbury Tales*. The Wife of Bath, the Miller, the Knight, the Pardoner, the Nun. They all occupy the same ground, under the same sky, and they tell stories to reflect that shared vision."

"Do you think the Wife of Bath is erotic?" said Marin. "Or is she knowledgeable of her powers? And what of 'The Miller's Tale'? Some of you think it's X-rated, don't you?"

Some of the Ole Misses seemed agitated. I could see Apryl starting at me and Maggie.

"You know," said Courtney, "that we are talking about a time in Europe when the idea of Beauty was everywhere. Chaucer's world is informed by Boethius, St. Bonaventure and St. Francis of Assisi, Giotto and the images of spiritualized beauty in harmony with nature."

"Do they know about Brother Ass?" said Marin, challenging us. "St. Francis called the body Brother Ass. Don't you know the true erotic impulse is toward an infinite beauty? You have become abstracted from Beauty."

"This is commonplace at this time," said Whelan. "There is an earthiness in story and everyday reality, but there is also a corresponding appreciation of art and the desire for ultimate perfection. They live in tension and balance. We see this in the High Middle Ages, with Chaucer, and then, of course, Dante. There is an ascent toward the beatific. It starts in courtly love and ends in mystical union."

"Our times cannot be erotic," said Courtney, "because our times are not sensual. You believe in concepts before you believe in the reality of things. Chaucer shows you things, and you call that pornography. But the denial of the senses and the embracing of nihilism is the ultimate pornography."

"There is more purity in 'The Miller's Tale' than in all of your philosophy, dear Horatio," said Marin. "I know you, you are offended at your own humanity, all you Mayflower screwballs, which is why the earthiness of Don Quixote or Chaucer makes you question whether you really are angels. Augustine read a famous philosopher, Plautinus, who said, 'Come out from the beauty of corporeal things.' Now, there is this tendency in the history of ideas to retreat from Beauty, the body, from reality and corporeal things. When will you cease to live in your heads and realize you have bodies? Can you even do ten push-ups?"

The 1132 guys all wanted to drop and give him twenty.

"We are accused of trying to lead you to a Western or Judeo-Christian viewpoint," said Whelan. "The truth is, we would just like to make it possible for you to look at the Venus de Milo and not blush."

Marin broke in: "There are a few Savonarola's out there, Chester. They're just waiting to burn it all down, have yourself a little bonfire of the humanities."

"With some natural piety," said Courtney, "you could realize that nature is better than your false eroticism. You could realize, like Boethius, that poetry and philosophy are better than CBS. Benedict left Rome when he saw where it was leading and fled to Subiaco, throwing himself into the thorns. And from that grew up the pride of our civilization—the Benedictine monastic orders of Europe."

I looked at Hogg. I imagined he thinking about Chalfontbleau. I wondered at the monks who had wandered there from Kansas, and Blaine who failed, and the other who left the monastery because of the attack on HIP. Become good pagans, become monks. Become a real human being. How could one come out from the beauty of corporeal things, and if one did, what would he find?

But I had failed miserably, and now a child in the womb might be blamed on me. It was a like a fake changeling tale out of a Shakespeare comedy. It was becoming difficult to keep track of the potential culprits. But the lecture had given me an idea.

XLIII

DESCARTES BEFORE THE WHORES

M AGGIE and I holed up at the Crossing to write the tale with a Shaeffer fountain pen.

"Tom really thinks the body is separate from the mind and soul," I said.

"In his case, it may be."

"He thinks the elect do not have to worry about what they do with their bodies."

"So Descartes got it right, then," she said.

"*Cogito ergo sum* is the modern dilemma, according to the professors."

"They're right," she said. "If you exist only because you are thinking, then all that is depends on you, and not on itself or God. Plato was not there, but his idea that the soul contained all that was represented in reality helps us get there."

"You really have been listening."

We were familiar as cousins. We could flirt and talk philosophy. I was Tom Jones with Miss Jenny Waters. "This 3.2 percent beer is practically rancid."

"Not like Zorn's home brew," she said. "His stuff would sell like hot cakes."

"You're brilliant. That's what I've been thinking."

"What?"

"Sell Zorn's home brew. Everybody loves it. We'll get the program out of any embezzling charges and be good pagans to boot."

"Embezzling charges?"

"Let's just say, I've been working on fixing the books with a little help from my friends on the hill."

"First, we have to deal with Chaucer. One prank at a time, eh?" She showed me some lines. She came up with the "The Miller's Tale" as the model for our naughty endeavor.

"This is perfect. Better than what I showed you," I said.

"The spelling's all over the map. Let me read this out loud."

A QUAINT TAIL
> *Whan wid Aprill you are shorta soda,*
> *For sore the nicht ee ain kan the rote,*
> *Ye hadde ne bathed and smeel of licour*
> *And wilted feelin like dried up fluor,*
> *Whan eek you smeel each ootheres breeth*
> *Ee hold yir nase, an swerven an th heeth,*
> *Ewayke ye fand not eech aqueyntanuce*
> *Ferrer alan strondes of spiritual avaunce;*
> *Who haveing ypreached engendred hir disgust*
> *At lust and merriement al as they wiste,*
> > *For havynge yful hir worldlinesse.*
> *Acht manne livinge in chierfulnesse*
> > *Fyndem hir in tyme Venus' maydenheed,*
> > *Upon the ers or full upside the heed.*
> *No padre could the burning ytch subside,*
> *No pardoner or summoner, or nonne or monke*
> *Getyng attencion by hots that squeel and honke.*
> *All acht of the compaignye wold go to chirch*
> > *For to fynde if hir mondes would fle the curs*
> *Jove's quoniam and quenynte fantasye;*
> *Er ectracacion from woman subtilly.*

The others cleared out. Middle English was too much for them.

> *Thar was a monk who in hir lyfe the seyde*
> > *Gave comfort for to hooly woordes to rede;*
> *Oon Swyn by name was he, so I gesse,*
> > *From martirs, or else leye told Ceys.*
> *Ceys was he ken and greet by a soun*
> > *Er belch come out and makken everych froun.*

"Not bad," I said, "but let's not get Descartes before the whores." She slugged me playfully. Some of my courtesy was leaving me as I drank. Maggie and I were touching more.

Many oother lydes compleyne and crye
For Eleyne the fleur makke greet envye.
Among womman her equal namoor could be found
  Us evern wight was lookyng to be oon,
Unfettered by the chayns of mariage,
But coyness stirred the noblesse corage
  Of these youthful consorts on the playne
  The mound of college found each oon ynsane,
  Prayyng to the goddess Venus yn the nyght
  Bright images of Eleyne to hire delit.
Moost fervent of al the monk, hem confess
  He knew the scripture of wommanlyness.
Swyn byat his breast full manie a tyme
  In habit sadd, chaste and tame.
Each knyght of hous longe to be a saynte,
Els they wont the richnesse of hire queynte.
Whan did Frede call his freres yn charitee
  To ask of them protectors for to be,
All knyghts of Mount Oread drewe to oon
  For festivities yn fulnesse of the moon,
Wyne and libations flowed, trewe and certayn
  Til mowre Swyn rede from St. Augustine.
High masse came through with bells, incense and beads . . .

"Are we getting carried away? I mean who would read this stuff un-less they were getting credit?"

"Who cares?" she said.

We went on with this knight's tale of farm fields and lovers' frolics to the climax.

Goon at large are we, but to what entreatie?
  What the region, what the clime, I seye,
  When Venus in jalousie rocks Oxford's walls
With waltzyng and champagne, the nyghte's balls,
Where professors corrupt the fayre youthe
  With all hir poesie and philosophic couthe.

"Now that is hitting close to home," said Maggie. The next part had been mine.

The fayre Eleyne preened hire riche harre
  In glasse that sheened hir beautee and ware
  Lyghte for angelic hosts, then did nyghte
  Permit to espye wenches for to dighte

And Swyn raises up to watch her ritual
    Of nakednesse, carnalitie I wol tell.
    Afeared, the twain rushed for covers warm,
    Away from knyghtly amour and from harm.
    As the knights broke into the chambre faire,
    Magpie grabbed in the dark for the monk's harre
    But ynstead grabbed a thyng moost shockyng eek,
The likerous end of hys unhooly steek.

Maggie laughed and spit out some beer on our work.

At wych she let out a powerful yelle
    To waken the dede who clepe in Hell.
And Egremont, who stood by the byd
    Found the naked Eleyne with cover on hire hedde.
He tried to kisse her fol lippes hastily
    When he also felt the long and pryvely
    Of the monk, until he bent back the cowl
    And heard the yiddish heathen loudly howl.
    'God forgive me, I am a synner, I convert.'
    And Egremont laughed loudly and let scape
The Jewe from this most unholsome jape.
    'Can you forgive me, noble Egremont?

Maggie stopped me. "Everyone is going to know this is about you."
"Exactly. They'll know I couldn't have written it."

    And if you woll, I will go to the convent.'
Aeneas fle into the room on wings of wynd
And filled the air with smells fol unkynd.
With him he carried a nakked monk, Swyn
Who in routh admitted his unkynde crym.
Then Ceys laughed fol cheerfully and drank
A flagon of meade until he was in the tank.
That nyght did Egremont propose on honde
To Eleyne hirself for her lyfe housbonde
So to put the Envye and rygt the compaignye,
    Knights, ladies of Universitee.
And everichon seye sooth it was trewe
    And none could the marriage of Eleyne regret
For it caused them to reduce the appetit
    For revelry, and now they could pray
    And study and thynk of love another day.
And thus did the Jewe come unto Jhesu Crist
    As the Knyghts heard him by a magpie, he list

Her for his sponsor, and Egremont agreed
But kept hire in ceremony upon his steed.
And al lived yn happyness all hir lyves,
Found contrie monastery and some wyves.

"Perfect," said Maggie, "and mean, too."

"Much of literature is the writer getting back at someone."

"All your study has paid off," she said.

"Grigson says that the practical joke feeds virtue, for it reveals the true nature of a person's vanity and defects."

"Let's get out of here," she said, bolting from her chair.

Once outside, we were becoming more flirtatious.

"I don't think Hogg can smell sins anymore," I said. Maggie leaned in close to me.

"You won't need special powers to smell my sins." I smelled her hair.

"Only lilac and a faint odor of beauty."

She grabbed my hand, I squeezed hers.

"And perhaps you smell *désirée amoreuse . . .*"

"*Mais oui,*" I said.

"Ou n'aime que ce qu'on possède pas tout entire," she said.

"Another one of your father's clichés?"

"No, that is from Proust: we love only what we do not have entirely."

"It must have been a good school—*Song of Roland,* Chaucer and Proust."

"I ran away before I found out."

"When?"

"When I was seventeen."

She opened up to me about her childhood, the death of her father, and her teenage crisis. We walked on campus as the sun set over Potter Lake. All was in conspiracy, the hot, red azaleas in florid bloom.

We could not resist each other and were soon embracing and kissing at the bridge where I drank vermouth with Chalmers. She tasted sweet, and I wanted more.

"Not here," I said.

We drove out to the country. I turned off the lights as we circled among trees on country roads. We came to the rock quarry where I had seen Apryl bathed in moondust. We took off our clothes and swam and frolicked in this star-filled theater. Then we embraced and, unlike my last adventure in the water, there was no doubt, no fumbling, straight to it, in the water, then up in the field above the quarry, angry with passion, as if each of us poured the other's confusion and frustration at ever being other than what we were as people into it. In the end, we were cast back to earth our old selves. Not one, but two separate, lost souls.

I dropped her off at Ole Miss at two in the morning. I took her up to the door and kissed her there. I looked into her eyes. No lies, no explanations, no strange avoidance of what we knew of our own "synne," caught up in our own parody.

"You are *très magnifique*, G. K.," she said. As I leaned over to kiss her again, I saw a light come on upstairs. I walked her inside, and we made out for all to see.

Apryl, seeing me bring Maggie in at that ungodly hour, all mussed and flushed, was the icing on the cake. I had come to the gate of the city, and there on the outskirts, I found revenge with a prostitute.

"Good night," she said as she disappeared up the stairs, noisily upsetting a plant as she went. Apryl stormed off to her room.

I was far from that person Professor Courtney had called me to become. But was I really this person who uses people? Behind the mask, I was still old Glaze living in a fraternity haze.

Suddenly I had the urge to flee everything. I realized I had reached the end of my journey here in Kansas. I was running from my father. Telemachus in reverse. My odyssey was at an end.

INTERLUDE

THE VISIONARY GLEAM

I HAD *to know and yet I did not. I called out to memory to explain why I was driven to far journeys, why I suffered in spirit on the wide sea of life, struggling to save myself and my companions; why there was still a burning within that would not be consumed. I knelt before the bush of knowledge. I came, I saw a vision. And I have been telling this over and over since, smelling it ever since. The smoke, the burning, the incense of memory, desire, and regret.*

In memory, we find reassurance as a child finds reassurance in the retelling of stories. Hansel will try again to find the way home, following breadcrumbs along the path; Peter Rabbit will somehow manage to learn his lesson. In a retelling, I might become G. K. Chesterton, the jolly warrior for civilization's lost verities. I might uncover a million treasures and love the work more than my pain. Where is it fled, this glory and dream of youth? That person in the picture thought there was something more, just around the corner, a shadow he could barely see but knew he had to grasp. The sea of faith had retreated; I looked across the vast ocean separating me from faith; did I even have a love to be true to on the darkling plain, or was I just looking for a supporting actress to be my Dover bitch?

Perhaps in retelling, in dressing again in a tuxedo, I can invest that person who was and remember, and hope that love is not betrayed; that you can possess the one loved without making her your prey, subjecting that one to your will and thereby destroying the impulse to love.

The book of numbers informs our life, but few can see them. I have been seeing numbers and smelling things. I have to carry a handkerchief everywhere I go. I cannot go inside the convent church because the incense would be overwhelming. I smell the sulfur. I got the disability from Hogg. I just wanted the marks gone, the memory, too. I wanted civilization to recede or whatever it is going to do without me, with its melancholy, long-withdrawing roar.

After I made full partner at Kenwood Carnes, I celebrated and bought a Patek Phillipe Perpetual Calendar Chronograph in 18 carat gold. I felt I could look into the inner workings of time. But was it worth the price of a house just to have a window into Swiss clockworks, as if I could somehow stop time? It brought me no closer to mastering the sweep of years.

The past never gives up the dead. Still, I long to see the incorrupt bodies of my college past. Just to be with friends in unguarded hours of youth, discovery, and spontaneous laughter. Maybe I have no more need to go inside here than I did at Chalfontbleau. Maybe what was written is not what is or must have been. I turn to leave, but behind me I hear the click of a gate, and I turn around.

BOOK III

THE ROYAL ROAD

We have reached at last, as the final result of that catastrophe three hundred years ago, a state of society which cannot endure, and a dissolution of standards, a melting of the spiritual framework, such that the body politic fails . . . Our various forms of knowledge diverge more and more. Authority, the very principle of life, loses its meaning, and this awful edifice of civilization which we have inherited, and which is still our trust, trembles and threatens to crash down . . .

— HILAIRE BELLOC, EUROPE AND THE FAITH

XLIV

VARIETIES OF RELIGIOUS EXPERIENCE

I WAS awakened from a hard afternoon nap by the noise of a door opening. A quivering jolt of air from a distant quasar, the ripples of a thousand iridescent skies, the moisture and tides exploding into a whorl of breath, and then a silent stirring of trees outside the window. An awakening. Or just another wind of April that had cast a spell over me.

As I considered my last month as a Jayhawk, I was still prolific in pranks with Chalmers and the Knights. I had concocted ten practical jokes: we put tacks on chairs, microphones in Barrows's bathroom tied to speakers on Jayhawk Boulevard behind the wing of the Jayhawk statue, and handbills of Finley with a goat's body and a rhyme on self-abuse.

"A Quaint Tail" not only had made its way around Ole Miss and HIP but was also a surprise sensation on campus. Soon, I found bootlegged copies in the kiosks where the *Jayhawker Daily* was dispensed. Apryl and all of Ole Miss blamed Swensen as the author of "Quaint Tail." I learned that Buntrock even read a section to his Chaucer class. Amid these musings, Patrick delivered some mail to me and set a paper down on my bed. I rubbed my eyes.

"Will you read my paper on Keats?"

"Sure." He did not leave. He sat down on my bed.

"What's going on with you?"

"I am in a cloud of unknowing."

"Stomach bothering you?"

"Sometimes I think Aeolus has taken up residence in my small intestine."

"The god of wind has visited the whole house. Is that what is really bothering you?"

"I am thinking I am going to leave KU."

"Let me tell you something, Bernard. You bring a dimension we needed, something to remind us that we owe it to ourselves to be better, to be more ourselves."

"What are you talking about? You guys have given everything to me."

"You've taught me to believe in my writing. Hogg thinks you were meant to help him with his vocation and usher in a new golden age of mysticism."

"Hogg thinks the trees are there to help with his vocation."

"Well, yeah . . . but this place would not be the same without you. Ross thinks he should be a parish priest because he's done so well with you, getting you to listen to Sheen and read De Montfort. Hell, DeBlasio writes better and appreciates poetry now. McDarby is less of a prick."

"Let's not get carried away."

"Even Clark laughs at his own conspiracies. You've made us better Catholics."

"Better Catholics?"

"It's like you said about Thomas Wolfe—sometimes you have to leave everything to find anything good."

"Sounds more like Chesterton," I said.

"You're becoming him more every day."

"I can't even figure out original sin."

"Take it from me: it's not so original," said Patrick.

"I know now there is good and evil, but I don't understand why."

"It's called *mysterium iniquitatis* for a reason."

We said together, "Because it's a mystery."

"Hey, there's a letter here from B'nai Brith." He handed me a letter.

"B'nai Brith . . . is everyone trying to convert me?"

He left. I opened the letter.

The Catholics for Free Choice, B'nai Brith
and Anti-Defamation League join in a
cooperative effort to rid KU of bigotry

Mr. Bernard Kennisbaum
1132 Ohio St.
Lawrence, KS 66044

Dear Mr. Kennisbaum:

Your mother has written us and informed us that you are Jewish. We are also informed that you have been in the Humanities Integration Program at KU. We understand you plan to testify at the upcoming hearings. We are sending this out to all students who may be the targets of brainwashing and other improper teaching methods of the professors of HIP.

If you have been considering converting to Catholicism as a result of your involvement in HIP, we ask that you consider the source of your interest and the amount of influences upon you, whether this is from your own free choice, and whether you have consulted with the KU administration, parents, and rabbis sufficient to make an informed decision about what you may be contemplating.

We are looking into a secret college graduate fund, SCHLAYEX, and would like to talk to you further about any knowledge you have of improprieties related to that fund.

We would be happy to talk to you and would ask that you go forward with courage in the testimony you will give.

Yours very truly,

Charlene Platzen
Father Sandy Smoot
Randall Dokes

Ever since I stopped going to CAPUT and told Barrows I was going deep underground, they had been trying to approach me. Swensen was alternately ashamed and proud that he was accused of authorship of "A Quaint Tail." Chalmers dropped by two days before the first day of HISS hearings. I showed him the letter. He beamed.

"Perfect. Now you can testify against the program—but not the SCHLAYEX funds." I looked at him, astonished. "There is no question what this committee will do. You have to be a good double agent, G. K."

"Like you were for Barrows."

"Sometimes you have to burn things to rebuild them."

"You will go down in flames along with the professors if the money isn't put back in SCHLAYEX."

"Are you accusing me of something?"

"Yes. You have used funds for yourself and put everyone else at risk."

"You want them knowing about your aunt Teresa and Marin?"

"That's a lie."

"That's what the poem is about. Marin has always loved her. That's the reason your father had a falling-out with her and Marin, isn't it?"

"Damn you!" I raised my fist to him. He smiled.

"You don't want everyone knowing Apryl's pregnant? Or that we caught her in bed with Finley? It would destroy Apryl and you."

"What was your role in Finley being in Apryl's bed?"

"Hey, I'm not the one carrying on with a prostitute. You still love Apryl, you pathetic pussy."

Chalmers had presumed on my desire to play infiltrator provocateur. That was fine, but now he was playing with my family.

"And you wouldn't want your embezzling to come to light," I said.

"You were supposed to take care of that."

"Too much to cover over in the journal entries. The account is missing thirty thousand. And I think you took it."

He flinched. "Listen . . . I didn't mean what I said about—"

"I have a plan to get the money back."

"How?"

"Sell Champoeg beer. It's already got a reputation all over campus."

"Brilliant . . . we could talk Zorn into giving up the recipe."

"Maybe we can say we'll pay for a public TL mass near the Campanile."

"But what experience do you have with sales?"

"I was the top salesman of carpet and linoleum the summer of seventy-six."

"Okay, I'll oversee production; you run sales and keep the books."

"I have to go to class."

"This is your real education," said Chalmers.

Apryl led the class in "Believe Me If All Those Endearing Young Charms," but I could not sing. I could not give her the same look—or see her as the sunflower sees the sun. Morning and night cast very different shades of light on her.

"Arnold felt powerless to be born, to use Hardy's phrase," said Marin, who had described the entire age of doubt and despair of the Victorians who had drunk the poison of scientism in place of faith. They were taking us deep inside the moderns, into James's *Varieties of Religious Experience* and Freud's *Civilization and its Discontents*. Marin took us right to the heart of Matthew Arnold's existential lovers on Dover Beach.

"You see, it is beyond that for you," said Courtney. "You are beyond wondering whether you can act, like Hamlet, or what happened to the world, like Arnold. You are trying to decide if there is any reality at all."

"The sea of faith was once too at the full, and round earth's shore lay like the folds of a bright girdle furled." Whelan rolled the lines off his tongue. "Think about that, 'the sea of faith was once too at the full.'"

Marin lit up a cigarette gleefully and waved it around as he spoke. "You know the parody of this poem, called 'Dover Bitch.' He really just wants to bed the girl." There were gasps from some. "He isn't interested in Truth. It is not even a valid religious experience. Yes, he feels, but does he really see?"

Yes, I was in it for the incredible hues, the wide palette of feelings. But the hard truth, the thing humans cannot bear much of, was that the sea of faith had retreated in me—if it was ever there at all.

"When you look for peace, are you sure you want peace, or do you want easy exits? What are you going to do when the lights go out?" Marin's acuity had improved since his drinking had subsided.

"You have to face the truth . . . and knowing that truth, you may have to take unpleasant action." Courtney had picked up on what Marin had said. "You may find that you are with someone or going somewhere in life and you have grasped part of the understanding of yourself. Arnold's man understands his ignorance, understands he has failed to grasp things fully, sees that the truth of existence sometimes is perceived like those distant lights out on the channel. He hears the eternal note of sadness that you read in Sophocles and in Virgil. So what is his answer? Despair?"

"You see," said Whelan, breaking the spell of Courtney's somber message, "for Arnold, it was a problem of faith waning. For you, it is a problem of reason and sanity waning. Some of you may be losing your minds over the noise of the modern world. Our lives are not lived on a human scale."

"Gather ye rosebuds while ye may," said Marin, and looked at me. "To virgins who make much of time, you don't look so good." I looked over at Maggie.

"There are rosebuds beyond the flower, beyond the opposite sex, beyond the fruits of nature," said Courtney. "There are rosebuds in our life. There is a time to gather . . . and we should not let anything get in the way. You cannot fail to grasp at the roses for fear that they are not roses—or that the thorns may hurt. That is the modern problem, the problem of Prufrock."

"Do I dare . . . and how should I begin?" said Marin. "All of you are worried about rolling your trousers up, about your little lust. You're all so proud of not being virgins. But by life's measure, you are virgins of time. You wonder if you made the right decision or if you can make the right decision. Make any decision. That is the poem of your life."

Maggie bore a wide, transparent smile. Marin had said, "If you don't really enjoy it, it can't be a sin"? With Maggie, it was a real sin.

"You studied Hamlet and Don Quixote," said Courtney. "Are they mad or are we mad? Ask yourselves what makes more sense: a guy standing on the cliffs overlooking a channel and deciding there is no hope or peace except sex or Don Quixote and Hamlet?"

"Moses supposes his bushes are roses. Are they? Is anything real to you?" said Marin. "Coke, the real thing. You want the answer to your indecision? Eat the damn peach! But first, do the basics, do those things antecedent to decisions, like making your bed. Connect to reality outside your heads for once."

"He's right," said Courtney, "you have to immerse yourself in the country, not the city. I'm from a great city, but I don't think anyone I grew up with had any conception of where food came from."

Marin jumped back in.

"If you can't face the reality of smelly farm animals, how are you going to deal with the cesspools of your life? When the wind is right in Dodge City, a few hours from her, you will encounter smells from the cattle operations that will knock you out. You know what that smell is? Do you? It's the smell of money."

Whelan came in with the final word:

"That's why we have the country fair each year, so you can connect to those elemental things that are part of the cycle of your lives. Come to the country fair and enjoy the arts of food and dance and song. You may not know experience is real until the moment . . . like a kiss. Your mind will tell you, and your heart will confirm."

Eat the damn peach was right.

XLV

CONVERSION OF THE JEWS

And you should, if you please, refuse
Till the Conversion of the Jews.

— MARVELL, "TO HIS COY MISTRESS"

"WE have been very concerned about you," said Rhoden. I looked at his twitching mustache. It was the Saturday before Palm Sunday when I met with the committee.

"That is why I have come to speak to you."

Dr. Littman smoked his cigar. Sharon Blaine sat fanning the air. Schmead tapped his large foot. Fruhling glared.

"Way I hear it, sonny," said Fruhling, "you becoming a real Catholischer like the rest of them."

"Not so fast," said Littman. "You've been playing all of us—the university, even HIP—for fools. I've seen his meshuggener type before. They don't have any identity. He's a shapeshifter. A zelig."

"He's turning Roman," said Sharon Blaine.

"He will never do it," said Schmead. "He knows if he testifies against us, he'll lose everything."

"Well, Catholic or not," said Littman, "you are knee-deep in kidnapping plots. You try to involve us, you'll be the shmendrick I took you for."

"What if I refuse to testify?" I said.

"You're our star witness," said Mrs. Blaine.

"This committee has no subpoena power. They cannot force a student to testify against his own teachers."

"*Sehr klug*," said Fruhling. "You think you are Mephistopheles, clever boy? Well, sonny, you will testify or you will be over, kaput."

"I don't care."

"What about your Fulbright?" said Schmead.

"It's over a year away, and a lot can happen between now and then," I said in noncommittal way.

"It's too late," said Rhoden. "We have relied on your testimony."

"I will not let you destroy my friends."

I started to leave.

"Get back here," said Schmead. I turned. "It seems you might have overlooked something." Schmead pulled out a piece of paper. He began reading a copy of the poem of Marin.

Littman raised his hand in the air. "You are within your rights. If you decide to maintain silence, so be it. We'll let you decide when the time comes."

I nodded and started to leave. I heard Fruhling say under his breath, "*Verdammt Katholisch.*"

φ

"*In illo tempore*," began the Gospel. In that time, Christ rode into Jerusalem on an ass, and the crowds cried out "Hosanna!" We were given palm branches to hold.

Broglio preached thunderously, counseling us to be wise as serpents and to sting the enemy who was throwing us out of the temple—saying they did not know us because we were not children of the world. The very bushes would cry out along Jayhawk Boulevard if the professors did not speak the truth.

It was Palm Sunday at Hess's farm. Dom Broglio had presided magisterially in gold-fringed robes with McDarby and Swensen as acolytes. The effect of the Latin Mass was of a magic act, with smells and bells, incense and chanting.

I stood outside the experience of the Mass, yet I recognized its ancient beauty. *Introibo ad altare Dei.* I approach the altar of God who gives joy to my youth. Joy to my youth: if only I could grasp it. There was incense, and it filled the living room and my senses. Then the reading of the Gospel. Was Hogg right, had I put the coal to the soul? When Dom

Broglio reached the *Munda cor meam*, the lead-in to the Gospel, Trish pointed in the Sears, Roebuck so I could follow the Latin and English.

It reminded me of the short time I had spent learning about ancient Israel: *I have loved, O Lord, the beauty of Thy house and the place where Thy glory dwelleth.* It caused a yearning to well up inside of me. It spoke to something deep-seated—a longing for infinitude.

But ultimately, my senses failed me. I saw bread—a wafer—where they saw the body, blood, soul, and divinity of the Creator. I saw a gold chalice holding wine; they saw the blood of the Redeemer offered up in an unbloody sacrifice. Calvary reenacted, as he said, "in memory of me." It was a hard doctrine, to see and not see, to accept and deny the senses, to rise above common sense to spiritual sense. It was a doctrine that had divided many and caused many to rise and fall. *I believe, Lord, help thou my unbelief.*

Apryl finally spoke to me after mass. I played like I was sick of her. Maggie and I pretended not to want to be with one another. Ever since I had taken up with Maggie, Apryl had wanted to see me.

We walked to the pond.

"Do you think Tom will go to the monastery?" she said. She carried a rosary and wore a lace-fringed collar on a purple dress. It clung to her like bark on a tree. It was holy and voluptuous. The sky was overcast. "He just really understands LaGrange and the unitive stage."

"Go, get thee to a monastery," I said, looking into Apryl's eyes.

"As to holy monks . . ." She quoted from *Romeo and Juliet*, as if I were crossing Shakespearean swords with her.

"I've renounced my father and denied my name," I said.

"You look really good now, Bernard."

"Thank you, I . . . have been taking care of Maggie." I wanted to see her reaction. She turned to me suddenly and kissed me on the lips. Blood was coursing, birds and insects watching. I reached for her, but she drew away.

"I heard you might leave us for California," she said, looking down slightly.

"Right back where I started from."

"You've barely given us a chance."

"You mean, I have barely given you a chance."

"If you convert . . . I will wait for you."

"Wait?" It was the first time I had challenged one of her tricks, one of her carrots held out for me.

"I suppose I should be asking you. I am trying to help Maggie, and you . . . you are carrying on and it is—"

"Are you prepared to judge me?"

I was almost to the point of confronting her with her crime with Finley. "I have enough on my plate just judging myself."

"I would marry Tom Hogg if he were not God's. He and Swensen are the only pure ones." I felt like showing her the remarks about her in Hogg's journal.

"Pure? Have you read Swensen's tale?" I knew Maggie had left it out at Ole Miss where it might be found. She flushed in embarrassment.

"That was just . . . a whimsical imitation of Chaucer."

"You're not thinking of going to the waltz with Pete?" Again, she said nothing. "Bob?"

She turned to me with glowering eyes. I saw it at that moment. It was why she burned guys at the house. It was why she played with our emotions and hormones. Sex was not a drive for her—it was a weapon.

"I wouldn't be so quick to talk about purity, Apryl, after the other night."

"The other night? On All Saints' Day. Yes, we were together in a way I've never been with another."

She was either a very good actress or this was an MFing miracle.

"What is really going on with you?" I looked down at her stomach.

"Haven't you learned the first thing about manners?" she said in a matron's tone.

"Isn't there a way back to that night for us?"

"I've wished for nothing else."

"Then why are you so distant?"

"Can't you tell me straight up whether you're really pregnant?"

"You're not that naïve . . . I can't believe I . . . gave myself to you."

"I mean, I'm having a hard enough time with the virgin birth, the immaculate conception, bulls praying rosaries. I don't think the search for faith can take another miracle."

"What are you talking about?"

"The only miracle I want now is to go back to that quarry with you that night, to have another chance."

She turned away, crying.

"I am thinking about this convent in France," she said.

The tears stopped as if a spigot had been turned. She turned and looked at me with coy affection.

"Bernard, you could still take me to the waltz."

"I can't believe I'm hearing this Little Bo Peep routine, talking about pregnancy one moment and going to a convent in France the next—now the waltz."

She straightened up and said, "There is still time."

She threw her hair back with a flick of her neck, spun around, and walked back to the house.

"Time for what?" But she did not turn back.

I sat on the palm fronds we had gotten from Hess inside. I smoked a couple of cigarettes. Only a goddess could lie that way and still walk in radiance. A basso profundo drawl knocked me out of my reverie.

"Thank God you're a country boy, Bernie."

Hess wore shiny cowboy boots and best Sunday clothes, with a white and gold vest and an old-fashioned watch on a chain.

"Cat got your tongue?"

"No, I think it's the Gorgon."

"Turn you down again?"

I shrugged. Hess watched her angelic form disappearing into the farmhouse.

"That is some filly there, boy."

"More like a bucking bronco."

Hess stared reflectively at his bean fields.

"Hard to square being a Catholic in this insane world . . . I think it's especially hard for us converts. Best to rely on nature."

Hess turned to me, his blue eyes blazing with honesty.

"This is my legacy after my parents died a few years ago in a car accident. After they died, I was a mess, living fast and reckless. Then I found the program, and I knew that in nature I could come back to myself. I won't lie to you, Bernie. I think the only way to make sense is to get away from the world. Out here, a man can think."

"I think this would be a great center for being sane again," I added.

Hess paused and looked sideways at me.

"G. K., you have a lot of insight. But you fail to see what is right in front of you. This is consecrated ground. I've known Beauty, creation, fruitfulness—a fellow can get his soul in order out here."

"Has Ellis gotten his soul in order? Rich thinks he was running away from a fight."

"Chalmers is too busy running into every fight."

"He doesn't want me to become Catholic at all now."

"You do what you're gonna do. Ellis has to leave, needs to be by himself, away from all of us. He's packed his things. We'll have a spare bedroom for you. Kansas is the right place for love."

"Maybe if I stayed out here for a while—to sort things out. It's peaceful."

Hess looked out at his lands. "All this is gone soon . . . the whole world, vanished. You gotta have a place where you can go to prepare."

"Do you really get by without electricity?"

"Men have been doing it for thousands of years."

"If you say so."

"I say so. And the prophecies about this place predict it."

"Prophecies?"

"The Indians called this the Place of the Cross."

"Why?"

"They saw a cross here. The Ottawa tribe. Over two hundred years ago."

"Karl, you ever have trouble with the doctrine of the virgin birth?"

"Don't get to thinking too much on it. Remember, Bernie—just keep your nose clean and everything will come out right."

He patted me hard on the back. "You stay with me, we'll keep you in that good shape for the waltz—and for the end of the world." He boomed out reports of laughter. "And you can help us get ready for the country fair, bail some hay, and help dig the pig pit."

"Pig pit?"

"For smoking the meat. You can help me dig it. Real man's work will do you good."

"Sounds like hard labor."

"We could also have you paint the stumps of the bulls."

I remembered what McDarby told me about chopping off the manhood of the bulls.

"I'll dig the pits and bail the hay, you paint the stumps."

At least I would not have to face Maggie or the guys at 1132. I didn't need an apocalypse—my world was falling down around me fast. Easter was a week away and the hearings were starting in a few days. The annual fair was in the middle. As Mom would say, "Oi vey, go away."

XLVI

FAIRE THEE WELL

Be glad of life because it gives you the chance to
love, to work, to play, and to look up at the stars.

— *HENRY VAN DYKE JR.*

H ESS and the girls of Ole Miss had managed to turn the spreading
green into a village with tents, lights, stages, a Latin puppet play that
was in full swing, square-dance lessons, cakes, breads, pies, Greek shish
kebab, cider, sleights of art, a log pull, two-man team sawing contests,
pumpkin carving, and calligraphy displays in Latin and English. One
booth sold brightly colored organic vegetables I helped grow, ploughing
fields with Belgians. I came to know real horsepower.

Trish hosted a booth featuring knitted coasters, assorted doilies, and
some cross-stitch patterns on pillows with scenes and quotes from the
Homer, Virgil, and Dante, and a detailed one with Venus on the seashell
and the phrase stitched in, "Born in Wonder."

"Did you do this?"

"No . . . an anonymous artist." Trish looked down. I purchased it and
put it inside Hess's house.

The pig roasted in the pit that I helped dig: its smoky burnt offerings
filled the air as did a beautiful soprano voice singing "Parting Glass." Hess
cut up the pig in generous slabs, tantalizingly tender, a smoky piece of
heaven. Diana and Maggie were twisting about a maypole with homemade multicolor ribbons flitting in the wind. Zorn sold his beer at a

booth with a long queue. Ross and DeBlasio cut the line. Hogg wandered around in a denim shirt and broad-brimmed straw hat, looking like a Mennonite.

"Alcinous would be at home here," said Grigson as he addressed a large group of current and former students of HIP. "We will have all the feast, including feats of strength, to test you—if you still have what it takes."

"The question is, do you still have what it takes, Russ?" said Whelan, breaking up the crowd. I saw Courtney eating a portion of the pig flitch, sucking on his fingers after each bite.

"I have this much," said Grigson as he threw his arms out in a thespian pose:

> *Dear lovely bowers of innocence and ease,*
> *Seats of my youth, when every sport could please,*
> *How often have I loitered o'er thy green,*
> *Where humble happiness endeared each scene!*

The onlookers whistled; some joined in the recitation of the Goldsmith poem. Roy Neis stepped up, dressed up as a rustic:

> *While many a pastime circled in the shade,*
> *The young contending as the old surveyed;*

I stepped up:

> *The boast of heraldry, the pomp of power;*
> *And all that beauty, all that wealth e'er gave,*
> *Awaits alike the inevitable hour.*
> *The paths of glory lead but to the grave.*

The group groaned its approval of the lines from Grey's "Elegy Written in a Country Churchyard." Always a *memento mori* in HIP.

Apryl had flowers woven in her hair and wore a loose-fitting dress with a festive design, browsing among handmade silver jewelry offerings. Maggie was nearby with McDarby and DeBlasio, drinking Champoeg and throwing darts.

"You look like a different person," Apryl said. Up close, I could see she was all dolled up with sparkling glitter. Hess had got me versed in country things, including the loss of twenty pounds.

"I barely recognize myself. You, on the other hand, are all sparkly."

"Goddess dust." She pointed over at the Anachronists table where they were applying paints and sparkle to kids' faces.

"Ah, Merlin and his tricks again. How about that smoked pig?"

"I didn't have any, not feeling that good," she said. I glanced at her midriff. A group cheered as music was struck up.

"Look, it's the contest!" she said with excitement. I looked at her quizzically. "Don't you know?" she said. "Every year, Karl has a greased pig contest, the scramble, and whoever captures it gets the first dance with the princess of the fair."

"Why did you and Finley . . ." It just came out. "Is it . . ." I pointed to her belly. I couldn't ask her if it was Finley's child. I decided to cloak it in a bit more of Grey's "Elegy":

> *The struggling pangs of conscious truth to hide.*
> *To quench the blushes of ingenuous shame.*

"What has Grey's "Elegy" to do with Professor Finley?"

"Didn't you read the Chaucerian farce?"

"Did you purchase my cross-stitch?"

"That had to take you a long time."

"Not really."

"I guess you just worked in a few stitches between lovers."

"If you have something to say, just say it," she said firmly. That was it, I was prepared to confront her finally.

We were interrupted by a great flock of voices. McDarby, DeBlasio, Swensen, and Chalmers all crowded up with a bunch of older students. They started taking off their shirts.

"Now boys, give everyone a chance," boomed Hess. We came to the place where all were gathered around a circular pen lined with straw.

"That's one dark pig," said Ross.

"That, children," said Hess, "is Haney, my pet pig. You've been eating his mother." The crowd groaned; a girl threw down her remaining piece of pork on a stick with a look of disgust.

"You all watch out—he is smarter than most of us and a little mean-er." The crowd made sounds of feigned fear.

Hess held up Haney as it squealed and wriggled. We stared at those who were still eating the sow mother of this pet pig.

"What, no brave men?" said Hess with his taunting bonhomie.

McDarby was the first to jump over the red fencing. Then Patrick followed. Apryl looked at them admiringly. A hand clasped my shoulders. Jimmy.

"If you catch the pig, I'll dance a jig," he said.

"Jews from LA don't have much in common with pigs."

I looked at Apryl. "We'll talk later."

"This pig is Jewish," said Hess, trying to pull me toward the gate.

"How can you tell," I said, resisting. People nearby were egging me on.

"He doesn't eat other pigs." He laughed so loud in my ear, it started ringing. Suddenly, I was hoisted over the fence by Hess, Chalmers, and Grigson. I took off my shirt. There was applause.

The crowd chanted:

"Wooo pig sooey!"

"Wooo pig sooey," I yelled back and bowed in several directions, finally toward Apryl, who nodded—but then, I bowed to Maggie. Before I could get my bearings, Hess shoved Haney under the fencing, and the dirty creature was off. Pursuers shot in all directions—helter skelter—until McDarby jumped, caught a hoof, and went twisting to the floor. The pig got away easily, leaving him straw-feathered and spitting.

Chalmers came aboard, running faster than the others, and waited until he'd cornered the frightened creature, letting others take tries. But Haney squeezed away, so thick was Hess's dark grease compound.

'What'd you put on this pig?" said Patrick, smelling his hands after he got up from a failed attempt at a porcine grab.

"My own secret blend of suet, Vaseline, and tractor grease."

"Nasty," said DeBlasio, wiping his hands on his jeans. Chalmers was quick to get Haney by the hoof, but the pig outsmarted him and curled up toward his arm and bit him.

"Bastard pig," said Chalmers, holding on. His switchblade came out in a flash.

"No!" yelled Hess. Girls screamed in horror.

But Chalmers planted the knife into the pig's thigh, causing the creature to let out the worst farmyard screech I'd ever heard. Somehow, the pig wriggled loose and started running like a wild boar hell-bent on revenge. Instinctively, I started for the gate, but I heard Haney at my back, rushing headlong, grunting, snorting, and oinking all at once, a terrifying danse macabre.

I turned; Haney went airborne. I put my arm up, he planted his snout on my arm, and we both went down in a disgusting display of wrestling, no holds barred, straw in every hole, grease everywhere, and untoward sounds coming out of both of us.

I felt an intense pain in my arm. I was holding one of Haney's haunches, and I could hear the crowd cheering, then I felt the wound Chalmers had created, and stuck my thumb into it. Haney let go his hold on my arm, and blood came gushing out, but I grabbed both his legs. Somehow, I managed to keep my balance and hold on to the pig. I felt intense animal rage.

Soon, I was spinning around and around with the pig and it was squealing, and the crowd was rhythmically chanting "G-K," anticipating what I was going to do in this Grunter-Roman combat. Then I let go, sending Haney flying high toward the gate.

Everything went into slow motion as Haney hit the gate and went flat to the ground, motionless.

"You killed Haney!" yelled a tall girl wearing a Franklin County Feed hat.

Hess ran over. I came over, a strawy mess. Then the crowd parted. We watched as one as Hogg moved to the pig. He took off his hat like a doctor arriving on the scene. He took out his rosary and kneeled down, speaking to Haney.

"Haney will live," he said as he got up.

The crowd made scoffing sounds. Hess crouched over his pet.

"I'll be damned!" he exploded.

Suddenly, I saw the hooves quicken and the pig scuttering and getting up, dazed. Suddenly shy of people, it retreated to the other end of the pen, trembling.

Hess walked over to me. He pulled my arm up.

"A winner by knockout!"

Cheers went up. I saw Marin smiling, standing near Apryl. Chalmers hurried over.

"Lucky fuck," he whispered.

"Rich, those who live by the knife . . ." I didn't complete the thought.

I had gone from what would have made me the skunk of the fair—to the hero. Someone struck up an Irish ditty. I looked over and Jimmy was dancing a jig. Then several maids, including Trish and Laura—and Maggie with them—came rushing over with a homemade healing salve that was being sold at the Anachronists booth and tended to my wound, wrapping the field dressing with maypole ribbons.

Then Apryl came over and took my hand. I pulled it back.

"Stupid. I'm Princess Nausicaa of the fair this year, you get the dance with me," she said, smiling like a goddess. "I never knew you were so brave . . ."

"But, what about you and Finley in bed?"

"Excuse me?"

"So someone else was in your bed the other day?"

"You're making no sense. Come on, silly, let's show them how to dance." She yanked on my arm, but I pulled away, walked over to Maggie, and held out my arm. She took it daintily. We started to walk toward the music.

"You pick a prostitute over me?" Apryl said. I looked back at her.

"At least she admits it," I said.

As I walked toward the crowd, they nodded to us with greetings.

"Odysseus. Nausicaa."

Maggie curtsied.

"Some fair, eh?" I said out of the side of my mouth, "Hogg rescues pig, boy gets girl."

She smiled. We waved to our friends as we approached the dance floor. Chalmers was standing by the stage, arms akimbo, seething.

XLVII

THE GLAND INQUISITOR

*B*ANG! The inquisitor's gavel came down. Finley looked around at the thronged room. It had been hailed as the new Scopes trial only instead of monkeys, it was Catholics.

Hess had brought me in on his Harley-Davidson, which he'd let me drive in the country. My hair was stiff from the wind. I felt my leathery skin from days in the sun, baling hay, and the glow of winning the pig fling, as they were now calling it.

I had a perfect vantage point to watch the gossiping crowd of HIPsters, townies, students, the gents of 1132, the gals of Ole Miss, pinched-faced professors, communists, Latin traditionalists, Wesleyans, Baptists, Pentecostals, local press, and two deaf-language signers. Jimmy Drungole flashed his gleaming smile at Finley and the rest of the panel. Trish sat quietly. Vice Chancellor Holloway sat nearby, impassively as a man sitting for a portrait.

"This is the Humanities Integration Systems Search committee's first hearing," said Finley, "to look into aspects in our report of academic improprieties. We are an advisory committee and will make whatever recommendations are called for. We will now proceed with the first witness *against* the program."

"We go no further until you recognize our right to speak," snapped Marin. Chalmers snickered as if he knew that Marin would do this. Maggie sat by him. Apryl was right behind the professors.

There they were, the triumvirate of tradition—Whelan with his quick eyes and impervious expression; Marin with his stout torso, his fisherman's hands, his manly appearance; Courtney with his sad but compelling visage, his Irish tweed hanging from this stick of a man.

Finley went off the record, pushing down the mute button on the recorder, and leaned over to his colleagues so that his beard mated with the thick beard of Stephen Pigg. Regent Dewain Schmead sat two rows in front of me, his legs sprawled over the chair. Near him sat Perry Hudson, adjusting his tortoiseshell glasses. I had not said anything to him in weeks.

Whelan rose, the bantam Irishman:

"You three committee members have no particular *reason* why we cannot be acknowledged here today and make a remark or two concerning our objections to this proceeding? We have our lawyer, Dom Angelo Broglio, who is prepared to give an opening statement on our behalf."

Whelan gripped a folder that had grown fat with correspondence. He lifted an eye above the black rim of his glasses and met the gaze of Professor Stephen Pigg, who taught constitutional law and denounced witch hunts and restrictions on academic freedom.

"This is not a courtroom," said Finley. "There is no need for lawyers." He conferred with his colleagues, who furiously gesticulated and whispered. Pigg seemed upset and kept nodding.

"Very well, Mr. Broglio," said Finley finally, exasperated. Dom Broglio bowed, inhaled deeply, then turned from the committee and addressed the crowd.

"I am Dom Angelo Broglio. A priest from Rome. But I am also lawyer, both civil and canon. And I am here to tell you about a travesty that you as Americans must appreciate. I represent three professors at the University of Kansas who are being burned at the stake. Their names are Paul Courtney, Chester Whelan, and Frederick Marin. They are all award-winning teachers. Paul Courtney, a distinguished professor of classics, was interviewed in *Atlantic* magazine. The university has been the torturer and executioner of these men, men whose reputations have been ruined, whose names have been dragged through the mud on account of their dedication to teaching the great works of Western Civilization.

"The university endorsed their humanities program at first. They provided thousands in funding, helped them to get an NEH grant of fifty thousand dollars, allowing it to be the pilot program for colleges within the university, and it was so successful and well regarded that the university recommended it for a federal grant. Parents write in overwhelming numbers—and you will hear each of these four hundred and seventy-six letters before I am through."

Groans rose from the anti-HIP section, cheers from the HIP section.

"Bit by bit, the administration has taken their funding, trying to starve them, but still, the program is quite popular. The university took away credits toward graduation requirements for Western civilization because of the so-called revolution these men were preaching. This 'revolution' for which they have been persecuted is the mere return to serious consideration of tradition and the Western canon!"

Pigg eyed Finley hopelessly. Finley leaned over to Schmead. Holloway looked mortified.

"But of the crime of proselytizing, they are innocent. They did not discourage students to become Catholics. After all, this is a university, a place of great thoughts and changing attitudes.

"These men stand for the principle of academic freedom, the freedom to teach as they see fit without interference from those who misunderstand this teaching or oppose it or just want to do away with it. If you allow this, you participate in killing Socrates, the first great philosopher accused of corrupting the youth. Now they are on trial for asking their students to think about their roots, their history, the great writers—for asking them to learn manners and regard for the opposite sex, instilling in them a sense of Beauty rather than a purely pragmatic view of the world. For this, they stand accused and plead *guilty*."

A thunder of applause erupted from the back of the room. Reporters scribbled madly. I saw Fruhling and Smoot from CAPUT. A few rows up, the prickly Saul Littman chewed on a cigar. Angry parents had seen their children defect to tradition.

A crimson Finley banged the gavel. Finley then stood and called out in a loud voice, "Professor Eldridge Buntrock!"

I was shocked. He was a friend of HIP from a distance. He had taught me Chaucer. He wore his best Harris Tweed sport coat, and his hair was not falling down on his face in strands as usual.

"Please state your name," said Finley.

"Eldridge Buntrock, professor of English at the University of Kansas."

"Why are you testifying?"

"Because I think the Humanities Integration Program, while making some contribution to learning, is the wrong idea for bringing students to a greater appreciation of their heritage and of great works."

"Are you saying they don't provide a good overview of Western civilization?"

"In their sampling of works and the way they have their students embrace poetry and works of literature, history, and philosophy, there is a kind of family-like familiarity, a breaking down of the necessary walls that we need in scholarship to provide students with objectivity, analytics, and aesthetic distance."

"Can you give us an example of this?"

"Yes. As I say, I try to get my students to look at the world differently than they are used to seeing it, and so do the HIP professors. But when it comes to the text, such as my specialty of Chaucer, I am interested in students really diving in, where the HIP professors seem content with festivals more than the deep dive into the inner workings of, say, *The Canterbury Tales* and the typology and mythology of the Middle Ages it represents."

"Are you saying they are teaching students humanities appreciation rather than scholarship and critical thinking?"

"Yes, students are given a false sense that 'the West is best.'"

"Is it the best?"

"That is complicated. As you know from running the Western civilization program, you have to look at many myths, many philosophies, and the great works of the East, the West, Native Americans, and Africans to see a pattern."

"So does this way of looking at things in your view have any backing among the community of scholars, a consensus?"

"Yes. Broadly, it could be found in the critique of Western culture by the French philosopher, Jacques Derrida, who looked at the binary or hierarchical approach to meaning and language in Western philosophy and literature and argued for a more holistic approach."

"But isn't this based in a kind of skepticism about the claims of Western culture to holding the keys to meaning?"

"I look at it as more of a celebration of all different cultures and languages and systems of meaning to find a synthesis."

"That sounds like an integrated humanities philosophy to me."

"I would like to see HIP do more of that—diversify its curriculum. Less dialectical truth finding, more synthesis."

"Thank you, professor." He sat down. Broglio rose. Buntrock's hair fell out of place a little, and he threw back some strands and rubbed his face.

"Professor Buntrock, it seems to me that you are saying that HIP is too popular, not scholarly enough, and that the students end up with the sense of real verities in the universe rather than being good cynics and modernists?"

"That's absurd. I worry that they offer the verities to the students as if they are fruit you can pick from the tree of knowledge."

"Well, do you deny there are verities?"

"No, only that we are dealing with the realm of myth, not scientifically provable truth, and it is well to make distinctions."

"So you think they do not understand myth?"

"Individually, these are marvelous scholars and teachers, but together, they form this unbreakable unit of rhetorical magic—they get carried away by their own message. It is an interesting conceit, this idea of experimenting with tradition. I must admit to it myself."

"Yes, you take students on romps through campus, no?"

"Romps, what does that mean?"

"Some have accused you of eccentricity in your teaching."

"What proof do you have for that?"

"You have had students on their knees smelling the Moses bushes on campus, haven't you?"

"Sniffing? I want students to occasionally get outside of class to explore the flora and fauna on campus, an idea that is supported in the Renaissance writers that I teach."

"So you think it's important to awaken a sense of wonder in students."

"The HIP professors do not have a lock on wonder. I want students to be open to the universe, to be able to look at things as if for the first time. My students have come to appreciate that faculty of the mind."

"Indeed. Some have accused you of having too much of a following, like Professor Courtney?"

"I have loyal students. Should we only teach those who despise us?"

"Maybe they have more than you?"

"Nonsense. These are respected colleagues."

"Didn't you lose out to them on the National Endowment for the Humanities grant that started HIP?"

"That was nine years ago." Buntrock rubbed his face several times.

"So you have always resented them, isn't that why you're here?"

"No! I want them to provide a more rounded view, with more viewpoints, more voices."

"And you would want to be one of those on the stage, another voice, teaching with them?"

"Well, sure, but not just me, even someone from philosophy and chemistry."

"Wouldn't that just be your version of integration of knowledge? Quantitative and horizontal integration rather than the vertical integration of all knowledge under the single notion of Truth?"

"Yes, that would be a pedagogical difference I have with them. I don't think the Truth is univocal."

"But you would teach students then that truth does not actually exist."

"I teach them to be critical and discover their own truths."

"Professor, if you show all viewpoints as equally valid, then you are in fact teaching that there is no superior way of thought or political structure or social organization?"

"I suppose."

"So you would teach relativism?"

"I prefer to call it a search for truth."

"And does the principle of academic freedom guarantee you the right to teach your version of the search for truth?"

"Absolutely."

"But you would deny the HIP professors the academic freedom to teach history and literature and civilization under the light of Truth?"

Buntrock went silent for a tense moment.

"You are turning my argument on its head."

"You are familiar with Alexandr Solzhenitsyn's recent commencement speech at Harvard University." He nodded in the affirmative. "In that speech, he warns of the loss of belief in Truth, or Veritas, as he points out about the motto of Harvard."

"Yes, we have all read his speech."

"He notes the tendency of the West toward a decadence of relativism weakening the West, its moral weakening to the point where individualism has resulted in a loss of courage and an unwillingness to fight against moral evils."

"I understand his views are colored by the terrible things he suffered in the Gulag. He sees the Renaissance as necessarily leaving behind spirituality and inevitably embracing pure materialism, but that is not my view of where we are. We are a free society and can express our views freely, which is no small thing."

"But what happens when freedom becomes license, when diversity, tolerance, and pluralism bring a society to disbelieve in evil and good?"

"Evil and good are in themselves relative concepts."

"Shouldn't students be offered a robust view of the West that shows the history up until our century of moral greatness in thought and action?

"It seems that we have come to a point in civilization where these matters are in question and we need to explore new paradigms."

"But is not the study of speculative paradigms better at graduate study level? Most of your students are not steeped in the classics to be able to really engage in that sort of high-level criticism, are they?

"I am thinking of some students who have had their development cut short by immersion in HIP and its satellite courses."

"I see you wish to impose your view of education on students just like you accuse these professors of doing."

"If I have to choose Truth or voluntarism and doubt, I would say it is best to present doubt to students."

"And you have the academic freedom to do that. As I hope you would extend to the professors Courtney, Whelan, and Marin."

"I am a vocal proponent of academic freedom, and for this reason, I have supported the right of HIP to exist, but I am here to question the wisdom continuing HIP with the religious turn it has taken."

"If they were to teach Buddhism and Marxism alongside traditional Catholic and Christian writers, would you have the same opinion?"

"No, I would support them whole heartedly. This is a great university where all viewpoints must be presented."

"Ah! Except one view: the traditional view of Western civilization." Buntrock looked at Broglio and said nothing for a moment.

"Thank you, Professor Buntrock."

Finley called a few more former students to testify. They told tales of woe, how they had—the unimaginable!—actually contemplated converting to Catholicism. They felt compelled to a way of thinking that was narrow and overly critical of the university and the modern world. In this light, the program appeared to be influencing students in a public university toward retrogression to religion. It was not looking good.

XLIX

THE FULLNESS OF TIME

" W E have a student witness who will corroborate all of this," said Finley. "I call Perry Hudson to the stand."

Perry marched to the front, looking right at me. Dressed in a light brown houndstooth and gabardine slacks, he sported a red tie with a little pheasant pattern, and a bright red pocket part kerchief. His shoes were two-tone black and tan loafers with tassels. He exuded central Kansas smarminess. He sat, crossed his legs, and enumerated his stay at the fraternity, then his scholarly pursuits.

"Why are you here to testify?"

"The HIP program is subversive. I see the University of Kansas being used to indoctrinate and undermine the whole purpose of higher education."

"What is that?"

"To create more searching minds. But they mock that and substitute their promise of a utopia of poetry and parties."

"As an English major, do you consider that to be bad?"

"I enjoy that sort of thing as far as it goes, gather ye rosebuds while ye may, and all that. But the professors are subtly encouraging students not only to follow them in their Catholic beliefs, but to reject their chosen studies in favor of a medieval regimen of literature and great books. Which are, in fact, great."

Finley turned red at being upstaged by this young pedant.

"You are talking in generalities. Do you know any students who fit your description?"

"I know some promising literary scholars, one who was cutting edge in a new discipline of deconstructionism. Another who had studied under Seamus Heaney, a great Irish poet, but when HIP came to Ireland with its ice cream truck of tradition, he left it all."

"Can you give us other examples?"

"They kidnapped a young man, Tom Hogg, in the program. He was in very serious mental condition, receiving treatment at Menninger's Institute.

He really had been spying on 1132 all this time.

"What symptoms?"

"Well, he sees visions and claims to smell people's sins."

I was more convinced than ever that the university had my journal.

"What happened to Mr. Hogg?"

"He is back in school, living in their den of iniquity, 1132 Ohio Street, when they aren't spiriting him to the country. They are shielding him from treatment and taking his exams for him. I believe the professors—Courtney, Marin, and Whelan—control these young men and women. Like a cult."

"Thank you, Mr. Hudson."

I rushed up to Dom Broglio and whispered to him. I stared at Perry. Butter wouldn't melt in his mouth. So I flashed him the secret Sigma Chi warning sign that cops were present, four fingers of right hand, thumb tucked. That got his attention. Broglio stood and approached the witness to cross examine.

"This is slander, to call them a cult. Why don't you tell the committee who kidnapped Mr. Hogg in the first instance?"

"His parents rescued him from the cult."

"What about the committee, CAPUT? They knew of this plan."

"I don't know about that."

"So we have established that a committee of parents had Mr. Hogg kidnapped, then had him deprogramed. Have you any idea how they accomplished this?"

"Therapy, I imagine," said Perry dismissively.

"They gave him electroshock and drugs to control his mind."

Perry looked rattled, but he was too well-studied not to have a comeback.

"Menninger's is the preeminent mental health facility in the U.S."

"Yes, Mr. Hudson. You would know," said Broglio. Perry looked shocked. "Haven't you yourself had treatment at Menningers?" Perry looked at me, then at Finley. "Never mind, Mr. Hudson, let's move on. How about hemp, do you know what that is?"

"Hemp?" Perry's preppy expression turned ashen.

"Yes, Hemp."

"It's a plant . . . it is used for rope."

"Do you have an agricultural background?"

"Agricultural?"

"You grew up on a farm in Butler County outside El Dorado, isn't that so?"

"Yes . . . your point?"

"Wasn't there a scandal among many farmers in the area a few years ago involving hemp?"

"What?" Perry was fidgeting in his chair and looking over at Finley and Pigg.

"Hemp or wild marijuana plants were planted all along the highway just outside the property lines of farmers, allowing a bumper crop of marijuana to be sold throughout Kansas, including here in Lawrence."

"I . . . am unaware of all that, I think something happened like that when I was in high school . . . as I recall."

"I see." Broglio looked back at me. I looked at Perry who nodded to me. I nodded to Broglio.

"Well, let's move on. Have you been spying on the HIP program?"

"Spying? I have been willing to provide my information to the University."

"But you are expecting a Fulbright scholarship in exchange."

"Well . . . those are hard to come by."

"But you're in the running."

"Many are." Perry looked at me, chagrined.

"I have no further questions," said Broglio. Finley stood.

"I have some questions."

"Why do you call it a cult?"

"HIP is not just a couple of classes on the humanities and great books. If that were so, it would have no hold on students. It is a total environment. They take an inexperienced, sensitive eighteen-year-old who is influenced by the professors in class, and he gets so involved that he ignores his other classes or drops them. They all go to parties where they drink copious amounts of alcohol. I know—I've been to them."

This drew laughter.

"They go to lectures, out-of-class meetings, Latin Gregorian chant. They take Latin classes offered through HIP. A few years ago, they spent an entire semester on a small, medieval Irish island, and many students converted there, or at the French monastery they discovered."

Then Margaret Schmead jumped in and asked some questions:

"You mentioned the alcohol and kidnapping. Were there any other kidnappings or druggings?"

"Oh, yes. They drugged a girl in the program, for sex."

"How is it you know so much?"

"I have spent time around them for a couple of years, gone to their parties, and one . . . friend from old fraternity days is now with them and I'm seeing the same things happen with him."

"Tell us more about this drugging issue."

Well, they had this party . . ."

I stood up and flashed Perry the secret Sigma Chi sign again.

"Go on, Mr. Hudson."

"That is, I don't really know but I heard they have a prostitute who joined the program."

The crowd erupted. Maggie looked at me, saddened. I looked at Apryl, who did not stand up or make any noise or gesture.

"All right, we have heard enough from this witness. We are in adjournment until next week."

Apryl got up and left. Holloway followed her. Schmead rose and stomped out.

I walked toward Quantrill's Crossing. I was intercepted by Chalmers and the gang from 1132. Chalmers held his knife at his side.

"I always knew you would finger us," said Chalmers.

"I think it was you."

"That's laughable."

"Why don't you explain to them how Finley could have known those things that were in my diary?"

Chalmers put the knife away. DeBlasio turned to Chalmers. So did the others. Chalmers raised his arm.

"Enough. I never had GK's diary."

"You blackmailed me with that. Now you've given it to them, and they're going to embarrass me, Apryl, the professors. You are a rat bastard, Chalmers."

"I'm telling you, I never had that diary, I just said that to have something over you."

"That guy had specific information about Hogg's kidnapping," said Patrick. "Writing his papers, all of that. And he's your old frat buddy!"

"Who do you think told them that?" said McDarby, "The hearing fairy? You were working with that committee."

"I didn't give them any of that," I said. "I gave them worthless misinformation for the past three months. Besides, who do you think fed Broglio the information he used on Perry to stop him from doing more damage?"

"That was good to see that pantywaist squirm," said Chalmers. "You have to find out who fed Perry the information. You have to testify."

"They can bring out things that you don't want coming out."

"Like what?" said Swensen.

"Things about Apryl, about Hogg. Can't you see they're going after Hogg?"

Chalmers shook his head. "I want to know who is behind this."

He poked me in the chest and rushed off. The other followed.

I identified now with the horror of Holy Week and the inability of words to suffice in the face of ultimate accusations. If confession was good for the soul, I needed a serious dose.

L

CULT FEET

"AND how many times, and to what effect . . . I can't do this." I smoked one of Hogg's Marlboros and held open a *New Key of Heaven* prayer book as Maggie and I sat in the back of the hearse looking out at the stunning Saturday in April.

"Hogg is getting worse," she said.

"How did Perry know so much about Hogg?"

"It doesn't take much to know what is going on in HIP."

"Maggie . . . I did not tell anybody about you." She looked into my eyes. "And I don't care what Chalmers says, I'm not going to be intimidated."

"So you'll become Catholic to spite him?"

"I don't know if I can."

"Vouloir, c'est pouvoir."

"To want . . . is to enable something."

"To want to is to be able to."

"You're like a French Sancho Panza."

'Quebecois."

"Okay, Quebec-sauce."

"Is that all I am to you, a curiosity?" She took my hand. I saw tears in her eyes.

"You are amazing."

"But you . . . love her."

"Love? . . . I'm beginning to wonder if anyone knows what it is."

"L'amour est comme le vent, nous ne savon pas d'où il vient."

"Okay, love is like the wind and we don't know . . . uh—"

311

"Nobody knows where it comes from."

"Your father really had a quiver full of sayings."

"That is from Balzac."

"Maybe Balzac will help me to convert."

It was two days since the first hearing, and all eyes were on me. I had tried to resist her, but I was weak. Neither of us stopped to consider the irony of her helping me prepare for my first confession.

"I am going to have to publicly decide whether all of this was a ruse of college life."

"We take on the identities we need to survive," she said.

"Right now, I'd rather be Nixon—anyone else but me."

"I have to confess something—"

"I'm the one supposed to be practicing for confession."

"What if you knew things about me that were unforgivable?"

"Is this in the catechism? I think I have to forgive if I am to be forgiven. Right?" She hugged me close.

"But would you forgive me if I said that—"

I pushed her away.

"We have to keep our hands off each other if this is going to work. Now, where were we? Impure desires in thought and deed?"

"And how many times," she said, snickering.

We had avoided going any farther than kissing. I knew Maggie was trying to reform herself. And I was not sure how much our fling was revenge on Apryl. How often it seemed that love and betrayal shared a common thread, two sides of the shield of youth.

"Roughly thirty-five thousand and forty lustful and impure thoughts."

Maggie cracked up and fell over in her seat. She looked good. But right now, I was just trying to get through this process and figure out what to do with the university hearings. Maggie was right to question Hogg's status in this world. Maybe he didn't belong in the university anymore. The professors were not responsible for every problem the students had. Hogg could not turn to his parents. Like me, he had no parents anymore; both of us were lost boys.

"I heard that Hogg made a wild bull pray the rosary."

"I was there," I said.

"I wouldn't be surprised if he raised Haney from the dead at the fair."

"Like the burning coals of St. Thomas?"

"What do you mean?" I covered my hand. She took my hand and looked at the scar.

"You're not good at hiding that."

"I thought Apryl was pure."

Maggie looked up at me, eyes of azure lapis and emeralds.

"Now you think she isn't?" she said.

"I know *I'm* not."

"I don't think you know what is going on in Apryl's soul any more than you do your own."

"I think Apryl betrayed the program . . . and all of us."

"Don't be so sure." Maggie was agitated. I knew girls could bond even in rivalry. I'd seen it in the sororities.

"She knows more about the committee and the administration than she pretends. She and the vice chancellor . . ."

Maggie looked up into my eyes.

"She really hurt you," Maggie said.

"Is this about my coming into the Church, or about over analyzing us?"

"I think you are ready for confession." She walked out in a huff.

φ

At St. Johns, I stood with the sinners, young and old—men and women taking instruction to marry a beautiful bride or to satisfy a curiosity about the faith. Drive-thru for your sins.

My heart beat wildly as I approached the box. I had been over and over it in my mind. How could I do the thing I did and then blithely come in and say I was sorry?

I walked in. The sun shone through the other side of the screen, and I could make out Father Connell's silhouette. I knelt on the pad in front of the screen. It was mysterious.

"Bless me, Father, it's been . . . never since my last confession."

"Go ahead," said Connell. I had worked through most of the commandments, the detailed examination of conscience. Lust had been a breeze. I told him how I had lied and pretended, been a fraud in a circle of hell not yet charted. I had something else to confess.

"I have fornicated on a number of occasions during college, maybe six times, no, eight—the last was recently, at a quarry, skinny dipping, and it was more than once. I guess that makes nine."

"Go on."

"This is going to sound strange, and I don't believe it myself . . . but I was with a different girl, same quarry, we were impure and did everything but, well . . . I guess everything . . . I'm not sure how—she says she's pregnant, but I have my doubts."

"She either is or she isn't."

"I don't know that we even had sex in any traditional sense . . ."

"Did you do the act to completion?"

"There was a completion, but I am not sure if it was us—or just me. Uh . . . we were in the water . . . uh, well, am I supposed to get into gory details?"

He cleared his throat. "Let's just say, this whole Church started in a cloud of mystery about a pregnancy, and look how that turned out."

I had to stifle laughter.

"You see, there are wounds in our souls, from original sin, but also from the self-created wounds, and God has the way to cure those wounds. But he sends us on a journey, like the Fisher King in the legend of the Grail, and we must seek after the things God has put in our heart to find peace and healing. His capacity to forgive is infinite, His love for you is deeper than an ocean."

I paused, touched by this speech. I started into the act of contrition: "O my God, I am heartily sorry for having offended thee," but I kept stumbling over it. I was still numb from seeing Finley in Apryl's bed and the image of them.

"Father . . . I am not sure I can finish the act of contrition. I don't know if I am really sorry. I don't know if I really have faith. I am guilty of dissembling, of fraud, of pretending to be all things to all people. Now they think I've betrayed the program."

"Have you?"

"Yes . . . no. I don't know. I'm no Judas."

"We're all Judases in the making. That's what sin is, a betrayal, the ultimate betrayal of our Father. Most Catholics have one foot in the Church, one foot in the world, sometimes dancing between the two with both feet. The sin of Judas was not forgiving himself."

I told him all of it, how I had been guilty of lust, consuming lust, and fornication, but then, in some ways, I had never been purer in all my life. But now I was giving into lust with another woman. I told him about hating my father and abandoning my promises in coming to KU.

"I can't find peace in all the upheaval on campus."

"In his will we find peace. God sees into our hearts. He brings us to a new order of creation. I will absolve you, conditioned on your having the requisite contrition and intent to amend your life. You don't have to do this just because you started on this path. That can be a long process, it was for many, like Chesterton."

Father Connell had given me the choice. Once again, I was turned in a real direction, away from polar opposites. Not this or that. But this *and* that.

When he pronounced the words of absolution, I felt or wanted to feel a complete release. In some ways, I felt more guilty. If I didn't have faith, at least I had spoken the truth for once. A new order of creation? That is what I thought Apryl was—or what she meant. That is what I thought HIP was. A new country. Yet this seemed far out of reach, so many mirages on the dusty plains. I couldn't face them back at 1132. I couldn't face Maggie.

I went to Kansas City to see my aunt Teresa. For some old-fashioned confession.

LI

TRANSMISSION PROBLEMS

" I TOLD you to let your parents know what you were doing." Aunt Teresa wasted no time when I arrived. Then she grabbed me and kissed me and hugged me.

"Look how that worked out."

"Made you lose weight!"

"I can work things out on my own."

"Then why are you here." Teresa gave me a wily look. Her gray eyes were cloudy.

"I have too many decisions to make. Like the Church. What made *you* want to be Catholic?"

"That's too long ago," she said.

"Dad is upset."

"He was closer than I to conversion, let me tell you."

"What happened?"

"Look, in those days, it was not unusual for people to go to the university, meet new people and switch religions. It wasn't seen as some faux pas."

"So if it wasn't such a big deal, why did I never hear about it?"

"Your father . . . and I, well—let's just say he left in a hurry, married your mother, got disinherited, and I had my heart broken."

"You and Marin?"

She nodded, in obvious pain.

"So Dad didn't approve?"

"You could say that. Fred was the ultimate Lothario on campus, even more charismatic than he is now. He changed my life."

"How?"

"His lectures on poetry were the crown of my education."

"Was he drinking then?"

"Yes, but even that was charming. I'm not sure there was a woman on campus who . . ."

"Who what?"

She just went silent. Then she turned to me.

"You have to decide what you believe. Who you are. Only you can do it."

"That is tough . . . right now."

"What is going on with you really?" she asked pointedly. "Are you still obsessed with Apryl?"

"It's more complicated now."

She studied my face. "Maggie?" I looked at her without having to say anything. She picked up the *Kansas City Star* and showed me a front-page article about the hearings. "They left no lurid detail out."

"I do not know who told them . . . it wasn't me."

"These hearings will lead to no good."

"I decided long ago I would not betray my friends."

"Staying faithful to your principles is harder than you think."

"You told Apryl I was something of a loner—no girlfriends."

"It's true. Now you can't put on the brakes."

"What do I need to do?"

"Apryl was perhaps a bit out of your league, but I think she really wanted to give you a go. But Bernie, Maggie is . . . a bit more experienced."

"Haven't you ever been involved with someone older, a little more experienced?" I searched her eyes for signs of recognition.

"There are things, Bernard, about the past that . . . are better left that way."

She looked out the window of her kitchen on the light streaming in, the same light she used for painting and thinking about life.

"What went on between you and Fred Marin?" She turned red. "I know he wrote poems about you."

"You should talk to Fred about that."

"I'm talking to you."

"Everybody had a crush on Fred Marin. Even your father worshipped him. But they had a falling out."

"Over you?"

She did not say anything, just crossed her arms. It made sense now—the great books, all the night-reading Mom did from Dickens, Longfellow, Yeats, Shakespeare, and my father all but banning literature from the house. Between the two of them, I learned to think of it as a guilty pleasure.

"You know, nephew, there are worse things than going to California."

"Are you still teaching me?"

"You have to understand that the people you thought were perfect have feet of clay. Women are not goddesses. Much as you want them to be. You must grow up."

"There it is . . . why I always keep coming back. You are my oracle."

We embraced. I knew my talk had dredged up painful memories from the past. She made me think about life: should I stay in school, go back to 1132, be a hanger-on to tradition and the Church, or watch as things fell apart at the university?

When I arrived back home, nobody was there. Patrick and I had been noticing that Hogg was different, not his old cheerful self. He smoked with less enthusiasm. He quoted Leon Bloy: the only tragedy was not becoming a saint. Hogg's only weakness now was for Jimmy Drungole, if not just for the gems of black poetry, the inimitable way Jimmy had of phrasing and spinning things.

I called Jimmy to invite him over. While I waited, I took Hogg's diary to the basement and read it in the Apryl room, as I thought of it. I was invading his privacy, but I thought in some way Hogg was the key to everything that was happening. In this chapel of feminine enchantment, I came to know the real danger to him.

> This morning, I gave thanks after a much need movement of my bowels. In my anger, I found solace . . . for I was led to the succor of a blessed distaff of the Middle Ages, Julian of Norwich. I put down her words in this journal in the hopes that it will remind me to give appropriate thanks in digestion as well as indigestion:

> A person walks upright and the food in his body is shut in as if in a well-made purse. When the time of need arises, the purse is opened and then shut again in a most fitting fashion. And it is God who does this. For God does not disdain to serve us in the simplest natural functions.

Luther was meant to and could only have done what he did from the privy, grounded in human nature. Perhaps through scatology, he was able to reach an eschatology. Perhaps mine may come through diabolical pills which change the body's functions. Perhaps I can be assumed bodily, in the twinkling of an eye, to change into a new form.

Now I think I should take the pills, an oblation, sacrifices of goats do not please Thee, and some day, he too shall come to Chalfontbleau. I pledge it, Our Lady of the Happy Death. For me, it is either the Lutheran Church or the monastery.

So all that talk of happy death, his hearse, the talk about the glories of the martyrs—it was a dance with death. Diabolical pills? A suicide in the program would be devastating at the hearings. I looked for drugs or prescription bottles but found only cigarette butts.

Hogg had been working all week on his thesis for his independent study under Professor Courtney, a defense of *Humanae Vitae: on the transmission of human life,* and the cultural changes effected by birth control. Hogg had tried to keep his mind on it and had even scribbled a few pages that I had read with dismay. I heard a stirring upstairs.

People were arriving for Courtney's catechism. I ran upstairs, stashing Hogg's journal under his mattress.

"Boy, what you been eating?" Jimmy Drungole stood in the doorway with Hogg. As I had slimmed, Hogg had gained weight. He tended toward gaining around his chest. People were commenting now on Hogg's chest and his thighs.

"My heart leaps up," said Hogg. "Our Lady is lovely as a cloud."

Jimmy laughed: "You been hanging out in Lake Country?"

Patrick stood up, looking around for his shoes.

"You said you got some poems for me—let's hear them," said Jimmy.

Hogg stood near him in the middle of the room. What came out was a medley of poetry we had learned in HIP:

> Sweet Auburn, loveliest lady of the lea,
> How sweetly flows thy Afton toward the wine-dark sea.
> We grant its loftiness the right
> to only stand and wait,
> or break at the crags of thy feet, O lovely,
> But I was sweet and twenty, no use to kiss me.
> Whan that April in silks goes

a brave vibration, each way, those
wreathed horns I see are Triton rising from the sea
That bares her bosom to the moon on Innishfree.
The winds that howl at all hours were ne'er given in vain
As long as I am in my bed again.
The professor and Ginger
The quality of mercy strains her,
if the mob at times strains
with reeking shard and linnet wings.
The liquefaction of a sword, a horse
Ere half my days, ring swich liquor across the snow,
and miles to go, and miles to go,
a three-hour tour, every wise man son doth grow.

"That is some messed-up verse. How'd you do that?" asked Jimmy. "You and I should take our show on the road, see if we can't make a load, you see what I mean, Mister Poetry Machine?"

I looked on with jealousy as Jimmy did a sweet little dance around Hogg. I heard a noise at the front door.

"Shit, it's Courtney," said Winston, and a mass scramble ensued—a taking of places in the living room, crossing of legs, then total silence. I took up a nearby copy of *Self-Abandonment to Divine Providence* and read like an upperclassman at Cambridge.

LII

NEW HOPS OF CONTEMPLATION

"You must lay the axe to the root of believing in scripture as your faith. As Catholics, you believe in Jesus Christ and his Church, not in a book."

Courtney was laser focused today. An entourage of students sat at his feet. The living room of 1132 was packed to overflowing. This was the catechism class, an informal talk he would give to any students (or non-students) to discuss certain fundamentals of being a Catholic.

Zorn and Hess had a full case of beer, notwithstanding that it was Holy Thursday. Apryl sat far from Maggie; she wore a jumper and had her hair braided like a Roman peasant. Roy and Meg Neis sat on the floor, cross-legged. Gretchen Olaf and Patrick sat together squeezed onto the couch. Corey Tartt sat next to Lucas Raleigh.

I was shocked how pale and drawn Courtney was. He must have really taken the fasting of Lent seriously. He had that transparency Hogg talked about—the skin of monks becomes like translucent wafers, as he put it.

"It is not enough to clear part of the ground," he continued, "to trim the branches of your heart. You must cut it down, that tree that chokes out your life, that chokes out your willingness to receive Grace and Truth. Homer has Odysseus at the banquet of Alcinous seeing something like perfection. It is a reflection of the perfection of the heavenly banquet, when we will all see as we are seen. The Catholic answer to perfection is the saints, those who, through Grace, laid it all down and reflected that perfection in their daily lives."

"Scripture is poetry, inspired words of the Holy Ghost. Use it to pray, to sing the chant, to ponder, but for God's sake, don't try to interpret it!"

Laughter erupted. I had been trying to understand the saints and scripture like a pelagian or a Bible Christian. I had been reading scripture like a manual, like a chemistry text. Authority was irrelevant.

My forebears understood the need to protect and preserve the sacredness of the word, the Torah. Yet tradition was still important, almost as important as the Torah, because it was handed down.

"You are used to anesthesia; all of the world has been since the pain of World War II. Now is the end of another era. First it was manifest destiny, then the work ethic, then technology. The heresy of Americanism coined by Leo XIII. The disintegration of your world inspired us to form this program eight years ago. You worry about a silly committee hearing, about the things that they would destroy: credits, brochures, trips—worry instead about what cannot be destroyed. Worry about the unquenchable hearing, the Last Judgment. It will be a Watergate hearing like no other, everything on tape."

We needed a little break form this intensity.

"We know from scripture, tradition—from revelation—that the city of God is not of this world. We are sojourners here below, and yet we act courteous and behave as citizens, but when we come to the gate of the new city, we will know if our name is inscribed in the book. And that book is not scripture but the book of the Lamb. The city of God has a gate, and you must pass through it."

Roy and Meg clasped hands.

"It saddens me to tell you they have invaded our ranks, have come between us and teaching. They have brought in students to testify. But you must know this, even among you in this room, there is an informer. After all, this is called Spy Thursday." Chalmers's eyes raked the room. My stomach fluttered and growled as it had not in a month.

"I am not bitter. For the university has preordained the death of HIP no matter what. We know that." Courtney stared. Apryl's eyes were tearing up. Was I the great Iscariot, after all this time? Was it I? Even if all would betray, I would not. I had been a spy, yes; but I wanted to be more.

"I tell you this not so that you can try to figure out who it is. If it is meant to be, you must pray for this person. This is Holy Week. We have to strip off the falseness of self, to be like Veronica and see the image of Our Savior on the veil of our broken resolutions. It is prayer, in silence, where you will discover the truth. Where God is. As St. Peter of Alcantara says . . ."

Here, he pulled out a little volume from the pocket of his tweed jacket and read:

"In prayer, by which he means real prayer from the inner man, from the heart—what we call mental prayer— 'in prayer the inward man is directed aright, the heart purified, the truth discovered, temptation overcome, sadness avoided, the perceptions renewed.' That is the gift I leave you for your future. So close your eyes and go into the chamber of yourselves, now with me, and silently see with the eye of the mind what is there . . ."

We sat like children of our times, cross-legged at an EST seminar or before the swami. We looked inward, meditating with the eye of the mind. Seconds became minutes. I squinted an eye open at one point to see countenances at once serene and frozen.

"You must go deep within yourself . . ." Courtney was reputed to be expert at mediation. It was said he had spent some time in Tibet with a real lama. "To go inside yourself, it is necessary to drop the assumed self, the false self that prepares a face to meet the faces around it . . ."

T. S. Eliot meets Siddhartha? Yet even as I used literary reference as a defense, I found myself drifting into a cottony cloud of mind.

"You find yourself encountering what is, no longer in the realm of the frivolous or conscious concern. You are going deeper into a state where you can encounter the *Is*. Let yourself encounter within you a little heaven. Go inside the hive of yourself and allow yourself to make honey."

Just as surely, I went into a deeper state of meditation, calm—maybe even contemplation—as we sat there a few minutes at the feet of this master of the classics. I began to see something, a glow, a red inner hearth of sorts, a cool fire burning, but beyond that or within that, I don't know what, was a peace, a sense of oneness or wholeness I had not experienced before. Everything dropped away, and there was only knowing or not knowing, my inner glowing. I felt like smiling. An inner sense of smile. I have sometimes returned to in moments of greatest strife. It has never failed me. Was it God? Was it being? Was it just the stripped-away power of the mind over the body?

He then led us through an Ignatian mediation where we were with Christ himself in the Praetorium, in the trial, and feeling what he felt and responding to Pilate, "What is Truth? . . . Prophesy who it is who strikes thee."

Everything was very quiet, especially us—our minds, our bodies in suspension. How long I was in that state, I cannot say. Whether in my body or in some astral state, a cocktail of Paul Courtney, Augustine, Plato, and Robert Lowell—I did not know or care. Because I was having a dialogue in that contemplative moment, and Christ turned to me and asked me, "What is Truth, Bernard?" He spoke my name. Was this normal? Then suddenly out of that silence and utter calm, we heard loud explosions like gunfire.

"Crap," said Zorn involuntarily as he scurried out of the room. Karl looked around, laughed his booming laugh, and said, "Holy beer." It came from the basement.

"As we come out of our recollected selves," said Courtney, and he gave us permission to laugh. As it died down, everyone looked at him. "As we return to our everyday selves, let us then pray the angelic salutation."

As they started into the Hail Mary, I ran to the basement to salvage the latest batch of Champoeg.

LIII

THE BACCHANALIAN METHOD

> When I speak of darkness, I am referring
> to a lack of knowing. It is a lack of knowing
> that includes everything you do not know or
> else that you have forgotten, whatever is
> altogether dark for you because you do not
> see it with your spiritual eye. And for this
> reason it is not called a cloud of the air, but
> rather a cloud of unknowing that is between
> you and your God.
>
> — THE CLOUD OF UNKNOWING, CH. IV, V. 18

M Y comrades of the heart came to the point of return from the odyssey into the land of the Achaeans. Youth waned and the promise
of four years, the conditional paradise of college, drew on apace to the
mouth of the river. We were soon to be cast out, foundering in the seas
of doubt and despair. I had been lost in the enchanted wood, and I had
hoped to be led to knowledge and understanding, but the leopard of vice
had kept me from knowing. I thought the eyes of her who became loveliness would lead me in the straight way, but the way seemed lost.

I went to see Professor Buntrock the next morning, hung over from
drinking the exploded batch of Champoeg, which no college student
would let go to waste. A Bach fugue played on his Rega P3 turntable with

Realistic speakers. When you entered his office, you inhabited a world of thought and of the higher aspirations of mankind.

"I never tire of *The Well-Tempered Clavier*," he said as if he were drinking the sounds.

He was holding my papers. "Chaucer's Quaint Tales" was a blatant rehash of neo-feminism I had taken from several books by a German critic on Shakespearean female roles; and one on Joyce as scatological scout of the modern world, called "Portrait of the Fartist as a Jung Man."

Buntrock handed me the papers. I stared at it in disbelief.

"Brilliant, Bernie, just brilliant. You say everything I can't."

He not only gave me an A+ on the project, but he said he had circulated it as a kind of underground anomaly that thrilled other professors. He encouraged me to ride this radical Bellerophon of HIP, the Pegasus of the past, to slay the chimeras of academe and modernism.

"When you testified at the hearings on HIP, it felt like you were talking about me when you said some students were being stunted by the professors."

"Never you. You have what it takes. You should go to graduate school. I have half a dozen recommendations if you decide to do so." For me, my junior year had started in jest but now was anything but. The answer to the university was to shunt its best to graduate school to churn out more high-sounding jests.

"I don't think my psyche could withstand that level of intellectual stretching."

He wanted me to become like him—an expert in textual dissection. As much as I admired him as a teacher, I could not exchange the prison of carpet and linoleum for a prison of deconstructed texts and philosophical tasting menus.

As I was leaving his office, he said: "I read that parody on Chaucer. Very nice." He didn't even ask if I had written it.

I came back to 1132, crestfallen. Hogg was struggling to reenter reality, at least the reality of 1132. The door was shut to him, and the harder he tried, the more frustrated he became. I clung to the notion that I could bring him back to reality, that I could heal him. I brought him to the HIP lecture to cheer him up.

"So you want justice?" Marin stood facing the class. "They aren't interested in justice, Paul," said Marin as he sat down.

"What did Aeneas see as his city burned?" said Whelan. "He saw the tears in things, *sunt lacrimae rerum*." He took off his glasses and began to wipe his eyes. "Don't try to deny the tears. But looking back on things, you need to know you have done what is right, what is just. What did Aeneas say to his comrades about their terrible circumstances? *Forsan et haec olim meminisse juvabit*. One day, we will look back on this destruction with joy. He takes his father on his back. He falls in love with Dido; he leaves her to follow his duty to found Rome, and she kills herself. That isn't exactly a series of happy endings. What Aeneas finds out, we hope you will find out too. That however wonderful this life is, and it is wonderful, full of so many beautiful and lovely things. It ought to work, things ought to pan out. But something is wrong. There is a fly in the ointment. Things get messy, even twisted and tragic in life."

"They forgot the lecture on Aeneas, Chester," said Marin. "Don't you know, you will look back even on all of this with *joy* unspeakable? You think this is tragedy, an American tragedy! It's not. You're seeing it all go up in flames. Joy. Have you ever had the joy of putting your father on your back and seeking new shores? You don't know anything about the child being father of the man until you do that!"

"Well, he's right," said Courtney in a reflective pose, "this idea that you can just testify and then everything will be all right. It's very American. Theodore Dreiser tried to capture American justice in his novel, *An American Tragedy*. What you end up with is not justice, but a sense of loss. A sense of revenge. Is education just a game you win or lose?"

I sat with Patrick and McDarby. Chalmers stood in the back of the class with Dom Broglio. Trish sat next to DeBlasio.

"This kid murders a girl he gets pregnant," said Whelan. "Part of the novel takes place in Kansas City, not far from here. We wonder if you understand the madness that love can create."

The modern dilemma. Follow your saint, and when she becomes pregnant, kill her. I wanted Apryl to get justice. I wanted Finley dead.

"We want to bring our leaders down when they have done something wrong," cut in Courtney. "You want a hearing every time you catch someone in authority telling a lie or fibbing. But that isn't justice. That is puritanism. We are not advocating corruption but, instead, justice. Which in Plato's sense, you may recall, meant mind your business. Is it our business to right every wrong at this university? Or only defend the one principle that is your birthright? The right of a professor to teach the Truth."

"So how do we find the Truth?" asked Whelan as he scanned the class with his penetrating eyes. "Through rhetoric in a court of law? Don't you have to believe in the concept of law and justice before you can have law? We believe in the law, but does the university? Perhaps we will find out, perhaps we will not. But we have to insist that you be students, and we'll be professors, and we'll try to separate you from all the controversy."

"There is something that does not love a wall," said Marin, "and you do not like that we are different from you, or that someone in authority is not an underling. You would like to tear down all the walls. What if there are no laws, asks Thomas More—what if we are just facing the devil without law? We have to let the devil use the system just as much as we do. Don't kid yourselves. You are controlled by nothing but rules. You violate all principle when it pleases you. Do you think the Greeks lived by the pleasure principle alone? Or did they find a mean, a balance by which to unite the Dionysian wine drinking with the Apollonian brilliance of intellect?"

"That's right," said Courtney, "some of you are bothered by what we are asking you to read. Euripides in his play, *The Bacchae*, reflects the group excitement of music, of dancing, of wine. Losing yourself in a physical wonder. We encourage you to drink wine, to dance, to listen to music. But some of you think that is sinful, while others think it is license to lose yourself in a cult of pleasure. You want to be traditional hippies with a little less hair. There is a via media—a middle way, a royal way."

I heard the music—Courtney's voice, mellow but infused with bittersweet pain.

"Love's compass turns, and you find yourself on an axis not of your own making or design. Have you ever stopped to consider the revolutions of love, the orbits of beauty? You find it in the other, as Dante said, in the love that made the sun and all the other stars."

At that, he fell silent, leaning his head to one side, balancing his fine chin on his cupped hand. Courtney held us captive: shaman, high priest, Fisher King. During this interlude, this shadow of reflection, Fred Marin sat calmly, not smoking, not moving, not posing in a fighting position.

"You have heard the oriental wisdom of old," continued our guide into the world beyond. "When the student is ready, the master will appear. But you have also heard that when the lover is willing, the beloved will appear. How many of you have stopped to consider why your bodies run wild and your spirits find no rest, why you feel this expansion in your being that can only be satisfied by 'the other?' Donne's poetry was nothing but a study of 'the other.' But can we dissect love or decline its verb? It is the final verb. It declines us."

"First you dance, then you die," said Marin. Nobody made a sound. "Don't you know that the waltz you are about to experience is about death? The soldier comes to the waltz in his dress uniform. The next day he must go into battle. These are rituals of death. That is why you study at the university, to contemplate the battle—and ultimately death itself. The inevitable hour."

"You are on the edge of discovery," said Courtney, who had not finished his thought. "Like Dante, you are asking yourselves how is this possible, how does Beatrice lead me on with her beauty and then make me feel so foolish because she sees it all, and I see nothing? Dante wants to return to the divided world of Florence where civilization seems to be running over the edge and into a pit, and you know you cannot go back and tell them all, for you will be seen as a madman. All you can do is quietly tell your song."

Courtney spoke as if in a different realm.

"You will see the roads extend before you, the path of least resistance in career and family, and some of you will take this, and some of you will lose the way, becoming so confused with the steps up the mountain, worrying that it leads nowhere. And some may turn from the muse and ask what good is it to you or your life.

"I would tell you only this: do not try to reach for the highest plane or the final story on the trip up the mountain. Return to Lady Philosophy in humility and to Lady Poetry, for by their attraction, you came to the mount in the first place, and that will carry you. The real is real if it is what it is. Do not abandon poetry but sing it all the days of your life. Never give up on your odyssey of wonder. Even if you find yourself lost in the dark wood of middle age, don't forfeit your treasure map."

Class broke up that day, and the group, Mississippi and Ohio, converged at the Crossing. But I needed to see Courtney.

LIV

THE GATE OF THE CITY

The best lack all conviction, while the worst
Are full of passionate intensity.

— *WB Yeats, "The Second Coming"*

I walked from Strong Hall across Jayhawk Boulevard to his office in the concrete architectural abortion of Wescoe Hall. The apple blossom had spun its brilliant web of white, and the cherry bud raged infernal with red; the nymphs of Mount Oread were spreading their wiles about campus.

His office smelled of musty leaves and old books. He was bent over a volume of Rimbaud, wolfing down a chili dog from a campus vending machine. I was surprised how a thin man like him could put one away in two bites.

"My doctor says I have to give these up. But I'm a New Yorker."

"What do doctors know?"

"So, you have finally come," he said bluntly.

"I find myself again at the outskirts of the city."

"How will you gain entrance?"

"A ruse."

"You can't fool Charon who ferries souls across Styx."

"At least I have Virgil."

"Have you talked to Professor Marin?"

Teresa said I should, that it might help me understand my father.

"No, I have not," I finally replied.

"The city is in flames. Priam is dead."

"I am a stranger invited in, an intruder." I was talking in parable with Courtney.

"Why can't you turn the key and walk through?"

I don't think I knew until I knew it right in front of him.

"I feel it is a shortcut. I don't think I can end my education like this."

"You mean, you want to go to graduate school?"

"No . . . is this all there is? Where is the idea of a university? I have few languages well, and I am pitiful in the fine arts and philosophy."

Courtney smiled. His face was paler, his blue eyes more opaque than I had ever seen them.

"You think you can get an education because you tasted at the well. But what you have to understand is that the reason you tasted it is because you could not have the education you wanted and still get to the gate."

"You mean you brought us to taste of knowledge but knew we could not have a classical education? So you led us to the love of God?"

"You see, none of you—though you are probably closer than most— have the grounding for a classical education. You needed a crash course. You will have the rest of your lives to fill in the gaps—language, philosophy, theology. That is not why you came here."

"For what, then?"

"For friendship, of course. It is right there in Aristotle. He says without friends, no one would choose to live *though he had all other goods.*"

I paused, dumbfounded. It is what he had talked about from the beginning—*The Odyssey*, Aristotle, Augustine, Cervantes. It was all for friendship.

"You have something they cannot take from you. You have become kindred spirits. With that, a man can live his life."

I nodded thoughtfully and then came to the real reason I was here:

"Do you think I am ready to come into the Church?"

He paused, looking neither at me nor away. I had asked him to be my sponsor.

"Do you know the Mass?"

I sat there for a moment, thinking. Courtney looked plaintively at me.

"Do you know who burned down St. Mary's Church?" I asked.

"Maybe I am responsible." I looked at him, startled. "Not directly, but by encouraging students to experiment with Latin liturgy. The kingdom is not of this world, but while we're here, there are many difficulties and disagreements about what to do here on earth. So Traditio Latinae created animosity, and some nut burned it down."

"I did not deliver HIP up for Finley."

"Someone else did."

"I once had agreed to betray you, but that was before I knew."

"They call you G. K.?"

"Yes."

"Chesterton was one of the leading Catholic apologists, influencing conversions, and he had not been received formally into the Catholic Church. It took him twenty years."

"I thought I could leapfrog up to the royal road. It is harder than I thought."

"Yes."

"Will it do any harm to wait?"

"They also serve who only stand and wait. I'll stand as your sponsor if you want."

Again, he looked down, smiled, and nodded. I walked out without saying goodbye, without needing to say a thing. With a Milton quote, he had given me permission to defer.

I do not remember seeing or looking at anything on my way home. I did not need eyes to come back to 1132, the womb of friendship. Courtney had given me the final lecture.

I had yet to reconcile with my father—and to talk to Marin. I did not want to have to face the severity of Marin. So I returned to 1132 filled to the brim with regnant springtime hope. But this ebullience was short lived.

LV

THE INEVITABLE HOUR

I T was our landlord who was the Hermes of doom. Ralph Penshurst came to tell us that his world had collapsed.

"Boys, can I talk with you?"

"Sure, we're only studying the most important events and words of history, but we always have time for you, Mr. Penshurst." I was prepping myself and Hogg for the comprehensive Western civilization exam. Hogg was doing fairly well with the secular names. But whenever we hit St. Thomas or St. Augustine, he froze. I shut the Western civ. notes, the canned stuff.

"All my investments were tied up in bonds and interest rate sensitive funds. It's come to this: I have to give you notice." Penshurst's face was white.

Notice to us was: look at her, take notice of her hips, her legs, the shapeliness. *Notice* had no legal significance to us. For if any of us had read in law, we would have known that here was a superior interest in the land.

"Notice?" snorted Winston, ever mindful of rents. A Sheen tape was playing.

"Boys . . . I have agreed to sell."

"Sell . . ." Ross could not go on. He had decided on a seminary on the East Coast. He turned off the tape recording.

"Yes . . . I'm afraid this is your last hurrah. The lease runs out at the end of July. But many of you are graduating anyway, right?"

We looked at him. Hogg was not. It was doubtful he would even pass some of his classes. Swensen was not. Zorn was leaving school to

333

get married to Martha and live in Oregon, raise hops, and mosey into a beer-happy sunset. I was headed West.

"I know you have a kind of . . . legacy here. You've been good tenants for almost ten years."

"Maybe we can make a deal with the new owner?" I turned to Patrick, pleading. "We have to save 1132—maybe we could buy it."

Patrick just shook his head. "You're in debt as it is for rent, how can you expect to finance the purchase of this place?"

"I don't know who the new owner is," said Penshurst in a befuddled tone. "Some agent who cannot disclose his principal. Besides, the price is too high, boys. In these bad economic times, it's a deal I just can't refuse." Penshurst scratched his head and let his weary eyes wander the room, to the blue and pink Virgin. DeBlasio looked up at that comment. I wondered if he could get a relative to lean on the buyer, take less, and force a sale to us.

Penshurst patted McDarby on the back and left with his head hanging down, swallowed up in the misty green of spring. The others were dumbstruck. I knew I had to do something. With the HISS hearings in full swing, graduation seemed now like a prison sentence of thirty to life with no poetry. The end was surely coming, the world was too much with us, the barbarians had breached the gate. And I couldn't help thinking that the information I provided had in some way lead to this debacle.

φ

And now it was before me, or rather I was before it: St. John's eighty-year-old brick cornerstone. Spindly-legged youths rushing to religion and marriage bounded up the steps, holding hands with their ripe fiancées. I was affianced to an idea, uncertain of the outcome, and it was the vigil of decision, the eve of conversion or destruction.

Palm Sunday's Mass was not the Latin Mass, the Tridentine rite that Dom Broglio had uttered like a dervish of old, spinning with the censor as white smoke rose above the gold-fringed robes.

But it was the entry into the Mass that had so captivated me at Hess's farm the preceding Sunday. It seemed so long ago that I had nearly entered the courts of the Almighty amid a cleansing smoke, where the priest in robes of gold had protected the sanctum sanctorum, the Ark, the great secret of youth.

Introibo ad altare Dei

Ad Deum qui laetificat Juventutem meam

I had ascended the mountain and seen a vision, a burning bush, and realized that in going up to the altar of God, I had encountered the giver of joy and youth. Determined to discover the secret of my youth, I had dabbled in the secret of youth and existence, of generative power and knowledge. But had I attained anything like faith?

Pater, si non potest hic calix transire nisi bibam illum, fiat voluntas tua.

I was moved by the sadness of the betrayal and the acceptance of the cup, not my will but thine. I was more terrified than ever that I might truly know what was on the other side of the veil at the altar. There in two pews were the girls of Ole Miss and the gents of 1132, smiling proudly, holding candles.

I just kept coming back to the realization of a person speaking to me in my contemplative journey. I really did not know there was anything out there other than my racing thoughts, my ego, or the brilliant cries of other lonely writers—until that moment. There was something there.

I was handed a candle as I walked into the sanctuary, smelled the warm vanilla air, and lighted my candle from the flame of another's as I stood at the back waiting for Professor Courtney. I knew that if he showed up, I would have to go through with it. My heart beat quickly. I saw sponsors going two by two into pews, entering the ark of their journey to eternity. I had to have my sponsor; I could not come in without him.

But he was nowhere to be found. I wanted to go through with it and drown in a ceremony of light, to know the culmination of a covenant made to my forefathers in Babylon, in Egypt, in Canaan. I wanted to find that center and enter the Promised Land. Moses saw the burning bush, but he never entered the Promised Land.

It was dark in the church. As my heart beat quickly and the organ began to play the interlude to the Easter vigil, I felt my breathing turning heavy. Soon, I could not breathe and moved silently as if impelled by a force within me and outside of me at the same time.

Before I knew it, I had slipped out the back, extinguishing my candle quietly in the vestibule. I crossed Kentucky Street and walked quickly up an alley. I turned to look back at the church. I saw a slender figure ascending the steps. Had Courtney come after all? I started back toward St. Johns. But I saw DeBlasio and Trish coming out and looking around, calling out my name.

I turned and headed back toward 1132 Ohio, got my car and drove out to Wells Overlook to view the stars on this cloudless spring night. I looked at the pulsating lights from the little city on the hill and realized I had passed by, had foregone something. Maybe in another year, maybe in a different time. Then, as if to rescue myself, I thought of my first night looking at the stars at Hess's place. Penelope would not mind a knight on horseback, even this Knight of Mt. Oread who had failed to sup the Holy Grail. Another cup awaited me.

LVI

ARISTOTLE IN A BOTTLE

A MINUTE can create an experience, which a moment may reverse. Our minute was coming to an end. For days, students from dorms and apartments around the area had been lined up around the block during the evening to get Champoeg beer. Soon we would have enough to do a wire transfer into an account in Europe.

It would be the last waltz sponsored by the university, in this union, under the auspices of the Humanities Integration Program due to cuts in funding. It was the site of the radical burning, now a radical turning, with Chalmers the common denominator. Now they were the radicals being burned down. Two hundred had already passed under the garland-and-flower-decked trellis. Chalmers had seen to it that champagne was added to the punch.

The lights were turned down low, chiffon dresses sparkled in the lambent wash of a thousand candles. Trish Ellsworth was responsible for the many candles. Corsages and bouquets abounded. Cuff links and rings sparkled. All the men looked uniform in their orderliness. Tuxedoes brought us fully into relief and raised the beauty of our partners to new heights in the dance on the broad parquet floor. I went outside of the student union and met Hess at his horse trailer.

When I came back inside, Beauty was afoot. Maggie was a quick study, a fine dancer, and fetching in her burgundy silk dress that Hogg had helped me to pick out downtown at Weaver's. This drew looks from the gals of Ole Miss. Then Apryl walked in, flowing like a waterfall in a wispy, lime-green chiffon that hid her belly.

Courtney stood by Whelan and Marin. Courtney beheld a constellation of his students turning and turning in perfect rhythm, the music and the man, the sparkle and the girl and the hair and the *profumo*, the delightful valence of music, man and woman.

At the right moment, Karl gave me Penelope, and Corey gave me the armor, greaves, mail, helmet, breastplate, and sword. The horse was festooned with a purple and gold blanket courtesy of the Society for Anachronism. I was an anachronism, reaching for a chivalry I hoped was there. Chalmers ran toward the horse and yelled: "Russ, what are you doing, you fool!" But I did not budge. I raised the visor slowly.

"It's me, Rich."

"G. K.? What the hell are you doing in armor? How did you even fit? You're going to fall off that horse and kill yourself."

Out of the wings, from the table where sat the professors and their wives came a shout of approval. I lowered the visor and urged Penelope forward.

"It is not I—I am No Man," I was calling out to the crowd.

"You are nobody without the Church," said Chalmers in a low voice, then he bowed to the crowd. Pockets of dancers, wallflowers, tuxedos, and parents began a murmur of discomfort.

"You're the one who insisted I not enter the Church," I said.

And Chalmers responded, "I knew you were a pussy."

"I haven't figured out the rules of Elfland."

"Did Grigson put you up to this?"

"Hess said we could use a call to arms."

"Get off that horse before it shits all over everything."

"She already relieved herself on the chancellor's lawn."

Chalmers smiled. "Carry on, Knight of Mount Oread."

I began to lift an arm to the helmet, the creaking metal of this imitation armor making a terrific racket. I saw Apryl approach, smiling at the sight of me in shining armor. Maggie smiled. They were my list field in the joust of youth.

"I call the fight," said Chalmers.

"À la guerre," said Corey.

"Listen to me, you sons and daughters of the program," I said in a French accent of sorts. "I was born in this age of iron—to bring in an age of gold."

Hogg ran in a frenzied cheer. He screamed, "I am your Sancho!" Soon, he was surrounded by students, lifting glasses to him and me.

Hogg, with the help of Russ Grigson, mounted up on Penelope. Someone gave me a champagne glass.

"We salute you, oh great teachers of the heart, and we swear our allegiance through this difficult war." *Hear! hear!* went up all around. I looked at Maggie, then Apryl. Jimmy stood by Apryl. Above were the erstwhile boardroom stowaways, leaning in a bunch over the railing, trying to get a glimpse of the professors and their armor-sealed companion. Patrick looked down and pointed at Jimmy standing with Apryl, holding her hand on the dance floor.

Hogg whispered in my ear. "You know what Sancho would do now?" I could not turn my head. "He would defecate off the horse."

After reading what was in his diary, I thought I had better get off that horse fast. I tried to make a lithe move, but instead the whole weight of the armor shifted and threw me off the horse. I came crashing down onto the parquet with a clatter worthy of battle. Then Hogg fell on top of me. Several pieces of armor came off and clattered in several directions on the dance floor. A chorus of laughter erupted. I sat up, popped my visor, looked at Hogg, and we both laughed.

In rescue, Diana Dietz stepped away from the shadows out onto the dance floor. Diana curtsied and rustled the hem of her robin's egg blue taffeta dress as if she were all packaged and ribboned as a gift to Paul Courtney. Swede stood next to McDarby, agog. Silence descended on the ballroom, and all looked on. Diana pursed her full lips and opened them. Slowly, the air filled with the gentle song of Ben Jonson, "To Celia":

> *Drink to me only with thine eyes,*
> *And I will pledge with mine . . .*

Hogg helped me up. Grigson led Penelope off the floor. Corey gathered up the armor. I sang with her in my baritone. Then the entire gathering of young and old met her chorus with sympathetic echoes.

> *Or leave a kiss but in the cup,*
> *And I'll not ask for wine.*
> *The thirst that from the soul doth rise*
> *Doth ask a drink divine;*
> *But might I of Jove's nectar sup,*
> *I would not change for thine.*

Glasses were raised. I looked at Marin, who had snuck several glasses of champagne. Courtney stepped forward reluctantly onto the floor, took the hand of Diana, and led her to a chair. He bowed to me. I bowed and made a creaking noise that generated another chorus of laughter.

"I had hoped to speak of lovely things this evening," began Courtney, "to tell tales of heroism and entertain by delight—like Odysseus to King Alcinous of Scheria. For those parents who have forgotten *The Odyssey*, Odysseus is on his way home after years of captivity and trial, and he has many adventures along the way, including washing up on shore and encountering the princess Nausicaa and then entering the palace of her father the king. And wherever Odysseus went, there were festivities, fine wine and music, and always stories. But finally, when he arrives at home, his wife Penelope's suitors have taken over his home and ravaged it, and they are trying to take from him all that was his, and his wife and son alone are faithful. So he must drive the suitors from her home. Tonight, we have Penelope here." He went and patted the horse's snout, which brought approving laughter.

"And I suppose tonight, I feel here a bit like Odysseus. There have been many adventures along the way, so many that I have delighted in those adventures. Yet when I think of my true purpose, the education of young minds and the assault on the castle that has been taken over by the destroyers of education, the modernists and skeptics, it is with pride that I observe the knight mounted on horseback, the fitting symbol of gentlemen warriors. And so, I raise my glass to all of you. I toast you, I commend you, and I say, 'Godspeed and ride on, roughshod if need be, but ride on!'"

Up went a cheer. I grabbed some champagne from a tray and drank. The orchestra struck up a reprise of "The Blue Danube" and couples drifted onto the floor. At this, the gents of 1132 came down en masse and found their dates. Swensen moved toward Diana, whose steps were blocked out perfectly, even as her eyes were fixed on him. Others paired off. Only Apryl and Maggie were left.

I walked toward them. Their eyes met mine in anticipation. Apryl had offered herself to me, but I could never know whether this was some new ruse to show the world she could not be conquered or whether the Lady Godiva of HIP was sincere. Maggie moved toward me. She was too eager. Things had happened so quickly, and yet, there was something radiant about her.

Finally, I turned and offered my armored glove. Maggie took it. We moved among the others. I tried to dance with her, but I could only move in half time. I saw Hogg dancing awkwardly with Louise Courtney.

"You are dashing as a knight . . . it's crazy, Jack."

"It's Jack-in-the-box to you," I returned. I twirled her and nearly fell over. She giggled as I brought her back to earth. I noticed her eyes, fixed as planets while they spun around, as the world turned into a gauze of swirls and colors.

"You dance well. You couldn't have learned this just with Diana's lessons."

"She's a good teacher. But you're right. The Ursuline sisters taught polka and waltz. You had to dance in my family."

'You move very well . . . in many ways."

She looked into my eyes with reproof, then sadness. "I wanted to talk to you about that."

"We'll have plenty of time for talk at the after-party." I looked around; Marin glared from the shadows.

"Marin is staring at us," said Maggie.

"Me."

"Why you?"

"Because it's time," I said bowing, and I walked from the floor. McDarby was now dancing with Apryl. I didn't care.

The brisk limbs and alabaster arms of youth smelled like candles. The older folks creaked their limbs and bursa to the point of bursting and thought youth had come back, the young men dreamed dreams and fled to the protected chambers above the dance floor. I looked above and saw the cavaliers of 1132 Ohio on the balcony headed to an upper room reserved for chancellors.

He was drinking champagne as I approached him. Easter was past. No more Lenten penances.

"Quite an outfit," said Marin.

"Not Nixon or a ghost in a sheet, but it will have to do."

"Hard to dance in that?"

"I would like to get out of it." I took off my gloves. Inside of one, I felt the poem, laced with sweat. I had brought it for this moment.

"A lovely dancer, Margaret," he said. "I wouldn't have left her out on the floor like that."

"No, you wouldn't."

"And I wouldn't have left Professor Courtney at the altar."

"I heard you're not so quick on the spiritual draw."

"You can't help Tom Hogg," he said, evading my slight.

"He just needs a little help on Latin."

"He's failing everything."

"It's not his fault."

"You mean it's not your fault," said Marin.

Tom was now a surrogate for whatever was between us. Why had he singled me out, what had I done? He was the head lion in the pride, and he let everyone know it. Now it was just him and me and two plastic glasses with hollow stems.

"You hate me for a reason," I said. "Because you feel guilty about Teresa."

"We saw you coming from a long way off, Bernard."

"'Louise, why are you grieving . . . is this April unrelieving?'"

His expression changed as if I had summoned the dead spirit of King Saul.

He drank and smoked and stared at me with something like scientific curiosity. He blew a plume in my face. I pulled out the damp poem from my glove and recited.

"'O Miriam, what is this impeaching, or an act of student teaching?'" I paused. "That doesn't really work. The meter is off, don't you think? May it should be, 'or is it just an act of student teaching?' Approaches a more anapestic rhythm."

He just stared at me, searching my eyes in the bluish haze of smoke and Strauss. Somehow in that three-four time beating within my veins, it descended on me as a revelation.

"Miriam . . . is that a reference to my mother?"

"I don't hate you, Bernard," he said finally. "But you might want to stop probing into past indiscretions. It has a funny way of bringing out violence in people."

My heart pounded faster as I stood my ground. I checked his hands to make sure there was no flash of steel.

"Why did you hurt my aunt Teresa?" His eyes narrowed. "That's who your poem is about, isn't it?"

He grabbed my breastplate and yanked a piece of the armor off with his bare hands. He showed his teeth. The unthinkable presented itself to my mind.

"Miriam Mintz. Were you . . . involved with . . . my mother?"

He said nothing.

"Is that why my father hates KU, why he transferred to Berkeley, why he didn't want me coming to KU?"

Marin leaned in.

"You think you know the answers? You don't even know the questions."

He threw down the armor plate, causing a considerable clatter as the orchestra brought the waltz to a conclusion. Several students and parents stared at Marin walked off, as if the noise was an accompaniment to the timpani drums of the waltz. I thought about my mother, Marin, the poem. And what did he mean about seeing me coming from a long way off? Did he have advance notice of coming to KU?

LVII

TOM WAITS FOR NO MAN

This is the point to which, above all, the attention
of our rulers should be directed, that music and
gymnastics be preserved in their original form, and
no innovation made . . . for any musical innovation
is full of danger to the whole state, and ought to
be prohibited.

— PLATO: THE REPUBLIC, BOOK IV

The waltz after-party at 1132 Ohio had gained the ascendancy and was *comme il faut* on campus. In this pageantry of passages, 1132 was ablaze with grins and wine; light and festive Athenas combined in the collaboration of moonlight and music. Girlish giggles, leers, strutting, exaggerated poses, and unreflected mating rituals. Wood floors do not a drawing room make, and this house had thrown off the shackles of propriety and even good taste as the evening wore on.

For a moment, I forgot the revelation, wrapped up in the creamy music of Stevie Wonder, mouthing words I could barely remember, but a wistful song about winter and fall, and being fooled by April. I was dancing in the middle of the room with Maggie—on a distant cloud.

Women came and went, leaving conversational crumbs.

"Order of the night . . . we just love your party, that we establish this order of the night, or knight, that we should all be Catholic in a kind of atheistic way . . . so that if God thought it proper to speak sometime—"

344

Stacey and Kim were laughing at their own jokes, even when nobody else understood them, while Gretchen Olaf and Diana Dietz flocked to a corner of the room underneath the scowling eye of the blue Virgin, staring at the isle of Lesbos, carrying on in their private language. Clark and Jacques were deep into Champoeg and Champagne stupors.

"What are they doing here?" asked Diana.

"They just walked in," said Gretchen, staring at the happy couple.

"Not very fulfilling." Diana's pun caused some blushing and titillation.

"They actually support HIP. They were in the program in 1971," Clark said. "One of them is a Jew."

Diana screwed up her face tight: "They say that a Jew destroyed St. Mary's church."

"Not this Jew," I said, holding up a matchbook and lighting a match with one hand, flipping a beant into the air. It landed on my lip; I lighted it and blew out a smoke ring.

Stacey grabbed my cigarette, sucked in, and blew out an enormous ring, double the size of mine. The girls clapped louder for hers.

"You know the last two popes were Jews," said Zorn, barely coherent.

"No," I said, "but the first two definitely were."

There was a long pause, and suddenly, Zorn spit out his sip of Champoeg, laughing so hard he fell down. Gretchen was also honking. Martha dragged Zorn away to the cheese table, a ruins of crumbled Ritz and jagged cheddar blocks. A Steely Dan song had just ended on Ross's high-tech sound system. Swensen picked up her scent and followed.

"O, mistress mine, where art thou foaming?" He swooned mockingly. Diana showed her disapproval of the alcoholic elation by pursing her lips and looking away. Ross changed the song to Waits's "Lonely."

"I hate this song—it's too sad." Swensen beheld Diana's stature. He moved toward her. The record changed again. The lilting rasps of Tom Waits's "Little Trip to Heaven on the Wings of Your Love" came moaning into the air. Swensen moved closer and started to sing with the music. Diana moved away, demure and desirable—huntress becoming the hunted.

Swensen grabbed her—the solid waist, the moving part of her. She became still, rigid, afraid. Although her hair was flowing and swirling with her every move.

Jacques stepped in my direction. Clark wandered across the floor to dance with Martha.

"Don't listen to him, G. K.," said Jacques.

"No, he's right. Someone burned down St. Mary's. Might as well be a Jew, right?"

"When you put it this way . . ." Jacques was stone cold sober. "Truly it is martyrdom, the Mass, St. Mary's, Lefebvre, the pope—all of it, just martyrdom."

"Yeah, but at least we suffer before we die," I added. At that moment Apryl glided into the room. "Speaking of suffering."

Apryl still looked glorious, her face a radiant planet. I tried to turn away from her as she approached. I watched as Swensen pulled Diana to himself and his lips met hers.

"Way, Swede!" Ross was barely conscious.

"All right!" yelled McDarby.

"Better than a Hurlbut!" squealed Winston. He had recited all of his extant poetry to Sue Hurlbut and Laura Hull. Maggie danced with Kozokowski.

"Lude-cididees." DeBlasio was clearer drunk than sober. Trish hit him on the arm. DeBlasio grabbed her and imitated the kiss they'd all just seen.

Chalmers came up beside me holding a highball glass in one hand and three cigarettes in the other, one of which had a crumpled handmade look. I smelled the rank plant.

"That wacky weed got me in a raft of trouble a couple of years ago," I said.

"Gather them while they may," said Chalmers.

"Schlayex!! . . . shlacks!" chanted the group.

"Beer sales are brisk."

"You keeping the journal entries straight?"

"No, crooked as hell," I gleamed. "Double entry heaven."

"Where's Hogg?" said Chalmers.

"I thought he was up here."

"You should be keeping an eye on him."

"I will," I said.

"You think you're too good to be Catholic?" said Chalmers.

"Maybe I should join Jacques and the TL's at St. Mary's."

"They never should have started TL. Better to work inside the system."

"Like you?"

He ignored my slight. He looked at Apryl, who mooned at us from across the room.

"Fat chance she will go for you now that you're not Catholic." I just stared at him, incredulous. "She's nothing special, G. K."

"You're nothing special." It was the Champagne talking. He walked off, toking. I tried to avoid Apryl after that, going from room to room, dancing, as things devolved into a bacchic free for all.

It was three in the morning when I awoke to Jacques lying nearby in a heap on the couch. My cummerbund hung around my neck like a lei. I was a pair of ragged claws, drunk and scuttling on the floor. Stacey was lying in Ross's arms. Broken furniture was strewn around the entryway. I could only recall gauzy images of DeBlasio and Swensen sword-fighting with chairs, and globs of peanut butter flying through the air.

"Perhaps it would be best for you to sleep these off." Jacques had helped Gretchen to her eighth champagne. Now it was down to cheap California Zinfandel.

"Ha! And give *them* the satisfaction?"

"Who is 'zem'?" asked Jacques.

"I tell you who is 'zem' . . . all of zem, that's who—these flibbertigib-bets." She hiccupped and laughed. She fell over onto the couch on top of a sleeping Chalmers. He wrapped his arms around her, smiled, and went back to sleep. She stayed there in his arms momentarily, then got up. She went up to Winston, grabbed a Champoeg from his fluttering hand and drained it. He had been quoting some Shelley to the unknown student.

"Drink life to the lees!" she shouted.

"What are all these kisses worth, if thou kiss not me?" Patrick looked around and laughed goofily. He sang along with the music, bobbing his head up and down.

McDarby and I sang out, "Winston tastes good, like a cigarette should."

Diana and Winston walked out into the frozen moonlight a few moments later. I joined them.

Hess was carrying on at the back porch about the Three Days of Darkness, for which he found a comparison in this very party. Maggie was asleep on the cadaverous couch on the porch.

"B-but what if it *is* the three days, right now? No, listen, and we have to hang out here, man?" said Hess.

"You would be able to create the village at your place," I said.

"Yes," he said, acknowledging what I thought was in the works. "Did we talk about this, Bernie?"

"Yes," I said, "between MF mounting several cows." The right question for Hess to ask was, did we talk about setting up a dummy fund for Operation Constantine.

Back inside, Lucas Raleigh was passed out on the floor. Last I recalled, I had the upper hand on his argument that Cranmer was really the pope's right-hand man and that the killing of priests in England was greatly exaggerated. I got up and made off for some other corner of the room.

There, to my surprise, I found *l'objet du desire* . . . one Apryl Elaine "Juliet" "Dulcinea" Jovey. She was in the arms of Jimmy, who was passed out.

Apryl looked at me. I was always ready for a trip to heaven—those heavenly auburn locks braided like Venus.

She reached up her delicate hand. I took it. The only sound was the recurring scratch of the stereo needle as it made its revolutions.

We went into the sweet night air of the balcony under the overarching canopy of an elm. Its swishing in the breeze reminded me of the passage of hours and days, of the abject approach of the end of flirtation—with her, the Church, the university.

And in her hand, in that ecstasy of hoped-for fulfillment, I could see myself in the Church, in its belly, its nave, extending outward, safe, living only on desire, love of this woman, this faith, this communion. It was this forgetting and remembering at once that made me overlook the past and want her again. The cocktail of youth was powerful, and I was drinking deep.

I led Apryl by the hand, through the dark to the stairs leading to the basement. As we entered the basement, the smell of Oregon hops was stronger. Boxes lined the walls. Back in the cave, the pots were brewing. This was my chance to find out why she had slept with Finley.

I led her back to the cave where I had seen her in the votive light and prayed she would be mine.

LVIII

INTERRUPTUS ANGEL

" S o you want me? Here I am." I reached over and pulled her closer.
       "Bernard, we have to talk about what is between us."
       "So we're here to talk?"

I felt the dankness of the basement; the half-light was appealing. Imagination stirred my mind to a congeries of images. I was near her, smelling her. Something stirred, a twitching urge. I hated it, drew toward it, swore it off, rationalized it, spiritualized it, sublimated and reconstituted it. I tried to think of Hogg, of the examination of conscience, of the four last things: Heaven, Hell, Death, and . . . Apryl.

Now her silken brassiere showed. She was pulling at my tuxedo, unsnapping things. She yanked at my cummerbund, and it snapped onto my face. Then she and I kissed again. I felt her warmth melting into me. Then she looked down at my nether regions. Nothing. I pulled away and put on my trousers.

"What are we doing? Alcohol and us? Why can't we be together sober?"

"Why don't you love me?"

"Love you? I can't tell you how many times I wanted to hear that."

"I thought at the fair . . . but you went off with her."

"A pig in a poke," I said as I pulled out a beant and tried to smoke. She put her hand on my hand and shook her head.

"Is it because I'm pregnant?" She cried. I let her cry. "I thought you would want me since it was your baby."

"Listen, I'm no biology major, but I don't think what we did would cause this. Maybe you need to talk to Finley."

349

"Why do you keep mentioning Finley?"

"Because you two slept together, didn't you?"

"No . . . what ever gave you that idea? You're the only one I've been with . . . in that way."

This seemed like a lost *Rockford Files* episode where Jim Rockford gets too close to one of his subjects during an investigation and she runs a scam on him.

"You want *her* now, don't you? . . . Do you love Maggie?"

"We are more like one another—both outcasts, scapegoats. Love has become one of Courtney's visions, always just out of reach."

"I love you. It took me a long time to figure it out."

"Where were you during this last year when I was pining for you?"

"You were?"

"As if you were not aware of everyone pursuing you, me most of all. It's been like some damned Elizabethan farce in which every character gets burned by the goddess."

"I had to think about things; that's why I stayed away at your aunt's. What happened . . . scared me."

"As scary as having someone else's baby and lying about it?"

"You don't want me because I want you."

"That's *your* game."

"I know how men are . . . they are happy only in the pursuit, but if you catch us, it's no fun, and once you've had us, it's over. You don't want someone who wants you."

"Someone messed you up good."

"Holloway."

"Maybe he's the father?"

"He's my father!"

"He's more obsessed with you than I am. That's why he's going after me in the hearings, trying to—wait, what did you say?"

She stood up.

"Albert Holloway is my father."

"Your father?"

"He and my mother split up when I was ten, and I vowed to find him and make his life hell. I wanted to tell you at the cabin but then it started burning down."

"So you came to Kansas to torment . . . your father?"

"Until I found the program."

"And then you decided to torment young men . . ." She just stared. It was a little too much Freud at three in the morning.

She drew closer to me and started kissing me. Still nothing stirred down there.

"Why do you love me?"

"You are independent, smart, your own person. And you know how broken I feel. I don't care if you are Catholic now. I know in time—"

"Wait. Whoa, sister. Only one you've loved? I don't think I'm the first or the last. This whole virgin thing . . . I don't know."

"I am a virgin . . . I mean . . . "

"I may be drunk, but I remember finding Finley in your bed during Lent. You were in the shower."

"Are you crazy? I never had Professor Finley in my bed or anywhere near me."

"I know what I saw."

"Well, it was not me."

She was good at this. She had planted a doubt. I was starting to feel sorry for her, even though she had manipulated and squeezed the life out of half of 1132 Ohio and now was going in for the kill with me.

"All I know is, we didn't have carnal knowledge."

"Don't you remember . . ." She leaned in close, stroking me, whispering in my ear. "Our night at the quarry . . . under the moonlight." She kissed me. She was starting to slip off my trousers. I grabbed her hand.

"Don't you remember, in the water, I was touching you . . ."

A light went off—that moment of ecstasy in the water. Could it have been that I prematurely . . . that I . . .

"Wait, you are saying my . . ."

"Seed."

"Like, what? A salmon . . . like spawning?"

"I guess some stuck to me as we got out of the water maybe."

Being that close to her, the touching, rubbing against her, the excitement, the anticipation, the alcohol, the waiting and fantasizing—could that possibly result in pregnancy?

I looked into her eyes. She seemed embarrassed, innocent. It was utterly arousing.

It started to fit, how pale she looked after going to Aunt Teresa's.

It was every young man's nightmare, being trapped by the passions that beset him. But I was writing a new chapter in *Fears of the College*

Man. I might as well ravish her right there since I was going to have to pay for the unfulfilled basement rite I had been pursuing for the last year.

Then I heard a sweet voice saying things, echoing my name, so I looked at Apryl, who looked in my eyes. It was not her voice—not a girl, not a boy. Apryl started kissing me. Still, I heard the voice calling out my name. And the words came back to me—this time, Courtney's voice in my head from the lecture on Augustine: "Not in rioting and drunkenness, not in chambering and wantonness, not in strife and envying; but put ye on the Lord Jesus Christ, and make not provision for the flesh, to fulfill the lusts thereof." These shadows in this basement of my soul were holding me prisoner.

I pulled away from her. "I can't." Was I saying that a second time? I heard the sweet voice approaching, echoing in the catacombs. I realized I had missed the message since the Halloween party. I was not supposed to engage in chambering and drunkenness—and lewdness.

Out of the darkness, a face emerged—beautiful, angelic. It was the face of the sweet voice in my head. Apryl pulled her blouse on, mortified.

"Have you seen Hogg?" said the apparition. It was Maggie. Her dress was rumpled, her makeup smeared.

"Huhn?"

"You were supposed to watch him."

I looked at her. She looked at Apryl. Her smile crumbled. Her old voice came back. "He's gone missing again, Jack." She started to leave.

"Wait . . . it's not what you think."

"Oh, I think it is, don't you think?"

We ran after her. The thought that Hogg had been kidnapped again and placed in a psychiatric facility was terrifying.

"We found these pills by his bed," she said.

"What are they?" asked Apryl.

"I don't know," said Maggie, "but they've all been taken."

I grabbed the bottle. Chalmers joined us from his search upstairs. We stampeded through the living room across barely moving bodies, a Waterloo of blunted desire.

Hogg was not among the tangle of bodies on the floor or couch. I looked out the window at the hearse in the alley behind 1132. Smoke was pouring out of the windows.

LIX

EGGS BENEDICTINE

"Has anybody checked the auto-da-fé?" I said. Chalmers rushed outside.

As we approached the hearse, a stammering voice called out from inside. We threw open the back of the hearse, and there lay Hogg, foam coming from his mouth. I put out a cigarette that was burning the carpet.

"Why must I battle with the flesh, Lord?"

Hogg looked at us and right through us, as if we were not there.

"The devil attacks, and I hurl shit at him—I will throw the devil into my anus where he belongs!"

Hogg was channeling Luther.

"Tom, it's us," said Apryl. She was in tears. "What's wrong with him?"

"Let's get him out of here," said Chalmers.

"How many did you take?" I asked Tom, holding up the bottle.

"All . . ." Tom lapsed again into incomprehensible mutterings. "Four score, *obsculta fili, gratia tibi,* upside the more perfect union, to Carthage I came, *arma verumque cano, sunt lacrimae* rarin to go for to carry me home, bags of shite covered over with snow, Whan that whore have perced to the roota, *cartaga delinda,* sterile, no transmission, barren sex, burning with unholy loves."

He fell gurgling on the ground like a machine whose engine had sprung a leak.

"Tom, man! Are you all right?" McDarby, Patrick, and DeBlasio had joined the party. Jimmy came up. "What the hell?"

Maggie was crying. "We have to get him to the hospital," she said.

"Maybe someone should call his parents," said Jimmy.

"Don't give him back to his parents," said Maggie. "That's the last thing he needs."

"It's his parents," I said, "and their damned deprogramming that's causing all this. They screwed with his computer."

φ

A doctor entered the waiting area. He introduced himself as Doctor Emil Carnow, an emergency medicine specialist.

"We've moved him to the fifth floor." He paused. We waited for more information.

"The fifth floor is where we send psychiatric patients."

"Excuse me . . . the psychiatric ward? What's wrong with him?" I asked. Maggie stepped forward.

"Don't do any goddamned electroshock on him, or I'll personally punch your lights out," said Chalmers.

"His parents had him kidnapped to Menningers; they gave him ETC," I said.

"I see . . . well, he checked out fine . . . physically. He's had some kind of breakdown. No drugs in his system . . . that is, no conventional mind-altering drugs. And no ethanol, of course, which I can smell on all of you."

"What does *that* mean?" urged Chalmers, a keen student of all kinds of drugs.

"Look, I know you guys are his buddies, but maybe this should wait for his parents who—"

"You tell us now!" Maggie had grabbed the doctor's arm and let go quickly. I pulled out the bottle of pills, looking at the label. The doctor took it and smiled.

"We did a blood gas workup . . . really had us going for a while . . . thought we had a genuine hermaphrodite, and there are some indications—"

"Cut the BS, Doc, and tell us something!" I said.

"It seems your friend has been taking anovulent pills."

We stared at him.

"Anovulent?" I said. "Is that what I think it is . . . ?"

Maggie picked up the thought.

"Estrogen, the pill . . . you know, Jack, birth control!

"Birth control . . . what for?" said Apryl.

"He's been taking estrogen, the only effect of which is to make him manufacture more sputum—and breasts in some men. I'd say he's put on a little fat in his chest area. No breasts yet." Carnow laughed nervously. No doubt he had seen funnier things in the emergency room, men with pins stuck through their members, women with pool balls where they didn't belong.

"Estrogen . . . are you saying he is trying to avoid pregnancy . . . ?" Chalmers trailed off.

"They are trying to make a male birth control pill to lower male hormones, but there is nothing commercially available."

"He was doing an independent study on *Humanae Vitae*," I said. The doctor looked at me vacantly. "It's a papal encyclical on artificial birth control."

"I see, performing some kind of experiment," he said. "I did a rotation in psychiatry in Boston and there was this man who was taking the pill. He thought he was a woman trapped in a man's body."

"What happened?" said Maggie.

"He grew breasts, had loss of libido, some other minor side effects."

"What did you prescribe for him?" I asked.

"We couldn't do anything for him. You can see Mr. Hogg tomorrow during visiting hours. We have him on fairly heavy doses of Thorazine. He appears to be very active and mumbled incessantly in Latin . . . something about St. Benedict saving civilization and the month of April. Is that somehow significant?"

We all shook our heads, pretending ignorance.

"Thank you, Doctor," I said. The others started to leave the emergency room. I hung back, and Maggie approached me.

"We need to talk."

"I want to have a word with the doctor first," I said. She hesitated, then walked out. This was no time for me to figure out my feelings.

"Doctor, you see a lot of weird stuff."

"Sure . . ."

"Sexual stuff, like this."

"Not like this."

"Well, I'm sure you've seen virgin pregnancies."

"No." He shook his head and scratched his chin, and then he smiled. "But I read about one in a journal."

"So it is possible? For people to get pregnant like, say, salmon?"

"Well . . . you mean spawning, in water, with the egg being laid in suspension?"

"Just for sake of argument."

"I'd say off the top of my head, very unlikely."

"How unlikely?"

"A one in ten thousand chance? I don't know if that has been tested empirically. Technically, all that must occur is the penetration of the spermatozoa and the ovum. No penile penetration is necessary for that. Spermatozoa can survive outside the body for up to thirty minutes. Depending on water temperature, it would be the perfect condition for it. So I suppose people could . . . spawn, as you say. I will have to raise this with a colleague of mine at the medical center in Kansas City."

"No need for that. It's a bet I have with a friend."

He looked at me as if he were back on his psychiatric rotation. I blew out the automatic doors of the emergency room. On the ride back, we considered the reality of the situation.

"It will blow over," said Chalmers. "He'll be fine. Let's just keep this under our hats."

I looked at the rearview. Chalmers scowled. I looked at Apryl. She looked away. The one thing none of us wanted to acknowledge was the unthinkable—the invisible, indiscriminate monster of mental illness. And the one thing I could not acknowledge—or conceive—was that I was the father of Apryl's child.

I could not help blaming Apryl for what had happened to Hogg. He had been following her around at the moment I intersected their universe, and Hogg never left off his obsession with her. She was playing him, playing me, playing Finley. I was going to burn Finley once and for all—even if it exposed Apryl to the whole world.

LX

OUTSIDE THE CIRCLE

> Blue as a sapphire from the Orient,
> The aspect of the sky shone forth serene
> From zenith to the rim of the horizon,
> So that my eyes were filled again with joy
> As soon as I had left that deathly air
> Which had so sore oppressed my sight and spirit.
>
> — DANTE, *PURGATORIO*, CANTO I

O UT on the extremities of the world, here, on the edge of education, at the border of life experience, if they could destroy investigation of Truth and culture in the name of protecting vested interests, then they had proved Galileo wrong: the world was indeed flat, there was no roundness to it, and if you strayed very far from the beaten track, you fell over the edge into a mindless black void of one-eyed monsters, department stores, best sellers, and A-frame churches. In short, the Inquisition was never more alive and in good working order.

As I entered the lecture room, Trish was leading the class in Burns's "A Red, Red Rose." Apryl sat on one side, Maggie on the other.

> *So fair art thou, my bonnie lass,*
> *So deep in luve am I;*
> *And I will luve thee still, my dear,*
> *Till a' the seas gang dry.*

Apryl looked longingly at me. I could barely mouth the words of the song. She had declared her love for me. I knew I should sit next to her, but I was still unsure what she was doing to me. Maggie sat down by me and Jimmy.

"I have been trying to talk to you," said Maggie.

"Are you going to tell me they have let the hostages go in Iran?" I was trying to entertain Jimmy. Maggie was getting frustrated.

"No. You are a hard man to find."

"'I was a freed black in Paris,'" sang Jimmy under his breath.

"I'm not about to let you off that easy."

"You're not aboot?"

She hit me.

"You have been too harsh with Apryl."

I shushed Maggie as the professors called the class to order.

"Don't look so glum," said Marin. "Your world is not ending."

"No, *our* world is ending," quipped Whelan, evoking laughter. The last couple of days of hearings had been brutal, students and faculty cataloging the parade of horribles: narrow-mindedness, conversions, proselytization at 1132 Ohio or Ole Miss, Latin masses, and wild parties.

"You should be happiest right now," said Courtney. He looked pale and seemed to be struggling to sit upright. "Recall the happiness of Boethius who is jailed for his beliefs but finds happiness in the knowledge of what is right and good. His consolation is Lady Philosophy. Don Quixote and Sancho, who have been scorned and kicked out of every inn, pummeled and robbed—are they defeated, do they go to a doctor and get pills for depression? No, they happily pursue their chivalric dreams and ever will.

"You have come to the end of a school year," said Whelan, "and it is possible it will be the last for you, or that our program will no longer be at the university. Most certainly, you will not be able to satisfy course distribution requirements through our course, and how many of you can afford to take eight hours next year without any real credits? Still, we are happy."

"Why," said Marin angrily, "why would we be happy? Well, at least we won't have to wipe your . . . noses anymore, will we, Paul?" Courtney looked sadly at the ground. "We are happy because the good life means rejoicing in the Truth. We are joyful because we are telling the truth. Have you heard a word we have said? The falcon cannot hear the falconer.

The center cannot hold. But after all this time, do you now know that the center lies outside the circle?"

Courtney deflected Marin.

"You have been pursuing an education that your forebears took for granted. It is what Plato started in his academy. Plato says in the *Laws*, 'Shall we begin with the acknowledgment that education is first given through Apollo and the muses.' He is referring to music and dance. Apollo, of course, is the god of poetry. You have wondered perhaps why the emphasis on poetry. Why memorization. Why begin each class with a song, as you did today. The answer is in awakening your memory and your senses and then your body in dance, which orders you to the whole, to the movement of the world—the universe, the stars—and brings into relief your lives as a poem."

"We are trying to tell you something," said Marin. "You are linear thinkers. Benedict fled the world, so did Boethius. You have been reading *Crime and Punishment*. Dostoevsky retreated from the world. Raskolnikov retreats from society as well. Is there a difference between a monk and an axe murderer? You read *The Brothers Karamozov*. What is the dispute between Ivan and Father Zosima? Who is the Grand Inquisitor?"

"What Mr. Marin is saying," said Whelan, "is that we did not have any higher aspirations than to awaken poetry in a generation that had lost all contact with reality. Everything in your world is unreal. You have lost touch with what is. At least if we could get you to believe in reality, we would have accomplished something."

"There *is* something," said Courtney. "That something is: this is the whole of this course. Or more properly, the fact that there is something and not nothing is the concern of your education. That is why Truth is so important. *Veritas sequitur esse rerum*. Truth follows existence. Truth follows from the existence of things."

"We want you more interested in things than in thoughts," said Whelan. "We want you to rub yourself in things, to smear yourselves in reality, in soil, bleared and smeared, smudged."

Courtney looked up at Whelan out of a reverie and shook his head.

"But when Boethius saw the collapse of the Roman Empire, when he wrote *The Consolation of Philosophy* from his prison cell, before they squeezed his neck until his eyeballs popped out, he was retreating. Saint Benedict was retreating from this same kind of world, into seclusion. Benedict knew it had all ended, that the civilization had spent itself, that something else was on the horizon. He retreated and rooted himself in the brambles, in silence, work, prayer, the elements, even pain. Raskol-nikov chooses evil out of desperation."

"Raskolnikov sees the poetry of murder," said Marin as he pulled out a beant and lit it. "He immersed himself in non-being, in the poetry of solipsism. But Benedict created a whole new civilization, a whole new classicism. You cannot rebuild education and society without poetry. It is the very seedbed of civilization. There is no salvation outside of poetry."

I thought of Hogg's discussion of the chosen—the *gnosis*, the elect—who are given the knowledge and then cannot sin.

"Well, if you like," said Courtney, "there are mysteries. We must look behind the obvious, even the second layer of meaning. Socrates does not make himself known to all. Nor does Christ make his points obvious. The parables contain seeds that contain mysteries that take a lifetime to unfold."

It was past the point when I could endure the mysteries; I had basked in them for years, reveled in the inexplicable, the unseen and unknow-able, the conundrums of a thousand Ecclesiastic and Solomonic sayings.

"You were indoctrinated long before we ever got you," said Marin with a sardonic grin. "You came from the *disintegrated inhumanities* program of the commercial world, innocent experiments of a thousand greedy companies, theoreticians in social planning, education, and so-cietal engineering. You had so many irrational and mandatory agenda positions ingrained in you, it was a wonder any of you could think a real thought. For this experiment with tradition, we are to be put to death."

The horn sounded. As I gathered my books to leave, Maggie grabbed my arm.

"We need to talk—now."

"Sure," I said.

She got up and we started into the aisle. Suddenly, I was face to face with Chalmers, and behind him were DeBlasio, McDarby, Zorn, and Sw-ensen. Chalmers took my arm and pushed Maggie aside.

"Sorry, we have a prior appointment with him."

ϕ

They led me down to the basement of 1132, where it was chilly and musty. They sat me in a chair. Light flooded in on me from a lone window. The faces of my friends were in shadow.

"That was quite a lecture," I said.

"Enough palaver," said Chalmers. "We heard about you and Apryl."

DeBlasio was punching his fist into his hand, warming up.

"I want to know about the beer money," said Zorn. "My family heard about my selling beer. They're cutting off my supply of hops."

"What right do you have!" said McDarby, his face tight as a nail.

"She was pure," said Swensen.

"After everything . . . after she burned every one of you, you still think she's pure?" They didn't say anything, but their faces looked angrier. "Look, I am not even sure I want Apryl."

"You've been carrying on with the whore, we know," said Swensen.

"You're completely under her spell."

"When this is over," said Chalmers, "you're out."

"Gone from our house," said McDarby.

"Gone from the program," said Swensen.

"Gone for good," said DeBlasio.

"I got news for you: the child is a miracle that I couldn't get even you guys to believe if the Blessed Virgin came down right now and explained it."

They circled in tighter. Chalmers took the first punch. Then DeBlasio. I sat there as I felt the blood flowing out of my nose. McDarby swung at my jaw, but I turned away and he missed. He was just coming back around when out of the shadows, a fist smacked McDarby in the side of the head and sent him flying into the wall.

"Patrick!"

He looked down at me.

"Winston, you stay out of this," said Chalmers.

"Wait," I said. "I didn't even have sex with Apryl, not in any traditional sense."

"You backstabbing sonofabitch," said McDarby. He raised his arm to hit me again.

"All right, all right!" I shouted at them. "You want a confession?" They looked at me hungrily. "I don't deny, I've been in love with her ever since I saw her that day. Outside of Strong. I've been drunk with it. I didn't mean to, but we fell for one another at that cabin Hess took us to. I had the opportunity . . . yes, we skinny-dipped, we fooled around, but . . . we didn't exactly have sex. It was more like swimming flirtations and touching. I swear, I can't explain it."

"Wow, you guys from LA really are perverts," said Swensen.

"All I can say is, she was willing to go all the way, but I pulled back."

"You expect us to believe that?" said Chalmers.

"Why wouldn't you mortalize?" said DeBlasio.

"Mike, I got to tell you, I'm not sure. I'll go a step further. I have been holding things back from all of you, playing both sides a little, thinking I could ride the razor's edge. And Apryl is trying to say she's pregnant and is having my baby, but we caught Finley in her bed—"

"Shut up!" said Chalmers.

"No, you shut up, let him talk," said DeBlasio.

"Are you kidding?" said McDarby.

"No, when we were looking for you and you were with Hogg and the Bull at the church, we went looking at Ole Miss, and there he was, the redbeard in Apryl's bed, and the shower was going."

"So who is behind this?" said Swensen.

"Ask Rich," I said.

"He's a good bullshitter, boys," said Chalmers.

"Go on," said McDarby.

"I just realized it—he's been running me like a perfect double agent. He gave them the journal. He set me up with Apryl, he got her to be with me, he drugged her."

"Don't tell me you knights are buying this," said Chalmers. They looked at me, then at him.

"You're a double agent," said Patrick to Chalmers.

"G. K. can talk his way out of anything. He didn't tell you he and Maggie are now an item." He turned to me. "You don't want to go down this road."

"Is that true about you and Maggie?" asked Swensen.

"I'm afraid so," I said. "I was pretty upset about Apryl and Finley. I don't care what you do to me. Besides, everyone but the janitor has read my journal by now."

Swensen looked at me and DeBlasio. If not Chalmers, then who?

There he was in the center, and we were circling him.

"You pussies would rather see the professors go down than a Jew who admits he was working against us."

"You are in the center, but you're outside our circle. Why don't you tell them about the money from the beer," I said.

"Yeah. What about it?" said Zorn. They grabbed him.

Chalmers struggled free.

"He's been pocketing most of it," I said, "so we don't have enough to reimburse the university fund, much less to save 1132."

He pulled his knife and backed out into the alley, cursing us the whole way.

"Fucking Protestants," he spat from the alley. "The money's for priests and monks. I brought you into the fold. You'll wish you hadn't done this to me!"

"Asshole," said Patrick.

I started for the door. "I deserve to be kicked out."

"What about British Writers? How am I going to pass?" said McDarby.

"He really does deserve to be kicked out," said Swensen.

"Come on, G. K.," said Patrick, "I need to bounce some ideas for my paper on *Karamozov*."

"What are we going to do about the mess Chalmers made for the professors?" I said.

"You write my British Writers paper and leave that to us," said DeBlasio.

"What's a little plagiarism among Catholics?!"

"In hoc signo vinces!" we yelled, putting arms around one another, cracking open some of the supply of Champoeg.

"To hell with his SCHLAYEX fund!" said McDarby as he swigged down a bottle in one pull.

"I have an idea to resume SCHLAYEX and keep the funds from Chalmers," I said.

"How are you going to do that?" said McDarby.

"I have created a dummy fund, at the monastery."

"You what?" said Patrick.

"The university is looking at that," said DeBlasio.

"Yes, but Hogg told me about another monastery in France, of nuns."

"Fontevrault," said Zorn. "But you can't involve them."

"Saints have hands that pilgrims' hands do touch," I said.

"What's that supposed to mean?" said Patrick.

"It means they will be chasing after nothing amounts, a reimbursement here, a journal entry there for purchased supplies, some visitor expenses."

"Sounds like you got it all figured out," said McDarby.

"Do you think she's really pregnant?" said Swensen, expressing what they were all focused on.

"Boys, I've seen bulls praying and chancellors swaying, and I don't know what end is up."

"God said Abraham would have offspring as numerous as the stars," said Swensen. "Maybe you have special sperm."

DeBlasio left out the back, laughing harder than I'd ever heard, repeating McDarby's line. That was a high moment in higher education, when I knew they were my friends regardless of what happened. Come what may, they would fight by my side; if need be, I would fall on the sword for them.

I had a plan now to locate the betrayer in the academic woodpile.

LXI

TRUTH ON TRIAL

Socrates is guilty of corrupting the minds of the
young, and of believing in deities of his own invention
instead of the gods recognized by the state.

— *The Last Days of Socrates*

I T was the third day of hearings. The crowd had come out to see
Courtney on the hot seat. Finley and Margaret Schmead started in on
Courtney, picking apart all his writings while he had been at Columbia
and those since his conversion. Finley tried to paint him as a radical.
Finally, they let Courtney speak.

"I have listened to the charges here and, frankly, I have to say that
if I were an outside observer, never having attended my classes and the
classes of my colleagues, never once having opened the great books, I
might think you were right—that we were brainwashing students and
hoping to cleverly lead them away from their beliefs into our beliefs.
When I see how successful we have been in seeing students impassioned
by poetry, literature, and philosophy, I am quite struck with awe at their
minds and their ability to see into the life of the mind with such poor
educational preparation.

"We have one of the most successful programs since Professor Jack
Hutchens at Chicago. Were we too popular? Is it the Truth you fear?"

"The Truth?" said Finley with a searing smile. "What do you mean? Your students see truth through their own lenses. Do you pretend you were not projecting belief onto them?"

"I do not doubt that a good teacher's beliefs are evident to a good student—the belief in Truth, the belief in the student's ability—but as for doctrine and religion, this is something that if you had spent any time in our classes, you would know is absent. We invite students to consider the contradictions in their own education, such as the doctrine they are taught that there is no single truth or the superiority of their scientific world."

"So you teach them to doubt the scientific method, the crown jewel of our civilization?"

"You are presenting an unthinking view of received wisdom. You espouse what Francis Bacon did to the university in the seventeenth century."

"You mean when he harnessed knowledge to science?"

"When he subverted knowledge to power. Students come to the university now repeating the cant they have been taught in high school and college: the mind cannot really know anything, there is no real truth that can be known but what can be measured or seen through a microscope. We ask them to think more deeply."

"Yet you have no experts in science or the history of science teaching them."

"That is something we also ask them to challenge, the argument from expertise. Are you not simply declaring such things to be true, and if they are true, can you demonstrate their truth in all times and all places?"

"But that is a broadside challenge to the primacy of hypothesis and experimentation."

"The university today pretends to be the keeper of what hypotheses and what possible outcomes are admissible. We offer a more rigorous intellectual examination, a greater embrace of student imaginations, and a greater sense of humor about the twentieth century's pretentions to ultimate wisdom. I am only trying to lead them to water of the intellect."

"So if your own students were to say that they only tried to follow your lead, that they were trying to imitate you, would you say you had failed as an academician?"

"We all imitate someone. You seem to lack respect for the ability of students to make up their own minds. In fact, these hearings are not about us but about the administration and its desire to control all messages to students."

"I can see why they call you the Midwest Svengali."

"If you are saying I am persuasive, I would only point to your position as head of the Western civilization program. You didn't get there by reading from a scientific-method textbook."

"Yes, there's persuasion and then there is forming minds to think only one way."

"In *The Republic*," rejoined Courtney, "Polemarchus comes to get Socrates to go to the home of Cephalus. He tells Socrates that he is outnumbered, that the young men can force him to go where they want. Socrates asks them if there is not another way, can they not use persuasion? We have tried to use persuasion to lead our students to turn from where they were going and consider the road not taken."

"In other words, to free them from their improper beliefs and suppositions."

"To give them *another way* of looking at things. A fresh perspective. In this case, of tradition, of the ancient thoughts and arts of their forefathers. You see, many of them are not even open to anything old and some, not to anything that does not come from themselves. They are trying to be themselves by imitating others trying to be themselves, but without any model."

"Are you that model?"

"I am just a teacher. We point to the greater models in literature, history, and philosophy."

"How would you characterize Tom Hogg, Professor?" interjected Schmead, apparently impatient of this philosophic strain. The HIP gallery collectively gasped.

"I would not pretend to characterize him. Not as you do."

"Yes, yes." Finley took back over and laughed, a laugh he used to perfection in Western civ. "But he was your student, after all."

"I feel the young man's anguish with his family, and my prayers are with him. Depression is a mystery. It is no respecter of persons. That includes half of those we read and study."

Courtney did not bring up Menninger's. Finley knew that there was no proof that it was connected to the university.

"We have here, professor, a selection from his diary that I would like to read and ask you to comment—"

"We object, Mr. Chairman, to this unprecedented bit of evidence."
Broglio had shot out of his chair and was calmly invoking the attention of
Pigg, who was sensitive to rules of evidence. Chalmers face had become
a volcano of pent-up rage; at Maggie; at Swensen; and at Apryl, whose
mouth was slightly open, eyebrows knitted. Their gazes turned to me.

I had the diary. How did they get it?

"There has been no foundation of personal knowledge, and this is a
gross violation of student medical privacy."

Pigg conferred with the others. Finley emerged and spoke:

"Father Broglio is right. We'll just call the young man. He's currently
in Lawrence Memorial Hospital. We'll have him here this afternoon."

The others looked at me. They knew I had gone to confront Barrows.

"No, I'd like to answer it from his diary," said Courtney.

"We object to—"

"Dom Angelo, let me answer," said Courtney.

Broglio sat down reluctantly. Finley feigned concern at the idea of
invading someone's privacy, then pursed his lips and read in a measured
tone:

> Paul Courtney is a modern-day apostle. He is Athanasius, or
> Benedict, poised at the entrance of the city, ready to flee at a mo-
> ment's notice. I could smell the fetid breath of the sinful student
> body. A body without a head, as St. Catherine says. I began to
> smell the sins of this society, and I listened to the pure words of
> Professor Courtney, the only true doctor.
>
> Generations to come will call me blessed and they will
> know Courtney was right and know that he was a saint.

Finley set the diary down, looking with a question in his eyes at the
spectators, then at Courtney.

"Many students imitate great men and women of the past, athletes
and saints, like Joe DiMaggio, or St. Francis. Tom is perhaps a little over-
zealous," said Courtney, the slightest note of remorse in his voice. He
looked really wan.

Broglio conferred with Marin. Broglio asked for a break, and the
panel recessed for fifteen minutes. Marin looked directly at me, but I
went outside for a beant.

"Who in the hell gave them that diary!" Chalmers was stomping
around, poised to hurt me while Marin conferred with Broglio, Whelan,
and Courtney. The guys from 1132 were looking at me.

"I did not give it to them," I said. "I swear."

"I told you you would regret siding with him," said Chalmers. McDarby just shook his head. "All you jerks with your diaries." They walked off.

LXII

DEATH BY ADMINISTRATION

W HEN the hearing resumed, Courtney looked sick. Broglio leaned over him, but Courtney waved him off to show he was fine. Finley started asking Courtney about conversions. The press perked up.

"What about Todd Livermore?" asked Finley.

"He died in a tragic accident on the Aran Islands. As I am sure you know, Mr. Finley. He died, and it was the worst day of our lives—and his parents' lives."

The audience turned as one to Finley, who did not miss a beat.

"He had recently converted to Roman Catholicism?"

"Yes, I was his sponsor. Is it a crime for a person of age to adopt religious beliefs?"

"Had he gone to Ireland with his parents' approval?"

"He was nineteen. He paid his own way and had a partial scholarship."

"Let's talk about that scholarship . . ."

Finley knew how to use a pause. He arched his eyebrows slightly as he looked down. Hubris dripped from his chin. Chalmers shifted in his chair.

"You had a fund set aside for students who showed exceptional promise?"

"You would have to ask Professor Whelan. I know very little about the fund."

"You know enough to have seen to it that Bob Littman, Corey Tartt, Arnold Truslow, Barry Weitz, and others received substantial help toward stays at the monastery of Notre Dame de Chalfontbleau. It came from this graduate school you allegedly set up . . . SCHLAYEX. What does it stand for?"

"It stands for School for Laymen of Excellence." Courtney colored as he said it. Finley was brilliant to have brought it out with Courtney.

With the details of the SCHLAYEX scholarships coming out, we knew the extent of the damage Perry had done.

"But as a result of that death, one of your promising students, Arnold Truslow, became a monk in France, and his fiancée became a nun in France."

"It was really something special . . . they found the monasteries on their own," said Courtney expansively, his eyes locking onto some distant city.

"But Professor Courtney, this was Notre Dame de Chalfontbleau, and just by coincidence, let us say, this is the same monastery where you yourself went and took simple vows almost thirty years ago."

"Yes, that is right," acknowledged Courtney. He lifted his head and leveled a fierce stare at Barrows: thick, dark eyebrows concealed his eyes. I sat forward on my seat. Courtney appeared to be flushed, to be faint.

"And yet you tell us you did not set up this fund to send students to the monastery. You expect us to believe that you did not use study abroad and federal and university funds and programs to direct students to this monastery?"

Courtney blanched. I felt the eyes of the section from HIP were on me. I knew I was on trial.

"I can only repeat. It was a coincidence . . . or—"

"Or what?" interrupted Finley.

"Or . . . providential."

"Providence. You mean something supernatural, Professor?" There was the slightest air of mockery in Finley's tone.

"I suppose that sounds old fashioned." He lowered his head. "Not every coincidence is chock full of providence. But the will of God can be seen in the smallest of things, as we learned from St. Therese of Lisieux. From Jean-Pierre de Caussade. I discouraged people from talking about the monastery or from going there, unless they felt absolutely sure."

"Because you knew you were promoting religion."

"Because I felt it a personal failure that I did not succeed as a monk, and I did not want people saying that Brother Martin or any other person who might follow him there was trying to do what I wanted to do but couldn't. And I did not want them to fail. I knew how psychologically damaging it could be."

"A personal failure. How could it be a personal failure to come back to America and be recognized as you were?"

"Perhaps it is difficult for us to understand Benedictine monasticism. We do not yet know the impact that the demise of monasteries had on civilization. Monasteries kept civilization alive for a thousand years, fostered learning, science, agriculture. But with the decimation of the monasteries and with the ruin of St. Benedict's rule came the rise of money and mercantilism, and with them came the Industrial Revolution; this ravaged our farm base and the family, fueling our own age of technological idolatry. Society can take only so many shifts of models, so much inundation of information. I fear we are in for another Dark Age."

Courtney looked at the panel, the spectators, pained and distant.

"Professor," Finley said with ridicule, "are you saying that monasteries were always bastions of fairness and learning? Have you not read Boccaccio?"

"Original sin has been around since the beginning. No place is without its flaws."

"Aren't you just sending students on a romantic escapade that has no hope of producing any results? Are you really telling them that unless monasteries rise again, we will see the fall of civilization as we know it?"

"I say that any learned person should know something of the monastic way and its significance to Western civilization."

"I can see why your students go to monasteries." Finley paused while he let his score sink in. Finley looked further on his list of peccadilloes.

"Ellis Blaine."

Courtney went pale again. Blaine had left for France as I came to 1132 Ohio. A Scot, volatile, who had wrestled with anybody who came in the door of 1132. That was in the days when Chalmers and Todd Livermore and Hess lived there.

"He is a student."

"He was a monk at Chalfontbleau."

"He went there for a time."

"He had a breakdown and hid at a farm in . . . Le Loup, near here. And now, he has disappeared. The committee tried to call him. You wouldn't know where he is?"

Courtney became ashen and drawn. I suspected that Blaine was the informer, that he likely had my journal and had turned it over to

Barrows. No matter how things swung, I was always going to be seen as the betrayer.

"Well, he took it hard that he did not have the fortitude for the life of a monk. It is a hard life. Even I was not suited to it."

"Professor, was Mr. Blaine supposed to help found a monastery right here in Kansas?"

Courtney looked shocked. "That . . . is news to me."

I looked at Hess, who reached in his boot—was he pulling out a shotgun? I knew they would think I had spilled the beans on Operation Constantine.

"What is your relationship to Ellis Blaine?"

"I was his teacher."

"You were his godfather, weren't you?"

The way in which the word came out spoke of back-alley meetings, kissing of rings—some ancient mafia. Courtney nodded.

"What was he before?"

"Presbyterian."

"A devout Presbyterian who never touched a drop of alcohol, and you sponsored him in the Roman Church, and he became a drunk."

I saw the contingent of protestors, concerned Jewish parents, the vice chancellor, and Sharon Blaine, cut you through with a glance.

"Some students are not good at handling drink temperately."

"But you encouraged students to drink in moderation."

"Yes. We thought it better to bring out into open what happens anyway, try to expose them to real wine in moderation."

"Blaine is the same student who went to your catechisms at 1132 Ohio Street, where he lived with the other Catholic converts."

"Yes. They call that catechism, but it is really just discussion."

The house of many revelations, incantations, and undulations. The house that Penshurst was selling. The house of my rebirth and house of my current confusion. Of near conversion, love and obsession.

"And this is well attended. Do freshmen girls take an oath of chastity?"

Courtney made fierce eyes at Finley. "Some do, I suppose."

"We will have a student testify that your fund, Slayex, was used to get Americans to France to be traditional monks—and then to start a monastery right here in Kansas."

I had told Holloway I couldn't get anything specific on a monastery. Courtney winced.

Then suddenly he slumped over in his chair, wheezed, clutching his chest. Marin ran up, pulled Courtney out of the chair, and laid him down on the floor. Courtney did not appear to be breathing. Dr. Littman rushed up and brushed aside the students who swarmed him.

"Excuse me, Professor Marin, I'm a doctor. This man appears to be in acute cardiac arrest."

Girls from Ole Miss cried out Ave Marias. Dr. Littman squatted, his large stomach protruding out from his shirt, and started pounding on Courtney's chest and administering mouth-to-mouth resuscitation. Nothing. He tried again, laboring over his huge gut. Then in an instant, Courtney's chest heaved, and he began shallowly breathing.

Soon, the ambulance arrived. Paramedics and emergency medical technicians ran into the room like knights errant in their flashy orange uniforms and bulky equipment. They clapped a green oxygen mask on him and took readings. A stretcher was wheeled in and placed next to Courtney. As quickly as they arrived, they left, wheeling Courtney to the ambulance. Reporters flashed pictures, and the excited crowd babbled.

Chalmers stormed out. Patrick, DeBlasio, and McDarby came up. I felt a tidal wave of guilt. I never thought anything I did could lead to this.

"I don't believe this." Swensen was thunderstruck. McDarby stared at me.

"You think Chalmers sold us out?" said Patrick.

"There's one way to find out," I said and walked off.

LXIII

THE TROJAN HORSE

W HEN I arrived, Barrows jutted out his jaw, folded his hands, and spoke slowly.

"You can't blame yourself for what happened to Professor Courtney. I've known about his weak heart for some time. He is stabilized, no?"

"They have taken him to St. Francis in Topeka. You have what you want now."

"What I wanted was to be free of these forces tearing apart the university."

"You mean great books?"

"I mean the media, the regents of the University. Like Dewain Schmead."

"Are you saying you do not control all that happens here?"

"Maybe you are learning something after all. We're all controlled by someone else. It should not shock you that the chancellor is not the chancellor."

"You wanted me because you heard of my reputation for upending others."

"Schmead could understand professors, tenure, committees, the Byzantine structure of budgets and financing from the legislature. But he cannot understand the mind of a young upstart from Los Angeles. And he has a personal stake."

"Personal?"

"His son was in HIP. A friend of Chalmers's, in fact. Lived in your house. Became a monk in France."

I recalled the name of Kludas Schmead from 1132's mailbox.

"And the kidnapping of Hogg? The deprogramming of other students?"

"All Schmead."

"How did you know about me?"

"*Glaze*, I think they called you. Your friend, Perry, was most helpful in that regard."

"I suppose he will get the Fulbright."

"Bested you by a hair." He grinned. I wanted to shatter that glass patrician jaw. "Of course, I do have some influence to award another one. If you give me all the information on the SCHLAYEX funding, we'll let you continue your bootleg beer operation. Study abroad in Italy is one of the better experiences, I hear."

I was licking my lips, but my anger overcame me.

"You bastard." He merely smiled. "You pitted me and Perry against each other."

"I love an academic joust."

"You gave me the poem by Marin, knowing it would lead to my aunt."

"I warned you to stay out of this. I am afraid your time at this university is over."

I thought he was going to have me expelled and call the police right there.

"You will transfer to Berkeley."

It was a shot below the belt.

"You have been talking to my father."

"And your mother."

My heart skipped a beat. "Why . . . why are you . . ." He looked across his desk at me and bobbled in his judge's chair. "Wait . . . you can't afford to have me testify!"

At that point, he opened a drawer and pulled out a package. He set it on the desk, opened it package, and pulled out—my journal!

I jumped up and tried to grab it across the desk. He pulled it away.

"Student druggings, burning things down, your father, mother, aunt, plagiarism, sex—this will ruin many people."

"That's mine!"

Barrows locked it back in his desk and placed the key in his pocket.

"All the paperwork is available from Mrs. Ellsworth outside. Once the semester is over and the transfer to Berkeley is complete, you may have this back."

I wanted my journal. I wanted to put it in my pants where it felt as if I had my armor once again to protect me.

"Screw yourself, Barrows."

"Are you going to testify?"

"Maybe I am going to tell the whole world about Schmead and HIP and all of this insanity. How you let it go on. How you knew Chalmers burned down the union and did nothing, how your ego is paramount over the interests of the university."

I started to walk out. When I looked back, he was on to other paperwork.

Nancy Ellsworth looked at me kindly as she proffered the papers. I declined them. She motioned toward Holloway's office.

"He would like a word with you."

"That's all I need."

"I think you had better go in there."

I shrugged, walked in, and found him perched on his desk with his hands folded.

"Apryl came to see me last night."

I stared at this walleyed man.

"She is in love with you." I looked into his eyes, fierce balls of light.

"She is a goddess, and all of us, including you, worship her."

"Why would she love you, Kennisbaum?"

"Maybe because she knows it drives you mad."

"Are you telling me you don't love her?"

"I'm twenty. What do I know?"

"But she is having your baby."

"That is . . . a matter of some dispute."

He sprang off his desk like a gyrfalcon. I went crashing over a chair and onto the floor. He had his hands on my windpipe, but he did not have the powerful hands of the Swede, and I flipped him over easily in a move McDarby had used on me. I let him up slowly. He got up and sat down behind his desk, a sprig of his hair standing on end.

"You know I am her father." I nodded. "You have to do the right thing."

"If you mean marrying her—"

"I mean, testify against Finley."

"So you believe me, that she—"

"Yes. And if this is his child, I will not expect you . . ."

"First, sir," I said, "I have to think through some things. Apryl is lovely—and manipulative and dangerous. She has burned practically every guy in HIP."

"Like her mother. I'm going to tell you something, son, but you can never tell her." I nodded. "Apryl's mother and I split up because Fred Marin and she . . ."

"So you gave Barrows the poem?"

"I found it among her things."

"Is her name Miriam?"

"No. It is Helen."

"Who is Louise in the poem?"

"Chancellor Barrows's wife." I was shocked. "Marin made the rounds in those days. I suppose we were all too afraid of him to do anything."

"So your ex-wife and Marin . . ."

"I never knew if she was mine or his. I raised Apryl as my own. I suppose I never forgave her. I drove Helen away."

"My God," I said. The more I looked in his blinkless eyes, the more I could see the galaxy of Apryl's eyes. He picked up a picture on his credenza and showed it to me.

"Your wife?" He nodded. She looked as much the goddess as Apryl.

"Marin knows she is my daughter. He has Chalmers protecting her."

"So Chalmers stole my journal?"

"He didn't steal your journal. Ellis Blaine did. He gave us much information on Chalmers. That boy is no saint."

"We wondered why he disappeared. What about Hogg's diary, who did that?"

He stared blankly at me, then shook his head. "So you don't want me to leave the university?"

"I want you to testify against Chalmers and Finley."

"Barrows will—"

"Forget Barrows. He loves all this controversy whether he admits it or not." He paused. "Kind of hard to decide who you want to hurt more, Finley or Marin."

I started to leave. I was fuming but uncertain what to do. Most of all, I wanted to confront Marin, the master manipulator behind Chalmers.

"Kennisbaum," he called. "The attorney general is sniffing around a potential illegal beer-running operation. Know anything about it?"

I started out the door again, thinking of the Hummer billboard. If I did Barrows's bidding, we would be in the clear on the beer.

"Remember, do not let happen to your child what happened to mine. Regret is a bitter pill."

I stopped, looked at him. "Do you think she is not going to burn you?" He looked back. Maybe it was worth it to him, to prove to her he was not the bad guy she thought him to be.

How was I to accept Apryl's baby as mine just because her stepfather wanted me to perpetuate that myth? I had not come this far to let it go and perpetuate another myth. But could I summon the courage to confront the one who, years before, started all this academic pandemonium?

LXIV

LIMITATIONS OF IMMORTALITY

And I could wish my days to be
Bound each to each by natural piety.

— *WILLIAM WORDSWORTH*

"WHAT have you and Chalmers done to HIP and to me?" I just blurted it out.

I found his office in the catacombs of Wescoe Hall and stood outside, staring at his name plate. Nothing remarkable in the name itself: Frederick L. Marin, Professor of English. It was the number on his office. I put my face up close to the plate, so close the numbers seemed larger than life: a one, a three, and then a two.

"Finally, you've come for the truth?"

For a man of fifty-seven, he was surprisingly virile. He sat in a plain chair surrounded by books, poetry, and pictures of famous men and women: Wallace Stevens, T. S. Eliot, Ezra Pound, Dorothy Sayers, Robert Frost.

"I always was here for that."

"In dubious battle on the plains of Kansas and shook his throne."

"What?"

"*Paradise Lost*. You've eaten of the fruit of that forbidden tree."

"Have I?"

"If you knew all things, would it make you better? Or do you just want immortality?"

"I don't want to know all things, just what went wrong. Why you hurt so many people." I had come to Mount Olympus, and the ground did not shake. The man behind the numbers.

"I knew you would come," he said with prophetic gravity. "Kansas is not a place one can hide from his past." Was he drinking? "From the foundations of the world, I knew you."

"That's from a poem of yours."

"Appeared in *Paris Review*, you know."

"'In your mother's womb I knitted our love.'"

"You know my poetry."

"It's overly laden with the biblical, yet it does contain a certain allusive power."

"Do you think it attains Truth, though?"

"It's overrated," I said.

"Your aunt says that."

"Teresa picked it up from you."

"Student teaching."

He was quoting from his own poem. I took out the poem. The evidence. He stood accused. I had found him guilty. Guilty of hurting Apryl, of hurting other men's wives, of hurting my aunt.

"In your mother's womb, I knitted you. Did you knit something in her womb?"

"It is the nature of sin. My father was a womanizer." He paused. "I am what I am."

"Some would call that blasphemy."

"Do you believe? Is there anything permanent, anything eternal?"

"I believed in many things. My mother's love is eternal."

He stopped at that, and then he looked at me in earnest.

"What do you want to know?"

"Are you Apryl's father?" He smoked his beant and stared.

"Haven't you hurt enough people?"

"Do you blame me for Professor Courtney?"

"Do you blame yourself?"

"I think I set all of this up," I said.

"Did you?"

"Or maybe you did—to get at me."

"Ah . . . Bernard, Bernard." He laughed to himself. "I am not Apryl's father. I know that I fathered . . . many, but she was not one. Her mother was amazing. When I see Apryl walking, it is as if her mother were my student again. He did not know the treasure he had. Look at me. Do you see any resemblance? She is a perfect reflection of Helen—Helen's eyes, Helen's mouth, her high forehead, her stunning jawline and hair. And Holloway's sleek nose. Nature's little joke to take that weasel and give him a goddess."

"What about the wreckage you caused in that marriage?"

"I am sorry for my sins. Are you?"

"I did not become Catholic because of my sins."

"You will learn some day that, Catholic or not, there are things beyond your control. You have to learn what they are and move on."

"Like alcohol?" I saw his eyes light up.

"For some. For others, just a litany of lesser-known sins."

"What sins would those be?"

"Insincerity. Dissembling. We saw the disguise—even without the Nixon mask."

"Why didn't you say anything?"

"We saw something in you; you had a birthright, and that was your mind, your imagination, and if we could give that back to you, reignite the pilot light of wonder . . . by living where you did, you received a greater education than we could ever give you by ourselves."

How right he was. There I learned to retreat from the world to a monastic infusing of poetic spirit. And we danced with Bacchus and the saints all at once. I felt as Catholic as if I had been a devout penitent, fleeing the crumbling civilization, returning to the Ithaca of the heart.

"Chalmers has gone mad."

"He's hard to contain."

"I have been seeing Maggie."

"Do you know what she—"

"People change."

"Some do."

"I told the university authorities about SCHLAYEX funds and Chalmers."

Marin's face tightened.

"They already knew about that," he said. "But did you give them Tom Hogg's diary?" I was fearful I would be disbelieved. I had lied to myself. But that I had not done. My stomach started gurgling.

"I read the diary. But I swear, you have to believe—"

"I know. I did."

"Why?"

"You do not understand war!" He slammed his hand on the desk and jolted my nerves. "In war, sometimes you must do things you would rather not do. We had to turn that over to divert them from other things they were onto. Even Chalmers does not know what I did."

I felt my face flush and all my anger welling up. "The monastery?" Marin nodded.

"At Hess's farm?" He was silent. "I was out there for a month."

"Paul has always felt that getting a traditional Benedictine monastery in the United States would do more to save the culture than a million liberal arts programs. Shock treatment to the heart of the country."

"That shock treatment sent him to the hospital."

"In case you were thinking about going to see Paul, don't. You will be turned away."

"I can't testify . . . it will destroy everything."

"I thought you came for the truth."

"I can't . . . the Attorney General will arrest me and everyone involved."

"Tell all the truth, but tell it slant," he said.

"My aunt Teresa won't talk about you. Why?"

He said nothing. I looked at the poem. *Helen, chemicals are the real price; For a little more, they'll throw in rice.*

"Did you get Teresa pregnant?"

"Do you love Maggie?"

"What does Maggie have to do with this?"

"You just have to see it for yourself," he replied.

"Why won't you answer me about Teresa?"

He laughed and lit up another beant. Then it hit me. It was too terrible to say. The chemicals were not for the pregnancy of Helen, but Teresa.

When I was sixteen, I had read a letter in my father's things from Aunt Teresa from the late 1950s. From that letter, I knew they had quarreled over something at the University of Kansas, and my father would not answer her letters.

"Did you procure an abortion for Teresa?"

"And you haven't thought about one for Apryl?"

That cut to the quick.

"You are talking about the nonexistence of a person in being."

"You are close to the truth," he said.

I thought of Apryl and the same situation she was in. I thought about the chemicals in *An American Tragedy*. As a Roman Catholic, she would never consent. How was I that different from Marin?

"You're holding things from me!" I found myself raising my voice. He smiled.

I turned and left. I had come to Kansas to satisfy a morbid curiosity about my father's past, and now, I wished I had not come this far. Barrows was right. It was over.

LXV

FOLLOW YOUR SAINT

I HAD packed, but before I left town, I sought comfort in the basement with Hogg's well-worn Douay-Rheims Bible. I recalled how Augustine practiced bibliomancy, opening scripture to a random passage and receiving the message from God. There in the garden of the basement, I opened the book, *tolle lege*, and my finger came to rest on a passage in the Old Testament from Daniel:

> And such as deal wickedly against the covenant shall
> deceitfully dissemble: but the people that know their God
> shall prevail and succeed.

I had deceitfully dissembled in the assembly. It had landed me in a den of lions. I looked again at the verse. It was the thirty-second verse. I took a second look at the chapter. The numbers hit me like a sledgehammer: Chapter 11, verse 32.

Had I become infected with a group madness, a mass hysteria? Was it saying I was wicked, or that I was through with deceit and that I would prevail, that 1132 Ohio would be saved? I closed the Bible, and, opening it again, I read:

> You are the light of the world. A city seated on a mountain cannot be
> hid.

The University of Kansas and Lawrence were a city seated on a hill, true. But I was not the light of the world. I had failed to hold the lights of the Easter Vigil. I looked at the verse. In relief, I read, Matthew 5, verse 14.

Two out of three. I closed the Bible again, opened it, and read out loud:

> The men of Nineve shall rise in the judgment with this
> generation, and shall condemn it; because they did
> penance at the preaching of Jonas; and behold more
> than Jonas here. No man lighteth a candle, and putteth
> it in a hidden place, nor under a bushel; but upon a
> candlestick, that they that come in, may see the light.

Marin was more like Jeremiah. Courtney was more like Jonas. Here again was the message about not hiding your light. I looked at the verse. Verse 32. I looked for the beginning of the chapter. My heart was racing: chapter 11, verse 32. Maybe this was all just a self-fulfilling fixation.

I would leave, all right, but not before I let my light shine for the whole world, not before I told Nineveh the truth. It no longer mattered whether Apryl was in fact Athena—or Medusa. My life may have been all in pieces, but I could put something right.

"Bernard," said Trish. "How are you?"

"I need to see Apryl."

"She's resting upstairs."

I rushed past her up the stairs to Apryl's bedroom, where I had caught her during Lent with the bearded inquisitor. I pushed open her door, and there she was lying on her bed, curled up. She raised herself when she saw me.

"Bernard." She beckoned me to come sit on her bed.

"Let's go."

"Where?"

"You'll see."

I took her to the emergency room. I asked for Doctor Carnow. They said he was on break. We waited.

"No, Bernard. Let's go see Tom."

"We wait." She was in tears.

Soon, Dr. Carnow appeared in his white coat.

"Yes, the young man with the birth control issue." He smiled. "He's been asking to see you. I was just getting ready to call you."

"We have another birth control issue?"

"Don't tell me *you've* been taking the pills." Apryl was crying. She ran down the hall.

"What is going on?" he asked me.

"Remember the matter I discussed with you, about whether a girl could get pregnant?"

"You mean in water, without actual intercourse?"

I nodded, totally chagrined.

"Oh . . . " He seemed to get the situation. "How far along is she?"

"I don't know. It could be from last October, if it is the water thing, or from late March with someone else."

"I see. She is not showing that much. But some women don't show until very late in the pregnancy.

"So, doc, can you tell the age of the fetus?"

"Yes, I will be able to approximate gestational age from a pelvic exam. But you are here for an abortion?"

"I dunno."

"Only if it's less than three months old. It must be in the first trimester. And not here. Aren't you people Catholic?"

"Mostly."

I went down the hall and found Apryl crying outside.

"The doctor will see you."

"I can't."

"Just for an exam. I want some answers."

I was not going to find out someday after leaving KU, somewhere ages and ages hence, that somewhere on this earth was a son I didn't know I had. Or a daughter who, like Apryl, would come back to haunt me in some place and some time of her choosing.

After leaving Apryl with Dr. Carnow, I thought about Hogg. Maybe we would go to see him. I thought about the Bible verse. Maybe the light we were hiding under a bushel was this child. Or had we set something into motion by our mutual consent? I reflected on love, which was different from obsession, different from a crush, different from lust and desire to be counted among your peers as having conquered—different from succeeding in the hunt.

Dr. Carnow finally came into the waiting room. He sat down next to me with a somber purse of the lips.

"This is going to be hard to understand."

"Tell me."

"She is not pregnant."

"What?" I felt relief. Then anger. "So she has made this all up!"

"No. She *thinks* she is pregnant."

"Excuse me?"

"All the signs point to it. She has not had her period for several months. She has a paunch. She has even experienced nausea."

"Then what is it?"

"It's unusual. It is commonly called a hysterical pregnancy."

"Hysterical? Are there tests?"

"We tested her blood, her urine—and I performed a pelvic exam. Hysterical, or pseudopregnancy, is the only possible diagnosis. It happens more often than you would think. We see this especially in college women. They have many signs of pregnancy—tender breasts, skipped menstruation, frequent urination, even distended belly. I have read about women who go into labor before the pseudopregnancy is detected."

"Holy crap."

"Well . . . There is something else with Miss Jovey. The hymen is intact."

"You mean . . ."

"She is apparently still a virgin."

"Apparently?"

"Well, I took it from your bringing her in that the two of you did something that involved your thinking she was pregnant."

"Are you sure?"

"We don't see too many virgins these days in college-age females."

I was stunned. What had Finley been doing in her bed? What had my Chaucerian satire and my assumptions about her been this whole time? Had it just been staged for me to happen upon? Had I been wrong—that wrong—about her, or had she done the same thing to Finley, taken him up to the point of consummation and burned him?

"She left," Dr. Carnow added. "She was quite distraught."

I started to leave to follow after her.

"She needs her space. You should go see your friend, Mr. Aquino . . . the one with the birth control pills. Tom Aquino." He smiled.

"Oh, of course, thank you." I had forgotten about the assumed name. We did not want the university kidnapping him again so easily.

LXVI

BUSH THAT WOULD NOT BURN

Hogg was lying in bed reading Garrigou LaGrange and cooking a
Marlboro.

"Bernard."

"Mr. Aquino, how are you?" He smiled.

"Filling up what is wanting in the sufferings of the body." He put out
his cigarette in a Styrofoam cup of half-drunk coffee.

"They let you smoke in here?"

"Kind of like a HIP lecture."

"We have to get you out of here—"

"We must suffer purgations in the spiritual life. This is my suffering,
my trial—to be accused of being mad. I am happy."

"If that is the measure, I'm in ecstasy."

"Really, are you receiving locutions?"

"Locutions?"

"Direct infusions of knowledge from the triune God—or conversations with an angel, yours or another's?"

"You haven't been telling the doctors here that you're having
these . . . locutions."

"Don't you think I know of their unbelief? How are they to know the
truth if they do not hear it."

At least he did not sound like a broken poetry record.

"I don't know about locutions, but I have had a lot of encounters
with . . . numbers."

"Numbers, really. Any involving the house?"

"Yes . . ."

"It is the number of rebirth, of a great movement, of what Our Lady has in mind for the program."

"I see." I didn't, but I wanted to understand. "I have not only seen the numbers, 1132, everywhere, I've been opening the Bible and alighting on chapter 11 verse 32 of different books of the Old and New Testaments."

"This is a great sign."

"A sign? I'm trying to get to the bottom of things, but all I'm seeing is numbers and strange events. Maybe I'm going mad."

"Being is itself a burden. That is why the vision of the I AM will always bring confusion to the proud mind.

"What about the birth control pills?"

"I took those from someone. Someone who needs you."

Who? Apryl? She would not take contraception.

"We learn through tasting, touching. The Jews thought Our Lord was preaching cannibalism. He was preaching the need to transform substance to substance. The history of faith is a history of God growing ever closer to His chosen until they become one with Him."

"You mean like voodoo? Take their pills and help women vicariously?"

I felt the scar in my hand. By fire, her virginity was preserved. Hogg grabbed my hand and looked at the scar. Then he looked up into my eyes.

"Our Lord is mighty. He will make virgins of the concupiscent, pure hearts out of the covetous. He makes all things new."

"So God is saying I should love her who was not pure?"

"Yes. It is His will that you were preserved by fire. You are part of His circle."

"His circle?"

"St. Bonaventure says, 'God is a circle whose center is everywhere and whose circumference nowhere.'"

"Then you won't mind that I read your journal," I confessed.

"I left it for you."

"Someone gave it to the university, and it was used in the hearings. Professor Courtney is in Topeka in intensive care. A coronary occlusion."

"It is His will."

"I want my journal, but they have it."

"You must pray to St. Anthony, patron of lost things."

Like my youth.

"Who do you think I prayed to when that mad bull chased me into St. Johns?"

"MF chased you?" I had never really understood what happened in there, with that rosary draped in the horns of the snorting behemoth.

"Yes, I probably shouldn't have let him out."

"No shit."

"But St. Anthony came through. It is one of his more famous miracles, the mule whom he caused to kneel at the altar."

"A mule kneeled?"

"Yes, but he did one better with MF."

"Mother Fu—" was all I could say.

"Is it His will that the program go down in flames, that we lose 1132, that Apryl manipulate all of us?"

"She has been planning to go to Fontevrault, the Sister House of Chalfontbleau."

"Apryl to a nunnery?"

"Cloistered convent, perpetual adoration. She knew the program must suffer and many would come to salvation if she prayed like the monks pray."

"She burned every one of us."

"We must all burn—if not in this life, then in the next."

I saw that she was bringing down our house, our program. She had been sleeping with the enemy—or pretending. She was preparing the grand finale arson of our amatory pursuits.

"I have to tell the others. I have to save 1132."

"The house is not ours. Unless the Lord build the house, they labor in vain who build it. *Nisi Dominus aedificaverit domum, laboraverunt qui aedificant eum.*"

He brought to me the words of vespers chant. I echoed it back to him.

"*Nisi Dominus custodierit civitatem, frustra vigilat qui custodit eam.*"

"Watch not in vain, Bernard."

"That I not be frustrated."

"Do not put up treasures where rust and fire destroy."

"Isn't it moth and rust?"

"*Pax et bonum.*"

He made the sign of the cross at me as if he were a priest on his death bed.

φ

I left and made my way back to 1132 Ohio to face my friends and give them the hope they craved. When I arrived, they were standing by the door with blank stares. McDarby stepped forward.

"I just got off the phone with Laura. She says you took Apryl to the hospital, and she's back there now in tears and won't come out of her room."

"I'll explain everything, but I have a plan to save the program and 1132 Ohio."

"Big talk," said Ross.

"Maybe we should run this past Marin," said DeBlasio.

"I've been to see Marin. He is the last person you want to run this past. He is part of the problem. No, I have to get up in front of the administration and tell all: the double dealing, the university bribes, the kidnapping, the plagiarism, the monks, Hogg, everything."

"You can't tell the truth," said McDarby. "They'd crucify us, and the professors would never forgive us."

"It's the one thing nobody has thought to do. It will set us free. It will save us—and this house."

"How?"

"They won't let me get too far. They will bargain. They will give us whatever we want. We will get a permanent source of funding; this will be a scholarship house. I know how they work. Barrows will have to give it to us."

"Sounds like a fraught plan right out of Dickens," said Patrick.

"And if I'm right, we keep the house. And it stays in the family for all time. I've been seeing visions, Bible verses."

"Bibliomancy," said Ross.

It was the one thing they could not resist. Patrick nodded. McDarby was not giving in that easy. Maybe my rhetoric was thicker than a Thucydides sandwich, but desperate times call for desperate measures.

"Saved by a Jew," said Zorn.

"Salvation comes through the Jews," said Ross.

"Salvation comes through L. A.," said DeBlasio.

"What about Apryl?" said McDarby.

"Alas, I love another. Apryl's yours. Still a vestal virgin."

"You mean . . .?

"In the fresh vegetable aisle. Only been squeezed."

McDarby stared at me for a moment ferociously, then his whole face broke into a smile.

"So you were telling the truth," said Swensen.

"I do once in a while."

We all believed I was going to give them back the house and their virgin damsel as well.

"Virgin, virgin, virgin!" We chanted over and over in a group hug, which quickly descended into a wrestling match and much drinking of Champoeg beer into the wee hours.

To hell with finals, to hell with the hearings, to hell with Chalmers. For another hour, we were a light shining in the Midwest, the city on a hill, and the mount was surrounded with cigarette smoke and fire and prayer of lusty youth.

Later that evening, I went to see Maggie. She understood what it was to be an outsider.

"I don't get how she can still be a virgin," I said. "I know what I saw . . . or maybe what someone wanted me to see?"

She put her hands on my shoulders as if to brace me. "You sound like a vampire," she said. "Enough talk of virgins."

"Didn't you have something you wanted to talk to me about?"

"Why don't we get a bottle of wine and celebrate your freedom from virgins?" she said.

A bottle of burgundy sounded pretty good right about then. We shared one over a candlelit dinner at the Castle Tea Room, where I told her how I was going to save the day.

"But enough about me. You had something you wanted to tell me, and I keep getting interrupted."

"Me? I think I already did, didn't I?"

"No." She looked nervous.

"I must have forgotten." She yawned. "I'm tired. All this wine. Besides, you have a big day at the hearings."

"Now if I can just screw up my courage."

"Pourquoi pas? You've screwed up just about everything else," she said as she got up.

LXIX

DEUS EX MAFIA

M Y life now was my journal. I was writing a new chapter every day in the ink of solidarity and friendship.

I strutted into the amphitheater of Dyche Hall as I had once strutted into the amphitheater of Strong, a player on a stage much larger than I imagined on that sweltering day. All eyes were on me as I swaggered to the front past the trimmers, Buntrock, the other professors—past the malicious lawyers of the ACLU and the raging parents of Jewish students went to a monastery, past the HIP faithful who wondered about my loyalties.

Finley, Pigg, and Margaret Schmead sat at the front, thick as thieves. I once again wore my Ben Gurion jacket, which had been in the closet at 1132 since my late winter transformation. I had expanded in all the stress. I passed by Chalmers, who sat apart from the guys of 1132 Ohio and the girls of Ole Miss, his arms crossed on his chest. Jimmy sat with Maggie.

There was Apryl. I now saw that she had given Hogg the birth control pills, pretending to be thinking of using them herself. She was Circe, turning us all into pigs.

I sat near the professors in the front. Marin looked at me as if he knew everything. Whelan whispered to Broglio, then Broglio to me.

"What do you want?"

Before I could answer, I heard a stirring, turned, and saw them come in at the back: my father and mother, flanked by Aunt Tessie, who was holding my mother's arm. Their faces were solemn. Marin looked at them, then at me.

"Well?" said Broglio.

"We can talk later."

"This hearing is back in session. Your next witness, Father Broglio." Finley looked right at me, taunting me.

"Behp." Broglio stood up, rustling his cassock ceremoniously. "We . . . have one last student witness to testify." I fully expected my name to come out, but instead: "Kludas Schmead."

Murmurs spread throughout the hall. In the front row, Dewain Schmead sat snarling. Next to him was an attractive redhead with no facial expression, his wife. They watched as their only son took the stand, clad in a plain black robe and dangling rosary beads.

His skin was pellucid, taut against his bones. He had an undergarment of giddiness about him.

"Sir, please state your name," said Broglio.

"Brother Peter of L'Abbaye Notre Dame de Chalfontbleau in Mondrin, France."

I watched Dewain Schmead. He was driving the committee. Without Schmead, Professor Courtney would not have had a heart attack.

"Your American-born name."

"Kludas Dewain Schmead II," he said. "Son of the Kansas University regent, basketball legend, and construction mogul."

He explained how he had heard a call to become a monk at Chalfontbleau when he was a HIP student on a study abroad for a semester in Ireland. He, Corey Tartt, Richard Chalmers, and Todd Livermore had visited France during spring break and had discovered an old monastery. Todd died after their return to Ireland.

"But were you a Catholic at the time."

"No, I was received into the Church in Galway by Father Shea."

"Did any of the HIP professors persuade you to go into the monastery?"

"Professor Courtney cautioned me that it was a hard life. The decision was all mine."

"What were your parents' wishes?"

"My father was against my going into the program from the start. He said it would hurt the university to have a regent's son in a Catholic program."

"Did they teach Truth?"

"They taught that Truth needed to be taken seriously, but the program was heuristic. They let us find things out for ourselves."

"But critics say it was brainwashing—just the opposite."

"Only the dirty parts that needed washing," he said to some laughter. "They taught us through Socrates that an unexamined life was not worth living. We came to see that the university official narrative that the inherited wisdom of the past was imprisoning the mind was itself a received wisdom of the present in preference to the past."

"They weren't making you think their way, like clever Svengalis?"

"I did not feel that way. Through reading, memorizing poetry, serious conversations as they called lectures, and other activities outdoors like stargazing, our hearts opened up slowly. If you open up your heart, the Truth will find it."

"That sounds a lot like romance, not education."

"Real education is an opening of the channels of your inner life of your active mind and your heart. They taught us to see the invisible world by showing us the beauty of the visible. In that process, I saw that verities of the past traditions were more liberating than the false narrative of the modern tradition. We didn't reject the modern world, but we learned to question it."

"What did you tell your parents?"

"I said it was not a Catholic program except with a small *c*, and it offered classical education, grounded in an appreciation of the best that has been thought and written."

"That sounds like what every student and parent should want."

"My father didn't have much use for liberal education. He expected me to learn more marketable skills to help in his business. When I went to Ireland, he cut me off. After that, the professors helped me out."

"With a fund that helped you pay off student debt eventually and go to the monastery?"

"Yes." He looked at his parents in the front row.

"Your father is a mogul, as you put it—a big shot in the construction industry?"

"Not much gets built without him and his labor friends in Kansas City."

"And he wanted you to take over the business. He was willing to give you 49 percent of his business. That would have been worth several million to you."

"You cannot give me enough millions to compare with the peace I have as a monk living in harmony with my brothers, praying for the world, working a garden."

"Did the program alienate you from your parents?"

"I truly gained an appreciation for their concerns, their sacrifices. I learned to really respect and love them, and my time in the monastery has intensified that love and appreciation."

"Then you have come back to give up the robes and take up your place in his business."

There was a long pause as he looked at his parents and the professors.

"No, I was kidnapped from the monastery."

The elder Schmead turned red. He stood and ran to the front. There was a lot of angry discussion. Finley spoke up.

"This will conclude the hearings at this time."

A hubbub erupted. Reporters were yelling questions.

"Schmead! Stop!" Everyone in the auditorium turned to see an imposing figure in the back at the main door. By him was Michael DeBlasio. They walked forward.

The figure had a grooved face, dark eyebrows and a full head of black hair, with an expression of paranoid vigilance. He wore a wide-lapeled silk suit. The deep vertical grooves gave him a handsome look that suggested ruggedness and complete control.

"You have no place here," said Regent Schmead.

"Dewain, you need to stand down," said the man.

"This committee demands to know who you are," said Pigg.

"Freddy DeBlasio." A hush came over the viewing section. They had all heard of him and the mafia operations on the River Quay in Kansas City.

"What do you want?" said Schmead.

"To talk to you."

"We have nothing to talk about."

"Yes, we do. Outside."

Schmead looked around.

"This hearing keeps going," said Freddy to the committee and to Broglio.

Schmead whispered to Finley.

"We will allow the professors to complete their case," said Finley.

Schmead stormed out with the DeBlasios. I wanted to follow to hear what they were saying, but I stayed out of desire for self-preservation.

"You may proceed," said Finley to Broglio.

"Thank you. Brother, you may proceed. What happened when you were kidnapped?"

"I overcame my captor. I was a football player and boxer in high school. I was freed in New York City and came here."

"Who kidnapped you?"

Margaret Schmead looked dismayed, her nephew in these dark robes bringing discredit to her role.

"I don't know."

"What did this person tell you?"

"He informed me of the whole scheme of the regents and Dewain Schmead to discredit the program, Paul Courtney, Chester Whelan, and Fred Marin and to take away our house."

"What do you mean—what house?"

"The house at 1132 Ohio Street. I lived there, as did Todd, and Rich, and others in the past. It has been handed down through each class of students."

"A kind of fraternity of the classics?"

"*Juste coma ça.*"

"How did your father propose to take away the Ohio Street house?"

We all leaned forward.

"They made the landlord an offer he couldn't refuse."

I saw the pieces now: a master plan to dismantle the program, first through funding, then through depriving credits to students, and then through Finley and the hearings. It was Schmead's men who had approached Maggie to set up Hogg so they could kidnap him. Schmead was the strawman behind the purchase of 1132.

"Thank you, Brother Peter."

A row of reporters scribbled furiously as Attorney General Hummer strode in as if someone had alerted him and his team of KBI investigators of the presence of racketeers. Finley saw him, and it did not take him much time to speak:

"Thank you, no questions from the panel. Unless you have other witnesses, these proceedings are adjourned, and recommendations will be prepared for the chancellor and the regents within sixty days."

Broglio looked at me.

"Let us have a few minutes to confer regarding additional testimony," he said as I rushed out of Dyche. I didn't know where I would go.

"Quo vadis?" said a chilling voice as I hit the outdoors and the smell of apple blossom. I turned to see Michael standing with his uncle Freddy, smoking. Moving closer, I saw he had an aquiline nose and reptilian hazel eyes. He had *predator* written all over him.

"I guess we're not the only ones classically trained," I said.

"I ain't. I saw the movie, had a thing for Deborah Kerr."

"I preferred her in *From Here to Eternity*."

"Listen to us movie buffs," said Freddy.

"Bernie," said Michael, "you got some loose ends to tie up in there, don't you?"

"I have nothing but loose ends. And Schmead, you and Uncle Freddy," I said, "and now Hummer with his goons. It's about as inviting as a tarantula's nest." I didn't mention the most lethal element of all, my parents.

"That's gratefulness for you," said Freddy. "We have a future monastic foundation to protect." I looked at Michael.

"So the whole monastery near Pompei was true? You want to support a monastery in Le Loup?" They nodded. "Hess's dream?"

"What can I say?" said Freddy. "We all have to support good causes, or what will become of us?"

"Ever hear of Operation Constantine,"

"Yes, but I could never figure out what it was," I said.

"Good, that's the way I wanted it."

"That was your money? From prostitution and gambling?"

"You ask a lot of questions." "

"I just want to know if I'm going to jail for washing your money?"

"Here's your answer: we need you to go in and testify and make sure they don't hear anything about Constantine, and then later you will help us wash some money in SCHLAYEX to make the books right and then some. Then it will make its way to a special project in Le Loup."

"I don't know."

"G. K., they know your name in Vegas. You showed us ways of double blinding ledgers to provide the law with a false trail, with fake bank accounts. And showing money going from the monastery to the sister house of nuns. That was genius. Where'd you learn that?"

"My father's stores in California. He hates paying taxes more than anything. The more you move around the money and jigger the ledgers, the easier it is to pass it off as capital improvements, supplies, returns, and starting a new store than never gets built. I came up with an imaginary new monastery that never gets built."

"Mai dire mai," said Freddy with a thick Italian accent. "Never say never."

I looked at him and Michael quizzically. "Just go back in there and steer them clear of any mention of Constantine."

"What about Chalmers, he's been stealing from the funds."

"We have plans for him." He and Michael exchanged mischievous looks.

I started to go back inside.

"Somehow none of this seems right. I came here for a classical education."

"This is classical, pure Machiavelli," said Freddy. Michael was laughing.

"My parents are in there and will not understand any of this."

"You should know better than me -- it's the sinners, not the saints, who end up at the table and make things turn out for the good."

"And Schmead, he's going to ruin the program and our house."

"We got Schmead covered. He'll back off or we'll tie up twenty rocks in downtown projects."

"Rocks?"

"He means *millions*," said Michael to Freddy's irritation.

"What about Hummer?" I said.

"From what I hear, all you got to do is give him something he's wanted for a long time," said Freddy with an evil grin.

"Like Chalmers," said Michael.

"What about our blood oath?"

"Our blood runs thicker," said Freddy. He pointed with his eyes to the doors back into Dyche Hall.

LXVIII

THICK AS THEBES

"Wait."

They were packing up; people were starting to leave.

"I would like to testify."

Finley looked at Broglio, then me. I saw my mother crying at the back, and I didn't know if I had it in me to go on. My friends all had question marks written on their faces.

Finley asked me some easy questions at first. That didn't last.

"You were an honors student?"

"One of your rising stars, as you put it."

"But you lost your scholarship after your first year."

"I voluntarily relinquished it."

He stared at me. If he wasn't going to mention the charges, I was not.

"Did you spy for the university to get your scholarship back?

"I gathered information for some elements in the university."

"You did more than gather information for the university. You went a lot further than that—coming into the Catholic Church."

"I went to confession, that is true, but I did not go through with baptism."

"You went through all that and didn't even become Catholic?"

"Missed it by that much," I said in my best *Get Smart* Agent 86 voice.

"What do you mean you worked for various elements in the university?"

"I worked for two elements within the university. Or three."

"Three? Explain."

"I worked for the chancellor tacitly. But . . . I met with the vice chancellor for academic affairs."

"Albert Holloway? He is but an extension of the chancellor. That's one element."

"Not exactly. He commissioned me to do something else."

"Something else?"

Now was my chance.

"To get rid of you and Professor Marin."

We both looked at Marin, who puffed a cigarette with his head cocked back.

"Excuse me, but you cannot smoke in here," said Pigg. Marin puffed away.

"But you did not try to do that?"

"Not Marin anyway." He thought he could go as far as he wanted with me.

"Because you came under their influence."

"Because I came under her influence!"

"Her?"

"Your girl." I had put together all the pieces now. He looked around. His "girl" was legion. Mindy sat there, jilted and pert. Terry Marker pouted. I knew I had all the ammunition I needed.

"You had her walk before me, follow me, and knew I would be hopelessly attracted to her . . . classic Florentine Renaissance art beauty."

"I have no idea what you're talking about."

"You slept with her, Mindy, and her, Terry Marker, and her, and her."

I pointed at them all, and Finley turned red.

"You were *my* spy!" he said.

The room inhaled as one.

"I told you I would not enroll in HIP." He had approached me the year before to discredit HIP. I would have his prized spot. It had to be Apryl, his girl inside.

"But you did enter HIP."

"Not because of you, because of her!" I pointed at Apryl. "Now I realize you were behind even that. The poem, all of it. You never expected I would be a double agent for Holloway, who knew of your sordid affair with his Apryl. And you did not know Apryl was his daughter."

"Apryl?"

Apryl was in tears, looking at me with imploring eyes, eyes I thought were asking me to stop. Finley looked around.

"I don't even know this . . . young lady. However, now that you mention it." He conferred with Margaret Schmead, looking at a folder. He pulled out a piece of paper. Margaret stepped in and took over.

"Yes, Mr. Kennisbaum," she said, looking down through a pair of reading glasses. "Is it common in the program for drugs to be used?"

"Drugs?"

"Yes, say, drugs for disinhibiting women."

I was flabbergasted. This was the last thing I expected. I looked over at Apryl, who seemed quite alarmed. Had she informed on us?

"I, uh, did not . . ."

"There are reports that a woman was drugged to make her more pliable." She cleared her throat as if she could not let the vulgarities pass her lips.

"I am not sure what you are talking about." Was it all going to come crashing down because I was trying to be the master of jests?

"Do you think nonconsensual sex is a form of rape?"

Apryl looked around. Was this rarest of flowers just another in a long line of accusers from the Old Testament to our day? I looked at Attorney General Hummer, who glared.

"Miss Schmead, I believe that there are many forms of non-consensual sex at the university."

"Do you now? Yes, like taking advantage of young women."

"Like teachers taking advantage of students."

I looked at Finley. I saw a few other younger assistant professors in the audience squirming in their chairs.

"We're here to talk about the humanities program."

I had to fight back. I pointed at Finley.

"That man, Finley, sleeps with his students, and I caught him in Apryl's bed recently, while he was investigating HIP."

Finely turned red and shot out of his seat. Hummer moved toward the front.

"You're through with all your violations of university code, your illegal sales off campus, your plagiarism," barked Hummer.

Apryl shot me daggers.

"How can you deny it?" I said to Apryl. "You have lied from the beginning. Were you teasing him as you were teasing us?"

"To think I loved you!" she said and strode out of the room. Holloway followed after her. She was walking again in slow motion, her beauty refulgent.

"That was me with Finley, in Apryl's bed."

It was Maggie who stood up now.

"You?" I looked at Finley, who was turning new shades of crimson.

"Rich had me lure Finley to her bed to compromise him."

I looked over at Chalmers in his leather bomber's jacket.

"Chalmers pimped you?"

"Now, wait, this is our proceeding," said Pigg. "This is out of order."
The viewers were rapt, on the edges of their seats.

I had not been caught in her evil net. I had done something terrible.
I had stolen her honor publicly.

And I thought of Maggie, still plying her trade. Hogg must have
taken the birth control pills from her. I got it all wrong.

Finley jumped up and tore into me again.

"So I'm looking at this report. Are you denying you drugged a girl,
kidnapped her, and had sexual relations with her?"

"Do you know who set you up, Professor Finley? Who got you on
film?"

I pointed at Chalmers. Finley scrambled through some papers,
looking at his colleagues for some help. I looked over at Chalmers who
shook his head, warning me.

"Rich Chalmers. Not only that, he was working for the chancellor."
Gasps came from the viewers. "First, he burned the student union, then
Barrows saw an opportunity to work in league with the agitators. Barrows
had to rein him in, and he tried to use me."

"Shut up, you quisling," said Chalmers, standing up in gunslinger
stance. "Don't forget what we have on you."

Then there was a glint of steel, a switchblade in its arc into the air
and its reentry onto the desk in front of me. I watched its pendulum
swinging, wondering how he could be so sure of the trajectory. It landed
right on the desk in front of Finley, as sure as it landed in front of me on
that hot August day. Finley looked agape as Marin stood.

"That's right, Finley. Let me talk, because you may yet escape the
judgment when you hear what I have to tell." I took out a cigarette and a
matchbook and lit the cigarette with one hand. Marin walked around in
front like it was his classroom.

"If all of you start throwing stones over kids sleeping with adults,
this is going to get very messy for everybody. I told Rich to do what he
did. He went too far."

"He burned down the union," I said. "Probably St. Mary's church, too. Drugged a young woman, hired prostitutes, embezzled—."

"Piss on you, Kennisbaum! Piss on all of you!" Chalmers stormed out, knocking over a chair. Hummer and his goons followed after him. I walked back to the front, taking the pose of a prosecutor. My mother was looking on, astonished.

"Embezzled what?" said Finley, trying to wrest control from proceedings that had gotten totally away from him.

"Uh . . . just spades winnings at the house." I did just what I thought DeBlasio wanted, take them right up to the edge but protect operation Constantine.

"Why did you set him on me?" I asked Marin.

"I wanted you to be in the program."

"This was *your* trap?"

"I let it be known to Chalmers who you were, that Finley was trying to get you to undermine HIP. He took it from there." Even in confession, he was fierce, a Hotspur.

"Why did you care about me? Because of my aunt, because of my father who was your student?"

"I had no children of my own . . . I had followed your career at KU, and your aunt Teresa told me about you."

"So you had Chalmers get Apryl to seduce me?"

"Nobody saw that coming."

"You mean, it was not an act."

"I love thee with a love I seemed to lose with my lost saints."

"You teach a kind of idealized love even she cannot live up to."

"You're talking about love and deception, disguises, and true love discovered. It's in everything we teach, especially Shakespeare," said Marin.

"But you make it all seem possible, but we're not up to it."

"That's not our fault."

"And Chancellor Barrows, he knew about your indiscretions. He had the poem?" He nodded. "You looked at me the first day of class. I thought you were talking to me, but you really *were* talking to me."

"Every student thinks that."

"You betrayed your own program."

"I helped things along."

"Tom Hogg is in the hospital now because of your 'help.'"

"He left. He was there voluntarily."

"Did you know Apryl is Vice Chancellor Holloway's daughter?"

"Yes."

"Was she your daughter?"

There was a hubbub, especially among my confreres.

"No."

"But you don't deny sleeping with his wife, Apryl's mother."

The onlookers were wide-eyed, the reporters scribbling.

"There is much I regret about that time period."

"My father hates you. My father was against my coming to KU." I was on a roll, no use to talk to me. "Did you have an affair with my mother, Miriam?" I looked back, and I saw my mother's look of shock.

"Why did you come to KU?" said Marin.

"I came here to know, about myself, my father. Why do you care?"

"I care because I wronged you."

I heard my aunt Teresa crying. My mother was comforting her.

"How could you wrong me?" I thought I saw tears in his eyes. "You had a child with Aunt Teresa, and she had an abortion. Is that it?"

Marin stared at me. My mother suddenly called out from the back. "Stop this!"

I looked at her, then at Marin, then at Aunt Teresa.

"Mom . . . what is going on?"

My mother wept. Marin could not speak.

"You are my son," said Teresa finally. The crowd hushed, all eyes on Teresa.

"I am *your* son?" I said gawking at Marin.

"She gave birth to you here in Lawrence," said Marin, "and your mother and father agreed to adopt you and took you to California when your father transferred to Berkeley."

I looked at my father, then at my mother. I turned to Marin:

"*You* are my father?" He looked down. "Aunt Teresa is my *mother*?"

"This is the end of the hearings—for real this time," said Pigg, bringing down the gavel.

My mother and father came to the front. I hugged them. My aunt Teresa walked slowly toward Marin. They embraced. Marin came over to me and placed a hand on my shoulder. I looked at the hand. I plucked the knife from the desk, holding it up in front of Marin.

"This is three times you nearly killed me with the knife." I carefully folded the blade back into place and handed it to him. "Do you mind? I'm spending time with my father," I said. Marin nodded and left the room.

Patrick and Jimmy slapped me on the back as they were leaving. Maggie stood back, watching.

"We sure got our money's worth," said Jimmy.

"Sorry," said Patrick.

"The truth isn't all it's cracked up to be," I said. I looked at Maggie as they left.

I turned to look my father in the eye.

"Well, son . . ." He did not seem to know what to say. "I never knew you had this much chutzpah."

"I guess I'm not half the Jew I used to be."

My mother laughed through her tears, and then my father cracked up.

"You seemed to know there was something here that you had to seek," she said.

"It was like righting his numbers, I just couldn't leave the journal unfinished," I said.

"We should have told you before you came here," he said, shaking his head. "Big mistake."

Teresa came over and put her hand on my chest, unmoved by my attempt at comic relief.

"You sure do have a flair for the dramatic, boyo."

"This stuff only happens in those nineteenth-century novels Mom reads," I said.

I realized how much of her was in me, that the bond we had these last three years was more than spiritual. We could not unpack what this meant in a few glib exchanges.

This odyssey did not unfold the way I ever expected. I had come to the right place to find my father after all.

LXIX

THE ONE THING

Presume not that I am the thing I was,
For God doth know—so shall the world perceive—
That I have turned away my former self.

— *Shakespeare, Henry IV, Part 2, Act V, sc. V*

INDECISION, the rock of Sisyphus, painful oversleeping, studying. After learning you had two sets of parents, finals were a snap. By comparison with the lingering of Apryl in my soul, my relationship with my father now seemed easy. A week later, after finals, Maggie intercepted me as I walked up the hill toward Strong Hall.

"Finals were a drag," she said. "Especially British Literature after 1800."

I just grunted, unable to muster enthusiasm for small talk.

"Apryl would like to talk to you," she said finally, her eyes on the ground. I looked at her. She saw the deep reproof in my eyes, her loss of status there. "So, it's that bad between us."

"Maggie—"

"Let me stop you. You think I used you. But I really fell for you, Jack."

"By sleeping with Finley?"

"I had no idea Rich was going to spring that on you."

"Why would you let Rich make you do that?"

"It wasn't Rich, it was DeBlasio. My price for leaving the life."

"I see." I was stunned.

408

"You should talk to Apryl."

"Apryl . . .?"

"She is innocent."

"Innocent?"

"Please see her. Or it may be too late."

"I have to see the chancellor." She looked at me with surprise. "I have loose ends before I leave." She teared up and stood in the street watching me as I carried my heavy load up Mount Oread. I could not look back.

I strode into Barrows's office without an appointment, as if he were expecting me.

"How were finals?"

"After the hearings, a joy."

"That was quite a performance. But I suppose you got a little more than you bargained for."

"As did you."

"I don't see it that way."

"We both lost."

"You lost a girl," he said sharply. "I, on the other hand . . . let's just say I am looking forward to great things here at the University of Kansas."

"How do you figure? You have a committee that set out to destroy students and a popular program."

"Transform a popular program. Finley is resigning and going to teach in Iowa, Holloway is out of the administration and is back teaching American literature, and HIP will be subsumed into a new college that I will design to provide classical education to students who want it. I will head it up."

"You . . . got what you wanted." He smiled with assurance. "What about Marin?"

"Your father? He'll take leave without pay for a year to dry out once and for all and put some distance between him, the university, and the hearings."

I started to leave in disgust.

"You will be wanting this." He opened a drawer. I turned and saw him holding out my journal. I snatched it and clutched it like a talisman, feeling its magical powers pass into my hands.

"All's well that ends well, is that it?" I said.

"Measure for measure, it could have been worse."

"Thanks for this." I held up my journal.

"Some good writing in there. Too bad you have to keep it to yourself. I assume you won't be talking about these matters publicly?"

"Not anytime soon," I said. I started to leave.

"You did just what I knew you would do, Kennisbaum."

"What?" I expected him to get in one final dig.

"Stayed true to yourself."

"You mean, turn on my friends, betray the best professors I ever had, and sully a girl's reputation, destroying my chance at true love?"

"Ah, youth, such harsh recriminations. You'll forget all of this in a year."

I smiled and remembered an old grudge. "Did Perry get the Fulbright?"

"He's a fastidious factotum who was also working both sides of the fence with Holloway. Nobody's getting one this year." He looked at me through his bushy black eyebrows. "If you will tell me it was him with the marijuana and you were protecting him, then I will have cause to expel him, and I might reconsider the Fulbright. We know his relatives had a pot operation along the highway. The pot circulating on campus came from that crop."

The real Barrows shining through. A picture flashed through my head of Hummer arresting Perry in front of everyone on Jayhawk Boulevard.

"I'm through with treachery."

"I almost forgot; your buddy Chalmers is expelled from the graduate school."

It figured. They had to shut down the SCHLAYEX account, but they never figured out the real accounts that Freddy controlled. I tried to leave.

"Kennisbaum, how is Courtney?" I turned to address him from the door.

"I don't know."

"That was not your fault."

I nodded, doubtful.

"Did you learn the truth from Courtney?"

"I am not sure."

"An agnostic." He narrowed his eyes. "A pity."

He laughed and went to the window and looked down on Jayhawk Boulevard, shoving out his jaw and peering down.

"Man's life is short, and he withers like the grass," he said like a Puritan preacher.

"Still, they keep coming to the hill," I said, "to the mount, thirsting for knowledge. Burning to know Truth. Will you give it to them?"

He looked at me vacantly. I turned and left. I said nothing to him about any scholarship or transfer, but later, I received by mail in a manila envelope my transcripts, a transfer agreement with Berkeley, and a copy of my official file expunged of any reference to suspicious activities at my old fraternity or in the new one, 1132 Ohio. I was just an honors student with high recommendations.

I came out into the brilliant May sunlight, onto Jayhawk Boulevard where I met Teresa and my parents standing by the bronze Jayhawk. I touched it one last time for luck. I saw my father do the same. I walked with them, arm in arm.

"Something is on your mind," said Aunt Teresa.

"Just a few things." She laughed. "I just don't know what to say to her."

"Which one?"

"Well, Apryl."

"You do owe her an apology."

"First, I need to see someone else at the hospital."

"The one with the miracles?" she said.

"I knew a fellow who lost his marbles at KU," said my father. "They packed him off to Larned, the state loony bin."

"Norm," said my mother affectionately. "It's not kind to talk like that."

"No, Tom has flown the coop, don't know where he is," I said.

"Then who *are* you seeing?"

φ

"You want de fof flow."

"Fourth floor, thank you." I wished I could be with Jimmy Drungole at the Crossing, mindlessly alive with word jazz. I went to the St. Francis Medical Center cardiac unit of eerie wheezes, collapsing and rising machines, and babbling blue beeps. The graphs displayed for passersby and cardiac nurses did not display the heart but instead made the case in electro-biologic plottings of random swerves of atoms to combine into something rhythmic and life-affirming.

I walked quietly in my white and blue Adidas racers and crept unseen among the pale and mummiform. An elderly woman, propped up in bed, was covered in tubes and an oxygen mask. She stared at me through wide, lashless eyes. A younger man stared, not at me, but into a void created by this atonal night.

One among the patients was reading, propped up on an elbow with tubes crisscrossing him like a marionette carelessly tossed on a bed, machines thrumming their sotto voce chorus. This man meditated on the text of the small hardbound book. It was Paul Courtney.

"St. Thomas?"

"That would be too obvious for one's deathbed. Maritain. On Beauty. He speaks of St. Thomas. The clear beauty of Truth. The greater beauty of being. Even in a place as dismal as this, you can meditate on Beauty."

"Where are the nurses, the doctors?"

"We don't need them. We have our friends." He raised an arm, feebly—the Punch and Judy show of tubes, drips, and monitors.

"I . . . let you down."

"My wife has been after me for years to exercise and eat right."

"Well, they do wonders now, with open heart and—"

He put up a hand. "You know what she said tonight when she visited, after the priest visited? 'None of us is getting out of this alive.' Her way of letting go." I laughed even as I teared up. He laughed, spreading a huge smile across his face, the kindest look I ever saw from him.

"Bernard, don't give up on yourself. You see in yourself only imperfection and missed opportunities. We see something else."

"What?"

"The jewel of youth, the promise of years. You don't know your own beauty."

"I don't know," I said. "So much I can't account for. Tom is gone from the hospital. I don't know if Chalmers has—"

While I was in midsentence, he grabbed my hand and shut his eyes. I felt his grip harden on me as his mouth curled into a wince.

"Follow the royal road."

"Royal?"

"Seek the one needful thing . . . the one thing necessary."

A monitor went off. He fell against the pillow. An intermittent beeping sounded, and a light show of blips and flashes draped my eyes. His grip tightened on my arm as he writhed on the bed.

"What is the one thing needful?"

He looked up in pain as the coda of alarms rushed on.

"Seek Beauty . . . seek the one."

Then he relaxed his grip, placed his hands over his chest, and looked placidly at the ceiling. I wanted to raise him on my back and take him from this hideous place, to 1132, where he could speak to us of the beauty of God's being until fate arrived.

I heard the rush of footsteps and voices. I darted behind a curtain and then out of a side door into bleakest Topeka night. I thought about stopping by Ole Miss on the way home. I felt an urgency to tell Apryl about Hogg and about how sorry I was—and that maybe there was hope for us. Somewhere between Lecompton and Lawrence, my resolve flagged. What could I say to them, that I went to see Courtney and then he had a fatal heart attack?

LXX

VIRGINS OF TIME

Even beneath the veil, across the stream,
Her loveliness surpassed her former self,
Just as on earth she had surpassed all others.

— DANTE, PURGATORIO, XXXI

AFTER Courtney's funeral service on campus, I spent some days of packing, trying to let the knowledge of events and persons sink in.

One of my first acts with my rediscovered journal was to paste a picture of me standing on the porch of 1132 in my tuxedo, holding a cigarette, looking every bit the suave man about campus. Right before the waltz, before it was all in pieces. At least, the picture made me look happy. These were the fairy gifts of youth, and I was afraid of their fading away. I hid the journal in a cubby in the cave of the basement.

Patrick and the others had excluded Chalmers from the house. They had taken my side. They actually found it cool that I was Marin's son, and that it was possible that Apryl was Marin's daughter, though I had told them that was untrue. Besides, it was a disgusting thought after all that had passed between us.

"You are still in love with her," said Patrick.

"Marin would always be between us."

"Conscience makes cowards of us all?"

"She is planning to leave K.U.," I said.

"You buying it?"

414

I looked at him. "It would be the ultimate burn." He nodded.

"Seems like she is the one who is more injured here."

"Don't be fair about her," I said. "There's nothing fair about her."

"She is fairest of the fair."

I had been thinking and dreaming of her. I had one dream in which both she and Maggie were naked at the rock quarry, vying for my affection.

I took a walk the next morning around the Campanile, looking over Memorial Stadium, when found myself walking down Mississippi Street. I felt my knees weakening, my resolve crumbling, as I mounted the stairs.

So many memories were wrapped up in my ventures to this house to seek the ultimate ecstasy with Apryl. I thought I had given her up. I was angry that I thought she had betrayed me and used me.

Sue Hurlbut answered the door. She looked at me for a long moment, her face sad and puffy from crying over Paul Courtney. She asked if I knew where Tom was. They were sick with worry about him; he hadn't made it to Courtney's funeral.

"What about Apryl?"

"You're too late. She's gone to the airport. Gone to France."

"France? When?"

"Her plane is set to leave around noon. I don't think you can make it."

It was only an hour and a half. I got the flight information. I had to stop back at 1132 to get my car in the alley. I rushed over the hill of Twelfth Street, huffing and puffing. As I reached the Crossing, I saw smoke rising. Once I reached Ohio Street, I heard sirens.

I walked slowly onto the scene of 1132 in flames. The fire seemed most intense in back of the house, the flames engulfing the basement and third floor. As I rounded the back of the house, I saw that my car had caught fire. I could smell beer and hops burning; I heard glass shattering as bottles exploded. Phaedo came running toward me. He jumped up onto his hind legs, whimpering some message. He smelled of smoke. He ran toward the basement door.

I ran after him, but Patrick came over to me and threw me to the ground. Michael, Bob, Swensen, Ross, and Zorn were outside, waiting for the fire trucks. Hess rode up on his motorcycle and rushed to our side.

"Anyone seen Hogg?" yelled Hess.

"I assumed he is in Kansas City," said McDarby.

"He's been hiding here," said Hess.

"You think Hogg burned down the house?" I said. I thought of St. Thomas and fire as the cure to impurity.

"Hell, no." Then Hess yelled at the house. "Chalmers!"

"Sonofabitch," snarled McDarby. "Arson and old Mace!"

"He tell you that?" I said.

Just then, I heard someone coughing inside the basement.

"Someone's in there!"

"I don't think so," said Patrick. I ran toward the back door. Patrick grabbed me again.

"You'll die," he said, pinning me down. I threw him off.

"My journal is in there." I kicked in the back door to the basement. Black smoke belched into my face. I rushed in.

"You're insane!" yelled Patrick.

I took off my Ben Gurion safari jacket and shielded my face from the inferno of flames and smoke. I was overcome with the acrid smoke, the burned beer smell, the hops. The basement was torn up as if from an explosion, glass shards everywhere.

I took in a mouthful of smoke. I put the Ben Gurion over my face. Back inside, flames licked books and old clothing. There on the desk by the window was my journal, open, as if someone had been reading it. I reached to rescue my journal from the fire, but I heard coughing and yelling coming from the cave. It was the best place to hide from flames, moist and leaky.

Back there, in the dark, I saw Hogg on the ground, curled up, muttering and coughing. I grabbed him.

"Brother fire," he said and looked at me with his dark eyes. He was holding his lighter. "*In lux perpetua*, Bernard." I saw burns on his arms and face, the cuts from flying glass.

I started to drag him out. He was resisting me. "Brother fire purges," he said, curling up in a ball. I tried to drag him further. I heard someone coughing. Patrick appeared suddenly. We heaved and picked Hogg up and carried him over our shoulders. Outside, we fell in a heap, gasping for air. Then I looked at Patrick. His face was black with smoke. He shook his head.

I ran back to the basement. Michael and McDarby tried to hold me back, but I threw them off.

"Crazy bastard!" said McDarby.

Back inside, the flames had grown higher, licking the edges of my journal. I reached with my burned hand right into the flames and grabbed it. I felt the sting of pain, the singe of flesh. I retrieved my journal before it burned. It was charred around the edges, a few pictures bearing the beginnings of heat and consumption. When I emerged, I fainted dead away.

I awoke to paramedics placing an oxygen mask over my mouth and nose. Men took axes to the basement. Other paramedics tended to Hogg. I felt in my pocket. I had Hogg's lighter. I felt around; my journal was nowhere to be found. Flames engulfed the upper storey. Water and ash baptized the air. We watched as the house burned hopelessly out of control.

The fire chief, a tall, burly man with a square jaw, a mustache, and large inquisitive eyes, approached us.

"I am Chief Matt Blair. This looks like a set fire. You know of anyone who would do this?" Blair looked at Hogg lying on a stretcher, crossing himself.

"Yes," said Hess, stepping forward confidently. We looked at each other. "Rich Chalmers."

"Likes to play with fire," I said. Hogg looked at me with nervous eyes. I clutched the lighter in my pocket. I heard some firemen on the radio calling out to police.

I looked at my watch. It was stopped. The time: 11:32 in the morning. Nobody would believe it or care. I put on my charred Ben Gurion.

In a minute, two cars pulled up to the curb. Kansas Bureau of Investigation. Out of one popped J. Barnett Hummer. I saw Chalmers in the back seat glaring at us. Hummer already had his man. Channel 13 filmed. Cameras were flashing. They weren't kidding about the illegal alcohol sales investigation. All the books, the hops, the bottles, the whole operation—all the evidence, up in smoke.

I started to leave.

"Where you going?" said Chief Blair.

"The airport."

"Why should I let you leave?" said the chief. "Besides, the attorney general is here; he will need you to answer questions."

"A girl is about to leave town."

Blair looked me up and down, charred, covered in dust and smoke. He saw how pathetic and desperate I was, and he was suspicious.

"I was just coming here to head to the airport to get my car." I pointed to it. "I gotta catch her before she's gone forever."

"She must be special."

"That ever I saw," I said.

McDarby, Patrick, Zorn, and Hess all echoed their grunts of approbation to the chief.

"You won't be going anywhere in that," said the chief, pointing to my Chevy in flames. Hess handed me my journal.

"Thought I would safeguard it. You best get out of here."

"I have to get to the airport—how am I going to see Apryl?"

"My Harley!" He ran to get his motorcycle.

I held the journal. I turned to head away toward the alley, but Hummer shouted above the din of the fire and journalists.

"Wait, you. I need to ask you some questions."

I shoved the journal in my pants. Hess's Harley snarled from the street. A belch of black smoke came out with a loud pop. I ran for the alley while Hummer shouted for me to stop. Two officers of the KBI headed out after me. I was running full tilt.

"Halt!" yelled the officers. Just then, Hess pulled up to the alley at the opening to Eleventh Street. I saw Michael running toward the officers to interfere with their pursuit.

"Hop on, boy." He got off and offered his shiny Harley-Davidson Sportster for me. I jumped on, familiar with the beast from riding it around the farm.

"Question internal combustion!" he yelled as he threw me his goggles. I revved the Harley for effect and peeled out.

I turned and looked back at the officers running and 1132 burning to the ground as I crested Kentucky and headed down onto the interstate at breakneck speed. As I pulled out, I saw Hummer by his car and Chalmers in the back. I smiled at him. He looked at me, stone-faced.

φ

I abandoned the bike at the circular Trans World Airlines entrance of Kansas City International Airport. I rushed inside and found a skycap who told me the gate where her flight was headed for Chicago O'Hare. He said I had best hurry, that they had announced the last call for that flight. I ran full out.

Just as I arrived, I looked through the window at the TWA 727 pulling away from the gate. I ran up to the tall glass and yelled at the plane to stop. I asked a stewardess in her thirties at the boarding area if they could stop the plane.

"Sir, the plane is already taxiing to the runway."

"It's an emergency." She looked me up and down, seeing the blackening covering me, smelling the smoke. My hair was bedraggled.

"A matter of life and death?"

"A matter of the love of my life."

She cracked a thin smile, remembering perhaps her own luckless affairs in a thousand ports.

She looked out as a plane began to take off, and said, "You're pretty young for that."

I rushed to the glass and watched abjectly as the plane lifted off the runway. I fell to the ground, my hands and arms plastered above me. There, through the smokey smears on the panes, with the truest contrition I had ever known, I wept. My last hope of redemption disappeared into a cloudless May sky. In a moment, she was a distant object hovering like a ghost on a midwestern horizon.

EPILOGUE

BOOK WITHOUT END

A l'alta fantasia qui mancò possa;
ma già volgeva il mio disio e 'l velle,
sì come rota ch'igualmente è mossa,
l'amor che move il sole e l'altre stelle.

(This high dream resisted my powers to fly,
as already my will and desire moved
– like revolving wheels turn as one – by
the Love that moves the sun and the other stars.)

— DANTE, PARADISO XXXIII, 142-45

I HEARD *about the program after Paul Courtney died. HIP continued as a smaller program, then was suffocated by Barrows's new program—CCS, Core Curriculum Studies. I finished college and law school in California, took a job in Chicago, and there I stayed. Some have preferred exile and wandering. Seeing Beatrice from afar and being burned by her on a bridge over the Arno ignited a dream and a passionate song that lives on. But once you have gone to the mount, wandering in a desert will never do; for you crave the epiphany of ordinary day.*

If I could disappear into a dream, it would be one of numberless recurrences of college when the mind was open to anything. Numbers did not contain us then, for they were infinity, singular, united. We were not Kantian knowers condemned to reason in a counting box, unable to transcend the binary code.

423

Now the numbers define everything. Like when I entered the market in the old center of Charleston when I was there for a bank merger. My eyes wandered to a leather vendor. I needed a new wallet. I opened one; the price was $11.32. I opened several more of differing varieties. All with the same price. I asked the owner of the booth why he would pick such a random number for wallets. He said in a lilting southern voice, "With taxes . . . come to twelve dollar even." In the lazy grammar there was grace and conservation of energy. He didn't want to deal with change. Maybe that was why I kept seeing numbers.

When I visited Kansas City last year to see Teresa, she was more blind than ever—and saw as clearly as she ever did. I never called her Mother.

"What are you going to do about all this in your past?" she said.

"I guess it is not going to go away on its own."

"He said, decades after the fact." She put her hand on my chest. "So what are you going to do to get past it?"

I turned at the click of a gate at Notre Dame de Fontevrault, the convent near Tour; a dove-skinned nun in wimple appeared and waved me back. She had eyes as placid as a mountain lake. She looked startled to see a disheveled man in a tuxedo. In her broken English, she conveyed that another sister, actually a postulant who had not taken final vows, Soeur Marie Terese, would come if I followed her. Once inside, she showed me to a waiting area in front of a grating. I waited, and another nun, closer to my age, with dazzling blue-green eyes, came to the grille. She stared at me for a time. I was just lost in her eyes.

"Bernard," she said. The voice startled me. It was the voice of Maggie. She looked the same—the eyes, the fair skin—except she looked younger than she should have.

"I have been here since 1992." Her French accent was thicker.

"I've been here since 1132."

"Long time to be in a tuxedo," she said. She looked straight at me as she had the first time I saw her at the Halloween party. Here I was in at French convent with a former prostitute with whom I'd had an affair. Here she was, pure, reformed, lovely in every way.

"I have not taken my simple vows yet."

"Does it always take this long?" I had left my country to avoid another set of vows.

"For some."

"Our hearts are restless," I said. She smiled at the allusion.

"In His will is our peace."

"St. Bernard?" I ventured.

"Close, but no, Dante."

"Right." Straight out of Paradiso. How could I forget?

"The light penetrates you the same, wherever you are, if you do not obscure it. Apryl left the convent years ago."

I think Maggie saw me blush. She knew full well why I had come.

She asked if I had heard from any of my old roommates of 1132. Just hearing her mention those numbers out loud made the whole dark memory lift, and it was once again a place of joviality and comradeship.

"It was a real disgusting house," she said, laughing.

"Transcendentally so."

She nodded and said, *"Have you ever gone back to Lawrence?"*

"Maybe some day."

"The search ends when the journey begins."

"Another famous saying from your Quebecois père?"

"My very own. I got it from being here."

"I thought after my marriage failed, maybe if I remarried . . ."

She silenced me with a look. This was no time for another confession.

"I live in Chicago. I see Aunt Tessie frequently in Kansas City, and she has asked about you."

She reached and took my hand. *"Bernard, I pray for you."* Tears flooded her eyes. I began to well up. *"Go see them . . . go to Le Loup."*

I said I would. What could I possibly find in Le Loup—Hess building a huge bonfire by the hedgerow, a Latin Mass, stars so close you could lick them, a girl by a pond surrounded by golden stubble fields under a giant harvest moon? I clutched my journal and left, hoping this experience would chase away the April phantoms.

φ

It is six months since the trip to France, blowing the metaphysical stink of thirty years off me. The decibels of desperation are lower. Hogg said once that I would go to Chalfontbleau and there would find peace. In a way, he was right.

I don't see the numbers anymore. My former fiancée did not ask any questions when she saw me at a fundraiser at the Art Institute. We sipped

Fumé Blanc and mused over the colossal Seurat, happily lost in the colorful points. Some partners were annoyed that they had come to my wedding only to find I had fled to France, but they spared me the humiliation of questions because most of their lives are in shambles. We have no fixed stars. Others have left for rain forests or tried to work among the poor in India to shake off the perplexity of prosperity—or to atone for an affair with an associate. I trudged on. Then one day I received a call.

"Bernard." *I would have known the voice anywhere, with that throaty, steamy longing sound. I place my journal in a drawer and lock it.*

"Apryl . . . how did—"

"Sister Marie. She wrote me that you were living in Chicago. I'm here."

"Here, in Chicago?"

"Yes, I live here now. Isn't that an amazing coincidence? I would like to see you." *During a long pause, I relive all of it.* "How about the Drake for high tea? It's not the Castle Tea Room, but it will have to do."

"Sure." *She gives a throaty laugh.* "See you at teatime."

I go early, waiting for her, admiring the white roses and filigreed drapery.

There she is, everything around us pales. She is walking again in a resplendent curvature of space, Lucretius in drag, a vision of loveliness, a glorious face as ever I saw. She draws closer—decked out to the nines in a luminous Dior outfit—a close-fitting white dress suit, her auburn hair slightly redder now from sun or highlights, pulled back in a bun, show-ing all of her magnificent Botticelli face, not like his Venus, but more like Madonna and Child, with a pomegranate, a little older, paler, less Venus, more noblewoman of Genoa from my second-hand Abrams Botticelli, on my coffee table. Downcast eyes.

She smiles and approaches, nipping me on the cheek with a fake kiss, smelling like heaven again. She grabs my hand and smiles. I hold her hands and feel the pent-up desire of thirty years surface.

"Bernard . . . Bernard. It is you." *Something is reflected in her eyes. Time? No, in the reflection of those eyes is—my gold Patek Phillipe.*

"Apryl, you look . . . amazing."

"You are . . . so distinguished—those glasses, the salt and pepper hair."

She tousles my hair. I feel a young thrill. She gives another throaty laugh.

"Are you going to stand here staring at me, or do you want to sit?"

"Would you mind if I just stared?"

She shakes her head, playfully scolding me as in times past. We sit in our cozy booth. I look at her straight on under a direct light over the booth: she is different close up. Time and fevers have burned something out of her. A perfect figure, attractive, yes, and desirable. But the halo of youth and ripeness has given way to something ordinary, blanched, not magical, just female; not Apryl Jovey, not the girl in the painting. All Apryl, and none of Apryl. Her erstwhile brimming sexual ripeness has run to a sporty, trim frame—kept through yoga or Tae Bo. Her breasts do not heave, as if someone had let the air out of them. Her teeth are perfect from treatments, outshining the rest of her like ivory and diamonds on an old woman. But her eyes, nothing has changed. I see Jove's nectar and wish to sup if only for old time's sake. My stomach tickles. We order tea, scones, and cucumber sandwiches.

"I am a cliché, a 'dink'—divorced, no kids. You?" *She looks up, says nothing.* "Had we but world enough and time." *I try to tempt her into an old mode. Apryl just smiles politely. I edge nearer to her.*

"You did chase me," *she says coldly, sipping her Mélange du Cap, leaving a smear of brick red on the bone china.*

"Even to France." *She looks quizzically at me.* "Figuratively, I mean." *Why lie now?* "When you left for France, I rode Hess's motorcycle to the airport."

"I never knew that." *She gets a dreamy look.*

"As 1132 went up in flames."

"I'm glad they never looked at Tom for that." *She looks into my eyes. I see something utterly foreign: fear.*

"What do you mean?" *I said.*

She looks around, distracted, as if she had another appointment. She places her hand on mine, mechanically. I pull my hand away.

"I rescued Tom from the cave. I took his lighter."

"Yes, you were gallant again. They think Rich burned it down but never could convict him." *Had she and Chalmers conspired in one last act? She had given up the program, was leaving it all, torched the house—maybe to cover up what Hogg was writing, maybe to avenge her humiliation, maybe to show everyone that she was supreme. I protected Hogg from anyone thinking he did it, and I partly believed Rich had torched our haven.*

"It was you? All these years, Rich and I carried the blame for sinking the program."

"You can't blame yourself for that." *It comes to me suddenly, like a flash of light.*

"I don't blame myself, not anymore. I guess I always knew Hogg burned down 1132. Or that you put him up to it. All this time, I couldn't show my face in Lawrence. Everyone thought I did it."

"Honestly, Bernie. You always were fanciful, writing in that journal. Besides, you're the one in love with fire and burning things down." I still bore the scar of her burn. No talk about Marin being my father or the scary thought that she and I may have been related.

"This has been fun reminiscing. I did have something I wanted to talk to you about today. How are you fixed for insurance, Bernard?"

I laugh and think of Fred MacMurray and Barbara Stanwyck in Double Indemnity.

"Why, are you going to kill me now?"

She lets out a cackle that makes someone at an adjoining table jump. Her throaty laugh has become grating.

"I understand you handle benefits for your firm."

"I was managing partner. Not anymore, but I still help with a few things. Ben Golden's your man."

She looks at me with those massive eyes, imploring. She still smelled like cinnamon but without the perfume. I knew that Golden and the team would eat it up, an old flame, hell, yes, we'll make this work. They'd see I was one of them. Being in business with Apryl was the next best thing to intimacy.

"I'm working with Northwestern Mutual Life, group benefits."

"You're kidding." I just can't do it, be her vassal in this way.

"Why would I be kidding?"

After everything, after a lifetime of longing and remembering, she comes to sell me insurance?

"It's an excellent company. I just never thought of you in life insurance."

"It's not just life, it's pensions, health, flexible savings plans. I thought I could shoot you a quote and help you do better than you're doing with your present plan. Which I checked, and you could do better."

I try to catch my breath. Could it be that the face that launched a thousand confessions is now an insurance agent? Circe with an actuary? Turning men into payouts?

"I'm the biggest producer now in the professional small company plans department, over ten million last year. I found my niche."

She has her niche—I have an unscratchable itch. If Golden got one whiff of her, she could write her own ticket: pensions, life, health, investment vehicles.

I want to say how I imagined meeting her like this a thousand times, but never in my wildest dreams did I think she'd come for a sale.

"I guess I thought you were here . . ."

"Oh, Bernie. I'm here to find out how you are doing, too."

"And to think I went looking for you in France last year."

"You're still quite dramatic after all these years."

"You didn't come here to check up on me, or to sell me. You came here for— forgiveness?"

"That's rich. After everything you did?"

"No, Apryl. You burned us all, you burned the program, you burned your father—are you here to burn me one last time?"

"You're not the only one who has thought about the past."

I am shot through with pain, the pain of someone hitting you in the softest place, causing you to confront the most shameful thing. I stare at my cup, stirring with the little spoon. It is all clear.

"You're right," *I say.*

She looks at me nervously. "Let's let bygones be bygones."

"No, you have . . . hit the nail on the head. I lacked the capacity to love, and that drove you away." *Tears form in her eyes.* "Like I drove away my first wife and left the second at the altar to go in search of you."

"Bernie, you don't have to—"

"You don't know it, but you came here today to release me from your spell. Don't you see—I'm no longer your slave. Thank you, Apryl."

She sits there looking at me for what feels like a full minute. Then I see the flash in her eyes. She stands.

"Great to see you, Bernie. Think about the insurance."

Suddenly I am up and am holding her close.

"Apryl . . . is this really all there is after what passed between us? I'm telling you I'm free. Nobody has as much in common as you and I. Virgil was right, we have looked back on all that happened with joy."

I am transported in the smell of her beauty, in the burnt orange of reflected moonlight bouncing off the quarry rocks under the wide and starry sky, naked and down to the quick of being. But she looks away, as if a curtain has come down on remembrance and tender things.

"You didn't want me. You had more than one chance." *A feral laser from inside her shoots me through. She feels the scar on my hand, leans against me, and whispers,* "You all had your chance. I could never marry a man. You worship yourselves."

I let go of her, and as quickly as she passed before me in Lawrence, Kansas, almost thirty years before, the hormonal arsonist is gone. I watch as she walks away in that liquefied vision, each gyration free. I, the master of jests, am the victim of the greatest jest.

φ

It is late September on campus when I return; the vibrating girls are out in their tight skirts and silken hair, as if they are waiting for some revelation in skin to consume them in carnal rapture. The slanting afternoon sun bathes the world in a mellow gold, the precious metal of memory. I feel the dangerous sensations of early manhood grasping, choking me off. I walk past a run-down Quantrill's Crossing down Twelfth Street to Ohio, waiting to see the portals to the pantheon of youthful longings. I have not been back here since yellow flames burned my youth away. I stop two hundred yards from the house. I had been avoiding a return to this place, avoiding the ghosts of self in an effort to keep them alive. Now I am ready to look, to encounter the past and deprive it of its power over me once and for all.

I see—nothing. A gaping hole in the ground, sentinels of sycamores and elms, a ten-ton truck making a delivery.

I rush over and jump up to the driver's door, hanging by a steel step. A grizzly man—bronze skin stretched tightly over a barrel gut, cigarette dangling from his lower lip—tells me to get off his truck.

"What's happening here?" *I say.*

"We're having a tea party."

"How long has this been a bare lot?"

"Tied up in court for years—some arson case, a real mess."

"Ever catch the fellow?"

"I don't know. Guy who was buying this went to prison."

"Schmead doesn't own it?"

"Yeah, that's the guy. After the indictment a plea deal, he took bankruptcy."

The toppling of a titan. I walk the grounds and kicked around some dirt, hoping for some relic, something that would reveal an archaeology of emotions, of the visions I once saw, the sensations, the awakening of wonder, the spectral madness of poetry and love. Those things had settled down now into a sediment of fact, of numbers, of dollars without sense, of knowledge without wisdom, as if an alien self grew out of that college self. Maybe time is a reverse alchemy, leaving only slag where once there was gold.

I find myself driving on Interstate 35 on my way back to Kansas City International. I come upon the sign that reads "Le Loup" near the entrance to Interstate 35. I drive toward Hess's farm as if some power has taken the wheel. But when I get to where his drive should be, I see a wooden sign that reads, "Notre Dame de Le Loup" and I turn onto that drive and see a glorious site: a native stone church and buildings, the neo-Gothic splitting a broad Kansas sky. I park by some other cars and enter the church unheeded. I am going to miss my flight.

I marvel at the intricate architecture, the columns and side altars, the lovely stained glass, the blue Virgin above the altar, the choir stalls, the smell. It has a musty, ancient smell, even though the buildings are new, save for a framed symbol hanging from a pillar, a P over an X with an inscription.

In hoc signo vinces.

The Constantine Cross. Operation Constantine fulfilled.

I had partied on this very hallowed ground. Is this crucifix the only symbol pointing to that sublime past? Where are the statues of the wild pig roasting or the pig fling pen or MF playing his luck with the cattle or a grotto of McDarby rolling in some haystack with a HIP lovely or me and Apryl at the rock quarry? I want to leave unseen as I was at Chalfontbleau.

An intonation breaks the vaulted silence. An organ, and then the sound of footsteps on stones, soft as a fox on a forest floor. I stir as if to leave. But people are coming into the church, farmers, men in suits, women with lace coverings. I can't resist the counter force, so I stay.

Then I see them, as in a dream, coming in twos. I count twenty-five. They flip back the cowls covering their faces. The first several, I do not recognize. Finally, I see Hess—a Marine short-cropped haircut and taut face. He appears happy, intense. Then Kludas Schmead, the son of the destroyer of 1132—the ultimate revenge, to be in a monastery twenty-five miles from his father's lost aggrandizements. And Jacques "Lefevbre, I would leave you" Gombault.

I see one of the stragglers moving slowly. Impossible. It is Tom Hogg! He is graying. I feel the worst kind of ache in my gut, an ache for the old days of Hogg and Swensen, of Courtney and the Greeks or Romans, of St. Augustine and Chaucer.

They begin vespers, and the dulcet tones bring back to me that whole world of late September shadows, the warmth and benediction of Ohio Street, the Latin chant at St. Johns, the lectures on campus, the catechisms at 1132, and the drinking and camaraderie—a civilization built on the ruins of the wasteland. Latin burns into me a sure knowledge of buried things:

Nisi Dominus aedificaverit domum,
in vanum laboraverunt qui aedificant eam.

Unless the Lord build the house. I had been trying to rebuild that house in my mind, had been trying to dissect the experience of youth. I knew that if I could rebuild 1132, I could live there again, even if only in my mind.

As vespers ends, I rise to leave undetected. As I turn around, there are Zorn and Martha—a couple, major benefactors of this place—Zorn winking at me as if he expected me to be there all along. Built, I assume, with his successful microbrewery franchise. At least, I hope it was not with mob funds.

Next to him is Ross in his priestly garb, with not so much a smile as a smirk. And behind them, Patrick Winston and Laura Hull Winston and their children. Patrick smiles at me, and his eyes disappear into his head. Swensen peers puckishly from around a column, all himself, holding a woman's hand—Trish.

I see the sunshine face of the priestly silver fox with a miter dancing over his smiling face—Archbishop Connell. As I leave, I notice above the doors the two symbols of Alpha and Omega, beginning and end. The only things missing are the numerals and Phaedo wagging his tail. I do not want to tax their charity or have to explain how I never entered the Church after all these years. Still Bernard the Agnostic, who, in spite of himself—and while committing all manner of crimes—somehow made all of this possible.

They begin to circle me. But I see her. She comes from behind a towering column near the statue of Our Lady of the Happy Death. Lovely as memory itself, better than memory, still young looking. Her eyes are large and clear. Maggie. She smiles, no longer framed in a wimple but encircled in purest dusk.

"Hello, Bernard."

"Maggie." She is no longer in a habit. Her hair is short, her figure perfect, her posture impeccable.

The others surround us. Circling me. As I had circled for years until I returned. The setting sun pierces the rose window above the altar. I look into its blinding light. I hear the slow strop of leather sandals on native stone. It is Tom Hogg, and he is joined by Bob McDarby, who comes from another corner of the church. I did not notice all of them, caught up as I was in the monks. It is obvious they all want me to stay. I feel my hand and am glad for the scar and the real memory.

I no longer see the perfect numbers. I want to recall with them ev-erything, how I got the girl. How I lost her, how 1132 Ohio was a center of culture. Right now, there is no time for recalling. No time at all. Just a gaze. And a song playing in my head:

> *Believe me, if all these endearing young charms,*
> > *Which I gaze on so fondly today,*
> *Were to change by tomorrow, and fleet in my arms,*
> > *Like fairy-gifts fading away . . .*

Is she the one which hasn't a why or because or although? I gaze into Maggie's pretty crystal-blue-green eyes gazing up at the window over the altar. This is a book that is writing itself in me. Then she is looking at me again, but still, I see the reflection—eyes that welcome and accept and for-give everything—and this to me is something like poetry and tender grace, is something like perfection.

Acknowledgments

While the events are inspired by a real humanities program and real hearings that sought to suppress the teaching of the ancients on their own terms, this is its own work of fiction, with its own world, its own set of controversies and characters, apart from the real world of lived lives. In an age of forgotten literary and artistic commitments, it is a mistake to substitute real experience of the author for events in a novel. The writer cannot but do what he imagines, artfully one hopes.

There are many who contributed to this work over, embarrassingly, decades. First, Professor Robert Carlson, who believed in this project and braved a mountain blizzard to deliver the first full manuscript and its author to safety. He has nurtured this work and I owe him a great debt of gratitude not only for being a thoughtful reader but a mentor and friend across the span of years.

Eric Brende has been a steadfast confidant, goad, source of inspiration, and friend. He provided much needed input. David Smith gave an important read and superb suggestions, as well as much needed encouragement without which this project might have died on the vine.

Others along the way provided food and drink to this pilgrim on his bumpy road to Jericho. I am indebted to writer, James Marinovich, who read the manuscript in an early stage and helped me to see the value in the story and the need for significant tightening. Tim was an inspiration all along, a friend and a fellow traveler in prose. Alan Hicks provided helpful input and encouragement.

I am indebted to Editor Ted Gilley who applied his expert editorial "Gilley-tine" and helped me see into the characters and story. My father and mother, Walter and Mary Ellen Bloch, believed in me and nurtured a lifelong love of language, art, story, and music. Finally, my brother, William, is a soul connection who first taught me the value of literature and has been an important voice of reason and encouragement on the tumultuous path to becoming an author.